TECHNA FORCE 20

Other Books BY Anton J. Stoerman

The Long Rutted Road

TECHNA FORCE 20

A Novel By

Anton J. Stoerman

Trafford Publishing

Order this book online at www.trafford.com
or email orders@trafford.com

Most Trafford titles are also available at major online book retailers.

Printed in the United States of America.

ISBN: 978-1-4269-7149-5 (sc)
ISBN: 978-1-4269-7150-1 (hc)
ISBN: 978-1-4269-7148-8 (e)

Library of Congress Control Number: 2011909525

Trafford rev. 06/13/2011

 www.trafford.com

North America & international
toll-free: 1 888 232 4444 (USA & Canada)
phone: 250 383 6864 ♦ fax: 812 355 4082

To My Dear Wife, Janet

ACKNOWLEDGMENTS

I wish to thank my daughter, Robin, for her wise guidance as a kindred soul concerning the workings of government and business in America, as well as her editing expertise; Gerald Thiell, Educator, for his fine editing efforts and considerable knowledge regarding word processor software; my granddaughters, Melissa, Kellie and Emily for their loving encouragement, and finally, my wife, Janet for her much appreciated guidance, encouragement, and countless hours spent in editing. Without their help this book would not have been possible.

PREFACE

I began to plan this novel after years of fascination with our great universe convinced me that earth is likely not the only planet upon which reasoning people live. Carrying that thought further, one might assume, I think that other civilizations could possess greater intelligence, and be far ahead of us in technological achievement. And perhaps they possess higher ethics and moral standards than exist on earth today. It is also possible that they have greater powers to protect themselves, or to persuade others to adopt a different way of acting.

These ideas, which some might consider hypothetical, or even too preposterous to imagine, could easily be reality, in my opinion. Combine them with what we have been told about an alleged extra-terrestrial landing incident near Roswell, New Mexico, more than sixty years ago, an incident that could well prove the existence of other beings and is still controversial, and you have something more plausible. Add the element of fear another planet might have of being destroyed by some country on earth, such as the United States, and you have exactly what this novel, Techna Force 20, is all about.

Anton J. Stoerman

THE STORY

An expeditionary force traveling in huge, black, very fast, starships from Techna Planet discovers Planet earth while on routine patrol of the universe. The force is called Techna Force 20 and its explorers, called agents, who are fluent in English, pick up a radio message that makes it very clear a country called the United States of America intends to attack and destroy any other inhabited planet in order to protect itself. The starship crews follow the radio beam to its point of origin, Roswell, New Mexico. The year is 1947.

Techna Force 20 agents all possess great powers, including the power to make themselves and their equipment invisible, and the power to terminate enemies using personal lasers. Over the course of many years following the discovery of earth, Techna Force 20 inserts hundreds of agents, operating invisibly, or in I-Mode, into every branch of the U.S. Federal Government, as well as into numerous large U.S. corporations. Through their intense observation and research, these agents become privy to all types of top secret information, much of which confirms the first radio message and points to a single mission: destruction of other inhabited planets.

Under the leadership of Commander Thor Berksten, Techna Force 20 sets out to make certain no harm comes to its home planet, or to any other inhabited planet, by American forces. Along the way, it discovers and acts on many problems in America that make life miserable for that country's private citizens. This is the story of Techna Force 20, and it begins in Earth year 2010, Techna Planet year 2623.

CHAPTER ONE

The Letter

February 11, 2010

To: Mr. Samuel Fischer, Producer, U.S. Sunday Review
        Continental Television System, Inc.
        29795 Continental Building
        New York, New York, 10001

From: Thor Berksten, Commander, Techna Force 20
        Roswell, New Mexico

Dear Mr. Fischer:

Do you recall all those UFO stories that began circulating around 1947, in the Roswell, New Mexico area? You know, the ones describing flying saucer sightings? Such rumors were rampant then and are often heard even today.

Perhaps you will also recall a newspaper article in the early 1950's that concerned the slaughter of every member of a KKK Klavern in their secret meeting place in a small southern Alabama town. This was justice done in retaliation for the brutal killing of a black male at the hands of this very Klavern.

Or, you might remember the trial of a white man for the vicious murder of an innocent little black girl, in which the defendant was found not guilty in spite of testimony by three people who witnessed the commission of this terrible crime. At the end of his trial the defendant suddenly dropped dead, apparently of "natural causes." Again, justice was done.

And more recently, you may be aware of numerous news accounts of people involved in the illicit drug trade being found dead.

Mr. Fischer, you might be wondering what these various events have in common, so I will tell you: Those reported UFO sightings were not really illusions at all, as claimed by your government. They were actual spaceships from another planet, my home planet of Techna, in fact, which is located five million miles from Earth. Those spaceships brought scientists to investigate Earth in 1947 and have been returning to continue their exploration at regular intervals ever since. Yes, it is true *and I can prove it.* In fact, five of our space ships are on Planet Earth at this moment, having recently delivered a very large group of agents whose reason for being here now shall become clear enough in good time.

The other three events were the work of members of our expeditionary force for, while we did not come to Planet Earth to be your police force, or your conscience, we are sworn to protect innocent people everywhere and are honor-bound to counter injustices where we find them. Reread the news articles for these events and you will find a common thread: each of the criminals was found with a small reddish circle with three black marks spaced equally around its circumference in the middle of his forehead. That mark is made by the weapon we all carry.

If you want to hear more please write me care of General Delivery, Washington,. D.C. 20090.

Sincerely,
Thor Berksten, Commander, Techna Force 20

*   *   *

Sam Fischer found the above letter on his desk when he arrived for work at Continental Television Headquarters, on Monday, February 15, 2010. It was on top of a large stack of correspondence waiting for his attention. What caught his eye was the letterhead, which consisted of the words *Sovereign Nation of Techna Planet,* in gold letters against a band of royal blue stretching across the top of the page. As he did first thing every morning, he stood at the desk, dressed in his ever-present tan tweed sport jacket over navy blue turtleneck, and briefly pawed through the correspondence. But his mind would focus only on the Techna letter. He had never heard of such a place and was intrigued by the name. Finally he took the letter in his hands, lowered his slender, five feet-six frame into the well-used oak desk chair and began to read. When he had finished reading he frowned, as if perplexed, then began to read the letter again, this time much more carefully, absent-mindedly stroking his close-cropped salt and pepper beard as he did so. Then he read the letter a third time, before turning toward the door to his office.

"Jesus, Margie," he shouted excitedly, though his secretary, Margie Peterson, sat not more than ten feet away, just outside his office, "Where the hell did this letter come from?"

"It was in the morning mail, Boss man."

"Well, get Mark in here on the double. This is hot!" (Mark Haddon was Senior Correspondent on the U.S. Sunday Review television show).

Haddon arrived a few minutes later, dressed to the nines, as usual, in dark grey suit, pale blue shirt and red stripped tie. Where Sam always had a slightly rumpled look, Mark seemed to have just come out of make-up. His snow-white hair and eyebrows were perfectly groomed and there was not a blemish on his well-tanned face.

Sam said "Good morning," and shoved the letter across the desk toward him. "Read this and tell me what you think."

Mark read quickly, then whistled softly. "What I think is, we gotta grab this guy damn fast and get him on the show."

No matter how often Sam encountered his friend and colleague he was always a bit startled by the sharp contrast between Mark's dress and manner of speaking. Haddon was from Mississippi and in moments of forgetfulness or excitement the clipped words, profanity and southern drawl just seemed to slip out. Fortunately, he never let that happened while he was in front of the cameras.

"Do you think he is legit?" Sam asked. "I mean, this is right out of science fiction."

"As if I know, Sam? He says he can prove all of it, so lets put him to the test. This could be a hell-uv-a-story. I want it! It has the makin's of the biggest thing to hit the tube in years, hell in the entire history of television! Can you imagine what it would mean to pull off an interview with a live Martian?"

"He's not a Martian, he's a Technian."

"Whatever. Our ratings will be in orbit, that's for damn sure. Right? Godammed right!"

"Okay, okay, don't bust a gut. I'll write him immediately. But he'd better be for real. What does he want from us? That's my question."

Mark shook his head from side to side thoughtfully, then shrugged. "Publicity, maybe? Guess we'll find out soon enough, won't we?" With that he left Sam's office.

*   *   *

Exactly one week later, Commander Thor Berksten got off the elevator at the 60th floor of the Continental Building and strode briskly across the long, elegant lobby toward the reception desk. The beautiful young woman with short auburn hair and large blue eyes, who was manning the desk, watched him from the moment he appeared, and now waited for him to approach. When he reached her station and smiled she knew she had never seen a more handsome male in all her life. He was tall—about six feet—slender but very well built, with jet black hair that clung to his head in small tight curls, and his eyes were the most intense gray. He gazed down at her, nodded, and said, "Good morning, Miss. I am Commander Thor Berksten, here to see Mr. Fischer. I believe he is expecting me?"

The young woman's face reddened with girlish embarrassment as she struggled to regain her composure. The sight of this magnificent young lion had swept aside her normally calm, confident demeanor. "Oh....Why, yes. Yes, of course. I'll announce you, Commander Berksten." With that she punched the number for Samuel Fischer's office—actually for Margie, his secretary—on the telephone console on her desk.

"Yes, Sarah?"

Sarah was still staring at her visitor. "Commander Berksten to see Mr. Fischer," she stammered.

"Very well. Is he a little green man with one eye in the middle of his forehead?"

Sarah wanted to say, *"definitely not,"* but said, "No, not at all," instead.

"Well, send him in so I can see for myself."

Sarah replaced the phone and pointed toward a door to her left. "You may go in, Mr. Berksten. Through that door, please."

"Thank you. By the way, I hope you don't mind my saying so, but you are very, very beautiful. What is your name?"

She told him, and he said, "That is the perfect name for you. In case you did not know, it is Hebrew by origin and means princess. You are, indeed, a princess."

"I did not know, Sir, though my mother is Jewish. Maybe that explains it. Anyway, I thank you for the compliment."

Thor nodded and said, "You are Welcome, Sarah, and I am pleased to have met you." Then he smiled and headed for the door.

Sarah watched him until he disappeared through the door, thinking, *Commander Thor Berksten, I don't know how I am going to arrange it, but I, Sarah Malloy, fully intend to spend a great deal of time with you.*

Margie had exactly the same reaction as Sarah upon seeing Thor for the first time, but being older and more mature she was able to hide her true emotions. Still, she had to agree with the receptionist: He was certainly no little green man with one eye. She greeted him and ushered him into Sam's office. "Please have a seat, Commander. Mr. Fischer will be here right away. Would you like coffee?"

"Thank you. Actually, I prefer tea if it is available."

"Of course. I'll only be a moment." *And he speaks perfect English,* she thought, wondering how in the world he picked that up.

When Margie returned with the tea, Sam and Mark were right behind her. They waited for her to give Thor his refreshment then advanced toward him. He stood to meet them.

"Morning, Commander Berksten. I'm Sam Fischer and this is Mark Haddon, Senior Correspondent, U.S. Sunday Review. Good of you to come." The three men shook hands then took seats around a large coffee table across the room from Sam's cluttered desk. When they were comfortable, Sam continued: "Well, that was quite a letter. Are you really from another planet—Techna Planet—is that how you pronounce it?"

Thor smiled. "Yes, Mr. Fischer, you said it perfectly and yes, I am from there."

"Funny, I thought I knew all the planets," Sam said, looking Thor straight in the eyes. "Never heard of that one."

"I am certain you haven't, Sir. No one on Earth has. Your astronomers would have to know exactly where to search."

"I notice the phrase, *Sovereign Nation of Techna Planet,* on your letterhead. Does that mean there is only one nation on Techna?"

"It does, Sir. Techna is very small—less than one tenth the size of Earth, or about 2000 miles in circumference. Most of the surface is covered by water, just as on Earth, leaving a land area only slightly larger than your state of Texas. I assure you, though, we are fully self-sufficient."

Sam rubbed his beard and nodded affirmatively. "Hmmm. yes, I gather that. Tell me, Commander, how did you discover Planet Earth?"

"Certainly. In our year 2560—that would be your year 1947— one of our starships picked up unfamiliar radio signals while on routine patrol and locked onto them. Those signals led directly to Earth—in fact, directly to Roswell, New Mexico, where you had a military installation at the time. Until then we had no idea another planet with an advanced civilization existed in the Universe. Being researchers at heart, we began to learn all we could about you, including your language. That took many visits."

Sam nodded. "That would explain how you speak our language so well. You really did your homework, Commander."

"Thank you. We Technians are a very thorough people."

Mark spoke now for the first time. "Commander, have you discovered other populated planets?"

"Yes. Four, so far. However, none of their mammals are much farther advanced than your ape species, as near as we can determine."

"What tests did you conduct to reach that conclusion?"

"To begin with, the lack of communication traffic from those planets, which we could see clearly from our starships and study at close range. Then by actually landing on them, as we did on

Planet Earth. It was then that we saw that they were much less advanced—though still well ahead of the little green people you joke about and we have never seen."

"Amazing. Absolutely amazing," Mark said. "But forgive me, Commander, if we are going to do business we need to substantiate your claims. You understand that we can't just take your word on all this. Your letter stated that you could prove your claims, so...."

"And I am prepared to do just that, Mr. Haddon. If we agree to do business, as you put it, I will take you to our base, which is inside Sardine Mountain, near Roswell, so you can see our starships, which is what we call Techna spacecraft, for yourself, and you will meet some of my expeditionary agents in their own environment. I feel certain what you witness will convince and amaze you."

"Sounds good to me," Sam replied. How about you, Mark?"

Mark nodded in agreement. " I have heard of Sardine Mountain. It's an old Army base, isn't it?

"Yes, Mark, that is my understanding."

"Right. Well, I guess we need to hear what you want from us, Mr. Berksten. How can Continental Television be of service?"

"By putting me on your television show. I want the citizens of the United States to know that we of Techna Planet exist and are little different from them. I want them to realize that we are able to come to their country—have come to their country again and again—with ease and without detection. Finally, I want them to know we come in peace, as far as the average person is concerned and mean them no harm."

"That sounds a bit ominous," Sam said. "You rule out harm to the average citizen but make no specific mention of American leaders. Do you intend to harm them? Also, in your letter you make reference to several events—the KKK, courtroom scene and dead drug sellers, implying that you were responsible for the demise of those people. In a sense, that amounts to harm to our citizens. How do you explain that in light of your claim that you mean our citizens no harm?"

"Mr. Fischer, I can only tell you we have grave concerns for the welfare of our own people. We see many problems in your country that might ultimately harm Techna Planet and are not being addressed by your leaders. We are here to protect our interests and will do whatever is necessary to do that. As for the incidents you refer to, it is as I said in the letter: we fight crime anywhere we encounter it. Now, if you wish, we can leave for Roswell immediately, where I will prove my claims. We should be back in New York before dark."

"What?" Mark blurted, "Back here by dark? How is that possible? We'd have trouble just getting a plane out of Kennedy by then."

"Ah, yes, gentlemen, but my personal transporter is waiting on your rooftop helipad as we speak...."

Sam and Mark exchanged surprised glances, and Mark asked, "You flew all the way from Roswell in a chopper?"

A blank look appeared on Thor's face. "Chopper? What is a chopper? I am not familiar with that term."

"Oh, I'm sorry," Mark answered. "That's American slang for whirly-birds, you know, helicopters."

"Ah, yes. I see," said Thor with just a hint of amusement in his eyes. "No, not in a chopper. Our transporters have VTOL capability. Are you familiar with that capability, Mr. Haddon?"

"Yes. It means vertical take off and landing ability."

"Quite so. Well, shall we proceed?"

"Let's do it, Commander Berksten."

"Fine, but please, call me Thor, and be sure to bring cameras along. You will surely want a record of what you witness today."

* * *

The transporter was a sleek white aircraft roughly the size of a Cessna *Mustang,* or small business jet, but was much more streamlined and advanced, with very stubby wings. Its pilot, dressed in a superb-fitting uniform of smoke blue with the same Techna logo in gold on royal blue emblazoned on his left breast, was waiting for them beside the aircraft's open passenger door. He saluted the three men as they appeared on the helipad.

"Are we ready, Jens?"

"Yes, Commander."

One by one they boarded the transporter and the pilot took his place in the cockpit last. There were six seats in the cabin, three across facing toward the rear and three facing forward, with a highly polished walnut table between the facing rows of seats. The seats were of the home recliner type, all upholstered in soft cream-colored Corinthian leather. Sam and Mark selected forward facing seats and Thor sat on the other side of the table facing them.

"Gentlemen," he said, "You must buckle your seatbelts just as you would on any other aircraft," and he buckled his as he spoke. When he was satisfied they had also complied he said over his shoulder, "You may leave when ready, Jens."

"Ready now, Sir," was the pilot's immediate response, and with that the transporter shot into the air as if launched by a rocket.

"Holy shit! exclaimed Mark, as his eyes grew as big as saucers. How fast does this thing go?"

Thor laughed. "At the moment we are climbing at about 1000 knots. In a moment or two we will reach our cruise altitude— between 60,000 and 70,000 feet—where our cruise speed will increase to around 5000 knots per hour. We should be on the ground in Roswell in roughly 30 minutes."

"Wow, this is fantastic," Mark said incredulously. "2000 miles to Roswell in 30 minutes and this thing is even quieter than your office, Sam."

Thor watched the two men with amusement. "That's because we power our starships—even small ones like this—with nuclear systems. They provide a huge increase in speed over other types of aircraft engines—including the most powerful turbo-jets, yet consume far, far less fuel. This transporter , which is used quite often, has flown more than 500,000 miles and is three years old, yet has never been refueled."

Then Thor continued, "Gentlemen, let me now prepare you for your visit. Soon you will find yourselves inside a huge underground chamber. The 579th Strategic Missile Squadron in your American Air Force constructed this facility in the early 1960's as part of development of a number of missile silos that once encircled Roswell. We believe this chamber was used to store and manage missiles, men and equipment required for this top secret Strategic Air Command facility."

"Yes," Sam said. "But it wasn't such a top secret. We learned about the missile silos, but the Air Force would not allow us near them. We also know about that mountain, though nothing was ever said about this chamber you talk about, Thor."

"Sam, there is much your government does not talk about, and that is exactly why we are now visitors to Planet Earth. But to continue, we were present in Roswell beginning in 1947, when we first heard of a massive Army Air Force Base—Walker Air Force Base it was known as then-- and also as Roswell Army Air Field later, being constructed here. We sent a starship to investigate. One of its small un-manned probe craft, dispatched from the mother ship for a closer look, malfunctioned in a severe thunderstorm and crashed near the base at Corona, New Mexico. That was the so-called 'flying disk' episode that was in all the papers around that time. You may have read those reports."

"Sure. The flying saucer with a crew of little green men," Mark responded.

Thor nodded agreement. "Right, except there were no little green men on board—no living personnel at all, in fact. The whole episode was blown up out of proportion to scare the American people. You still see versions of the event on television today. Such programs are in the _Unsolved Mysteries_ category, you know. People seem fascinated by such stories. But of course, your government knows the real truth—that life exists on other planets—as a result of that flying disk incident at Roswell, because they could not deny the existence of that disk on the one hand, or identify where it came from on the other. The U.S. Government has been frantically searching the universe for years to locate us. Why do you think your country has a space program--why it has the manned space shuttle program? In our opinion, there is no question its objective is to destroy Techna Planet, and any other planet found to have human life on it."

"Does this search and destroy effort concern you, Thor?"

"No, it does not concern us because you are not even close to discovering our planet, and probably will not be for another thirty years. You simply don't have the equipment needed for true space travel yet. So we watch and wait. It is not our purpose to destroy your planet, Earth, which we could do in a heartbeat today _because we are that advanced, technologically._ But make no mistake, Techna Planet will not be destroyed by your government, ever. We are here to see to that."

"And," Sam interjected, "I suppose that is why we have been brought here today?"

"Exactly, Sam. As people say in your world, *The best defense is a good offense,* right?"

"Let me ask you a question that has been on my mind, Commander."

"Of course, Sam."

"Why did you choose CTS *Sunday Review?* There are several other Sunday programs using the same news magazine format we use. Why us and not them?"

"Ah, that is easy to answer. We wanted a program with a large audience, as well as a penchant for telling the story truthfully, no matter the consequences. In our opinion, you meet those requirements very well."

"I appreciate that, Commander. We do try very hard."

Conversation in the transporter ceased at this point, for Thor could see that his guests were deep in thought concerning all that they had heard. Let them absorb that part first, he thought, for there is so much more they must know in order to help us accomplish our mission.

*   *   *

27 minutes into the flight, Jens said, "Commander, we are starting our final approach to Roswell. Please prepare for landing." He then banked the aircraft sharply left from its heading of 245 degrees and began a rapid, turning decent. Two minutes later, the craft slowed perceptibly, then settled gently to the ground. There was no sensation of having landed on a runway, no change in engine noise, no feeling of bumping along as wheels encountered concrete expansion strips. It was more like floating down and down, then settling softly to earth. Sam and Mark stared out the windows of the transporter and saw that they were, as Thor had indicated, no longer outside, but inside a well-lit structure. How had this happened, they wondered? There had been no delay once they landed while hanger doors opened, yet they had transitioned from swift flight to being at rest—apparently inside

the chamber Thor had mentioned. What manner of people could accomplish such a feat? The two men exchanged knowing glances as if, in reading each other's thoughts, they had learned the answer simultaneously.

Thor's voice brought them back to the present. "Gentlemen, as you can see, we are inside the Roswell chamber, which is our home base on Planet Earth. For your information, no one detected our flight here from New York, because we made that flight in *I-Mode,* which means we were invisible to other aircraft and to radar installations. We are able to accomplish invisibility by using advanced stealth technology strategies, such as shaping that minimizes shadows, and body illumination that allows Techna aircraft to blend into the surrounding background. We and the transporter have now returned to *V-Mode,* since, in this secure facility, there is no need to be invisible. There are other aircraft in this chamber at this moment, as well as hundreds of men and women. Ordinarily they, too, would be in V-Mode because, in here, there is no need to conceal them. However, when you leave the transporter seconds from now, you will see no sign of people or equipment at first. That is because I want to demonstrate our substantially advanced ability to remain invisible at will. Once you have witnessed an apparently empty cavern, I will show it to you as it truly is. Shall we begin our tour?"

In answer to his question, Sam and Mark rose at once and made for the transporter's open cabin door. Once outside, they found themselves inside a massive, free-span concrete building more than 700 hundred feet long and 350 feet wide. They knew they were underground but still found it hard to believe.

Sam was first to speak: "Incredible. Absolutely incredible. Washington does everything first class, doesn't it?"

"Yeah," Mark answered. "And we never heard a thing about this part of the Roswell story. "

Thor, who was standing off to one side waiting patiently for his two guests to absorb the scene before them, now said, "Would you gentlemen like to see what is really in this facility?"

"We are more than ready," Sam responded.

"Very well," and with that, Thor waved his right arm as if to say, *and now I present…*

Instantly, it was as if a huge stage curtain rose, or they had stepped onto a huge movie set, for there before them was the most amazing sight: five huge starships at rest in one long row, all painted dull black, surrounded by clusters of ordinary-looking people who were doing various types of ordinary work.

"These are our largest starships, gentlemen," Thor explained. "They are about 100 feet in diameter and stand three stories high—roughly 30 feet. They are capable of speeds up to 50,000 miles per hour outside Earth's atmosphere, move virtually without sound and are usually visible only to Techna personnel. We will not make the mistake of landing in V-Mode again, as we did here in Roswell, in 1947."

"My God," Sam mused. "We've been invaded and nobody has a clue." Then he turned to look at Thor. "Our radar doesn't pick you up?"

"No, Sam. As I said, our ships are invisible to all radar. We Technians are also invisible most of the time while on a mission, unless we choose to show ourselves. You were both invisible, as was I, except to each other, during our trip here today."

Sam and Mark exchanged knowing glances, for they recognized immediately the implication of Thor's words. A large foreign force was on the ground—on American soil—without government clearance, without even government knowledge. It could move about the country freely, with great speed without detection and, at least potentially, do great damage to facilities and humans. It could monitor the most confidential, sensitive government meetings in Washington, or any other location, capture such proceedings on video and audio media and use that information for whatever purpose it chose. Both men saw clearly that, for the first time in history, the United States was now facing a foe with immense power, without the means to defend against that power.

"Thor, you realize, of course, that we must report this to the U.S. Authorities," Sam said.

"Of course. But they will not be allowed to see what you are seeing today."

"But we must show Washington the pictures we take here," Mark responded. "That includes any pictures of your starships, your agents working here, us with you and the starships, the workers—everything."

Thor smiled. "Gentlemen, you may even photograph inside the starships, if you wish. I asked you to bring cameras, remember?"

"But don't you understand that Washington will come after you?" Sam asked. They'll send an army here. This place will be thick with soldiers, tanks and planes."

"Of course, " Thor answered, waving his arm in a wide arch as before, "But this is what they will see." Instantly the massive cavern was once again an empty structure. Even the transporter that had brought them here was gone, as was their host. Suddenly they were standing in the middle of nothing, totally alone. Thor let them absorb this change for a minute or two, then raised the curtain, as it were, once again. There were the starships, the workers, the transporter and Thor, himself—all as before. "So you see the major element of our power. How does one attack an invisible enemy? Your government, for all its vast resources, is powerless against us. It is our hope that your leaders will comprehend that and meet our simple demands. Now," he continued, pointing toward the first starship in line, "Shall we have a look inside this one? It is my flagship."

* * *

The three landing wheel legs of the starship were about seven feet long when fully extended, allowing adequate room to walk beneath the craft to a drop-down staircase at its center. They climbed the stairs and found themselves in a large lounge-type area furnished with comfortable chairs and sofas, as well as conveniently located tables. People were playing cards, or reading, or talking in small groups—even watching American television on a wide screen TV! The area reminded Mark of lounge areas on cruise ships he had been on and was every bit as plush.

"This level also contains staterooms and sanitary facilities for the crew and passengers," The Commander said as they passed through the lounge area. "We can house up to 200 travelers, two to four to a room. "

22

They were now walking along a long curving passageway with many doors along each side, much like the corridor of a hotel, or the passageway of cruise ships. From time to time, Thor paused to open a door, saying, "These are typical staterooms." The rooms were not elaborate; each was about nine feet by ten feet, with either twin beds or twin double bunks, chairs and storage lockers, just enough room to sleep.

From there, they climbed a central staircase in the middle of the lounge to the second level. Here they saw an immaculate dining room with tables and chairs lined up in neat rows, and beyond that, the ship's galley, or kitchen. Men and women in clean, white uniforms were busy preparing the next meal.

Next they were led along another passageway very similar to the one on the first level. "On other ships, this level would also house passengers and crew members," Thor explained. "But here, many of these rooms are used for office space, meeting rooms and so forth, as well as for communications and navigation equipment." He opened one door to expose a young woman, smartly dressed in the same smoke blue uniform as Jens, the transporter pilot, sitting at her desk. She stood and saluted as they appeared at her door. "This is Manta Sames, my Personal Aide. She is the one who keeps me on track, and does a superb job. I would be lost without her." Manta blushed and thanked her boss and the group chatted briefly. Then Thor showed his guests his own small, well furnished office just beyond Manta's desk, before they continued their inspection of the starship.

As they continued along the passageway, Thor opened a second door. Inside, a half dozen, similarly dressed men were seated at a long conference table. All stood and saluted Thor the moment he appeared. "As you were," he said. The men relaxed a bit but remained standing. Thor introduced them one by one, then turned to one agent he called Truls, who was obviously the group's leader. "These visitors are here to inspect our operation. How is the meeting going?"

"Commander, our plan should be ready by day's end."

Thor nodded, watching their faces, seeing in their eyes much more than his guests knew. "Good. Carry on," He replied, closing the door as he, Sam and Mark left the room.

Their next stop was the ship's communications center, or CIC, for Combat Information Center, which was housed behind two sets of doors forming a light barrier. They entered through the first door, closed it, and Thor tripped a light switch on the wall that dimmed the lights. Then he opened a second door, saying, "We go through this procedure because CIC is kept semi-dark and is lit by red lights, as you can see, to make it easier for the communications people to read their monitor screens."

To Mark, who had been communications officer on the aircraft carrier, *Ronald Reagan,* the room was very familiar, and every bit as sophisticated. There were the green radar screens with their sweeps constantly rotating in a slow circle, the men and women sitting at computers, and the radio operators wearing large headphones. In the middle of the room was a large table spread with charts, and beyond it one crew member standing behind the ever-present glass status board, which was covered with undecipherable numbers, letters and special symbols. A large GPS-generated map of the United States covered most of one wall. All in all, it was a Combat Information Center fully capable of dealing with any military problem, and he wondered how the Technians had acquired so much knowledge, so much technological capability. All along, he thought to himself, we believed human life existed only on Planet Earth. My God, this story is going to stand the entire world as we know it on its head.

When they had finished their tour of the second, or mid, level, Thor guided them back to the central staircase and up to the ship's top deck, which he called the 'bridge.' Once again Mark was reminded of the *Reagan,* for Thor's flagship bridge was just as impressive. The huge curving control console on the bridge seemed to stretch forever below a long row of windows, and was equipped with a vast array of dials, switches, chrome levers and video monitors. This bridge was truly the equal of any naval vessel he had ever served on. Because the ship was at rest, very little activity was taking place, but he could well imagine it in action and thought how thrilling it would be to observe the passing universe through those windows which now looked out only upon the huge cavern.

The remainder of their tour was given to inspecting engines, generators and other vital equipment, which Thor was careful not to explain in too much detail, and then they were back in the transporter, heading swiftly back to New York.

"Well Sam, Mark, what did you think? Did this tour convince you that we are real?"

"Yes," Sam responded. "We are not only convinced, we are very impressed." Then he turned to Mark. "How would you feel about pulling next Sunday's program and doing one entirely on this story?—give it the whole show, I mean. I know it's short notice—this is Monday—Only five days."

Mark nodded agreement. "Boss, I would have no problem with that, and I agree it needs an entire show. But we gotta give Washington a heads up first."

"Oh sure, absolutely, but not too much of a lead. It's a story that has to be told and if we give Homeland Security a chance they will block us. I'll contact them an hour before the show."

"Okay, Sam, let's go for it. Thor, what about you? Can you meet that schedule? You will probably have to be in our studio every day this week."

"That, of course, is exactly my wish, and your schedule will be no problem. Just tell me where to be and when."

The three men shook hands, as Mark said, giving voice to his thoughts, "This is going to be the story of the century."

"Please prepare for landing, Commander," Jens called from the cockpit, and minutes later the transporter touched down gently on Continental's rooftop helipad.

CHAPTER TWO

The Meeting

At six p.m., on Sunday, February 28, 2010, the White House Communications Center received an email message marked "Urgent, deliver to the President immediately." It was from Samuel Fischer, Continental Television System, and it read: "A subject of great importance will be broadcast at seven p.m. tonight on CTS *Sunday Review*."

At 6:10 P.M., Howard Fields, President of the United States, read this message, delivered by Jack Brill, his Chief of Staff.

"Hell, Jack," Fields answered, "CTS is always claiming they have something important to say. This ain't nothin' new. Mildred and I are goin' to the Kennedy Center tonight, as planned. Call if anything comes up."

"Yes, Mr. President," Jack responded. He was used to his boss's habit of never taking anything seriously, and knew better than to argue. He returned to his office, flicked the television to the CTS channel, and busied himself with the ever –present stack of situation reports. No matter how hard he worked, the stack never got any smaller. He had long since given up any hope of having a personal life. His wife had left him years before, and took his two children with her, rarely to be seen by him. At 45, balding and overweight, he no longer bothered with trying to date other women. There wouldn't be enough time to develop a meaningful relationship anyway, he reasoned, since virtually every waking hour of his life was spent at the White House. Sunday was just another work day. When he heard the TV announcer's familiar

CTS Sunday Review greeting, he paused in his work, pushed a button on his remote control to start the DVD recorder out of habit and sat back to watch.

There on the screen was Mark Haddon, whom he knew very well, since the two talked frequently. Mark was one of the few news personalities Jack trusted. He was hard-driving when it came to finding out what the government was up to, but Jack knew him to be fair and open in his dealings with people. He listened and watched as Mark introduced his guest, a man he did not recognize, whose name, according to Mark was Commander Thor Berksten. Not an unusual name, Jack thought, probably Danish or Norwegian, The guest was tall, with broad shoulders and black hair, and he was dressed in a dark gray business suit that appeared to be very expensive. Jack sensed that he was a man of considerable means, and wondered why he had never heard the name before. President Field's administration made it a point to cultivate powerful, wealthy, influential people, and this man certainly seemed to fit that category. One thing that bothered Jack was why a man dressed in business clothes would have a military title. He made a note on his ever-present "to-do" pad to follow up on that.

Now there was a tight shot of a very serious-faced Mark Haddon on the screen. "Ladies and gentlemen, tonight we bring you a story so startling, so incredible, that you might not believe it. We didn't either, when we first heard Commander Berksten's story. But he quickly convinced us by allowing *Sunday Review* Producer, Sam Fischer, and me to witness first hand what you are about to view, and to photograph at will. We accepted his invitation and now we bring what we saw to you. You see, ladies, and gentlemen, Commander Berksten is not from Planet Earth. That's right, you heard correctly. Not from Earth. He comes to us from another planet—*another inhabited planet, as a matter of fact*—called Techna Planet. He will not disclose its exact location in space, except to say, it is five million miles from Earth. Furthermore, he told us his researchers have discovered four other planets, all with mammals living on them, though except for Techna, none have life as advanced as ours."

Jack's attention was totally on the television program now, and his hand was on the telephone.

"Here are photographs Producer Fischer and I took last Monday, at Roswell, New Mexico," Mark continued, as he displayed a series of graphically vivid color video shots of strange-looking aircraft. "This is the same Roswell that has been in the news again and again, because of numerous claims of UFO sightings. Friends, Sam and I saw these so-called flying saucers with our own eyes, and took these photographs with our own cameras! These are not trick photos; they are real, only the space ships you see here—Commander Berksten calls them *Starships*—are so much larger and more sophisticated than anything described before. Sam and I touched them. We toured the inside of one of them, as you can tell from the videos, and what's even more incredible, we met and talked to many of the more than 2000 Techna crew members at this secret base near the New Mexico desert."

Jack didn't need to hear any more. He punched a button on the phone that put him in contact with the Secret Service office. "This is Brill. Get the President back here immediately. We have an emergency." He hung up without taking his eyes off the television.

Mark Haddon was still showing photos of the starships. There was a long shot of all five lined up in a row, obviously in some huge building, with workers scurrying around them like so many ants. Then the images of the starships and people suddenly dissolved into pictures of an empty building and barren, lifeless desert, before reverting to the original scenes a few seconds later. These transitions took place as Mark was saying, "As these videos show—and let me say again, they are not camera trickery—the people of Techna Planet can make themselves and their equipment invisible to our eyes at will. Commander Berksten calls it going to *I-Mode*. CTS cameras were rolling as these transitions took place. In case you missed the significance of that, consider this: Techna agents could be anywhere in the United States at this very moment, and none of us would know it. Commander, will you please demonstrate what I have just said?"

In response, Thor disappeared from the television screen instantly.

Speaking to nothing except thin air, Mark said, "Thank you, Sir," whereupon Thor reappeared, sitting in exactly the same pose, in the same richly upholstered chair, with the large CTS oval logo in maroon and white behind him and so familiar to millions of television viewers everywhere.

"Commander Berksten, could your agents be in the White House at this very moment?"

"Yes."

Without thinking, Jack Brill looked around his office, as if searching for an intruder, then his eyes darted swiftly back to the TV screen.

"Would government officials and staff members see them?"

"Not unless they considered it advantageous to show themselves."

"Could they be in the halls—the Houses of Congress, the Justice Department?"

"Mr. Haddon, our agents *are already imbedded in every Government office in Washington.*"

"And how long have they been there, Commander Berksten?"

"A few have been in Washington for twenty years or more, but most were assigned in your year 2000, our year 2613, to watch and listen, to record and report back on significant events, but never to disclose their presence."

"How many are in place today?"

" That information is classified, but the number is substantial."

"Tell me, Commander: Why have you come to our land and why do you have our Government under such heavy, clandestine, surveillance?"

"Mr. Haddon, there are a number of reasons. Basically, it comes down to a lack of trust. You surely know that your President, Howard Fields, like his brother, Frank, before him, has a master plan to convert the entire world to a democratic form of Government modeled after his right-wing Christian Coalition concept. Though that is never said in so many words, the message is clear in every speech. What the proponents of this scheme are careful never to admit in public, but we learned by monitoring private meetings, was that this grand plan pertains to the entire universe, which, of course, includes Techna Planet."

"I take it, then, that you are against a democratic form of government."

"Not at all. Techna has always been a democracy in the purest sense. What we are against is any plan in which someone else—another nation or another planet--dictates what will be the best form of government for us."

"Then, what, Commander, are you just trying to protect your form of government?"

" That is a major reason. We absolutely support separation of church and state, as the United States did, at one time, but sadly, no longer does. Right-wing religious conservatives literally control your Government now and dictate Government policy as well as action. And surely you can see that many of your so-called televangelists are enriching themselves on the backs of thousands of poor, gullible Americans. We see a time when such tainting of Government and taking advantage of the less informed could contaminate the entire universe. We will not allow that to happen."

"Second and of equal concern to us, your Federal Government no longer subscribes to the concept of separation of powers. Your last President—and his successor—have taken unto themselves far greater power than your founding fathers ever intended, without so much as a whimper from Congress, which had those powers taken away. Techna Planet's governing system mirrors yours, or rather did, before this happened. We see nothing but disaster in giving any President that much power . And to make the situation even worse, your CIA is now the President's very own private, secret, spy system."

"Also, your country has become a decadent society. You have uncontrolled addictive drug distribution. You have massive corporate greed--in fact human greed permeates every fiber of your society, or so it seems—drug use is part of that; corporate corruption is part of it. Then, too, and just as serious, you have unpunished killers and rapists everywhere. These problems are already spreading to other countries on Earth; we believe that in time they will also spill over to the entire universe. That is of great concern, for it could involve Techna Planet. We will never permit that. "

"Well, let's see, Commander, you are not very complimentary about religion as we know it. Are you atheists?"

"No."

"Agnostics?"

"Perhaps. Religion is such a subjective thing. It is true we are not convinced of the existence of this God you worship-- this God no one has seen or touched. In all our travels through space we have not encountered the place you call Heaven, where your God apparently resides. Instead, our people learn to treat others as they would like to be treated, to help others in need and to defend those who are less strong than themselves—I believe you used to call it the *Golden Rule* here on Earth. That is what we believe religion should be and it is certainly our religion. I assure you, we do not want to force our beliefs on your people; we simply want to prevent you from forcing your beliefs on us. Your religion is really money, Mr. Haddon. Your unquenchable quest for money, coupled with a serious lack of ethics and morals constitutes a major problem you must fix. "

"Or what?"

"Or your country, itself a great empire, will suffer the same fate as other great empires of the past, such as the Roman, Austro-Hungarian, French and all the others. Some students of empires are already saying the United States will be destroyed by its own vast military empire, which is a run-a-way giant with over 1000 bases in at least 130 countries."

"That sounds very much like a threat, Commander."

"It could seem that way, I suppose. But I am simply telling you, or more precisely your Government, that we do not intend to become another Iraq, another sovereign country invaded by your country without provocation."

"But, Commander, we are in Iraq to fight terrorists. Surely you understand that."

"I understand no such thing, Mr. Haddon. In my opinion you are there because of money; in this case oil money. President Fields wants you to believe terrorism is his cause--that's his cover--his rallying cry. He portrays any one or any group he sees as a threat to his goals as terrorists. By this time tomorrow, I will be labeled a terrorist in all the news media. This tactic is a bit like crying wolf. But if the wolf does not attack as predicted, the people no longer believe there is a wolf. That is the case with terrorism. No one believes terrorists lurk behind every bush anymore. You invaded Iraq to gain control of its vast oil reserves for the American oil companies. That is the truth of it."

31

"Well, Commander Berksten, you have certainly given us a lot to think about tonight. It seems to me you are against everything that makes America unique—our form of Government, our religion, the way we do business, our ethics and morals--everything. The only conclusion I can draw from this is that you are here to remake us into something more acceptable. In fact, to put it bluntly, you have invaded our country to suit your own interests. Is that not the case? You are forcing your beliefs on us. Are you any less fanatic, any less the aggressor? "

A faint smile appeared on Thor Berksten's face. "We are certainly not here by invitation, Mr. Haddon, just as you are not in Iraq and Afghanistan by invitation. Your Government's invasion of those countries was based on claims that they had weapons of mass destruction and that those weapons were pointed directly at the United States. That claim has never been proven. To say it plainly, you are aggressors. You have more nuclear weapons than any other country, yet you cry foul if another country develops one. You look down your noses at other religions, particularly Islam, because you perceive them as different. And where you find great wealth, you steal it. Call us invaders and fanatics--if you wish, Mr. Haddon, but we strongly believe that our cause—to keep Techna out of your hands—is just. Your Government cannot say that about the Middle East. "

"Ah, but you will get an argument from our President on that point."

"No doubt. We expect opposition and are fully prepared for it. In fact, the message I would like to send to President Fields tonight is that we are a much more powerful force than any your country has faced before, even more powerful than you are. After all, we have been at it 613 years longer than you have on Earth. But as I told you earlier, Mr. Haddon, we come in peace. Yes, we have issues your country must address to assure us that you will not try to destroy Techna Planet. But those issues can be easily met and we hope that can be done amicably."

"That sounds very much like an ultimatum, Commander."

"I am afraid it is an ultimatum, Mr. Haddon. We use our great power to benefit others in a positive sense. Your country's way of doing business does not. Thus change in your ways is necessary.

I intend to do whatever it takes to carry out my mission, which is to protect Techna Planet."

"Thank you, Commander. Ladies and gentlemen, I think we have just witnessed one of the most startling events in history. As always, the mission of CTS *Sunday Review* is to keep you informed. This is Mark Haddon. Thanks for watching."

*   *   *

Jack Brill sat in stunned silence for several minutes. "Godallmighty, it's happened," he muttered to himself finally. "We've been invaded. Fields said it couldn't happen if we took the fight to other nations. Guess he was wrong on that, too." He looked around the office again, as if to see if he was being watched. A sheepish look crossed his face, for he realized that, if what he had just seen on television was true—and he had to assume it was—he would not know if he was alone or not. He would never know from this day forward.

The phone on his desk rang and brought him back to the present. "This is Brill."

It was the duty secret service agent he had spoken to earlier. "Sir, the President says to tell you he will talk to you when he returns from the Kennedy Center performance. You are to remain at the "House," (inside slang for the White House). " He is sure whatever you have to tell him can wait."

Jack said, "Thanks," and slammed the phone back into its cradle. Then he shook his head in angry disgust and muttered, "maybe a good shakeup is what's needed around this place, Howard, baby. And I think you are about to get one." Then from long years of practice, he set himself to the task of preparing for the fire-storm that was sure to come as a result of what CTS revealed tonight. He didn't blame the organization, Mark Haddon, or Sam Fischer. They were just doing their job. But he knew it was going to be a very long night. Then as if to signal the start of another round in a prize fight, the phone rang again.

"Brill, here," he answered.

"Jack, Bob Watson here. Can you put me through to Howard, please?"

Jack knew immediately what this call was about. Bob Watson was the Very Reverend Robert Watson, one of the most powerful televangelists, and a close friend and supporter of Howard Fields. "Sorry, Bob," He said. "The President is away from the House right now. Can I have him call you when he returns?"

"Yes, absolutely. It's very important. We've got to stop this maniac CTS had on the *Sunday Review,* before he destroys all we've accomplished. Give Howard that message, will you? And tell him to call me immediately."

"Yes, Sir. I will."

In quick succession, he handled another two dozen calls over the next hour or so. All of them were from powerful people who had supported President Fields and expected a great deal in return.

Gordon Hausemann, CEO of United Motors called to express his desire to sue this Techna Planet bunch in court.

Peter Bigham, President of Delta Phamaceuticals called. He was angry and wanted the President to send troops to Roswell immediately.

Victor Moseman, Rector of St. Paul's Evangelical Church called to warn the President that the devil had finally got a foothold in Washington, and his name was Thor Berksten.

Bertram Phillips, Secretary of Defense called to let the President know the military was on full alert and ready to carry out his orders.

And so it went. In between the near- constant phone calls, Jack logged each call into the electronic message center that would print a list for the President when he was ready to receive it, while kicking himself for not ordering in some of his aides to help field the calls. But, he reminded himself, he hadn't received much of a heads up on this matter himself. He intended to burn Mark Haddon for not providing greater detail, not that it would do any good. The news media had no responsibility to give advance notice of stories; it just did so out of common courtesy.

As Jack well knew, any more detail than was given by CTS and the Government would have used all its power to try to kill the story ahead of time. It was always a cat and mouse game.

* * *

Thor, Sam Fischer and Mark Haddon huddled in Sam's office where they had watched the program—taped earlier, of course. Afterwards, Mark turned to Thor and asked, "Well, how do you think it went?"

"I think it went very well, Mark. Couldn't be more pleased. Let's see how your Government reacts."

"My guess is, troops are already on the way to Roswell to destroy your starships."

"Perhaps, but as I said the other day, they must be content to destroy only sand, sagebrush and jackrabbits."

Laughter filled the office, then Thor said, "Let me express my sincere appreciation to you both for your help, and for such a fine presentation. My country will not forget." They all stood and shook hands, and he continued. "Now I must go. There is much work to be done."

"Okay, then, Commander. But whatever you are going to do, I hope you will let us in on it first."

"You have my word, Sam."

*   *   *

As Thor was on his way out he passed the CTS reception desk, where a young woman was on duty. From a distance and at that angle she looked like Sarah, who had been on his mind more and more, and he was excited at the prospect of seeing her again. But as he drew closer he realized this woman was not Sarah, so he hid his disappointment and greeted her with a simple "hello," as he walked toward the elevators. Uppermost in his mind at that moment was the forthcoming confrontation with the United States Government. As much as he preferred otherwise, Sarah would have to wait.

*   *   *

His pilot, Jens Petersen, was standing, as always, at parade rest next to the open hatch of the transporter. The whispered hum of its powerful engine reached his ears as he approached, and he knew without asking that all was ready for take-off. Jens had been with him for over ten years now and had an impeccable service record. Thor reminded himself how fortunate he was to have one so loyal, so dependable. "Sorry to be so late, my friend," He said. "The meeting took longer than I expected."

"Not a problem, Sir,. I watched the show on our monitor. Hope you don't mind. You were very impressive."

"Thank you, Jens. No, I don't mind. I was pleased with how the show went, but of course, the real proof will come when we see the results."

"Where to, Commander?"

"Well, let's see, why don't we pay a visit to the White House?"

*   *   *

They landed on the South lawn of the White House a few minutes later, unseen and unheard. Thor, in I-Mode now, crossed the lawn from the invisible transporter on foot, strode down the long covered walkway leading from the main building to a door adjacent to the Oval Office. The door was locked and guarded by sophisticated electronic surveillance gear, as he knew it would be, but there was no need to force the door; he simply passed through it, soundlessly, undetected, and in an instant he was inside the most famous building in America, within a few feet of the most famous office.

At the far end of another long corridor he could see the curved door to the Oval Office. It was open, and he could hear voices coming from within. One voice was loud—angry—almost shrill; the other, softer—patient—soothing. He entered through the open door and recognized President Howard Fields and Jack Brill, his chief of staff, from photos shown on television and in newspapers numerous times. Fields, who was standing behind his massive carved walnut desk, had drawn himself up to his full five-feet-five-inch height and was pointing a scrawny finger across the desk at Brill. "Listen, Jack," he was saying. "This whole thing is just some kind of crap dreamed up by that lousy Jew, Sam Fischer, to make me look bad. I ain't fallin' for it and that's the end of it! Understand?"

Brill had faced his boss's anger many times before, and had no fear of him. It was his job to pound some sense into that thick, white-haired skull, so he stood virtually toe to toe with the most powerful man in the world, and shouted right back at him. "Howard, look at the DVD, for christsake! Every time we have a crisis around here you don't want to face it, and then we get—you get—in trouble for doing too little too late. Look at it, goddammit. This is just too real to be contrived. You need to understand, Mr. President: This Thor Berksten, this Commander from that place called Techna Planet, is claiming an invasion of our damned country. If he is talking straight, and I believe he is, you'd better damn well get on it and get on it fast. Jesus, man, at least get DHS (Department of Homeland Security) and FBI on it, to check it out. What the hell is wrong with putting some people on a plane to Roswell right now?"

"And look like a stupid fool when they come up empty? Whose side you on, Brill?"

"Low blow, Mr. President. I'm always on your side. If you don't know that after twenty years, I might as well walk."

"Yeah, yeah, sorry, didn't mean it," Fields said as he slumped into his dark red leather chair. "But where's the proof of this Techna planet thing? We've explored the universe pretty good, it seems to me, and we ain't found a sign of life out there. Now this guy shows up and claims he's from outer space—another planet. You gotta admit, Jack, that's a hell of a stretch."

"Okay, so you're not going to look at the video," Jack responded. "I can't force y…." He paused in mid-sentence as the President turned to stare at something to his left. There was a look of stark disbelief on his now colorless face. Jack followed his gaze and saw the reason immediately. A man was standing just inside the doorway of the Oval Office. Not just any ordinary man, not a White House staffer, not a Government official. President Fields obviously didn't know who the man was because he was pointing his finger at him and shouting, "Who the hell are you! How'd you get in here? Jack, get the SS (Secret Service) in here right now!"

Jack recognized the intruder immediately. It was Commander Thor Berksten, whom he had seen on *Sunday Review* a few hours earlier, and he signaled the SS via his hand-held pager even before Fields went ballistic. Carl Huff and Meredith Rice, the two agents on duty just outside the Oval Office, arrived instantly, with Glock automatics drawn. The moment they appeared, Thor disappeared. One second he was there, the next he was gone. The SS agents never saw him.

"What's the problem, Mr. President?" Carl asked.

"That man! That terrorist!" The President yelled. "There, by the door! Are you both blind? Arrest him! That's an order!"

Carl Huff, a wiry six-footer who had seen just about everything that could happen in his thirty years in the Service, turned to stare at the door through which he had just entered, then gave Jack a perplexed look as if to say, what's wrong with HIM this time? Then his gaze shifted to Fields. "Sir, There's no one in here except Jack, but we'll find him. There's no place for him to hide in here. What did the guy look like?"

The President shrugged and was about to speak, when Jack said, "I can describe him. He is tall, with black hair, and is wearing a dark business suit. He was on *Sunday Review* tonight.

He claims to be from another planet, and he looks just like one of us. He was very convincing on the program and, among other things, demonstrated his ability to become invisible instantly. I think we just saw him prove that. He's still in this building; I'd bet on it—probably still in this room—but my guess is , you won't find him."

Meredith Rice, who was as tall and as lean as her SS partner, and had lovely brown eyes and black shoulder-length hair, was watching Brill intently as he spoke. "Did you record the show, Mr. Brill?" She asked.

"Yep," Jack replied, handing her the DVD he had been trying to get the President to watch. "See for yourselves."

"Great! We're on it," Meredith replied.

"Right." Jack said. "He's on a mission. The DVD will explain it. Check it out."

In unison, the agents said they would, and left the Oval Office.

As soon as they were gone, Thor reappeared. "Yes, Mr. Brill, I am on a mission." Then he faced Fields. "Mr. President, I came here tonight to get your reaction to my appearance on the CTS program, and I see that you refuse to accept reality. No matter. The fact is, I am here. What your Chief-of-Staff has been trying to make you understand is that I also brought an invasion force with me from Techna. I can bring thousands more if necessary. Effective immediately, you can no longer run the United States as you see fit. I am now your commander-in--chief and will have a say in every decision. You will either conform to that reality or be removed from office. So will every other Government official, if that is what it takes. When I return to this office—and that will be very soon—I will lay out my terms in detail. I encourage you to consider them very seriously." And with that he disappeared again.

* * *

Contrary to Mark Haddon's prediction, President Fields did not send troops to Roswell immediately. For two critical days he agonized over what action to take against the invisible man who invaded his office, which is to say he did not agonize for one moment over the fact that *the country he swore to protect had been invaded,* because, in his mind, America was invincible. No enemy would dare attack it, so he did not consider that possibility at all, notwithstanding the fact that his own people claimed otherwise. His anger was directed at the invasion of his personal office, and he worked up quite a head of steam over that invasion, considering it an affront to his personal privacy. What angered him even more was the threat of removal from office, an office he intended to hold forever, no matter what term limits were imposed by the *Constitution.* The Oval Office was his, his alone, and no one was going to deprive him of it.

But the members of his cabinet, as well as Congressmen and Senators from his party, saw the real threat and were deeply concerned as soon as they viewed the DVD. One by one and in groups of two, five, ten or more, they visited the Oval Office and joined his Chief-of-Staff in urging the President to act for the country, not just for himself. On top of that, all his close supporters, the hundreds upon hundreds who had called, were clamoring for swift action. So, in the end, yet still reluctantly, he made the decision he should have made 48 hours sooner, and gave his Secretary of Defense, Bertram Phillips, permission to seek and destroy Techna Force 20 at its base near Roswell. Within an hour, F-22 fighter/bombers were in the air.

* * *

Meanwhile, the entire Secret Service unit, having been alerted by agents Carl Huff and Meredith Rice, was busy searching every inch of the White House. Needless to say, they did not find the intruder. Thor left the House immediately after his meeting with President Fields, and was back in his flagship at Roswell long before Fields issued his attack order. Through messages from Techna Force 20 agents assigned to monitor the President's every move, Thor was aware of all the Washington activity resulting from his visit to the White House. That Fields had ordered an air attack did not surprise him in the least; it was what he would have done had he been in Field's situation. He issued instructions to keep the massive rolling doors covering the opening to the underground hanger 400 feet below the peak of Sardine Mountain closed at all times, except when starship launch was required. Once closed, the sloping doors, covered with vegetation that matched the desert . landscape perfectly, and lined with four feet of steel armor plate on the inside, concealed and protected the huge hanger. Techna Force 20 was secure from any attack.

*   *   *

Two F-22 Raptor fighters from the 531st Fighter Squadron, Holloman AFB, near Alamogordo, New Mexico, each armed with AIM-120 air to ground missiles, were launched at 0600 hours on March 3, 2010, with instructions to find and kill Techna Force 20. In less than ten minutes they were circling the Sardine Mountain area, apparently their primary area of search. They made several passes at 5000 feet above ground level (AGL), as a TF20 transporter, operating in I-Mode, watched their every move from high above.

"They are looking hard at Sardine, TF20 Com."

"Roger, transporter one. They probably know from old records that this facility is here."

"Affirmative. Will continue to observe and report."

"Very well, transporter one."

*   *   *

"Raptor flight leader to wing. See anything?"

"Negative. Looks like barren desert to me."

"Concur. Raptor leader to base. On station at Sardine Mountain. No sign of military activity of any kind. Nothing to kill. Repeat, nothing to kill."

"Raptor base to Raptor leader. Re-transmit. Re-transmit. Message received as no evidence of enemy intrusion. Confirm that?"

"Affirmative, Raptor base. We see only desert. Nothing unusual."

"Hold one, Raptor leader. We are checking."

"Roger. Raptor flight standing by."

*   *   *

"Transporter one to TF20 Com, the Raptors are still circling. At times they drop to around 500 AGL for a closer look. They do that as they pass our southeast quarter."

'Roger, transporter one. That confirms they are looking for the hanger doors."

*   *   *

"Raptor base to Raptor flight leader."

"Raptor flight leader, roger."

"Turn to 330 and prepare for attack. Sardine Mountain has hidden doors leading to an underground hanger. On that heading they will be dead ahead and at ground level. Signal when in position."

"Roger base."

"Raptor base, we are 330 and ready to launch."

"Fire all missiles now, Raptor flight."

*   *   *

"Transporter one to TF20 Com. The Raptors just fired two AIM 120's each."

One by one the missiles slammed into the mountain. Each left a large crater and a huge cloud of dust. Inside the mountain Thor and his agents heard the muffled "frumpf, frumpf, frumpf,

frumpf as each missile exploded, but there was no shockwave and no damage.

*   *   *

"Raptor flight to Raptor base, missiles fired. Report four craters, otherwise no visible result."

"Very well, Raptor flight. Return to base. Looks like a false alarm."

*   *   *

Transporter one reported departure of the Raptors to TF 20 Com.

*   *   *

Before the Raptor flight returned, their base commander alerted Secretary of Defense, Phillips, in Washington concerning the failed Sardine Mountain mission. Secretary Phillips reported that message to the President immediately.

"Bertram, are you telling me we can't disable a military facility we built?"

"Sir, all our records indicate that the underground Sardine Mountain facility was deactivated and destroyed years ago. This Techna Force 20 would have to rebuild it from scratch, and the Raptor pilots saw no evidence of construction anywhere near the mountain. TF20 is either a hoax—and I doubt that-- or it is located someplace else."

"Well, I thought it was a hoax from the beginning. It is beyond my imagination as to how a foreign invader could get through our defenses. I only ordered the planes to check it out because all you people insisted. I know terrorists when I see them and as far as I am concerned this ain't no terrorist action, so tell everybody to stand down."

"But Mr. President, what about the photos? They sure seemed convincing to me. Surely we should do more than just send two fighter/ bombers to investigate."

"Bert, we'll do that when we have more proof."

"Sir....."

"Dammit, stand down! That's an order."

"Very well, Mr. President. You're the boss.

"Right! And don't forget it."

*   *   *

The TF20 agent on duty in the Oval Office recorded that entire conversation between the Secretary of Defense and the President, then promptly reported it to Commander Berksten in his starship at Roswell. Upon hearing this news, Thor walked out of his office and stood at his personal aide's desk. "Manta, please call my Group Leaders to a strategy meeting at 4 pm ."

Thor's organization chart for TF20 listed six units called Groups, each staffed by 200 agents. Group One, headed by Truls Heyerdahl, was responsible for monitoring and affecting all branches of the U.S. Federal Government. Heyerdahl was a huge man--well over six feet tall and 250 pounds—with thick blond hair the color of wheat, and eyes of the deepest blue that seemed to twinkle with every smile. He had been chosen for this mission because of a strong background in political science.

Group Two was headed by Siran Missirian, a beautiful woman, just 26 years old, with long black hair and eyes like deep pools of black onyx. She had graduated from Techna Planet's exceptional school of business with highest honors and was wise in the ways of American business well beyond her years. Her responsibilities included preventing huge corporations from controlling the U.S Government, plus insuring that all U.S. businesses operated in an ethical manner.

Group Three, headed by Captain Arne Klein, was in charge of eliminating religious influence in Government affairs, with emphasis on eradicating so-called televangelists. Klein, 35 years old, who had been one of the first Technians to arrive on Planet Earth, graduated from the California Baptist College, not with the intention of becoming a minister, but merely to learn the inner workings of American religion. He was a very quiet man, small and almost frail in stature, and wore thick horn-rimmed glasses to aid his poor eyesight.

Group Four, was commanded by Assim Agassi. His duties included assuring fairness in the U.S. legal system. Among his various duties was the task of making sure criminal sentences were carried out promptly. As with all group leaders, he had been chosen for this assignment because of his applicable education and training. Assim was a serious man with black hair and eyes and a dark olive complexion. At 45 years old he was the senior member of the expedition. He had a reputation for getting things done, no matter how difficult the assignment.

Group Five was the responsibility of Erika Varga, a tiny beauty of five feet two, with short auburn hair , green eyes and a ready smile. She was assigned the task of protecting the rights of the American middle class, as well as various minority segments of the population.

Group Six, under Guri Kohn, held approximately 800 agents in reserve, for use by any other group needing reinforcements. The need for additional agents was great, particularly in Groups One and Two, so Guri was kept very busy allocating agent resources.

*　　*　　*

Promptly at 4 pm, Thor's senior officers, Truls Heyerdahl, Siran Missirian, Arne Klein, Erika Varga, Assim Agassi, and Guri Kohn, arranged themselves around the polished walnut table in the flagship conference room. Thor was waiting for them, as was Manta Sames, who always attended and took notes on her laptop.

As was his custom, Thor thanked them for taking time from their busy work schedules for the meeting. "I know this is a difficult time for all of you. You signed on for this mission to Planet Earth knowing full well that it would be a long and trying journey filled with danger. You have committed to stay four years and still have three to go. We ask a lot of you, I realize: separation from your families on Techna, disrupting your personal lives. I can only say I believe it is for the best of causes: preservation of our planet and our way of life. Yet I want you all to know that I am so grateful for what you do. I could not ask for a better staff. Now, shall we begin? Truls, why don't you start?"

Truls Heyerdahl nodded. "Right, Commander. I think it is obvious to everyone in Group One that President Fields has no intention of ending the war against Iraq. Not only is it in its seventh year, but Fields is on record as actually wanting it to go for another fifty years. In other words, a permanent war or, if you will, a permanent take-over of that country . I am convinced he plans to do the same thing World-wide, because in his supreme arrogance, no country is capable of managing its own affairs and, in the interest of peace, must let the United States do it for them. Going hand in hand with that position is his desire to be President for life, President of the World. At least that is the way it looks to me. He knows the cost—which is already at $5 trillion dollars, and the U.S. has lost over 10,000 American lives. He does not care about the cost in terms of dead soldiers or in dollars—he just keeps saying it's all worth it. We know he's wrong, but the only way we will stop him is to send opposition forces to Iraq, so that is what we recommend."

"You mean Techna forces, Truls?

"Yes, Sir. We won't need a large force, you know. A couple of Starships and maybe 200 agents. We warn Fields that we intend to take out strategic facilities in Iraq, and give him a very limited time to order complete withdrawal. If he doesn't respond, we act. Our suggestion is that you pay another visit to Washington and lay it out for him. In the meantime we will position our resources."

"Sounds like a good plan, Truls. I will go to Washington on Friday, March 5. Can you be ready by then?

"No problem, Commander."

"Siran?"

"Afternoon, Commander. This coming Monday, March 8, Group Two will begin concerted efforts to eliminate control of the U.S. Government by large corporations engaged in petroleum, pharmaceutical, health care and war materials manufacturing. Our first act will be to order the approximately 20 major corporations we have targeted to stop buying the President and Congressmen with their campaign funding. The CEO's of these companies will each receive notices from us to cease and desist on all election campaign funding effective immediately. They will deny they are doing it and go running to the House and Senate members they support so generously, for help in stopping TF20, of course, but we have a mountain of evidence proving they own the Government. Our notices put them all on notice that the practice must stop right now, that we have the resources to stop it, and that we will use every weapon in our arsenal to do just that. In my opinion, we will have to use our weapons of power; I do not expect these men to agree to our demands without a fight. Owning the Government is just too lucrative for them.

"Very good, Siran. I know you have a very big present for them if they resist, right?"

"Sir, let me just say they will not think it is Christmas."

"Assim, what is happening in the legal and justice arena?"

"Commander, as you know, we have been working on the problem of large prison populations in the U.S., and are making excellent progress in developing our proposed plan, the major element of which is to take the lead in doing what the Government should have been done in the first place. We will be ready to present it to you in about three weeks. Shall we set it for March 29?"

"Done, Assim." Then in order, Thor heard progress reports from Group Three leader, Arne Klein, on the problem of fraudulent activity in religious organizations; Group Five leader, Erika Varga, on the suffering and rapid disappearance of the American middle class. Finally, Group Six leader, Guri Kohn, reported that he was gearing up training of reserve agent forces in anticipation of having to send them into 'battle' in one way or another, on the problems Captains of other Groups were dealing with, and asked that he be kept current on all plans to disperse reserve agents. He received assurances from all other Group Captains.

Thor adjourned the staff meeting at 5:00 p.m., pleased with the progress his TF20 Officers were making, and retired to his office. At 6:00 p.m., Manta handed him printed minutes of the meeting. He read them quickly, thanked her for excellent work as usual and said, "Have a good evening, Manta." Then he sat back and put his feet on the desk. There was so much to be done, he thought to himself. The withdrawal from Iraq, including the question of how best to use the returning troops, was a huge undertaking. He had a plan, but there were still many unanswered details.

Then there were the major problems with separation of powers in the Government, and with corporation control of Government. Will our plans for solving those problems work, he asked himself then after a bit more contemplation he decided everything in that area was on track.

Next he spent an hour going over his plan for dealing with the anticipated horrendous uproar from American citizens that was bound to result from TF20's solution to reduction of the prison population. They are a strange nation, he thought; they are against crime but refuse to enact penalties that would stop it.

*   *   *

On Thursday morning, March 4, Thor arose at 4:00 a.m., showered and donned his freshly pressed uniform, then ate a light breakfast of fruit, a bit of cheese, a slice of wheat bread and strong black tea. At 6:00 a.m., he placed a call to Sam Fischer at CTS *Sunday Review.*.

"Good morning, CTS Sunday Review. My name is Sarah. How may I direct your call?"

"Good morning, Sarah. This is Thor Berksten, Commander, Techna Force 20. I would like to speak to Mr. Sam Fischer. please. But before you connect me, I have a question for you."

"Is that right?"

"Yes. If you are not busy for lunch, tomorrow, will you be my guest?"

"That would be nice, Commander Berksten. My lunch hour is noon to 1:00 p.m."

"Until tomorrow then, Sarah. I am really looking forward to it."

"So am I, Sir. Hold please while I connect you to Mr. Fischer."

Sam Fischer came on the line in just a few seconds. "Hey, good to hear from you again, Thor. What can I do for you?"

"Good morning, Sam. If you have some time around 9:00 a.m. tomorrow, I'd like to stop by your office. I have something I think you might find interesting."

"9 a.m.? That's good with me. Any clues?"

"Just one. I am going to give President Fields an ultimatum."

"About what.?"

"Sorry, Sam. See you tomorrow morning."

Next, Thor came out of his office and stood at Manta's desk

"Will you ask Jens to prepare the transporter for a flight to New York and Washington, he said. I need to get there by 9 a.m. their time, tomorrow."

"Right away, Commander," Manta responded, and reached for the phone.

------///------

CHAPTER THREE
The Ultimatrum

On March 5th, at 8:45 a.m., Thor Berksten exited the elevator at the 60th floor of the Continental Television Building and made the long walk toward the CTS reception enclosure for the second time. As before, receptionist Sarah Malloy's eyes never left him.

"Good morning, Commander, Mr. Fischer is expecting you."

"Ah, the beautiful princess, Sarah," Thor responded. It is so good to see you again."

"Thank you, Sir. I thought you had forgotten us. It seems so long since we last saw you"

"Dear lady, it has been only a month, and I assure you I did not forget you for even one moment. Are we still on for lunch?"

"Yes. I'll be ready at 12."

"Great. See you then," Thor said, as he strode toward the door to Sam Fischer's office.

*   *   *

Sam's secretary, Margie, was waiting for him. "Good to see you again, Commander. Sam is wandering around here someplace. Just have a seat and I'll round him up. Your tea will be here in a moment."

Thor thanked her and walked into Sam Fischer's office. Sam appeared a few minutes later with Mark Haddon in tow. The three men shook hands, as Sam said, "Well, Thor, how are you? You've been sort of quiet since our last visit."

"Yes, I can see that it would seem so to you, but actually we have been very busy preparing for our work here in the United States. And, of course you must have heard that President Fields sent two fighter planes to find and destroy us. They left four craters on the face of Sardine Mountain when they fired missiles at us. But there was no damage and, as I told you when we last met, they found only sage brush and jack rabbits."

This was met with chuckles from Sam and Mark, after which Mark asked, "So, Thor, what happens now? When do you plan to begin your campaign to protect Techna Planet, and what can you tell us about that plan?"

"Actually, Mark, that is why I am here today, and I will lay out our plan for you in a moment, but first I must tell you the scope of our effort is much larger now. During research conducted over the past month we have uncovered irrefutable facts proving that your country is itself in great danger."

"Danger? What kind of danger?" Sam asked.

"Danger of complete collapse from the financial weight of funding your vast military empire. You do know just how huge that empire is, right?"

Sam nodded. "We read the Pentagon's Base Structure Reports, Thor. As I recall, the U.S. has something in excess of 1000 military bases scattered across 130 countries. The justification given to us is that the bases are needed to protect us from terrorists."

"Yes. There has been a massive military build-up since 9/11/2001, all because of the attack on the World Trade Center then. One single attack. To be sure, it was a terrible incident, but does it justify the costs you have incurred?"

"They're damn high, I know that much," Mark said.

"Right. The bill for Iraq and Afghanistan alone is now approaching $5 trillion dollars, not to mention the loss of nearly 10,000 American lives and tens of thousands of Iraqi's. And there is no end in sight. Fields is now talking of keeping troops there for 50 years. Factor in the additional trillions of dollars to keep all the other bases running and you have a staggering number. "

"Where do you get all these facts, Thor? I know you didn't just make them up."

"No, I didn't make them up, Sam. I have agents imbedded in the Pentagon. They are very sharp people who have access

50

to every cell in that vast complex. Also, as I am sure you are aware, your internet contains a huge library of information that is put there by Government agencies to satisfy requirements of the Freedom Of Information Act. It's all there, a bit difficult to dig out at times, but readily available. The sad thing is that so few Americans bother to look at it. Don't they care what is happening to their country?"

Sam and Mark exchanged knowing glances, and Mark answered. "That is a question we have been asking for years, Thor. It's as if they just don't want to be bothered. They're too damn wrapped up in getting on with their daily lives. For entertainment, they would rather watch the crap on TV, play games on their I-pods, or hang out with friends via their laptops. Join the army? Forget that! People get shot in the army. But, hey, what does all this have to do with protecting Techna Planet?"

"Plenty, Mark. To feed this hungry military giant you must borrow huge sums of money, and your primary sources are China, Japan and India. How long they will be able to sustain your vast appetite is anybody's guess. Plus, you have another problem:"

"Which is?" Mark asked.

"Which is, the dollar is losing ground fast against the Eurodollar. At some point, China, Japan and India may refuse to accept dollars in repayment of your debt and demand payment in Euros. Do either of you know where that could lead?"

Sam nodded. "Sure. The United States would be in the tank. Dead. That would be the end of us."

"Right. The American Military Empire would die and take the entire country with it. China would take over the U.S. Or, maybe split it with Japan and India. Your ways of governing would also die, to be replaced by—more than likely—China's form of Communism."

"Aw, come on, Thor," Mark growled. "That seems pretty far-fetched to me."

"It is not far-fetched, at all, Mark. Money controls everything. You know that. Ultimately, China, Japan and India will control all the money. They already control most of the manufacturing expertise the United States used to own. They are buying more and more of your agriculture products—corn and wheat—leaving precious little for American tables, and at a lot higher cost. You want to know why all this concerns me, so I'll tell you: It is because my adversary would no longer be the United States which for all its faults, still has a degree of ethics and morals that make dealing with you possible. The countries that are likely to take you over have far different philosophies, making my battle to protect Techna Planet infinitely more difficult. Furthermore, I would probably be fighting to preserve America, at least in the beginning of the collapse, which adds another layer of complexity."

"Okay, Thor," Sam asked. "What can we do about it?"

"Gentlemen, we must put the tiger back in its cage. By that I mean we have to drastically reduce the U.S. military establishment, and confine it to land owned by the United States. The job of the military is to protect your country, which includes the 50 states and Puerto Rico. Nothing more."

"It can't be done," Mark said. "Hell man, how do you fight a military juggernaut that big? Especially now, since Fields controls the CIA, which gives him his very own secret police force?"

"Mark, we fight it step by step, and we will begin with Iraq and Afghanistan. That's why I wanted to meet today. Forget about the CIA. Techna Force 20 will handle that problem. Sam, when I asked for this meeting you wanted clues as to what it would be about. I said it would be about giving President Fields an ultimatum. Let me explain. This afternoon I will visit Fields in the White House. I know he will be there; my agents keep close tabs on his every move. During that meeting I will order President Fields to begin rapid withdrawal of troops and equipment from Iraq immediately."

"You will order him!" Mark gasped.

"Yes. You see, when I left here the last time, I went directly to the White House and walked into the Oval Office. I made it that far by operating in I-mode which, as I explained to you before, allows me to move anywhere at any time without being seen. Once in the Oval Office, I switched to V-mode. Fields was arguing with Jack Brill, his chief of staff, who wanted him to send troops to Sardine Mountain and root us out, and Brill was not winning. Within seconds of my changing to V-mode, Fields spotted me out of the corner of his eye and went ballistic. He screamed for the Secret Service to arrest me, but when the two SS agents arrived I was nowhere to be seen, having reverted to

I-mode again. The agents thought Fields had flipped, but left after assuring him they would find me and deal with me. Of course, as soon as they left the Oval Office, I, who had been there the entire time, once again appeared in V-mode. Fields was jumping up and down, livid with anger, and demanded to know how I dared to invade *his personal office*, and what I was doing there. I told him I was there as his new commander-in-chief, and that henceforth he would be taking orders from me. Watching his reaction was quite a sight, indeed."

"Gawddamn!" exclaimed Mark, reverting to his Mississippi origins. "Sure would'uv liked to see that!"

Sam chimed in, "Yeah, that must have been some meeting."

"Exactly. You gentlemen would have enjoyed it. Anyway, today he gets that ultimatum. He must get out of Iraq, and I have numerous options to force him to do it. I will present those options to him at the meeting, on an as required basis. All of them involve destruction of American facilities, equipment and, possibly American personnel. I am not going to tell you now what those options are, but if you recall, I said in our first meeting here that I would do whatever is necessary to achieve Techna objectives. You can use your own imagination. Better still, why not come with me to the White House this afternoon and watch the fun personally?"

"How can we do that, Thor. Fields isn't issuing invitations."

"Simple. I will take you in with me. We take my transporter, land on the White House lawn, walk to the West Wing, and enter the Oval Office, all in I-mode. Once inside, when we are standing in front of Fields huge walnut desk, I revert to V-mode. If you want, I can make you two reappear as well. That's up to you. Then," Thor said, grinning broadly, "We let the games begin."

"Fantastic! Man, that is just fantastic! Mark yelled. "Whadya say, Sam? Let's do it. What a story this will make!"

"It is a good way for you to get the story, Sam, if you are interested. I think the American people would want to know. They certainly have a right to know. Who better to tell them than CTS *Sunday Review?* Are there any better reporters than you and Mark? Tell you what. I am going to have lunch with your lovely receptionist, Sarah Malloy, if you don't have a problem with that—no talk about any of this with her—but a man's life can't be all work, you know. Sarah and I will try to get back here at 1:00 p.m., when her lunch hour ends. I will pick you up at that time and we will be at the White House in minutes. How does that work for you?"

"Just fine, Thor. We'll be ready. We would prefer to be visible to the President though. CTS always tries to operate in the open."

"So be it, Sam. It is always better to deal openly, especially where the people's business is involved. I will 'introduce' you as it were, when I think the time is right."

"Great. Oh, if your lunch takes longer than an hour don't worry about it. One thing, though: I don't think Mark is too happy about you taking Sarah to lunch. He's had his eye on her forever."

Thor looked at Mark. "Sorry, old friend, but she is off limits to married men."

"How'd you know I'm married?

"Need you ask, Mark? By the way, you won't need cameras, at the White House. My agents will be hiding in the bushes so to speak, and will have plenty of photos for you. See you at 1:00 p.m. or so."

*   *   *

It was five minutes to twelve when Thor returned to the CTS reception area. Sarah, now wearing a long toffee-tone cashmere coat and knitted white beret', was standing outside the enclosure talking to the woman who was there to relieve her. She smiled, and, for him, the lobby filled with sunlight. Thor knew he had never seen a more beautiful woman in his life.

"Hi. Ready to go?" he asked. She nodded, and waved to her replacement. Thor took her arm and guided her toward the elevators, saying, "How do you feel about flying?"

She looked up at him. There was a question mark on her brow and a look of concern in her lovely blue eyes. "It's not like it used to be. Why?"

"Because I don't want to waste one moment of our time together and we will get to the restaurant I have chosen much faster in my plane."

Sarah had heard about his personal transporter. As with any company office, there were no secrets at CTS *Sunday Review*. "And just where *are* we going, Commander Berksten?"

"Please, Sarah. Call me Thor."

"All right, Thor. Same question."

"Cape Cod. Have you been there?"

"Oh, many times. Boston is my home town and our family always summers on the Cape."

"Then you must have been to the Coonamessett Inn in Falmouth."

"Of course. It is one of my favorites. I love the food"

"Wonderful. So do I, and it is such a beautiful place.

"But how did you discover it, Thor?"

"I was in Boston on business. The people I visited suggested we dine there. I found the Inn delightful, and loved it immediately; it has such a great, relaxing environment. Actually, I fell in love with all of the Cape. If I were to build a home in the United States, it would be there."

*   *   *

By this time they had reached Thor's transporter on the rooftop helipad. "Sarah, this is Jens, my personal pilot. All set, Jens?"

Jens bowed to Sarah and said, "Ready, Commander."

Sarah and Thor boarded the aircraft. He helped her fasten her seatbelt, then said, "Sarah, this aircraft takes off vertically, and does it very fast. You may feel as if you are being driven through the floor when we lift off, but do not be alarmed, it is normal, and the sensation is brief. Then he took his seat across from her, and signaled the pilot to take off. In spite of his warning, Sarah's eyes widened and she gripped the arms of her chair tightly for a second or two, as the sleek transporter became airborne. "Oh, my, this is exciting," She said. "How fast are we going?"

"We cruise at 5000 knots, but won't be up long enough to reach that. This flight will last only about five minutes."

"Amazing. Can I ask you a personal question?"

"Certainly."

"Are you married?"

"No. There was someone, once. But she couldn't handle my being away so much. When she learned that I could be on this mission for five years she broke off our engagement."

"Couldn't she come with you?"

"Yes, but she didn't want to be millions of miles from her family that long."

"Ummm, yes, I can understand that. Why did you accept this mission, Thor?"

"It is my job, Sarah. I was ordered here by the Prime Minister of Techna, who also happens to be my father. From the time we discovered Planet Earth, he has worried that our lovely planet might be invaded. So he sent me here to make sure that does not happen."

"Do you think you will be here five years?"

He shrugged. "I think it might be much longer—maybe even a permanent assignment. Perhaps you do not realize it, but your country has many problems that could impact Techna Planet. They must be resolved if I am to ever leave here."

On the cabin intercom Jens said, "Commander, we will be landing in one minute."

"Very well, Jens. Sarah, the destinies of Earth and Techna, and in fact, the entire universe, are inextricably linked together. The problems of one planet are the problems of all others"

*   *   *

The Maitre d' took them to their table in a quiet secluded nook off the main dining room. Commander Berksten, Albert will be your waiter. Would you care for cocktails?"

"No, thanks. We are short on time."

"Very well. Your meals will be served immediately."

Thor thanked him and said to Sarah, "I took a chance and ordered two of the house specialties, Lobster Bisque and Baked Chatham Scrod. Are you okay with that?"

"It's perfect. How did you know those would be my choices?"

"Just a hunch," He answered. "Now, what about you? I want to know everything."

"Well, as I said, I was born and raised in Boston--Brookline, actually. My father is a successful Irish Catholic lawyer, and my mother is a Jew who became a Catholic. I have a brother, James, who is also a lawyer in my father's firm, and two older sisters, Celia and Ellen, who are homemakers. I graduated from Harvard with a degree in journalism and the hope of becoming a writer. That hasn't happened, yet, and may never happen. I like New York, and love my job with CTS, but miss Boston and my family terribly."

"It is a short flight to Boston. You could visit often."

"And I do, but it's just not the same. We are a very close family. Do you have brothers and sisters, Thor?"

"Four sisters, all married with children."

"Uncle Thor. That has a nice ring."

"Thanks, I like being uncle. At last count I had seven nieces and three nephews. When I am home they keep me pretty busy."

"How old are you, Thor?"

"34. You?"

"26. Would you like kids of your own?"

"Sure. Some day." He looked Sarah straight in the eye and continued, "When I find the right girl." He wanted to add, _I think I have,_ but decided it was too soon to say that.

"What is it like, living on Techna Planet? I still find it hard to believe there is life anywhere but on Earth. Our education and religious communities have not prepared us well for this shocking development."

"Yes, Sarah, I agree. And you know what? I predict we will eventually discover many more planets with intelligent life. It is inconceivable that in so large a universe that is not the case. Anyway, to answer your question, life on Techna is very much as it is here. If you were there now, you might have difficulty telling the difference, except that our planet is much smaller than Earth. Of course, life on Techna developed much sooner—613 years sooner-- than on Earth, so, technologically, especially in electronics and transportation, you would see much greater advancement."

"I would love to see Techna, Thor."

"That can be arranged. In fact, I will be going home on business a month from now—I do that every six months. If you can get away for three weeks—that's one week to get there, one week to explore and one to get back to Earth--I would love to have you join me. It's like traveling by cruise ship, Sarah. Your very own private stateroom, great food, and about 200 other passengers to talk to."

"Why do you have so many passengers?"

"We try to rotate agents every six months. This mission, like most, is hard on personal relationships. I suppose it is much the same as for men and women in your military; they need a break, a chance to spend time with their families."

"That sounds like a vacation I should not pass up, Thor. Let me see if I can work it out."

"Wonderful, Sarah. I will stay very positive."

* * *

Albert brought their food at this point, and they ate quickly, talking all the while as if they had known each other for years. Sarah had been taken by Thor the moment she first set eyes on him, and now realized that she might already be in love with him. There were many rumors about him at CTS. Rumors to the effect that he was a very powerful man who would stop at nothing to accomplish his mission. But there were also rumors that indicated he had high moral and ethics, and was not just a ruthless tyrant. People said he could and would kill if he considered the act justified. Sarah, who was not against capital punishment per se, decided she needed to hear more from him on this subject before making a judgment, but already found it difficult to believe he could be a cold-blooded executioner. She could only hope that he would give her future chances to learn more about him, and took his offer of a trip to Techna as a good sign. She made a promise to herself not to let that opportunity slip away.

Thor had similarly warm feelings about Sarah. He saw in her eyes a woman of great gentleness, warmth and kindness. She was so beautiful that just watching her took his breath away and brought excitement to his heart. He knew he would ask her out again, and soon. He knew, too, that she would want to know about his work, and that, eventually, the methods he was forced to use to carry out his duties could become a serious issue. How to deal with that subject when it did come up was a perplexing matter deserving of a great deal more thought, but he was determined not to let it become an insurmountable obstacle to their relationship.

*   *   *

They returned to the helipad on the roof of the CTS building just after 1:00 p.m., and Thor escorted Sarah back to her work station. As they walked toward the reception enclosure he told her how much he had enjoyed their brief time together, and said, "I would love to see you again soon. Would it be all right if I call you?"

"Yes, Thor. I had a wonderful time."

When they arrived at the enclosure he hugged her and said, "It will be very soon, " then he walked quickly toward the door to Sam Fischer's office. Less than ten minutes later he reappeared, this time accompanied by Sam Fischer and by Mark Haddon.

*   *   *

The transporter flight to Washington was very short and, as Thor had promised, they soon landed on the south lawn of the White House, unseen and unheard. Nor did anyone see them as they walked toward the White House, or down the long corridor toward the Oval Office, and they were soon standing in front of Howard Field's desk, behind which sat the most powerful man on Earth. He was slouched in his chair with his feet on the desk, taking a nap. Thor reverted to V-mode and lost no time in waking him up. "Good afternoon, Mr. President," he said loudly. The greeting startled Fields and made him instantly alert.

"What the.... YOU! How the hell did you get in here again?"

"As I told you during our last meeting, I have many powers."

"Well so do I and this time you won't escape." With that he pressed a button hidden under the desk, and simultaneously yelled loudly for the secret service agents. The same two agents who had been on duty before were there in seconds but saw only the President.

"Yes, Mr. President?"

"Arrest that man!" Fields said, pointing across the desk. You let him get away the last time. Don't let it happen again! Get him!"

"Who, Mr. President? There's no one in here but you."

"Arrest him! I order you. Or get someone in here who is competent!"

Jack Brill, who was always alerted by the same buzzer Fields used to call his security guards, entered the office at that moment. "They're right, Howard. You're the only person in here. What's going on?"

The President's face was livid with anger. "That man, that Berksten guy—the one who invaded my office before—is here again. What the hell is happening to security around here?"

"Security is fine, Howard. It's you. You see terrorists behind every tree. You're getting more paranoid by the day." Only Jack Brill could talk to Fields that way, and he wasn't afraid to do so.

"Godammit, Brill, I know what I saw. Now sweep this building from top to bottom. This time I don't want any screw-ups, understand?"

"Right," Brill said, nodding to the secret service agents, "we'll get on it now." Then he dismissed them with a wave of his arm. As soon as they left, Thor who, along with Sam Fischer and Mark Haddon, had witnessed this scene, now returned to V-mode and said, "Mr. President, you must learn that you cannot control me. I am your commander in chief, remember? I am here to give you orders, not the other way around. Is that clear? By the way," Thor continued, as he made the two CTS men visible again, "I brought friends with me today. You know them, of course. Sam Fischer and Mark Haddon from CTS *Sunday Review.*"

Fields was beside himself and he stared at Sam and Mark in disbelief. "You brought the media into this? Don't you know what we do here is top secret? These bastards," He screamed, pointing at Sam and Mark, "will spread it all over the world."

"As they should, Mr. President. Government cannot be allowed to operate in secrecy, as you have done far too long. You do recognize freedom of the press, right?"

"Not when it comes to Government business, I don't."

"Well, Sir, it specifically applies to Government business, and from this moment on you will not keep secrets from the people. That is also an order."

"Listen, you son of a bitch. What do you mean, order? Nobody gives me orders. I am the Supreme Leader of this country. I give the orders around here."

"Not anymore. From now on you will do as I say or be removed from office. You are simply too incompetent to be allowed to make major decisions—any decisions, for that matter--on your own. Now, here is my first directive: You will initiate an immediate withdrawal of all troops and equipment from Iraq. You will start that process this very day."

"Like hell, I will," Fields shot back. "I will not quit there until they accept democracy, and what are you going to do if I don't? Kill me?"

"I hope that will not be necessary, but it is definitely one option. I have many others. You are a blind fool if you expect me to believe gaining democracy for Iraq is your objective. You want that country for another strategic military base, and for its oil. Now, Sir, you will comply with my order or subject your country and your armies to severe consequences. First, I will destroy your new, billion dollar Green Zone Embassy in Baghdad. That will happen within the hour today, so you need to send an alert right away to get all the people in that complex out of there. If they stay, they will die."

"Do you think I believe that?"

"You better believe it. One of my powerful starships is on station over Baghdad and I have already given the command. If you don't believe me, let the destruction happen--and it will--in about 45 minutes. Perhaps that will convince you. If it does not, my next target will be the entire Green Zone. The third will be your fantastic super carrier, *Ronald Reagan*. I will send her to the bottom of the Persian Gulf with all hands and her 50 F-18 aircraft. I have more choices, as well. So, Mr. President Fields, you WILL order commencement of withdrawal today, one way or another."

"Go to Hell, Berksten."

Thor took his smart phone from its holster on his belt, opened it and punched a button with his thumb, then put the instrument to his ear. The call was to Group One leader, Truls Heyerdahl in Baghdad, who answered right away.

"Commence the Embassy action, Truls," Thor said.

"Wait! Now you stop that!" Fields yelled.

"Well, Mr. President? Hold up, Truls"

"I don't think you have the guts to carry this out, Berksten."

"Howard, I think he does," Jack Brill warned. "You should consider his demands very carefully."

"Keep out of this, Brill. I know what I'm doing."

"Well, at least play it safe and get our people out."

Fields stared at Thor, then turned to face his chief of staff.

"He's bluffing. That's what I think."

Brill's face reddened. "Look, dammit. Even if it turns out he is—and I don't believe it for a minute—you had better err on the side of caution. Get the people out!

"Yeah, and what will the media make of that?"

In answer, Brill turned to face Sam and Mark, who were standing to one side of the president's desk. "Why don't you answer the question, Sam? What *will* you do with what is happening here today?"

"We will put the entire story on *Sunday Review,*" Sam responded. "We will let the people of America know that, finally, someone with courage to act is going to end this exercise in futility. Frankly, we will not be very kind to you, Mr. President. As you know CTS has never supported this war. If it were not for this man," he said, pointing to Thor, "There would be no end to the carnage; you don't want to stop it. And," he said, "We believe the people will be exuberant in their praise—maybe not the powerful corporate guys who have made a fortune feeding at the public trough—but the little guys, the men and women whose lives will never be the same because of your stubbornness and poor judgment. But they won't praise you, Mr. President. They will praise this man from Techna Planet, Commander Thor Berksten. You'll serve out your term as President—if he lets you—and vanish into obscurity.

Fields glared at the head of CTS *Sunday Review*. "I can stop you, you know. I'll pull your broadcast license. Disclosing secret information is a crime."

"Oh, I don't think you will do that, Mr. President. You still need us-- the media, I mean."

The President sat slumped in his chair, shoulders drooping, head down, eyes staring at the top of his desk for several minutes. Then his head came up and he looked straight at Thor. "Okay, Jack. You win. I'll call the Secretary of Defense and tell him to order evacuation. And I'll also tell him to order *Reagan* to shoot this man's goddamn starship out of the sky."

"Go ahead, Mr. President. You have 45 minutes," Thor said. Then, speaking into his smart phone, he said, "Truls, commence operations in 45.minutes."

"Very well, Commander."

*   *   *

Truls Heyerdahl stood on the bridge of his starship as it hovered high above the American embassy in Baghdad. Though darkness had settled over Iraq, he could see several thousand people, visible as small specks in the glow of the starship's powerful landing lights, scurrying from the embassy complex and climbing into a fleet off waiting trucks.

"Captain, incoming missiles!" a lookout warned. "Many SAMS!"

"Very well. They can see us because of our lights, We go to I-Mode now. Begin defensive measures, and commence firing.

Instantly, brilliant laser beams streaked from starship gun ports, piercing the night sky. None of the SAMs found its target, of course. A few drifted far off course and headed for deep outer space. Those that would have hit the starship had it been visible to them were destroyed by the lasers long before they reached the starship's location.

A communications officer called COM-1, standing next to Captain Heyerdahl and wearing headphones, warned the Captain that F-18 fighters had been launched from the aircraft carrier *Reagan*. "Very well," the Captain responded. "Same procedure. They are blind to us, but give the order to kill them, anyway."

Com-1 transmitted the order. About a minute later, he said, "Captain, 4 F-18's destroyed."

*   *   *

In Washington, a Defense Department communiqué was handed to President Fields, informing him that 20 SAM's and 4 F-18's had been lost in a failed attempt to bring down the Techna starship.

*   *   *

When the 45 minute deadline was up, Captain Heyerdahl gave the order to fire. Instantly, four laser bursts streaked toward the embassy. The buildings, each six stories high, exploded in a huge cloud of smoke and dust. When the wind carried the debris' away, all that could be seen where the once beautiful embassy had been standing was a monstrous pile of twisted steel and broken concrete. He turned to COM-1 and said, "Notify Commander Berksten that our mission has been accomplished."

*   *   *

Thor's smart phone signaled him just after 2:00 p.m. He listened carefully to the short message, returned the phone to its holster on his belt, then turned to face President Fields. "Your new embassy has been totally destroyed. It exists no more," he said. "Now, are you ready to start withdrawal, or not?"

"Never! And you will rue the day you took on the United States Government."

"Yes. However, we do not believe that day will come. For now you need to evacuate the Green Zone or 25,000 Americans are going to perish. That is our next target. We attack at dawn."

Fields did not respond. In his eyes there was a mixture of fury and fear. He didn't believe what was happening to him—to his great plan to make Iraq the new American satellite country. How, he thought, can I face my supporters—those powerful corporate leaders—who are already impatient to build factories and oil refineries there? In the beginning, he had hoped that winning the Iraq war and converting that country to democracy, a project started by his brother, the President before him, would bring him great fame and fortune. Instead it had become like a heavy lead anchor around his neck, dragging him ever deeper into the depths of despair, making it more and more difficult to pretend that all was well in the White House.

Jack Brill was watching the president intently. Through years of working with him he could almost read his mind. Jack knew Fields was not worried that 25,000 people might be killed; his fear was that his grand plan was doomed, and he was desperate for a way out. It was the possibility of losing an opportunity for even greater wealth that paralyzed him at this moment. "Howard," he said, "You'd better evacuate. This guy means business. Get those people out. Send in the C-17's and get them out of the Green Zone."

"Where do I put them? There is no other secure location."

"Bring them home, Howard. It's over."

"What's over? The war isn't over. It has to go on."

"Mr. President, I think the war *is over.* You just need to accept that."

"Are you telling me one man can dictate how I run this country—change our whole way of doing things?"

"No, Mr. President, I'm saying he has already done it. Game, set, match. We are finished. You are finished. When this story gets out—and Sam just told you it will—the Federal Government as we know it is done forever."

"Bullshit, not on my watch," President Fields blustered. Maybe we lose the Green Zone, but we fight on." He pounded the desk with his fist and shouted. "We must fight on! We will fight on! We will stay the course in Iraq! Then he pointed at Thor. "That guy is a terrorist. He has invaded us. We kill terrorists, Brill."

Bertram Phillips, Secretary of Defense, who had been summoned by the President, arrived in the Oval Office at this point. The President nodded to him and said, "Bertram, I want you to stop the takeover of our country by these Techna terrorists. Use all resources. Send our best space shuttles to find Techna Planet. Destroy it. Locate their base in New Mexico;

You botched that assignment once, now get it done. The survival of our country is at stake."

"Do you realize what you are asking, Mr. President? Locating a planet we have never even heard of before could take years, not to mention billions of dollars. You say use all resources? Hell, Mr. President, we don't have any left. Our army reserves are nil. We are spread so thin now that we could not fight an illegal town rally. And where's the money coming from?"

"Where it always come from. We borrow from China. You have your orders, so get to it."

"Sir, that order is virtually impossible to carry out."

"Bertram, if you think you can't handle it, resign and I'll get somebody else."

"Mr. President...."

"Howard," Brill argued, "Bert is right. If you order him to go after Techna Planet you have to give him the resources to do it. And, as he says, you don't have any resources left. Rescind that order. Concentrate on withdrawing from Iraq. The people want it. Congress wants it. Iraq has been doing business its own way for over 2000 years. In my opinion, you will not change that country today, tomorrow, ten years from now, hell, even 1000 years from now. The losses we suffer daily are not worth all the oil they have. Furthermore, what do we need with another military base? We already have hundreds of them scattered all over the world. I say, give it up. Order withdrawal to begin. If you don't, we lose the Green Zone tomorrow morning, possibly along with 25,000 lives. Next he'll sink the *Reagan*, and after that who knows what else he will do? The fact that he destroyed the Baghdad Embassy should tell you something about his ability to do what he threatens to do, and about his determination. And if nothing else gets your attention, think of the money getting out of there will free up. $12 billion a month can solve a lot of other problems for you."

"Maybe you should resign, too, Brill. You're against me, Bertram is against me, everybody is against me."

"Howard, " Brill continued, "If you want my resignation you can have it. I suspect that Bertram feels the same way. But our job is to advise you and that is what we are doing. I have been against the Iraq war from the beginning. You know that. It was a mistake. A very bad mistake. Let's cut our losses and move on."

The President raised both arms palm out and brought them down hard on the desktop. "Alright," he said, "I'll make one concession. I'll order that all non-combatants be transported back to the States. But I will not order withdrawal from Iraq. Bertram, see to it, will you?"

"As you wish, Mr. President."

Thor said, "Mr. President, in the interest of saving lives my force in Iraq will delay attack one day. We strike at dawn the day after tomorrow." He then transmitted that order to Captain Heyerdahl in Baghdad before adding, "But do not think this is the end of it. You must begin to withdraw all forces and equipment from Iraq immediately. In just 40 hours you will lose the Green Zone. Soon after that you will lose one of your great aircraft carriers. Every day I will deprive you of military resources you depend on in your futile attempt to conquer that country. You cannot win against Techna Force 20." Then, speaking to Sam and Mark, he said, "Gentlemen, our business here today is finished. It is time for us to leave." The two CTS men nodded in agreement and, along with Thor, disappeared into I-Mode before walking unseen out of the White House.

* * *

On the short flight back to New York Thor quizzed his companions about the White House meeting.

"Commander, " Mark replied, "To witness the workings of the Government first hand is every news man's dream. Damn, that was a very huge pleasure. You agree, Sam?"

"Absolutely. Thanks, Thor, for inviting us. You gave us a great scoop."

"But can CTS use what you learned today, Sam?"

"You bet, Commander. We can't put the story together in time for this week's *Sunday Review,* but I don't see that as a problem. We'll add a teaser news item on it this Sunday, then do full coverage next Sunday. In fact it will be a much more powerful story then, if you carry through on your threat to destroy the Green Zone and the *Reagan.*"

"It is no threat, Sam. I have to say, though, that I have never met a more stubborn person than Fields, or one as stupid."

"Yeah," Mark responded. "But members of our Government aren't known for their smarts, Thor. My take is, he doesn't see what you are yet, or any threat to his Iraq project. He's back there right now prodding Phillips to get that attack on Techna Planet going. He wants to kill you immediately, but hell, he doesn't even know which course to send shuttles out on."

Thor nodded in agreement. "Any course he chooses will be a failed course. Our starships will be there to intercept. We will make sure Fields never finds Techna. Remember the destruction of *Columbia* some years back? Well, you could see a recurrence of that disaster."

By this time the transporter had landed on the CTS rooftop helipad. Thor shook hands with Sam and Mark, and waited until they disappeared into the building. Then he said, "Now we go home, Jens."

* * *

Back on the base beneath Sardine Mountain, Thor looked up to find Manta Sames standing in front of his desk. "Hi, Manta. You look like you have a problem."

"Yes, I do. We are running out of money, Thor. American money, for food, lodging and all the other things we have to buy here."

Thor nodded. "Yes, I know it takes a lot to provide for 2000 agents, Manta. Ask Assim to come in. He may have an answer to that problem."

Assim Agassi, head of Group Four, was responsible for American legal affairs, and his assignments covered a broad range of activities. He appeared a few moments later and the two men exchanged greetings. "You wanted to see me, Commander?"

Thor responded by telling him about the shortage of American funds.

"Glad you asked, Commander. We are on it. Our agents are everywhere in Mexico now, looking for illegal drug shipments. Intercepting those shipments will be our best source of funds."

"How does the plan work, Assim?"

"We know how the drugs are shipped here and from which points. The largest shipments cross American borders in trucks. There are so many shipments the U.S. Border Patrol is overwhelmed, primarily because they have virtually no advance knowledge of specific shipments. But our agents, unseen as they are, circulate freely in areas of illegal activity. When one of them discovers a shipment about to be made he or she simply stays with it all the way in, until it reaches its American sale point. We let the transfer take place, then take possession of the money—a lot of money, and destroy the drugs. It drives the drug lords crazy, and we have all the cash we need and then some."

"Sounds good to me. It does get drugs off the streets, and it does solve our money problem. When can it be put into operation?"

"As a matter of fact, we intercepted our first large shipment a little over a week ago. Netted $2 million dollars and destroyed the drugs as soon as the new owner took possession. Now he is after the seller, who he thinks is cheating him. The result will be one dead drug lord and a reduced supply of drugs."

"It is a good plan," Thor responded. "Why don't you give Manta the news about the money part."

"Thanks, Commander. Do you have time for another matter?"

"Sure do. What's up?"

"We are ready to solve the death row problem in American prisons and need to know when you would like to start."

"Very well, Assim. I need to do something on that first. How would March 19 work for you?"

"Not a problem, Commander. Agents are in position. We will start then."

"Good. I think it is going to be hard for Americans to understand, but it is in their best interest."

*   *   *

Soon after Assim left Thor's office Manta came in. "Nice to know we have funds again, Thor, and that we will have a ready supply from now on. But where will I keep all of it? Not in a bank on Earth, certainly."

"No, not in a bank here. The Americans will soon know what we are up to where the drug business is concerned, and will be looking for the money. If we put it in one of their banks they will surely find it and take it. That would deprive us of badly needed funding, thus giving the U.S. Federal Government leverage over us we do not want. Keep on hand what you need for a month and send the rest home to our bank on Techna. I anticipate that we will be collecting very large amounts of cash. Keep just what you need from any such sources, then move the remainder to Techna on the next flight. If nothing comes in from Assim, and you need to replenish your supply, send an order with the next starship run to Techna and the money will be brought to you."

Manta said, "Yes, I understand," and left Thor's office.

* * *

Thor next checked with Truls Heyerdahl, who had returned from Baghdad, concerning the status of withdrawal from Iraq. During that call, he learned that little progress was being made. Republicans in the House of Representatives and Senate were doing everything possible to block Democrat Bills on the subject. Though the Democrats still had enough votes to pass the legislation, they lacked a sufficient majority to override a veto by President Fields, a veto that would surely come. This news troubled Thor very much. He understood the reasons for the U.S. Constitutional provisions that made participation of all three branches of Government in law-making activity mandatory, but in his mind, filibusters and political party majorities were being disgracefully misused and must be abolished.

The Republicans are like puppets on strings, he thought to himself. They are pulled this way or another by their handlers—the corporations who want the war to continue so they can make bigger profits on war planes, tanks and ships, or by other handlers who want no Government oversight of their operations. He knew the only purpose of the war was to satisfy corporate greed. Iraq was a sovereign country that had not attacked the United States, yet it was being systematically destroyed, and its citizens were being slaughtered, by U.S. forces. If there was a more evil crime, he could not think what it would be, and he vowed to make correction of that problem a priority project, with or without President Howard Fields.

* * *

Following that call, he met one on one with Siran Missirian, Group Two Leader in charge of corporate affairs, Arnie Klein, Group Three Leader on religious affairs, Erika Varga, Group Five Leader on the state of the American Middle Class, and Guri Kohn, Group Six Leader responsible for the movement of agent reserves. He listened patiently as each in turn updated him on progress in their respective areas of responsibility, and was very pleased with their reports.

Next, he called Sarah Malloy to see if she was available for an evening out on Saturday, March 12. To his delight, she accepted.

Finally, he looked at the various stacks of documents and reports on his desk and decided they could wait until tomorrow. It had been a very long day and he was growing weary. He left his office and stopped at Manta's desk. "Please have Jens prepare the transporter for another trip to Washington."

"When do you want to leave, Thor?"

"Six in the morning," he answered, and headed for his stateroom where he collapsed on his bunk and was instantly asleep.

CHAPTER FOUR

The Awesome Power of TF20

On Sunday, March 7, 2010, CTS *Sunday Review* Senior Correspondent, Mark Haddon, gave everyone listening a brief report on the visit he and Sam Fischer made to the White House with Thor Berksten, Commander, TF20. "In that visit we learned there will be some very important developments concerning the war in Iraq this week. Next Sunday's program will be dedicated to the full story. That's March 14, at seven p.m. eastern time. You don't want to miss it."

*   *   *

At dawn, Monday, March 8, 2010, a series of brilliant green laser flashes ripped into the Green Zone of Baghdad. In minutes the four square mile area was a mass of burning rubble. 6,000 American military personnel perished because their President would not allow them to evacuate. In terms of lives lost, it was the worst day of the war. President Howard Fields, who never rose before 9:00 a.m., was awakened by Jack Brill a few minutes after 6:00 a.m., Washington time, and given the news. He grunted, rolled over, and went back to sleep.

Captain Truls Heyerdahl carried out the attack as ordered by Commander Berksten. He waited all day in his starship high above Baghdad for some sign that loss of the American headquarters in Baghdad made Fields realize the hopelessness of his situation. Receiving none, he issued orders for the second phase of the attack.

*   *   *

At dawn, Tuesday, March 9, 2010, the mighty aircraft carrier, *Ronald Reagan,* CVN 76, was struck by laser beams on her starboard side, just below the water line. The beams, fired by Heyerdahl's Techna Force 20 starship, easily cut through the carrier's outer hull of heavy steel plate, as well as the inner hull, which was equally strong. The gash left by the lasers stretched from stem to stern, and seawater flooded into the ship. *Reagan* began to list to starboard almost immediately. Scramble alarms caused pilots and launch crews to rush to their planes in a frantic effort to get fighter protection into the air, as the vast flight deck tilted at an ever steeper angle with frightening speed. Only ten F-18's made it off the deck before the slope of the deck made further launches impossible.

Next came the abandon ship alarm, and 5,000 members of the ship's company struggled to leave the giant, fatally wounded vessel. They knew not to try to jump from the starboard side, although it was now much closer to the water than the port side, because of the risk of being pulled under by vacuum created as that side of the ship settled into the water. The portside edge of the deck and hanger deck were now much higher, and any jump from there would be very treacherous. Planes and other equipment began to slide off the low side of the flight deck, further imperiling crew efforts to escape. Many crew members soon lost their footing and frantically grabbed at anything to stop their slide, to no avail. They, too disappeared over the side of the ship. In less than 30 minutes one of the most advanced warships ever built rolled over and started her long final voyage to the bottom of the Persian Gulf. Incredibly, 3,500 of the ship's crew managed to escape. But 1,500 others, who worked deep within the vast hull, had no time to make it topside and perished with their ship, as did 50 F-18's and other assorted aircraft.

Once again Jack Brill had to awaken the President early and give him the bad news. *Reagan* was gone. And again, President

Fields, leader of the United States, rolled over and went back to sleep without a word.

Brill returned to his West Wing office where news reports of the attack were already flooding his television set. Angry and troubled by the President's reaction, he tried to think of a way to make Fields respond to this disaster. He was so deep in thought that the sudden ringing of his telephone startled him. He snatched it from its cradle and said, "Brill, here."

"Jack, this is Bert Phillips. What was the President's reaction to the news from Baghdad this morning? What's he going to do about it? Any direction?" Phillips sounded very concerned.

"Bertram, he just grunted and went back to sleep. Nothing will get him out of bed this early, I guess."

"Christ all mighty, doesn't he realize how serious this is? I've already had calls from the Senate Majority Leader and the Speaker of the House, asking what the hell is going on. We haven't told them about Techna Force 20, you know, which in and of itself is a big problem. Howard didn't believe Berksten was for real, so he didn't consider notification necessary. But we have to tell them now."

"I know, Bertram. You're right. I'll probably get my ass kicked, but I say, call the Congressional leaders together immediately."

"What action would you recommend, Jack?"

"Hell, Bertram, it's not my decision."

"I know, but what would you do if it was?"

"I'd pull out of Iraq in a heartbeat. This war has been a disaster."

"Thanks, Jack. We think alike, you and I. I'll get back to you." With that he hung up.

*   *   *

The Secretary of Defense went to work as soon as he got off the phone with Jack Brill. In a hastily arranged meeting with the leaders of the House and Senate he laid out the entire scenario that had taken place between President Howard Fields and Commander Thor Berksten. The leaders already knew about Thor's appearance on CTS *Sunday Review*, but though there had been rumors and they had made inquiries, they had learned nothing of the subsequent meetings between the President and Thor. The fact that Fields had received an ultimatum from an invader from another planet—had even agreed to move people out of harms way without informing Congress—infuriated them. But their fury then was nothing compared to their fury concerning destruction of the Baghdad Embassy, the Green Zone and the *Reagan*.

Senate Majority Leader, Edward Reynolds, shook his head in shocked disbelief as he listened to Phillip's account. Reynolds, a tall, powerfully built man of 65 from Virginia, with a cherubic face made permanently red by too much Irish whiskey, a thick crown of pure white hair that seemed never to have been combed, and intense blue eyes that bored into anyone facing his questions, was now more angry than at any time in his more than 30 years in the Senate. In a booming voice, he said, "This is the result of giving Field's predecessor too much power in time of war. Now we reap the wild wind, as the saying goes. For Fields to engage in discussions with a foreign power that is threatening to take over this government, without the advice and consent of Congress, and then to suffer such terrible losses of life, not to mention loss of costly facilities, puts him in a position of having exceeded even his broad authority in Iraq. He is not the person to lead our great country—never has been. I fear it is time to consider removing him from office."

Katherine McDonald, Speaker of the House, listened intently to what her Senate counterpart said. A product of Harvard Law, she graduated summa cum laude, then headed her own, very successful law firm for 15 years, before answering the call to public duty. She was no friend of Howard Fields. With 15 years in congress under her belt, including five years as Speaker, and a record of being one of the best experts ever on constitutional law, she had proven her great debating ability against House colleagues time and time again. More than once she stood toe to toe with Fields, as well. He was no match.

When Reynolds finished speaking, it was her turn. "Ed, you may be right about that, although, from what Bert just told us, it seems we now have a replacement for Fields, whether we like it or not: This man from Techna Planet. This Thor Berksten. Is he for real, Bert?"

"No question, Katherine. He could be in this room right now, listening to everything we say. His ability to become invisible at will is one reason he is so powerful. And everyone in his so-called Techna Force 20—he claims there are 2,000—has the same power. As far as we can determine, these people are virtually indestructible. Furthermore, according to Sam Fischer and Mark Haddon, of CTS *Sunday Review,* who toured the TF20 base near Roswell with Commander Berksten, TF20 has the most advanced equipment we have ever faced. Their starships are awesome. They are capable of moving at up to 50,000 miles per hour, have unmatched laser fire power and, get this: they can also be made invisible."

"Where, exactly, is their Roswell base, Bert? And, if we have pin-pointed its location, why haven't we destroyed it?"

"Katherine, CTS says it is hidden in Sardine Mountain, where we once had a secret military facility. The President sent F-22 Raptors armed with AIM missiles to wipe it out. They didn't find a thing."

"One thing that has been bothering me is why didn't CTS give Fields a heads up on the program they ran with Berksten present.? They certainly had an obligation to do that."

"They did notify us. Jack Brill got the word from Mark Haddon before the program aired and instructed the secret service to contact Fields immediately. He was attending a performance of some kind at the Kennedy Center. Fields told the agent to tell Brill that he would take the matter up on the following day, which was Monday."

So, because of another example of his blundering, we are now under siege. Bert, I can't believe this is happening."

"Believe it, Katherine. We have never faced anything like this before."

Edward Reynolds focused his steely-eyed stare on the Secretary of Defense. "Bert, what does Berksten want? Do we know?"

"He has said repeatedly that his mission is to keep us from finding Techna Planet and contaminating it as we have—so he claims—so many nations on Earth. That is a given. How that connects to Iraq is uncertain. He has made it very clear that he wants us out of there immediately, and that he will stop at nothing to make that happen. We also have indications that he wants us to give up all U.S. military bases on foreign soil worldwide, so he is evidently focused on reducing our military dominance. Understand, that there has been no actual ultimatum on that as yet. Beyond that, we don't know what his plans are."

"Bert, we are not exactly weaklings," Katherine said. "Do you think he can really force us to do his will?"

"Yes. You do know, I am sure, how heavily fortified the Green Zone was, right? We knew he was going to attack it, because he warned us in advance. He even gave Fields time to get everyone out of there before the attack because he didn't want human casualties, which tells me he has a humanitarian side, at least. Fields agreed to remove some 19,000 civilians, but left an army of about 6,000 soldiers and marines in there. When the laser attack came we answered with all weapons, but hell, our guys couldn't even see their starship, or locate it by radar, let alone shoot it down. In less than five minutes it was all over.

Yes, I absolutely believe he could easily take our country away from us—become a dictator, as it were—if he wanted to."

"But you don't think he wants to, is that it?"

"Right. I think he is pursuing his stated mission, which is to protect his planet from us. He doesn't want our country. But make no mistake. He is persistent. He is thorough in his planning. He is used to getting his way. He also has bigger guns than we do. When he gives an order don't expect him to back off. In that first CTS program he said he would do whatever it took to protect Techna Planet. He meant it, Katherine."

The Congressional Leaders exchanged glances, then Edward Reynolds said, "What do you want from Congress, Bert?"

"I want you to clip Field's wings; take away his war powers. I say, respectfully, that his brother should not have been given those powers in the first place. I say further, that when Howard took office it should have been without them. If you don't rescind them, Fields won't give up, and we will have a bloody disaster on our hands. Thor Berksten will see to that. Once you have control, you can, and must, stop this war."

"Thank you, Mr. Secretary, for being so candid." He looked directly at the Speaker. "I think Katherine and I feel as you do, that the war must end. But you must realize that the President has strong Republican support for it in both houses. It is a cash cow for many of their constituents. God knows we have tried to end it."

"I know, Ed. The Democratic majority is still razor thin. Even if you prevail, the President will veto the bill, and you don't have the 66 and 2/3rds votes to override him. However, I think I can guarantee you a different outcome this time.

"What do you mean, Bert?"

"I mean, this man from Techna Planet will not allow any member of Congress to block withdrawal efforts again. If I may make a suggestion, why not tell the Republicans that?"

Katherine nodded in agreement. "Now that's a good idea. What do you say, Ed?"

"I'm all for it. Let's go twist some arms."

*   *   *

The meeting took less than one hour, but for the first time, Bertram Phillips had reason to hope. He knew Fields would be very, very angry when he learned that his Secretary of Defense was meeting secretly with Congress, and might even fire him. "So be it," He thought. "Invading Iraq was not my idea. Fields tricked me into believing he could end the war in a month, as another President had done years before, without great cost or loss of life. He lied, and I was a fool to believe him."

Commander Thor Berksten, who was standing less than ten feet from Phillips, unseen, as he had been during the entire meeting, smiled knowingly. He, too, was pleased.

*   *   *

Later that day, Thor called Sarah Malloy to ask her if she could have dinner with him the following Friday, which would be March 12th. She seemed very happy that he had called, and accepted. "Suppose I pick you up at your home at seven p.m., Sarah. Would that work for you?"

"Perfect. I live in the Regina Arms Building at 73rd Street and Central Park West. 21st floor. Maybe you could land in the park; it's just across the street."

Thor laughed, and said, "Great idea, Sarah, and by the way," He added, "Being with you on the Cape was wonderful, just not long enough. It will be hard to wait until Friday night. Also, there is something we must talk about, then."

"Oh, What is that, Thor?"

"Sorry, dear, there isn't time now. Friday will have to do. See you at seven. Goodbye for now."

Sarah hung up the phone, wondering what it was he had to tell her. It could be about taking me to Techna Planet, she thought. We talked about that. Or maybe he is going to leave Earth sooner than expected. I do hope that is not true. Or...he is going to propose, but no, it is much too soon for that, though I certainly would not mind. He did call me 'dear.' He hasn't done that before....

* * *

On Thursday, March 11, Thor decided to pay another visit to the Oval Office. When he arrived around 10:30 a.m., the office was empty, and there was not the hustle and rush one would expect in such a crisis. The Techna agent on duty told him Fields was in the basement gym, where he always was this time of day. "You can set your watch by him, Commander. He does the same thing, at the same time, every day. What is going on in the world outside this building never seems to concern him. Once he gives the order to do something, he never dwells on it. He just moves on to whatever is next in his mind. I have not heard him say a word about the Green Zone or the sinking of the *Reagan,* and there has been no indication that he has changed position because of those events."

Following instructions the agent gave him on where to look for the White House gym, Thor walked directly to it. Fields was alone, dressed in track clothes, riding a stationery bicycle. As he slowly pedaled the bike, he watched a rerun of M.A.S.H., an old program about a battlefield hospital in Korea in the 1950's, on a television set a few feet away. It was a very funny episode, but the President showed absolutely no emotional reaction to it. Thor watched him for a few minutes, marveling at Field's ability to isolate himself from reality. His intent had been to speak to the

President again, thereby putting more pressure on him to agree to withdrawal. But he concluded that no urging was going to sway Field's thinking. so he left the gym without announcing himself.

* * *

At a few minutes to 7:00 p.m. on Friday, Thor's sleek transporter landed unseen on the manicured grass of New York's Central Park. Thor emerged wearing gray slacks, blue shirt and navy blue blazer under his black top coat. He walked briskly, head bent against the cold March wind, crossed Central Park West Avenue, to the Regina Arms building. The uniformed doorman called Sarah to announce him, then took him to the row of elevators in the lobby. "Any of these will take you to her floor," He said, motioning toward the elevators.

Sarah had chosen a simple, but elegant, black knee-length dress with ribbon-like shoulder straps. Around her neck was a string of pearls, and a single matching pearl adorned each earlobe. She stood in the open doorway, framed by the soft glow of many lit candles in the apartment. When he caught sight of her, Thor was momentarily overwhelmed by her loveliness. She smiled, took his hand in hers and said, "Hi. Please come in."

"Sarah," he responded, "You look absolutely stunning tonight."

"Thank you, Thor, care for some wine?"

"No, I think I will wait. You have a beautiful home, by the way."

"It was my father's home away from home when he practiced law in New York. When he closed that office he gave this apartment to me. It is much larger than I need, and I certainly could not afford it on my meager salary at CTS. But I do love it and its location."

"I can see why. Shall we go?"

Thor helped Sarah with her coat and felt the softness of her body as his hand brushed her shoulder. It was a sensation he had not experienced in a very long time; one that he thought quite wonderful. They walked hand in hand to the elevator, then to the transporter where Jens was waiting, as always. He bowed and said, "Good evening, Sarah." Then he helped her board the aircraft.

"Do you mind going back to the Cape, Sarah? I have chosen the Daniel Webster Inn, in Sandwich, for dinner tonight, if that is all right with you."

"Oh, yes. I love that place. You seem to know all my favorite haunts."

"Well, my dear, I think it is more likely that we have very similar tastes. I suppose I could have discovered that through secret investigation, but there was no need. It is just a sense I have."

* * *

The flight to Cape Cod took only minutes, as before, and soon they were seated by the fireplace, enjoying the restaurant's wonderfully comfortable old polished wood and red leather atmosphere. After asking Sarah about her preference, Thor ordered a fine Merlot' wine. They held their glasses up and he said, "To us, Sarah."

She smiled and nodded as the glasses touched.

While they waited for their meal to be served, Thor said, "Now, as I mentioned over the phone, there is something I must tell you. This concerns business and normally I do not discuss business plans with anyone. But where you are concerned, I make an exception. I do it because I feel something about you that I have never felt about anyone before, and because I don't want anything to come between us. All right?"

Sarah nodded and waited.

"I am sure, Sarah, that you have heard rumors about me around your office; rumors that might indicate to you that I am a ruthless man who will stop at nothing to accomplish an objective. "

"Yes, Thor. I have heard such rumors."

"Then know this, Sarah. Everything I do is to correct a wrong that I see; an injustice, if you will. The war in Iraq was, and still is, a gross injustice committed against all Americans. The world sees your Government as a bully, to say nothing of the terrible cost, and the potential danger to Techna Planet. I must right that injustice."

"By the same token, I must right other injustices, such as the failure of your country to carry out death sentences of people convicted of capital crimes, for by not doing so, your Government is condoning crimes against innocent people."

Then he told her that the sentences on all but 163 of the 3,500 people on death row in state prisons would be carried out by his agents, on his orders, in just seven days.

Sarah listened carefully and was silent for a long moment. Finally she said, "I appreciate you telling me. A part of me—the woman part—the part with the natural impulse to protect human life, finds your decision distasteful to say the least. But the part of me that is a lawyer's daughter knows that what you say is true, and recognizes the need for capital punishment. My father, who is a corporate lawyer and did not fight in the trenches of criminal law, thank God, would readily agree with your plan. I have heard him say the same thing so many times: justice must be done. So I agree with you, too, Thor. But tell me, why do you exclude the 163?"

"Because they vehemently proclaimed their innocence, and the other death row prisoners did not. We carried out our own investigations—each of them most intense and detailed-- and we found that these 163 were telling the truth. To protect their lives we will remove them to a safe location, then get their sentences overturned. They will not spend another day on death row."

"That pleases me, Thor, but tell me, what about all those prisoners consigned to life in prison without parole? Do they not constitute an injustice, too?"

"Yes, Sarah. And we must deal with that problem at some point, as well."

She placed her hand on his. "Thor, I know how hard this was for you. But you don't need to worry, because I believe in you and support you. You see, my dear, I am in love with you; very much in love with you."

"No, Sarah, are you serious? We have known each other such a short time. How can you be so sure so soon?"

"I've never been more serious, Thor. I know. I knew it the moment I first saw you."

"Well I, too, feel something very special is happening between us; I just cannot identify it. Maybe I do not know what loving someone feels like., and that scares me."

"Don't worry, Thor. I understand that many men have that problem. Give your feelings some time. I hope it turns out that you feel as I feel, but if not, we can still be friends."

He took her small hand in both of his, brought it to his lips and kissed it. Then he looked deep into her eyes and said, "Sarah, I believe I have discovered a very wise and wonderful woman. Maybe it is time to make that trip to Techna Planet that we talked about the last time we were together. What do you think?"

"I think I would like that very much. Just say when so I can arrange it with my boss."

"Good, I will do that very soon."

* * *

At that point their food arrived, and they chatted about many things as they ate, feeling as comfortable with one another as if they had been friends for years. They were lost in each other, oblivious to everyone and everything around them, and the time passed all too swiftly. Thor paid their tab and they walked out to where Jens had landed the transporter. "Feel like a walk on the beach?" He asked. "It is a beautiful evening."

She looked up at him and smiled. "I would love that, Thor. Let's take our shoes off."

He laughed. "Of course we can, if it is not too cold on the beach. Do you know, Sarah, I have never done that?" He looked at Jens who nodded in return. In just minutes the transporter touched down on Mashpee Beach, using only the light of the full moon, Jens watched as Thor and Sarah walked hand in hand just at the water's edge. They did not remove their shoes, and in fact wore their top coats because of the icy winter wind. They are like children, he thought. It is good to see the Commander relaxed for a change. I think he will not need me tonight.

Sarah and Thor walked nearly a mile, to a rocky outcropping that terminated the beach. There they found an ancient log that had been washed up by the waves ages ago, and it became their throne from which to gaze upon the huge orange moon now slowly settling into the Atlantic ocean.

Thor put his arm around Sarah's shoulder. "This has been the most wonderful evening of my life, Sarah. With you I can shed my burden for at least a little while. It is an experience I have never had before."

She snuggled against him, and said, "Yes, I feel the magic, too, and I don't want it to end. Are you busy tomorrow?"

"No."

"Then why don't you stay with me tonight? Come home with me. I really need you to do that. And tomorrow I will show you my New York."

"I would like that very much, Sarah. Are you sure I will not be imposing?"

"No, not at all. By staying you will make me very happy. I'll even fix you breakfast."

Thor gently cupped her face in his hands and kissed her for the first time. Then they watched the moon disappear into the sea, before walking back to the transporter.

* * *

Thor woke at his usual very early hour, and looked fondly at the lovely sleeping beauty lying next to him. Her beautiful auburn hair was slightly disheveled and her breathing was even and soft. She was lying on her left side, as if she had fallen asleep while watching him. He lay there for a long time, just looking at her, marveling at her, never wanting to leave her. Then slowly he slid out of the bed and quietly donned his pants and shirt, which were draped over a chair, picked up his shoes and stockings, and made his way to the kitchen, There, after searching unsuccessfully for tea bags, he eventually found the coffee supply, and made what he hoped would be coffee, for he had never done that before either. But it was hot and turned out very strong. He poured a cup and carried it to the living room, where he sipped it slowly as he watched the people scurrying about far below the window. After several moments, he felt soft arms around his waist and turned to find Sarah, still in her frilly nightgown. "Good morning, my dear," he said. "I did not hear you. You snuck up on me."

She hugged him tightly. "I intend to do that at least once every minute from now on."

"But won't that keep us from doing anything else?"

"Uh huh. There is nothing else that matters. Are you hungry?"

"Starving. Whatever we did last night gave me a huge appetite."

She looked up at him with a slight pouting expression. "You don't remember what we did?"

"Oh, I remember, angel, and it was an incredibly beautiful experience. I only hope I was a gentleman."

"You were everything I thought you would be; a perfectly fantastic man."

"Then perhaps we should do that again some day."

"Now?"

"I said some day. First I must regain my strength."

"Alright, then make yourself comfortable while I do breakfast."

Afterwards, they spent the entire day exploring Manhattan Island, with Sarah acting as tour guide. She took him to quaint shops in out of the way side streets, upscale boutiques along the avenues and boulevards, Central Park, antique stores, and New York's famous piers, where huge passenger liners were preparing for wherever their journey would take them.

They rode the subways and experienced the city's taxi system and took ferry boats to Staten Island and The Statue of Liberty.

Thor was amused by Sarah's virtually non-stop chatter about the history of these places; it was obvious that she knew them well. It was also obvious that she loved the excitement of this vast city; and that she loved telling him about it.

They ate cheeseburgers and drank Cokes in a tiny basement bistro, wandered through colorful Greenwich Village streets, and enjoyed an early dinner of linguini in wine sauce at a wonderful Italian restaurant called Trattoria Dopo Teatro, in the theater district.

During the taxi ride back to Sarah's apartment, and though Thor still had not declared his love for Sarah, they talked on and on as lovers will, discovering characteristics about one another in the process, and Saturday ended as Friday had ended.

* * *

On Sunday morning, after a passionate goodbye to Sarah, Thor walked briskly to where the transporter was waiting in Central Park. Jens was standing at the cabin door, as usual. "Sorry to keep you here so long, old friend. I should have planned this better."

Jens smiled. "It was no problem, Commander. I flew back to Roswell, and slept in my own bed for two nights. Most relaxing. I returned here at 6:30 this morning."

"You deserved the rest, Jens."

"Where to today, Commander?"

"Back to Washington. To the Capitol."

Thor strapped himself in and said, "Ready when you are, Jens."

While in the air, Thor received a call from Assim Agassi, Captain of Group Four, who wasted no time getting to the point of his call. "Commander, we are tracking a large drug shipment. 200 kilos of heroin, 300 kilos of cocaine, and another 200 of marijuana. Combined street value, almost $30 million dollars. The truck is also carrying a load of illegal clothing knock-offs from China. The cartons that cargo is in screen the pod containing the drugs."

"At the moment, this shipment is still in Mexico, but we have one agent inside the trailer of the 18-wheeler and two more following in an invisible car. The drop point is San Diego, and as soon as the deal is made we will take the money and burn the truck. Not only will the drug lords be unhappy, so will the Chinese. They have a deal with Washington bureaucrats to look the other way. Losing so profitable a shipment—I mean just the clothing—will not sit well. In fact, they will see it as a broken promise and will be furious."

"Are you worried, Assim?"

"Not in the least, Commander. We need these raids—many of them—to stop illicit drug activity. This one will help get Washington's attention."

Thor said, "Right. Good work. Keep me posted," and terminated the call, pleased with the news, saying to himself, "things are beginning to fall into place for us."

*   *   *

The transporter landed just as Thor finished the call from Assim. He took the many steps to the Capitol building two at a time, and soon found himself in its awesome central rotunda. Following directions given to him by Bertram Phillips, he made his way down a long passageway, easily bypassing security stations in his invisible state. The sound of voices coming through an open door led him directly to the small room where the Congressional leaders were to meet. The voices he had heard were those of Senate Majority Leader, Edward Reynolds, Speaker of the House, Katherine McDonald, and Bertram Phillips, Secretary of Defense, who had already taken seats at the conference table. Thor positioned himself in the front row of the section reserved for media people and spectators, and waited.

Soon, two more men he did not recognize entered the room. Phillips called one John and the other Murray, and from that information, Thor judged the two to be, John Raider, Senate Minority Leader, and Murray Rosenthal, House Minority Whip.

John Raider was about five feet nine, and weighed 165 pounds. He kept his salt and pepper hair, which had originally been red, short and in the crew-cut style. His face was clean shaven, his eyes were blue, and he wore an expensive-looking tan suit and stripped brown tie. He was in his sixth term in the Senate and was a strong conservative.

Murray Rosenthal was as opposite from Raider as could be in appearance. He was short, not more than five feet five, very heavy at 260 pounds, and had black hair streaked with gray that looked as if it had never seen a comb. His suit, which was black, was rumpled and smelled of perspiration. His eyes were dark brown and seemed larger behind his thick, horn-rimmed glasses.

His appearance was misleading, however, for he was a brilliant student of the Constitution, as well as a shrewd orator on the House floor. Politically he was far to the right on most issues, and was well known for favoring corporations over individuals.

Based on what his research had disclosed about these two Republican members of Congress, Thor judged them to be non-receptive to his plans. "No matter," He thought. "There is too much at stake here, so I will have to change their minds."

*   *   *

There was a cordial, but wary exchange of handshakes, and Bertram Phillips began the meeting with, "Lady and Gentlemen, I thank you for taking the time to meet today, and apologize for stealing your Sunday time. But we must take up a matter of extreme urgency, and I felt it could not wait even another day." He then asked Edward Reynolds if John and Murray had been briefed about recent related events.

"No, Bert. I thought it would be better to do so today."

"Very well. Perhaps we should start there, Ed."

Reynolds nodded agreement then glanced toward Raider and Rosenthall. "You both know that Planet Earth has had a visitor from outer space—from Planet Techna— to be exact. I believe you watched the CTS *Sunday Review* program February 28 of this year, when a man named Thor Berksten, claiming to be from Techna Planet, appeared. His title is Commander, Techna Force 20, and he told us then that he has 2,000 agents on Earth, and that most of them are in the U.S. If you saw that program, you already know that he demonstrated some pretty impressive powers, not the least of which is the power to become invisible and to make his equipment invisible, at will. Since then he has proved all of his claims again and again. He has entered the White House several times unseen, has informed the President that he, Thor Berksten, is now in charge of our Government, and has issued an ultimatum to Fields to get out of Iraq immediately."

Both John Raider and Murray Rosenthal looked surprised. "Ed," Murray said, "We know about this Berksten's appearance on CTS. We watched the program. But I have not heard about the other stuff—the taking over of our Government and the ultimatum. Have you, John?"

"No. This is shocking news. Who the hell does he think he is, coming after the most powerful country in the world?"

"John, Murray, wait till you hear the rest," Ed continued. "As I stated, on March fifth, less than a week ago, he gave Fields an ultimatum to withdraw from Iraq. Fields refused, so Berksten destroyed our new Baghdad Embassy. To his credit, he first warned Fields to get our people out of those buildings, which the President did, and then he bombarded it using sophisticated laser weapons. There is nothing left of that $600 million dollar investment. Did you know *about that?*"

John Raider looked incredulous. "Do you mean to say, Berksten did that? Fields told us it was an attack by Osama Bin Laden."

"John, a lot of us have been fooled by such claims for a long time, as you know. But it was Berksten, and there is more. He also told the President to either begin withdrawal immediately, or risk destruction of the Green Zone and the aircraft carrier, *Ronald Reagan;* his next two targets. Fields refused again, telling Berksten that nobody ordered him around. But, at the urging of Bertram, here, and Jack Brill, he did agree to remove non-combatants from the Green Zone, as Berksten asked. That saved 19,000 civilian lives, but both assets were destroyed, with the loss of 7,500 military personnel, and 50 F-18's."

"My God," Murray Rosenthal gasped. "Fields lied to us about that, too. He told us those targets were also destroyed by Bin Laden."

"Wrong, Murray and John," Katherine McDonald interjected. "Fields just doesn't want to face facts. He apparently thinks Thor Berksten is an aberration . According to Bert, who has been present in the Oval Office with Fields when Berksten was there, he definitely is not. He is a very real threat to our country, and so far we've found no way to stop him. Am I correct, Bert?"

"Indeed you are, Katherine."

"So now we have a dictator in America?" Murray said rhetorically. "How can this happen?"

"Hold on, everybody, Reynolds said. "Berksten may not be as great a threat as you think. Let's go back to basics. He wants to protect his planet from take-over by us. Can we honestly object to that? He wants us out of Iraq. Isn't that what we should do, anyway? He wants us to remove our military bases from other countries. Is that so bad? Think of the huge savings we would have in cost, and how much better we could use that money."

"No, Ed. That's what you Democrats want. You have never believed America was in danger of attack. Republicans see it quite differently."

"Come on, John. We were attacked only once: 9/11. One attack does not justify such a huge expansion in our military."

"It could happen again."

"That's just the point, John. It could happen again, and we would not be able to prevent it even if we blanketed the earth with military. There are Bin Ladens in every crack in the earth."

"Gentlemen, gentlemen," Bertram Phillips said. "There is no use debating this. John and Murray, if you can't get your people to cast enough votes to give us a majority the President can't override by veto, Thor Berksten will do it for you."

"Yeah?" Murray challenged. "What's he going to do, start breaking arms and heads?" He laughed at his own quip.

"He will probably do worse, Murray, like start killing off Republican members of congress, then force us to replace them with people who support withdrawal"

"Bullcrap. That's against the Constitution."

"Ours. not his, " Ed responded. "You guys better take this man very seriously. Tomorrow we absolutely must have a united force in both Congressional chambers to put through Bills on withdrawal; Bills the President can't override, or I predict there will be hell to pay."

"Whoa. Wait a minute, Ed. We don't take orders from you."

"They're not my orders, John. They're Berksten's. I suggest you not forget the Green Zone and the _Reagan_, Sir."

Katherine McDonald looked hard at John Raider and Murray Rosenthal. "We need your help on this, guys. Ed is right when he says Thor Berksten will not let us stop his plan. Do we have your support?"

There followed a long moment of silence while Rosenthal and Raider conferred in whispered tones some distance from the others. Then the two men returned and Murray spoke. "Katherine, Ed, Bert, John and I have agreed to call our Republican members of Congress into special session immediately, and try to convince them it is time to end this war. You understand, I am sure, that we cannot give you a guarantee."

"I do agree with Murray," John Raider responded.

Katherine nodded agreement. "Gentlemen, please tell them we can't have less than a 66 and 2/3rds vote of approval on this matter. The President must have no room to veto this Bill. If we fail, there will be bloodshed in this building and in the White House. Of that I am convinced. You said it Murray: Thor Berksten is a dictator. My advice is don't cross him."

* * *

Thor left for Sardine Mountain immediately after the Sunday Congressional meeting. On the way, Assim Agassi called to report that the large drug shipment to San Diego had been intercepted. "I am on my way to deliver $15 million dollars to Manta; that is the wholesale price the buyer paid. The truckload of drugs and knock-off clothing is but a pile of cinders in a truck stop. I think both the seller and the buyer will die before sunup tomorrow. Now we are monitoring an even larger drug action which originated in Columbia. It looks very promising for us."

"I am pleased, Assim. Our war against these terrible drugs must never end. They are too much of a temptation to American big business. Keep up your fine work." He replaced the phone just as the transporter landed.

* * *

On Tuesday, March 16, 2010, as Thor was going through reports from other Group Captains, Truls Heyerdahl, who was monitoring activities in Congress in his absence, called to let him know that Republicans had caucused, but had only agreed to listen to Democratic proposals, not join efforts to stop the war. "They want to hear what the President says tomorrow, when he addresses a joint session of Congress, Commander. We now know his theme will be that America must continue the fight because the threat of terrorist activity is greater than ever. We have also learned that he will point to us—TF20—as a major source of terror. Of course, as you are aware, all of Congress probably knows by now that Bin Laden did not cause the recent destruction in Baghdad. They, especially Republicans, are very angry with Fields for lying to them. I think he will have a very difficult time convincing Congress to go on, but it appears he does not plan to give in. You should also know, Commander, that Congress intends to use the full force of the United States Government against TF20. They are also quite angry with us for what we did in Baghdad. Orders have already gone out to NASA to start developing spacecraft that can match our starships."

"That will take years, Truls."

"I agree, Commander. We always assumed they would come after us; now we know they are serious."

"It is quite understandable, my friend. This country is not accustomed to being invaded. They are a proud people and will fight us hard, but our cause is just and not contrived. We will be ready for anything they throw at us. Keep up the good work. I will return to Washington tomorrow for the President's speech to Congress."

Thor hung up the phone and thought about his conversation with Truls for several minutes. He was most pleased with Heyerdahl's performance. I like his ability to remain calm under adverse conditions, to plan missions well, and carry them out smoothly, he thought. And I also like it that he is not afraid to speak his mind to me. He should go far in our organization. At that point his thoughts were interrupted by a call from Assim Agassi.

"Greetings Commander. Everything is ready for the prison mission which takes place on Friday, the 19th. I will call you with results Sunday night."

"Very well, Assim. I know you and your Group have worked hard on this. By the way, good job in San Diego. We are already getting feedback on reactions to our drug raids—from some not-too-surprising sources. "

"Oh? By any chance are they coming from certain Government agencies and corporations, Sir?"

"Yes. You knew?"

"No, not exactly. But we have been warned on both raids that high-powered individuals would be coming after us. Your news ties in with that."

"Well, good, Assim. Flushing out such people was one of our primary objectives, right? Once we know more—their names, for example, we will let the world know who the scumbags are that profit from illicit drug traffic."

"Nothing would please me more, Commander."

"I know, Assim. And I am very pleased with you. Your work is most impressive."

Thank you, Sir."

Thor terminated that call then punched the numbers for another. Sarah answered almost immediately. "Hello," he said. I hoped I would catch you at home. Are you well, Sarah?"

"Oh, Thor. It is so good to hear your voice again. Yes. I am well—now."

"You were not well before?"

"A woman needs her man, my dear. I cannot be well unless I am with you."

"I see. In that sense I have not been too well myself. How many weeks has it been since we were last together?"

"Not weeks, years. It seems like years. Where are you?"

"At my base in New Mexico."

"Will you be in or near New York anytime soon? I really must see you."

"As a matter of fact, I will be there March 16—in Washington, that is. If you have an opening in your dance card on Friday, the 19th, I would love to have you join me on a visit here, to my base for the weekend. Do you think that will work for you?"

"Yes, Thor, I would love that, but do I not get to see you sooner?"

"Perhaps. Much will happen during that week. Suppose I call you every night while I am there. No promises, but maybe we can squeeze in dinner along the way."

"That would be wonderful, Thor."

"Great! We will leave it at that, and I will pick you up Friday at six p.m., if that is all right."

"I'll be ready. How do I dress for this event?"

"Casual, My Love. It will be a very relaxed, casual week end."

"Sounds wonderful. See you at six."

Thor returned the phone to its cradle. Then he walked out of his office and stood in front of Manta's desk. "Do we have a starship going to Techna around mid-April?"

Manta studied the flight schedule which hung on the bulkhead beside her desk. "Yes, there is a flight leaving here April 16, arriving Techna April 20."

"Good. This flagship will join them on that trip, with one guest, leaving Techna April 26, for our return to Earth."

"Very well, Commander. May I have the guest's name?"

"Sarah Malloy."

That was a name Manta had not heard before and she made a mental note to chastise Jens Petersen for not telling her. The fact that there was now a woman in Thor's life did not bother Manta in the least. Jens was her man and she loved him very much, but it was, in her mind, his duty to report everything the Commander did and with whom. Jens never did, of course, but she never stopped trying to gain such information. Now she smiled up at Thor and said, "I'll make the arrangements right away, Commander. I love the name Sarah, by the way."

"You will meet her on Friday, Manta. I am bringing her here for the weekend. You will like her, I think. Which reminds me, ask Jens to prepare for a trip to Washington and New York tomorrow morning."

"What time, Sir?"

"Nine a.m. will be fine. And Manta, please prepare a nice stateroom for Sarah. You know what women like."

"I'll be glad to do that, Commander."

CHAPTER FIVE

Message For Congress

It was ten a.m. on March 15, 2010, and Thor waited unseen just to the left of the podium in the House Chamber on Capitol Hill, as members of the House and Senate slowly filled the room to hear the President's speech on Iraq. The scene in the room which would soon hold 535 high government officials, if every member attended, reminded him of the beginnings of a social gathering, rather than an important and very serious business affair. From his vantage point he watched as Congressional members—seemingly ever in motion—moved about the House floor, that surprisingly small space between the massive, tiered platforms of desks forming the podium, and the circular array of member seats, stopping here and there to shake a hand or pat a back or laugh at some amusing comment. To him, the ever-changing human ebb and flow was not unlike a school of circling sharks in search of prey.

Prior to coming to the House Chamber, he had paid a surprise visit to the office of the House Speaker, Katherine McDonald. As he entered she paused in her examination of a thick sheaf of papers and looked up at him. "Can I help you, Mr. Berksten?"

"I see you know who I am."

"A lucky guess. Nobody around here seems to have a photograph of you but I've heard about you, of course, and have been expecting a visit from you. Actually, I feel rather left out."

"Oh?"

"Yes. Seeing as how you have visited so many other Government officials, but not me. No matter. Let me guess why you are here today: It is because of the joint hearing and the President's speech, right?"

"That is correct, Madam Speaker. I want to address Congress after he gives his views and, of course, I want you to introduce me."

"Well, both requests are quite impossible, I am afraid. You see, we don't allow anyone to address the assembly after a Presidential address. Second, you have no standing here; you are an invader, after all. Besides, if I introduce you it could be construed as an endorsement." She shook her head from side to side vehemently. No, the whole idea is quite out of the question."

"Madam Speaker, I understand your concern, but I must speak today—with or without your introduction. I will wait in the Chamber until the President finishes, then make myself visible. When the members see me, I think they will listen to what I have to say, if for no other reason than to satisfy their curiosity. It would seem to me, however, that my appearance before them would be less traumatic, less chaotic, if you formally introduce me. You can, of course add any disclaimer you wish."

"In other words, you will have your way regardless."

Thor nodded. "The war in Iraq must end now. The President refuses to end it, which leaves me with two alternatives: Convince Congress to end it—or resort to more force and bloodshed, which is definitely not my preferred option. The United States Government, of which this body is the third house, must be made to understand that I, as Commander of Techna Force 20, am now a major player in U.S. politics. I expect Congress to comprehend that fact today."

"You have already caused too much blood letting, Mr. Berksten."

"Yes, but not by choice. As I just said, I prefer peaceful resolution, to violence."

The Speaker fell silent for several seconds. Then she asked, "Just what do you expect to accomplish here today? Democrats support withdrawal and Republicans don't. How do you plan to change their minds?"

"Madam Speaker, let me just say I am certain Congress will give you at least a 92 percent vote in favor of withdrawal after today."

"Preposterous, Mr. Berksten."

"Are you a gambler?"

"No, but I'll take that bet. There is a limit to what anybody can do in this situation, even a dictator."

"Please, That is a title I do not seek, for it implies someone who acts to enrich himself. I do not. I merely wish to protect my home Planet—Techna Planet. Your country seeks to rule the World, including the universe. I have the power to stop you, and I will. So, Madam, will you introduce me, or not?"

"Very well, Mr. Berksten. I am aware of your heavy-handed ways and do not want today's proceedings to become a circus. So I will introduce you—and disown any part in your plan—then you will have 30 minutes to state your case—which you will lose, of course."

Thor thanked the Speaker and left her office.

*　*　*

President Field's speech began much as it had on so many previous occasions, with reference to 9/11, then his oft-repeated claim that Iraq was an ally of Osama Bin Laden, then his reminder of the terrible things Saddam Hussein did to his people and would have done to Americans given the chance. "Make no mistake," He said, "These terrorists hate us. Bin Laden hates us. Saddam hated us. They were all out to destroy our country and our way of living. As Commander-In-Chief I could not, will not allow this to happen." He paused there as supporters—mainly Republicans— rose as one to give him a standing ovation. Then he continued, "And now we face a new threat, a new and more powerful enemy, no doubt hired by Bin Laden and his band of outlaws, and they have come to destroy us. They call themselves Techna Force 20 and claim to be from another planet. They do not play by our rules, I assure you. I have met their leader, whose name is Thor Berksten. He forced his way into the Oval Office several times. He actually ordered me, the President of the United States, to get out of Iraq! He threatened to destroy our new Embassy in Baghdad, as well as the Green Zone and the mighty aircraft carrier, _Ronald Reagan_. Of course, by now you know that he, on orders from Bin Laden, carried out those threats because I refused to comply with his evil demands, and he killed thousands of our brave fighting men and women in the process. Make no mistake, ladies and gentlemen of Congress, I will not rest until thugs like this are themselves hanging from the gallows!"

At that point Field's supporters rose again, and this time there was an even greater thunder of applause, mixed with what sounded to Thor like the growling of angry animals, and this ovation lasted much longer than the first. Fields waited patiently at the podium, smiling, basking in the effect he had had on a large part of the audience. Finally, he raised both arms high in the air in a signal to let him continue. "My friends, this is why we must not give up the fight in Iraq, and why we must extend it to Iran and Syria, if necessary. This is why we must remain strong militarily. This is why we have armies and military bases around the world. To fight terrorists, that's why. And I include this Techna bunch when I say terrorists, because that's all they are—terrorists, terrorists, terrorists! So we will take the fight into outer space now. Find this Techna Planet, if it exists, and destroy it. All of mankind will thank us, let me tell you. Give me your continued support and we will win this battle against terror." With that he left the podium to the sounds of a mighty roar of applause once again and made his way up the aisle to the back of the House Chamber, shaking eager, outstretched hands as he walked.

Katherine McDonald waited at the podium for the noise to subside and the President to leave. She looked around for some sign of Thor. He was not yet visible but she assumed he was in the Chamber and also waiting. Finally, when Fields disappeared through the double doors, she gaveled the House to order. It was a slow process, for many members were still excited and anxious to talk to their colleagues about the speech. But as she continued to tap her gavel slowly, rhythmically, firmly, all of the members finally took their seats.

"I thank the members of the Senate and the House. Now I have a surprise for you. Today, for the first time in our history, as far as I know, we are allowing another speaker to follow a

Presidential address in this great hall. I do not support this individual's views and purpose in any way. I merely ask you to listen and judge for yourself." She waved her arm to where she thought Thor might be waiting. "Ladies and gentlemen, Mr. Thor Berksten."

Thor, standing exactly where she expected, first appeared as a hazy figure surrounded by a greenish cloud. The cloud moved to the podium, then cleared to expose a tall young man with black curly hair, dressed in a perfectly fitting dark business suit. At first sight of him there was absolute silence in the Chamber, and the eyes of every member were upon him. It was clear they did not comprehend who he was. Then slowly the realization sank in and the look on their faces changed to anger. Silence was replaced by soft murmuring sounds at first, but those sounds quickly rose in volume and changed to the unified growl of 535 angry people. Their reaction neither surprised nor worried him. He waited for the angry outburst to subside, but when it did not, when member after member stood to point toward him and shout obscenities at him, he decided to give them a small example of his power. He raised his left arm to the horizontal and directed it toward one of the standing, shouting members. A brilliant green laser beam shot from his fingertips and struck the man in the chest, knocking him down, but otherwise doing no harm. Then he moved his arm to another standing member and directed the laser beam at him. That man was also sent crashing backwards into his seat. Thor's next target was a woman who was literally screaming at him. Once again the laser beam streaked from his hand. She, too, found herself unceremoniously dumped into her seat.

Now, staring intently at those assembled, Thor raised both hands in a signal for quiet. Instantly, the verbal attacks on him stopped. "Members of Congress," he said, "I come in peace today to ask for your help, not to attack you. Your taunts do not bother me in the least for, as many of already know, there is nothing you can do to harm me or my agents. What you just witnessed were very small examples of the power we members of Techna Force 20 possess. Yes, we came to Planet Earth in peace, but do not doubt our will to carry out our mission here. What is that mission? Originally, it was to protect Techna Planet from harmful invasion by countries on Planet Earth, primarily the United States and Russia. That remains our first duty. Once here, however, we found that the tentacles of your country have already reached far beyond your own borders. You have nearly 1,000 U.S. military bases in 130 other countries, as well as major armies in many of them. You have invaded—without authority or cause, I might add—the sovereign country of Iraq. That invasion has been very costly. Thousands of American military personnel have lost their lives needlessly; many more thousands of Iraqis—both military as well as civilian—have been killed, and this unnecessary war has cost your country nearly a trillion dollars. Now your President threatens war against Iran and Syria. These sad events are the result of this Congress relinquishing its constitutional power to declare and execute war on other countries. Put simply, you gave that power to an unscrupulous President who has used it very badly."

"Finally, your country is deeply committed to exploration of outer space. That commitment , while not objectionable to us under ordinary circumstances, cannot be condoned given the reach of your armies, your record with respect to Iraq, and your expressed desire to destroy Techna Planet."

"We wonder why you have this great yearning to be what will only become another failed empire."

"We wonder why you have not used your vast resources to improve the lives of Americans, instead of putting thousands of young men and women, both military and civilian, in harms way and squandering trillions of dollars on military operations rather than on improving the lives of your civilian population."

"Have you ever considered how much good you could have done had you kept your young men and women at home and used those trillions of dollars to improve the lives of your own people? Your school system is in shambles. Your medical care system is in even worse shape. Would it not be better to use the 12 billion dollars you spend every month on Iraq to better these services?"

"Ladies and gentlemen of Congress, it is too late to save those lives lost, or those trillions squandered, but it is not too late to stop the hemorrhaging. With the full support of my small army, I will stop it if you do not. All you have to do is cast enough votes for withdrawal from Iraq so your President cannot sustain a veto. I want, and will insist on, at least a

90 percent affirmative vote to withdraw. If you do not meet that objective on your own, I will give you a laser show quite different than the one you just witnessed, one that will replace every dissenting member of this body with someone who thinks in a more reasonable manner. You have only to consider what Techna Force 20 did to your new Baghdad Embassy, the Green Zone and your fantastic aircraft carrier to know that we mean exactly what we say."

"Furthermore, withdrawal from Iraq is not our only demand. You must also close all military bases on foreign soil and return those armies and their equipment to the United States. Military personnel who lost their civilian jobs when called to duty can be put to work guarding your borders, if nothing else."

"Members of Congress," Thor warned, "You have no more pressing business than what I have just outlined here today. I caution you to concentrate your efforts on these matters. Do not make it necessary for me to return to this Chamber." Then, without waiting for a response, he vanished from the podium.

* * *

It was clear that Thor's appearance at the joint session had as great an impact on the members of Congress as any other in its history. They sat in stunned silence after he disappeared. Many had heard of him and his exploits, yet even then had not comprehended the extent of his power. But seeing him in person, and hearing his words first hand, put everything in perspective. To these members, he was the greatest force they would ever have to contend with.

And contend with him they did, but not in the manner he expected or desired. By Wednesday, March 17, after visiting the House and Senate chambers much of each day as a silent, unseen witness, Thor was forced to admit to himself that his speech had virtually no effect. The two Houses of Congress, each debating on its own, acting as if they had never heard of Techna Force 20, went about their business in their usual way, with battle lines drawn between the two factions in each House; Democrats on one side, Republicans on the other. It was just as it had been for decades and, as in the past, virtually no progress was being made on the question of withdrawal from Iraq, or on any other matter. Their output would not fill one page of the Daily Record.

For Thor, accustomed to rapid, decisive action, it was an intolerable way to run a country, and totally unacceptable under the circumstances. Thus, on Wednesday night, he met with Truls Heyerdahl and instructed him to provide a list of all members of both Houses of Congress who were objecting to withdrawal. "Truls," he said, "We have to fight the log jams that exist, or we will never accomplish our objectives." Then he outlined for his Group One Captain exactly what he had in mind, and to Truls it was a brilliant plan.

Late Friday afternoon, just prior to leaving for New York and his date with Sarah, Thor received a call from Truls. They talked for almost an hour, during which he listened to the implementation of his plan Truls had worked out. At the end of their conversation, Truls said, "Commander, I believe we have covered all the exits, as they say. Everything is set. You will not recognize the United States Congress, and will be amazed, I think, as to how well they have learned to work together. By Monday night I expect to be able to report major progress."

Truls, I knew I could count on you to handle this very difficult assignment."

"Thank you, Sir. I understand how important this objective is to our overall effort. I will call you late Monday night."

"Call me no matter the hour, my friend."

*   *   *

After talking to Truls he called Siran Missirian, Group Captain in charge of overcoming the power huge corporations have over the U.S. Government, to see how things were going on that project.

"Commander," she responded, "This is going to be much more difficult than we thought. Corporations have extended their tentacles very far. Not only are they calling the shots on what Congress and the President do, they have virtually taken over every Government agency and bureau. Did you know that all major agencies are headed by people placed there by businesses?"

"Yes. President Reagan was a big supporter of that policy, but it actually began many years before he got into office, and it was a huge mistake. Because of that practice of drawing on corporations for highly skilled people, and also because of the lobbying corporations do constantly to win tax and tariff concessions, Government contracts, and all kinds of other favors, the Federal Government has put it self into a terrible position."

"I can confirm that, Sir. And I think it all started when Calvin Coolidge said '*The business of America is business*.' Somehow that statement got translated into 'The business of Government is business,' and the American people have taken a back seat to business in every way, since. I am convinced this policy is the reason the U.S. has gone from three classes of citizens—poor, middle class and wealthy, to just two classes, poor and very wealthy. The average American must struggle mightily just to live even a meager existence, while the rich live in multi-million dollar mansions and drive very expensive automobiles."

"Exactly, Siran, so how do you think we should solve this?"

"Commander, we must change the way Government thinks. We must replace the existing crop of corporate-grown leaders in Washington with agency and bureau leaders who understand that the primary responsibilities of Government must be security, and providing those services its citizens need but cannot afford themselves. As long as Government officials listen to lobbyists instead of citizens, we will not change the way things are now."

"Then where do we find Government leaders who are honest and able to ward off corporate suitors? Do you have a plan?"

"Yes, Sir, I do. I think we must draw from the ranks of our own Techna Agents to fill key Government positions. It is clear that Americans do not have the will, ethics and morality to say no to corporate money. We already have agents imbedded in every agency. I recommend that we train them as *doubles*, then put them in charge."

"Siran, I like your thinking and your plan. Please work with Guri Kohn on that. I will alert him, and he can help you."

"I intend to work very closely with Guri, Commander."

"Good," Thor said. "I look forward to hearing from you on this very important project.," and terminated the call.

*   *   *

Being with Sarah was to Thor like coming into a warm building after a bracing walk through a winter blizzard—or, like stepping out of gloomy shadows into brilliant sunlight and being greeted by the fragrance of millions of fresh-cut flowers. She was his safe harbor, his one brief interlude in an otherwise pressure-charged life. Her smile, her delicate beauty, the feel of her in his arms, always eased the burden he carried, instantly. It had been that way the first time he saw her, and every time since, and this Friday night was no exception. She was dressed in dark blue jeans and a cream-colored top with tiny lace detail along the bottom edge—a simple, casual, but on her, beautiful outfit, that was perfect for the weekend he had planned.

They dined in a small, not-so-crowded, out-of the way bistro one short block from Central Park West, and caught up on the events in each others lives since their last meeting. Sarah had heard a rumor that her boss, Sam Fischer, missed talking to Thor, and asked him to call Sam. Thor promised to do that the following Monday. She covered in detail the events of her days, relating all the things that happened, all the things she thought about in his absence, conversations by phone with her mother and father, brother and sisters in Boston, their desire to meet Thor, her hope that he could visit the family in Boston soon, how much she missed him when they were apart.

Thor listened intently to her every word, nodding in agreement here and there, promising a trip to Boston when possible, seeking greater detail about her family, for he was as interested in hearing about her life as she was in telling the story. And, when he could get a word in edgewise, he told her about his experience with Congress, including his speech there following the President's address, though he did not disclose the plan he and Truls had devised. She was astonished to hear that he had actually addressed Congress. She squeezed his hand and seemed genuinely pleased with "her man," as she put it.

After dinner, Thor took the small, wheeled travel bag she brought to the restaurant, and they strolled back to Central Park, to where the transporter was waiting. Jens Petersen smiled and bowed to Sarah, then greeted her warmly. He seemed so very pleased to see her with Thor again. To Thor he said, "Everything is ready for take-off, Commander."

"Very well, Jens," Thor replied, as he helped Sarah into the little starship, assisted her in fastening her seat belt, then took his seat beside her and fastened his own belt. Then he said, "Ready when you are, Jens."

As on past trips to Roswell, there was very little time for talk—just thirty minutes and they would be landing there, but Thor used that time to prepare Sarah for what she would see on her visit, being careful not to disclose any of the special arrangements Manta was preparing. When he explained that they would spend much of their time inside a mountain, her eyes grew big with anticipation. Then he said, "We can also visit the vast desert surrounding the base; it is quite beautiful this time of year because many desert plants display their delicate flowers only at this time, before the summer heat arrives. And then there is the City of Roswell, if you like, or even Albuquerque. But I fear you may find them quite disappointing after New York, my dear."

"Thor, I want to experience everything that is part of your life, even Roswell."

Thor smiled. "Well, I will bet you do not remember what Roswell is famous for, do you?"

"Quite wrong, dear man. We studied Roswell at length in journalism school. It is famous for little green men with one eye in the middle of their foreheads. We even listened to old 78 records of radio broadcasts on the extra-terrestrials, and read newspaper accounts with photographs of those little guys. I'll bet you never heard of 78's."

"Oh, but I have, little one. I probably listened to the same ones you did. By the way, I will also bet you never imagined you would be dating one of those little green men some day, right?"

Sara took his hand in hers and smiled. "You don't look anything like them, Thor. You are quite handsome to me."

"Thank you, dear lady. Roswell is famous, though. It is famous as the first landing site of so-called extra-terrestrials in 1947. Of course, people did not know then that those little green men described by the news media were from Techna Planet. Actually, they were not little at all—just normal size—and they were not green with one eye in the middle of their forehead. You see, my father was

Commander of that starship. The irony is that no one really saw any of them, or the starship that brought them to Planet Earth, for two reasons: One, they never landed, they hovered, and two: even in those days we always traveled in I-Mode. What they found—the wreckage the news media made such a ruckus about--was from a small, unmanned probe craft launched from our starship, just as I told Sam Fischer. The news people even fabricated little dummies out of green plastic and gave them just one eye, trying to convince the public their story was true."

"That is so amazing. I wonder if Sam was one of those news reporters. He started in radio."

"I do not know, honey. That could be. It was right after World War II, and there was a great deal of talk about invasion from outer space. Knowing Sam, I would not be surprised to learn he was right there in the middle of broadcasting such reports."

Through the transporter's cabin speakers, Jens announced that they would be landing in three minutes. "Please fasten seat belts," he said in his usual calm voice.

*   *   *

In spite of Thor's efforts to prepare her, Sarah could not believe the surreal scene inside Sardine Mountain. It reminded her of science fiction movies she had seen and she had the strange feeling of having been transported to another world. The five huge black starships lined up like houses on a street formed the backdrop for the movie, while the workers, all dressed in neat blue uniforms, were the actors. But before she could fully comprehend this vast panorama that stretched before her she felt Thor's hand on her shoulder. She turned to find him standing next to another woman—a very beautiful woman with shoulder-length red hair and green eyes, dressed in the same smoke blue uniform she had seen Thor wear on occasion. "Sarah," he said, "this is Manta Sames, my Administrative Assistant, Without her I would be lost. Manta, Sarah Malloy. I believe I would be lost without her, too."

Though neither Thor nor Jens noticed, the two women sized each other up from head to toe, practically with the speed of light, and Sarah felt an immediate tinge of jealousy. Then they hugged one another and Manta said, "Hello, Sarah. I am so glad to meet you. From what Thor has been telling me I expected someone very special, and you are."

"Thank you, Manta. That is a wonderful compliment. I must say, you, too, are everything Thor said."

"Well, you know men. They always exaggerate."

"Not this time, Manta. If anything his description of you was a gross understatement."

"Whew! I must hear more about that. Come, I am sure you would like to freshen up. I will show you to your stateroom." Then, looking at Thor she said, "After that, if it is alright with you, Commander, I will give Sarah the mini-tour of your flagship."

"Perfect, Manta. That will give me time to catch up on a few items of business. I will join you in the lounge in say, an hour?"

* * *

Sarah and Manta walked away toward the first starship in line, chatting like old friends. They climbed the central stairs leading to the main lounge, just as Sam Fischer and Mark Haddon had done just over one month earlier, then they walked along the curved passageway for several feet. "I am afraid," Manta explained, as she paused at one door, "that our facilities might not be up to your level, Sarah. Fortunately, one of our larger staterooms was available—it may not be what you are used to in Brookline, but it even has a window, wonder of wonders, if you like watching people work on aircraft." She opened the stateroom door, and said, "I think you will be quite comfortable." Then she looked at Sarah and smiled knowingly. "It even has its own bathroom, plus, it connects to Thor's stateroom, so you can keep tabs on him."

They both laughed and Sarah said, "Brookline was in my past, Manta. I live in a tiny apartment in New York now; I think this room might actually be larger. It will do just fine, and I just love the flower arrangement. Where ever did you find red roses this time of year?"

Manta smiled. "I do go shopping in Roswell occasionally, when Thor unlocks my chain. And I have discovered a delightful little flower shop there." She placed Sarah's travel bag on the bed and said, "So, if you do not mind, Sarah, I will wait in the lounge, you know, the one we just passed through, alright?"

"Thank you, Manta. I'll only be a moment."

* * *

When Sarah returned to the lounge she saw Manta seated in one of two upholstered chairs off to one side. She took the other chair, pleased to find hot tea waiting on the table between them. As a white-coated waiter poured for them, she said, "Manta, I am curious about one thing."

"Oh, what is that?"

Well, it is none of my business but why didn't Thor choose you?"

Manta laughed. "Thor and me, did he not tell you? We are practically brother and sister. We grew up together—Jens too. When Thor's mother died—I think he was only about fifteen at the time—I helped raise him. He is a wonderful man and I love him, not as a man, but as a brother. Neither of us has ever considered what you suggest."

"I am sorry, Manta. Please forgive me. It is just that you are so beautiful and...."

"Thanks for the compliment, Sarah. You are not so bad in the beauty department, yourself, so you need not worry. He's all yours, and with my blessing. I guess he told you about Darien, though, right?"

"Darien?"

"Yes, Darien Lachsa. We all thought she and Thor would marry someday, but that did not work out."

"He did mention another woman in his life, someone he was very fond of but, as I understand it, she could not handle his having to be away so much, or the thought of him being on this mission for as much as five years."

"That would be Darien. Fact is, she did not want to be away from her family that long. She is still not married, by the way; maybe she will never find the right man, I do not know. You do understand, do you not, that Thor's work will always take precedence over personal matters?"

"Yes, Manta, and I can deal with that. Thor seems to think he will be here, on Planet Earth, much longer than five years. I like that because this is where my family is, but I also understand that he could leave tomorrow."

"This assignment might well be lifetime for him, Sarah, but what if he is required to leave tomorrow? After all, he is next in line to take his father's place as Prime Minister of Techna. If Karl, who is Thor's father, and holds the position for life, were to die tomorrow, even though he is only 60 years old, and Thor decides to return to Techna what would you do?"

Sarah answered without a moments hesitation. "I would go with him, if he asks me to go."

"Then, dear girl, I think you have found your man, and a wonderful one at that."

"Do you really think so? I mean, I already know I am in love with him, but is he in love with me?"

"Sarah, Sarah, if Thor did not feel something for you, you would not be here today. He would not disclose this facility to anyone he did not trust completely. Let that be your clue. So do not worry. He is a man, remember? Committing and declaring love comes very hard for them."

"Yes, I am beginning to realize that. They are so very different from us."

"I agree. Their loss, though, their loss."

Sarah nodded in agreement. "Manta, what is Techna Planet like, in case I do end up there?"

Manta started to answer, then saw Thor walking toward them. When he reached them, she said, "Thor, Sarah just asked me what Techna Planet is like. Care to field that question?"

"Sure. Sarah, have you ever been to St. Augustine, Florida?"

"Yes, I have. My father took us there one summer on vacation. I remember it as a wonderful old city with delightful homes along the ocean front, and along its narrow cobblestone streets."

"Very good. That is what Techna is like, sort of, St Augustine is about 470 years old, Techna is 613 years older than Planet Earth. We have many beautiful old buildings and some very narrow, very ancient streets, and the people of Techna like it that way. The difference is in technology—high speed public transportation everywhere, every conceivable electronic aid to ease living—what they say about Kansas City, that everything is up to date there, is true of Techna, as well. Perhaps this is a good time to say I would like you to see Techna personally. Would it be possible for you to get away for about three weeks starting April 16?"

"Oh, Thor, I would love that so very much. Can you arrange that? I mean...."

"It is already arranged on this end. Manta took care of it. I have to go then, and I do want you to go with me. Just say the word."

"I'll have to talk to Sam, of course. But I am sure he will approve. I will call him from here."

"Good. Say hello for me and tell him I would like to see him on Monday, if possible. He turned to Manta and explained, "that is Sam Fischer of CTS *Sunday Review*."

Manta nodded and said, "I remember. He was one of the first two Earthlings ever to set foot in this starship." Then she looked at her watch. "Oh my, " she said. "I did not realize that it is nearly midnight. Sarah, I guess our little tour will have to wait until tomorrow. Sleep well and I will see you in the morning. I think I will call it a day."

"Good night, Manta, and thanks for everything you have done for me."

Manta smiled and walked away.

*   *   *

As of March 19, 2010, available records indicate that the United States had 3,309 prisoners on the combined death rows of 37 state prisons. Many had been there for years—some up to 20 years—for crimes that should have demanded virtually immediate retribution. That situation was rectified late at night on this date, as Thor learned via a smart-phone call from Assim Agassi.

As usual, Assim lost no time getting to the point of his call. "The executions were completed a few minutes ago, Commander. We commuted the death sentence of 163 prisoners we determined to have been convicted in error, and they are now in our protective custody. But 3,146 finally paid their long overdue penalty."

"How did it go, Assim?"

110

"Quite well, Commander. We had Techna agents in each prison—in most of them the small number of death row convicts required only one agent, though in states such as California, Florida and Texas, where the numbers were much higher, we had several agents. They carried out their assignments most efficiently, moving invisibly and silently from cell to cell. The prisoners suffered no pain, and the guards did not hear a thing.

The only indicator of what caused death was the small red circle with three black dots forming a triangle within the circle— the mark of our lasers—on the forehead of each prisoner as he slept. At the moment, guards still see nothing out of the ordinary; what has happened will not be clear until they do bed checks at midnight. Then the world will know."

"It is as we planned, Assim."

"Yes. Is Truls Heyerdahl in place?"

"He is waiting at the Bureau of Prisons in Washington, and will make the announcement as soon as you call him."

"Good. I will do so now, Commander."

"Well done, Assim. I know it was not a pleasant duty, and you carried it out to perfection, as usual."

"Thank you, Sir."

*   *   *

When Truls received the call from Assim, it was well after midnight in Washington. Only security guards and one junior Bureau official were in the Bureau of Prisons office. Truls placed a one-page report, printed in large type, with the Techna circle-triangle logo featured prominently in the top center of the page, on the desk of the Bureau Director. The report stood out as the only item on an otherwise clean black lacquered desk, and it was not long before the security guard for that sector of the building spotted it and sounded the alarm.

By one a.m. on March 20. every senior Washington official had the news—every official except President Howard Fields, that is, because of his strict rules against being awakened for any reason before nine a.m. Thus, long before he got out of bed, the story was featured on all five a.m. television news programs.

Howard was about the only person on Planet Earth who did not get the word.

This event, more than any act committed by TF20 since its landing in Roswell, finally captured the attention of the average American. They yawned when Thor appeared on CTS *Sunday Review*. His widely published visits to Washington stirred no public interest. There were no cries of outrage when one Techna starship caused massive destruction to men, machines and facilities in Iraq. But because 3,146 convicted killers and rapists who had escaped equitable punishment for so long, and who, unlike most of their victims, had enjoyed things like three meals a day, free television, free laundry, and visits from friends and relatives, long after their victims were dead and buried, finally paid the price for their crimes, then, and only then did Americans become very angry. Truls thought them a very strange people.

When his report to the Bureau of Prisons Director became fully public, including the news that 30,000 LWOP (Life Without Parole) prisoners were also scheduled to die at the hands of TF20, American citizens became a raging mob in most cities and towns in the country. What the loss of thousands of lives and billions of squandered dollars in Iraq did not do, this "slaughter of helpless prisoners, " as the press put it, accomplished: the awakening of Americans to the realization that their country had been invaded. Cities everywhere struggled to deal with furious, unruly, placard-carrying crowds, for whom television news flashes became the rallying cry. Newspapers were flooded with letters to the editors. Political leaders appeared on television talk shows, protesting the heinous crimes of these terrible invaders from Techna Planet, and there was a universal demand for an immediate end to the invasion. But what American Government officials—including those who protested loudly on television—knew was that the invasion by TF20 would not end anytime soon, and would probably affect the lives of people permanently.

*   *   *

One group that protested so loudly and vehemently about the executions of death row prisoners was the International Union of Prison Guards, with thousands of members, more than 30,000 just in California. Without prisoners to control, these guards would soon be out of work and lose their $80,000 annual salaries. Of course, the state never guaranteed them lifetime employment, but the guards, and their unions, had come to believe the state had a moral duty to do so and never expected things to be otherwise.

Publicly, union leaders tried to display sympathy and concern for their members, but in closed-door meetings it was obvious that their main concern was loss of union dues, for that meant union leaders would soon be out of work, too. The leaders tried to make the argument to the state that they had a lifetime contract. That argument failed. No politician enjoys saying no to constituents, but even in Government, where money flows like water and there is little accountability, it would have been a real stretch to keep guards on the payroll when there were no prisoners to guard. Thus, the union's house of cards collapsed, setting off a chain reaction of bankruptcies and business failures throughout its sphere of influence. Naturally, this left a lot of angry—and well armed—people who vowed to track down TF20 and put an end to its invasion. Clearly, this group of Americans still did not comprehend how futile such an attempt would be.

*   *   *

Another group of Americans, whose members were making a very good living, in fact—through more than 525 televised religious programs that filled 11 television channels 24 hours each and every day, were also very angry. These so-called televangelists were quick to jump on the outcry bandwagon, but not because they felt sadness for the dead prisoners. They saw in this event a chance to win more converts, and of course, an increase in donations to their already vast treasuries. Their televised religious programs— especially those featured on Sunday morning—blasted Techna Force 20 for the cruelty of its executions, ignoring the possibility that keeping people in prison cages for long periods—many for life—could be construed as the most cruel form of punishment of all.

Of course the televangelists were careful not to mention the history of cruel punishment methods Christians used to control their flocks in the Middle Ages.

For Arne Klein, Captain of Group 3, the TF20 Group responsible for religious reform, the outrage of televangelists was a perfect launching platform for a campaign he had been planning for months. He had watched all televangelists in action many times, and knew their methods of operation, their emotion-filled prepared messages, almost better than the preachers themselves knew them.

Arne and members of his Group had also spent long hours in places none of the religious program viewers ever saw: televangelist's very private, insanely opulent, homes and offices. TF20 agents sat in on meetings where the evangelist's messages were rehearsed and refined over and over, in the presence of highly skilled coaches bought for huge salaries from unscrupulous public relations companies, until those messages could be delivered before the cameras as convincingly as is humanly possible, without the use of scripts or teleprompters.

Group 3 agents carefully recorded example after example of the luxurious living that went on behind the vine-covered walls and massive wrought iron gates, beyond which lay another world, a world of Rolex watches, Mercedes and Lexus automobiles, hand made Italian leather shoes, and silk suits costing thousands of dollars each. They were frequent, uninvited, unseen witnesses to extravagant parties and dinners in the palatial homes, all of which contained the most expensive furniture, the finest paintings, the most valuable works of art.

Arne understood what the typical member of a televangelist congregation could not understand: that almost none of the monetary contributions received were ever distributed to those in need. Virtually every dime went to the personal lifestyle of the televangelist and his or her family. The whole enterprise was one gigantic ponzi scheme long overdue for exposure, and he could hardly wait to make that happen.

*   *   *

For Sarah and Thor the week-end went by all too rapidly. It began with a Saturday breakfast in the starship's dining room, at a table shared by Group Captains Siran Missirian, Erika Varda, Assim Agassi and Guri Kohn. Thor explained that his other two Group Captains, Truls Heyerdahl and Arne Klein, were on assignment . "They will be very sorry they missed meeting you, Sarah," he said.

"Well, I am sorry, too. Hopefully there will be another time." She was surprised and extremely pleased to find in Siran and Erika two obviously intelligent women, yet so very young, holding such responsible positions. The two men, Assim and Guri, were equally impressive, in her view, and she began to understand how Thor could manage so many huge tasks yet remain so calm. It was as he said: the key is to have the right people in charge. But she sensed that only a leader with great confidence in himself could do that.

After breakfast Thor took Sarah on a complete top-to-bottom tour of his starship, ending at the bridge. At one point, when they were completely alone he took her into his arms and kissed her passionately. "I am so pleased that you are here with me this week-end, angel, but I must admit, you are very, very habit-forming."

Sarah clung to him and responded, "I certainly hope it is an addiction you cannot break."

He smiled, then a serious look crossed his face. "I must also tell you something, dearest. Last Friday night we carried out the execution of most prisoners on death row. I did not want you to get that news from someone else."

"Thank you, Thor. As I said, the woman in me is sad, but the lawyer's daughter understands that it was necessary. Are you prepared for the backlash?"

"Yes, and unfortunately it has already started, especially from the prison guard's union—but also from televangelists. But we will deal with it. In fact, that is why Arne Klein is not here; religious fraud is his assignment. And by the way, Truls Heyerdahl is in Washington working to convince some stubborn members of Congress to vote for withdrawal from Iraq. Otherwise, he would be here to meet you."

"Well, that means I'll just have to make another trip out here."

"Yes, and very soon I hope. Very soon. Now, dear lady, enough about work. I have a special surprise for you."

"Oh, I do love surprises, Thor. What is it?"

"The rest of this weekend with me in beautiful, romantic Palm Springs, California. Have you been there?"

"No, and I have always wanted to see it. That sounds wonderful."

"Good, we leave immediately, dressed just as we are. Palm Springs—the natives call it the 'Springs—'is a very casual place. We will stay over until tomorrow night , and leave from there to return to New York, if that is alright with you."

"It is fine with me, Thor. I'll go pack my things."

Thor lifted a phone from its cradle on the bridge console. "Hello, Manta. Is Jens ready?"

"Yes, Commander."

"Very well, we will be there in ten minutes."

*   *   *

As Sarah quickly discovered, there is no place quite like Palm Springs, especially in winter. Flowers of every variety, lovingly maintained in formal gardens bordering walks, driveways and parking lots were at their absolute beautiful best at this time of year. They thrived amidst patches of greenery composed of hundreds of exotic plants against a background of huge palms that rustled continuously in the gentle breezes, and formed a frame for towering San Jacinto Mountain rising majestically in the background. The mingled fragrances of all this vegetation filled the air with a heady natural perfume.

Thor and Sarah checked in at the tiny, but very posh, Willows Hotel which nestled in a beautiful garden on South Tahquitz Drive, where each of its eight rooms bears the name of someone famous who had stayed in it while visiting Palm Springs. Their room was named for movie actress, Marion Davies. As with most rooms in this beautiful Mediterranean Villa, it was furnished with the best hand-made antique furniture, fine linens, hand-made tiles, and very expensive accessories. Sarah was amused and pleased to find only one king-size bed, for she took it as a sign that "her man" wanted to be close to her tonight.

From the Willows, it was just a short walk to Le Vallauris, a wonderful French restaurant, as well as to all the sights, sounds and shopping that lined both sides of South Palm Canyon Drive.

The night was warm, with a gentle breeze whispering softly through the palms, so they elected to dine under the stars in the restaurant's secluded tree-canopied courtyard. Their Maine Lobster Ravioli with basil cream was superb. During their meal, Thor mentioned that he had heard about a local live theater group called the Palm Springs Follies. "I am told that they put on a fantastic performance here at the Plaza Theater. Would you like to take that in tomorrow if I can arrange for tickets?"

"Oh, yes, Thor. I would love that. It sounds very exciting. But, and I hope you don't think I am being nosey, aren't you spending too much money on this trip? I mean, I am enjoying it so very much and all, but our room must have cost you a small fortune, and this restaurant , this fabulous restaurant, another fortune. It's just that I don't want you to think you have to do this on my account."

"Honey, believe me, I do not make a habit of living this extravagantly but you are very special to me. So is our time together."

"I love to hear that, Thor. Do you mind another nosey question?"

"Not at all."

"Well, you don't seem to have a source of income and I know your operation must require great gobs of money. How do you support it and yourself?"

"Sarah, that is a very fair question, and you have a right to know. As a member of my father's staff, I receive a substantial annual stipend that is paid by our country. Unfortunately, that money is not recognized on Planet Earth, so it is held in trust for my future use. In the meantime, as you so astutely point out, I must have funds to support our operation here, as well as myself. Just to pay 2000 Techna agents each month requires millions of dollars, and of course there are many other expenses. Fortunately, we have discovered a great source of funds from another of our projects on Earth."

"Oh? What project is that?"

"Illegal drugs. Millions of people on Earth, especially Americans, and more specifically, young Americans, are being destroyed by drug addiction, as I am sure you know. This disease will be the total destruction of your civilization if not stopped soon. Techna Force 20 is dedicated to stamping it out, and we are succeeding very nicely. That eradication program falls within Assim Agassi's responsibility. You met him this morning at breakfast."

"Yes, I remember Assim. A very impressive man."

Thor nodded in agreement. "He is amazing, to be sure. And last month his agents brought in more than forty million dollars in confiscated drug money."

"Goodness, Thor. That is incredible. How does the eradication program work?"

"Well, my dear, it is quite simple, really. Assim has many Techna agents stationed in Mexico, and they are constantly on the alert for news of drug shipments about to be made to the United States. The agents work in teams of various sizes, and when a pending shipment is located a team will insert itself unseen into the operation. As soon as a shipment crosses the border , and the exchange of drugs for money is made, we destroy the heroin, cocaine, opium or whatever, and confiscate the money, then leave the scene and let the buyer and seller fight it out. Usually they are furious because each believes the other has cheated."

"Amazing. You destroy the deadly drugs in the process, which hopefully helps discourage future production. It is a fantastic system, dear man."

"Thank you, Sarah, but it is Assim's system, not mine. Now, if there are no more questions, may I propose a tour of the avenue?"

Sarah smiled and took his hand in hers, and said, "Plaintiff rests, your Honor."

They left Le Vallauris and strolled hand in hand slowly along South Palm Canyon Drive, stopping here and there to examine the wares inside one of the many art galleries, or just to window shop. Along the way, Thor spotted the Plaza Theater and they turned into its quaint Spanish courtyard and stopped at the ticket office. He was able to purchase tickets for good seats in the center balcony, his preferred viewing location. Then they walked slowly back to Le Vallauris' piano bar to sip a glass of wine and enjoy the soft mellow mastery of pianist Paul Diamond. While they were there he played songs such as *Some Enchanted Evening,* by Rogers and Hammerstein, *Somewhere My Love (Lara's Theme)*, by Jarre-Webster, and *Stranger On The Shore*, by Acker Bilk.

Paul's closing number for the evening was one of Thor's favorites, *The Music Of The Night*, from *Phantom Of The Opera*, by Andrew Lloyd Webber. When he heard the opening strains of that beautiful musical number he walked the few steps to the piano and put two twenty dollar bills in the tip jar. Then he leaned over and whispered something in the pianist's ear before returning to Sarah. He held out his arms to her and she came into them immediately. They began to dance. They danced around the piano bar several times, then out through the courtyard dining area, oblivious to the stares of late-night diners, then across quiet West Tahquitz Canyon Way to the Willows, through its lobby as the lone night clerk watched, then down the short corridor to their room. For one brief moment Thor made them invisible and they passed through the room's closed door, just as the last notes of *Music Of The Night* drifted away on the night's gentle breezes.

Eventually they slept, locked in each other's arms as one, until long after the morning's bright sunlight filled their room.

CHAPTER SIX

House Cleaning Begins

Though no one witnessed the landing, Truls Heyerdahl's starship arrived at one of the parking lots adjacent to the Capitol building, late Saturday night, March 20, 2010. By 10:00 a.m. the next morning, the starship's lounge/dining hall contained 160 very bewildered Republican members of Congress; (130 members of the House, including ten women, and 30 members of the Senate, all men). Each had been tranquilized by Techna Force agents, then forcibly brought to the starship in I-Mode. Now, having revived for the most part, they milled around in the unfamiliar circular space and their voices grew louder and more angry by the minute, for they were not accustomed to being treated like just so many cattle.

Then a huge man, well over six feet tall, entered the area and walked calmly to the lectern directly in front of them. He was dressed in a smoke-blue uniform with gold lettering on the left breast, and he had the thickest thatch of wheat colored hair any of them had ever seen. He leaned forward slightly to speak into the microphone. "Ladies and Gentlemen, please take your seats and let me have your attention." He waited patiently for them to do as he ordered, and when they were seated and reasonably quiet, he said "I am Truls Heyerdahl, Captain of Group One, Techna Force 20. I am responsible for you being here, in my starship, today. Why are you here, you wonder? Well, I will tell you why: You are here because you have refused to vote in favor of troop withdrawal in Iraq. Today, each of you will be given a chance to change your mind on how you will vote. When your name is called, a member of my staff will escort you to another area, where you will be given your options. As I call...."

"This is an outrage," said Congressman Will Sizemore of Tennessee. Holding us like this is illegal, and you know it. Where is my cell phone? I want to call my office now."

"All cell phones have been confiscated. They will be returned to you when you leave."

"So you really are just a band of dictators, after all," yelled an unidentified voice from the middle of the pack. Do you know what happens to people who deliberately interfere with members of Congress?"

At that point a tall statuesque woman elbowed her way out of the crowd and stood in front of Truls. "How dare you try to intimidate members of Congress," she said, in a loud voice. I demand that we be released immediately. Just who do you think you are?"

"Ah, yes, Senator Swift, from the state of New York, I believe. Senator, we dare because we can. If you have kept up with the news lately you know about the power of Techna Force 20. You know, or should know, that it was us who destroyed your new Baghdad Embassy, as well as other Iraqi facilities, plus one aircraft carrier. You know, or should know, that we destroyed the F-22 Raptors that attacked our base in New Mexico. You should also know by now that it was Techna Force 20 agents who carried out the executions of more than 3,000 death row prisoners very recently. Yet, still you question our power? As our leader, Commander Berksten, told you in the joint session of Congress recently, you must now accept that we are major players in United States government efforts—all such efforts, including the Iraq war, which must stop now. Since President Fields will not stop it voluntarily, it falls to you to take away his power to continue it—power you should never have given him in the first place. Withdrawing from Iraq is vital to your planet and to ours. We need every vote in Congress to deprive him of that power. You 160 members assembled here today are the only ones insisting on continuing the war. That is unacceptable to Techna Force 20, so you are not going anywhere until you change your mind and agree to vote yes."

"Dictator, dictator! " Someone yelled.

"And," Senator Swift continued, "If we refuse to change our minds what will you do, kill us, as you did those poor soldiers in the Green Zone?"

Truls held up his arm and snapped his fingers. "No, Senator, we have something entirely different in mind for you. Let me show you what I mean."

At his signal another woman appeared and stood next to him. She was an exact duplicate of Senator Swift in every detail. She looked exactly like Swift. Her hair was the same, her clothes were the same, her face was the same. "Senator Swift, take a good look at this woman, who is a Techna agent, for, if you refuse to cooperate she will take your place in the Senate starting tomorrow, and *she will vote yes*. She will also take your place in your home, and I assure you, your husband, Charles, will not detect any difference--not in voice, appearance or actions." Truls let his eyes roam over the tightly packed crowd of angry faces. "Ladies and gentlemen, we do not have a double for just Senator Swift; we have one for each and every one of you."

"Those of you replaced by a double will, on the other hand, make a five million mile journey to our facility on Prison Planet. You could be there a very long time and, let me tell you, it will not be a pleasant experience. We do not segregate prisoners by gender. We do not prepare prison meals or wash your clothes; each prisoner must do that on his own. Nor do we have television. That is how we will deal with any of you who refuse to cooperate today. However, there is a way you can go home right now, if you are interested."

Senator Swift stared at her double in disbelief, fully recognizing the ramifications. But she heard every word Truls uttered. "And what is that way?" she asked.

"Any one here who agrees to vote as we wish tomorrow may leave now. But be warned. If you violate that agreement the punishment we mete out will be worse than anything you can imagine. Anyone interested in that arrangement? If so, please stand now."

Approximately 85 of the 160 stood, including Senator Swift, who had started to sit down, but changed her mind and stood with them. All 85—30 male Democrats, 45 male Republicans and 10 female Republicans--were escorted out of the starship and freed.

Then, in groups of a dozen or so, Truls began calling the names of the 75 male Republican members remaining. As a name was called, that person was detained, and a doubles agent, who was a perfect copy of him, stepped forward to take his place. All 75 of the men stubbornly refused to reconsider. None of them would see their families again. Thus, of the original 160 members taken to Truls' starship, 85, including all 10 women, agreed to change their vote to 'Yes,' on the question of ending the war in Iraq and were released. 75 male members who refused to change their vote were replaced by doubles and confined pending their one way trip to Prison Planet.

*   *   *

On Monday, March 22, 2010, the House of Representatives first debated then approved a Bill to rescind Presidential power to declare war on other countries, making their decision retroactive, to apply to the Iraq and Afghanistan wars. Next, they approved a Bill ending both current wars as soon as troops and equipment could be removed. The vote was 90 percent in favor on both Bills, 10 percent against. When the two Bills reached the Senate, the vote was 95 percent for and 5 percent against. Thor won his bet with the Speaker Of The House, Katherine McDonald. She was amazed. Never had she witnessed a vote so powerfully one-sided. Democrats in the House had a comfortable majority, yet this bill was supported more than she ever thought possible. Then she remembered the words of Commander Thor Berksten and understood why it happened. How he did it was a matter of great curiosity for her and she made a mental note to follow up on that question right away.

*   *   *

Edward Reynolds, Senate Majority Leader, could not believe the vote in his Chamber, either. What would make Republican Senators who were so against stopping the war vote to stop it, he wondered. He was pleased, of course, but did not understand how it could happen. He called Katherine McDonald, and was then even more amazed. "I think I know how it happened Ed," she said. This is Thor Berksten's work. He spoke after the President at the joint session, remember? I did not tell you before, but he came to my office before that session. He said he needed a 92% favorable vote, and predicted we would get it. The House missed that number by only two, but the vote was still far more than was needed to win. Your Senators did even better with a 95 percent Yes vote. That's pretty close to his prediction. I don't know how he managed to bring it off, but I for one sure intend to find out."

"Yes, Katherine. It sure would be interesting to find out. I'll do some checking on my side and let you know what I find. When do you want to present this to the President?"

"Right away. How about tomorrow? I'll set it up with his Chief of Staff."

"Sounds good to me. Let me know what time."

"I will, Ed, and by the way, Congratulations. We did it. I don't know how, but we did it. Fields won't be able to overturn this vote, that's for sure."

"Yes, Katherine. This is a great occasion."

* * *

It was a great occasion for Thor, as well. He had been in both Houses of Congress at various times during the vote, and knew the outcome as soon as Katherine McDonald and Edward Reynolds knew it. What concerned him was how the President would deal with the news. Technically, he had no choice but to go along with the decision but, as Thor was all too aware, he was a crafty politician who managed to get his way more often than not.

He called Truls and thanked him for doing such a great job. "What changed their minds the most? " he asked.

"It was two things, Commander. The news about our executions of death row prisoners was one. I think that event, as much as anything else, made them realize just how powerful we are and how serious. Then, when we presented the doubles it blew their minds. We sent 75 to Congress, you know. It was not so much that they could be replaced in Congress by a look-a-like, or even that they could end up on Prison Planet—in my opinion, none of them comprehended the agony of that place, how could they? What really got to them was that they would be replaced in their homes. Doubles is a very effective tool, and I recommend keeping it in our arsenal."

"Yes, I agree, Truls. Were any of the female members of Congress replaced?"

"No. Not a one. They were not about to allow another woman in their home. By the way, Commander. 35 members of the House reneged on their promise to vote yes. Before that we had—or thought we had-- a one hundred percent yes vote."

"What do you recommend we do about them, Truls?"

"I think they should also experience the meaning of doubles, Sir."

"Agreed. Will you see to it?"

"Yes, Sir. Right away."

"Good, dear friend. Again I congratulate you on a job very well done. The President will be advised tomorrow some time. Then we will see what he does. Take care."

* * *

After his phone call to Truls, Thor left immediately for New York to visit Sam Fischer at CTS *Sunday Review,* where, once again, he made the long walk from the elevator to the reception desk, and once again Sarah Malloy never took her eyes off him.

"Good morning, Commander Berksten," she said formally. It is good to see you again."

"Yes, dear lady, it has been much too long." He took her hand and kissed it. "Yes, indeed. Much, much too long."

Sarah smiled knowingly, and rang Sam Fischer's office.

"Yes, Sarah?" Margie answered.

"Commander Berksten to see Mr. Fischer."

"Send him right in. Sam is waiting for him now."

"You may go in, Commander."

Thor thanked her and disappeared through the now familiar door.

Margie greeted him and said, tea, right?"

"You have a good memory, Margie. Yes, tea will be just fine."

At that moment, Sam Fischer came out of his office. "Hey, Commander, good to see you again. It has been a while."

"Yes, it has, Sam. I see you have been very busy telling the world about Techna Force 20, and all of its activities. Excellent *Sunday Review* program yesterday."

"Thanks, Sam replied, as he escorted Thor back to his office. "Anything new for me?"

"Well, let me see. Do you know what happened in Congress today?"

"No, haven't heard. What happened?"

"They voted to end the Iraq war. The House vote was 392 yeas versus 43 nays. The Senate vote was 95 yeas against 5 nays.

The President will get the Bill formally tomorrow, so I ask you to keep this quiet until then.

"Sure thing. Wow, that's over 91%. A record. Fields will have a tizzy."

"Probably, But what can he do? He is trapped. It is long past time to end that terrible war."

"Yes, Thor, I agree completely."

"Not only did they vote to end both the Iraq and Afghan wars, Sam, they also approved a Bill rescinding the President's power to declare war on anybody."

"Wow! That is super significant, Commander."

"And I have news on our televangelist effort. We have had agents imbedded in many of those organizations for some time. Our investigation has been most enlightening. To put it bluntly, they constitute the biggest ponzi scheme your country has ever seen."

"Can we help you with that one, Thor? Maybe do a good expose' with lots of facts and figures?"

"Yes, Sam. I think that would be most appropriate. If the public can be made to understand that 99% of their contributions go into the pockets of the televangelists, and virtually none goes to the poor, perhaps these empires will come crashing down."

"Are those numbers accurate?"

"Very accurate. I will see that you get our final report, which details it all. That should be ready later this week."

"And nobody else gets it, right? We get an exclusive?"

"Always, Sam. I know you will put the information to good use. And on another subject, illegal drug sales, you barely scratched the surface on the size of this problem yesterday. Want to know more?"

"Hell yes, Thor. We don't have anybody inside those organizations, so information can only be catch as catch can. What do you have?"

"Agents on the inside. We know about every large drug shipment before it ever reaches the United States. We have confiscated more than one hundred million dollars worth so far, and have destroyed every kilo of drugs before they can be distributed. But the best news is that we have put buyer against seller—each thinking the other cheated—and they are killing one another left and right. Good riddance."

"God, I'd love to have that information, Thor. The people need to know. Give me a chance and we'll tell the world."

"Done, Sam. But we are not talking small fish here. Most of the sellers are very bad people. South Americans, mostly, all millionaires. And the buyers are large corporations—all American. They are the ones converting your people into raging druggies. You will be stepping on some pretty big toes."

"Hell, Thor, that's why we are here. Why *Sunday Review* has been so successful all these years. We inform on rats so the people will get the word. Man, you are a gold mine. Together we can do a lot of good."

"Exactly. That is why I came to you back in February, Sam."

"What else are you into, my friend?"

"Well, we have a large investigation going right now on corporation control of your Government, but it will not be completed for some time yet. I can tell you this much: it will be a bomb shell. We will name names and explain how they gain from such control. I think it will anger the general public beyond all imagination, and send a lot of vermin running for cover."

"Thor, we can help on that, as well. Let me know when you are ready. One thing I'd like to know, by the way: What happens to the drug money you confiscate?"

"It is used to fund our operations, Sam. Techna Planet currency is no good here, as you probably know."

"I see. Hell, that's just poetic justice; use their own money to put them out of our misery."

"Exactly. Well Sam, I must leave now. There is much to do. Has Sarah talked to you yet?"

"About what?"

"About giving her three weeks off so she can accompany me to Techna Planet in April."

"No, but she can have the time. We will get by somehow. She's pretty special to you, isn't she?"

"Thanks, but please do not let her know I said anything, and yes, she is very, very special to me."

"She is a wonderful woman and if you try to steal her I will kill you."

Thor laughed, but said no more. The two men shook hands and Thor left. On his way out he stopped at the reception desk and said goodbye to Sarah. "I will call you soon, my angel, " he said. "Very soon."

"One minute from now would not be soon enough, Thor," she replied.

"Well, in that case, what would you say if I asked you to go to dinner with me tonight?"

"I would say yes, but only if you stay over."

"Then it's a date. I don't have to be in Washington until morning. Pick you up at your place at seven?"

"I'll be ready, Thor."

*   *   *

Jack Brill walked into President Howard Fields bedroom at 9:00 a.m., on Tuesday, March 23. "Mr. President, you have to get up. The Speaker of the House and the Senate Majority Leader will be here at ten o'clock this morning to deliver the results of the vote on Iraq."

"Why so damned early?" the President grumbled, barely awake.

"Early for you, maybe," Brill replied. Then he said, "most people in this town have been awake for hours, I think you are going to have a bad hair day, so you better get yourself together." Then he left Fields to make himself presentable.

*   *   *

Katherine McDonald and Edward Reynolds entered the White House right on schedule, and they, along with John Raider, Senate Minority Leader and Murray Rosenthal, House Minority Whip, who came with them, were ushered into the Oval Office by Jack Brill. Standing to one side of the room but invisible was Thor Berksten. Fields appeared at ten minutes past ten a.m. "Katherine, Edward, John, Murray, good to see you." He shook hands with all of them then said, " I understand you have something for me."

"Yes, Mr. President," Katherine replied. We are here to present the results of a vote on ending the war in Iraq." She placed a black leather folder on Field's desk. "The House voted 392 to 43 in favor of immediate withdrawal, while the Senate vote was 95 in favor to 5 against. Furthermore, you no longer have the power to declare war or engage in war against any country without first gaining Congressional approval. The approval you received previously has been rescinded."

"Preposterous. You can't do that. I'll veto this as I have before."

"Your veto will be overturned this time, Mr. President," Edward Reynolds said. "The vote will be the same. We are here to instruct you to begin immediate withdrawal."

The President looked from Katherine and Edward to John and Murray, as if searching for support from at least one of them.

"Mr. President," John Raider said, "I am afraid this is official. We could not prevent the vote. There is simply no support for continuing the war."

"Well, you don't 'instruct me' on anything, people. I am the President, for Christ's sake."

"Perhaps instruct is too strong a word, but you will have to comply with the will of Congress, nevertheless, Katherine said. "Now, good day to you, Mr. President Please do not force us to commence impeachment proceedings." With that the four members of Congress left the Oval Office.

*   *   *

-

President Fields was beside himself with anger. He paced the Oval Office with his hands clasped behind his back for over an hour, as Jack Brill waited for him to issue instructions.

Finally he said, "Get Phillips over here now. And ask Bob Watson, Gordon Hausemann, Peter Bigham, Victor Moseman to come, too. I want to talk to Phillips first, then with Watson, Hausemann, Bigham and Moseman. Following those two meetings, schedule a meeting of the full Cabinet—all 13 of them."

"Yes, Mr. President," Brill replied, and left to handle this order. It would, he knew, take most of the day, if not longer, to round up the people Fields referred to.

Bertram Phillips came to the White House right away and he and the President met for well over an hour. The subject was how to comply with the Congressional decision by withdrawing, if the President did not prevail in efforts to avoid any such decision. Fields told Phillips he intended to go to the Supreme Court, if necessary, in order to get the decision overturned. Phillips replied that he did not think going to the Supreme Court was a good idea, or that they would even go along with that plan. "There is already a great deal of public anger over how you have used your war powers, Howard. Even though you appointed a number of Justices, I am afraid they will balk at vacating an act of Congress, especially one supported by so many members. You could lose that round and be even further in the hole."

"Well, they owe me, by God, and it's payback time," Fields said, angrily.

"Yes, I know, Mr. President, but there are limits to what they can do under the Constitution."

* * *

The next meeting, with Bob Watson, powerful television evangelists, Gordon Hausemann, CEO of United Motors, Peter Bigham, President of Delta Phamaceuticals, and Victor Moseman, Rector of St. Pauls' Evangelical Church, was much longer—more than three hours. Watson, Hausemann and Bigham wanted the war to continue, not because they believed it could be won, but because it was immensely profitable for them and their organizations. "Iraq has been a gold mine for us, Howard," Hausemann said. "If we lose those big contracts for tanks and other war material it could signal the end of United Motors. You can't let that happen. We are counting on you to keep it from happening. Those bastards in Congress don't understand. All they are interested in is getting reelected."

"Come now, Gordon," Moseman replied. "Surely you can give up something to stop this senseless killing of young soldiers. Besides, it is a war we cannot win. You know that."

"Hold it, Victor," the President said. "I think the war can be won. We are winning now, in fact. We'll get a democracy there without a doubt, though it may take additional time."

"Victor, winning or losing is not the question, anyway. This is business we are talking about. Howard asked us to retool most of our automobile plants to produce military equipment. We did that, and now he wants us to take a bath in the middle of the contract. I can't agree to that."

"It may be business to you, but I think you are all riding a dead horse. It is time to call a halt to this war, and to Afghanistan, too."

"And just forget that Osama Bin Laden attacked the World Trade Center, right?"

"Even if you kill him there will be another Bin Laden to take up the fight."

"Maybe Howard will pay for you to retool back to cars," Gordon, Bigham interjected. "Would that satisfy you?"

"Hell no. We are in a major recession right now and nobody is buying cars. We need the war, dammit."

At this point, Gordon Hausemann made a motion to continue the war. The vote was four in favor, with Moseman abstaining.

The President was very pleased with how it turned out.

* * *

The President's Cabinet, consisting of four women and nine men, met with Fields on the following day, March 24, 2010. After the President made his opening remarks, Bertram Phillips, Secretary of Defense was first to speak. He confessed to the other members that he no longer felt the war was sustainable, and that if the President wanted his resignation he could have it.

The four women, Margaret Bridges, Secretary of State; Linda Foxworth, Secretary of the Interior; Sylvia Patterson, Secretary of

Commerce and Labor; and Veronica Miller, Secretary of Education, all felt that the war should be ended for humanitarian as well as monetary reasons.

John Dawson, Secretary of the Treasury, made a strong argument for ending the war based on purely financial considerations. "We are spending twelve billion dollars every month over there, with no end in sight. The bill to date is over one trillion dollars. Now, in addition, our country has been hit with the greatest financial meltdown in its history, and we are committed to helping various banks and other financial institutions to the extent of one point five trillion dollars more. Mr. President, we simply cannot sustain that level of monetary outflow. It will bankrupt the country if we continue spending at this pace, and that is not an exaggeration."

"Hell, John, it's only money. What are you worried about?"

"Mr. President, we will not be able to pay the interest on over two point five trillion in loans, let alone finance a continuation of the war in Iraq, plus the war in Afghanistan. And we have been saying this for over a year; it should not be a surprise."

"Yes, John, you have been Mr. Gloom and Doom , but I think you are dead wrong. We are winning. We will win in Iraq. And we will get Bin Laden.

"Mr. President, I have to agree with John," Margaret Bridges said. I have been in Iraq and Afghanistan numerous times, and as I have reported to you in the past, we will not change more than 2000 years of tradition in the Middle East. All of the nations there are tribal, and any attempt on our part to change that will fail, as it has again and again for hundreds of years. We killed Saddam Hussein, but now a new strong man is taking his place. Will he be another vicious dictator? We don't know yet. But he sure is shaping up that way. Eventually we will catch and execute Bin Laden, but will it end with that? I don't think so. I think there is already someone waiting in the wings to take over for him. It will go on that way forever, it seems. We tend to lose sight of the real cause of unrest in that part of the world."

"And just what is that, Margaret?" Fields shot back.

"Well, what put us in this position with respect to the Middle East was the decision back in 1948, wherein we, along with France and Great Britain decided to give part of Palestine to the Jews, thus reinstating the country of Israel. That is the real reason we are hated over there—and will always be hated—by Arabs in all Muslem countries. They don't trust us, so why would they be willing to adopt our form of government—a democracy. It is my contention that they will not. So, if you are putting it to a vote, I say lets get out of the Middle East and move on."

"Margaret, I think you are over-emphasizing the Palestine-Israel event. I simply do not accept that," Fields said. "Any other thoughts on the subject of withdrawal?"

"I feel the same way, Mr. President," said Sylvia Patterson, Secretary of Commerce and Labor. We need to bring the troops home. However, there is a problem even then. Most of the nearly 150,000 over there are called-up reservists who left jobs they think will be waiting for them when they come home. Unfortunately that will not be the case. Many are on their second and even third tour of duty, and have been away from those jobs for years now. It was not, and is not reasonable to expect employers to hold them open; they have businesses to run, after all. So most of the 150,000 soldiers we bring home when we do withdraw will not find jobs—especially now with the unemployment rate hovering around eight percent. Therefore, I believe we should consider keeping them on the military payroll unless, or until they do have civilian jobs. We can't simply dump them on an already over-burdened labor market."

"But what will we do with them, Sylvia?" Veronica Miller, Secretary of Education asked. Even with re-education we cannot place too many of them in jobs."

"Well, none of you want to hear this, but I like the suggestion that Commander of Techna Force 20, what's his name, Thor Berksten, is supposed to have made: Put them on our borders to help prevent illegal immigration."

"Listen, all of you," Fields said firmly, "I don't want to hear that man's name ever again. He is just one of the many terrorists we face, and a primary reason why we need to keep our forces in Iraq."

"Mr. President, you can't be serious, Bertram Phillips responded. "Thor Berksten and his band are not going to go away. He is for real. He proved that in Baghdad. He proved it with the death row executions. I think he was a major player in this phenomenal Congressional vote, though we don't yet know just how he did it. No, Sir. You simply cannot, and must not, count him out. He is no aberration."

"Well maybe not, but he ain't gonna tell us how to run this country, Bertram. I won't allow it. Now let me see a show of hands. How many of you think we should pull out?"

At once nine hands went up. Nine in favor of withdrawal, four against. The President was grim-faced as he spoke to those with raised hands. " Okay, that is your opinion. I'm not bound by what you recommend, as all of you know, but I thank you for coming today, and for your candid suggestions. I'll let you know what I decide." With that he stood up, signaling the end of the meeting.

Thor, who had been in all three meetings, in I-Mode, was the last to leave the Cabinet room. He had concluded early on that Fields planned to continue the war, even in the face of opposition.

*   *   *

Wednesday evening he called Sarah Malloy to tell her how much he had enjoyed the time with her Monday. "You have become a very essential part of my life, angel," he told her. It is getting so I want to be with you every day."

"That is music I longed to hear, Thor, and nothing pleases me more than to hear you say it. When will I see you again?"

"Possibly on Friday, But I'll have to confirm that later."

"Wonderful. I'll be counting the minutes."

*   *   *

On Thursday morning, March 26, 2010, Thor was back at the White House, waiting in the Oval Office for the President to wake up. This time he had another Techna Force 20 agent with him. The two men waited patiently and unseen.

Fields appeared just after ten a.m., shuffling slowly into the room, looking as if he had not slept all night. Jack Brill followed him in. "Mr. President, you have a full agenda today," he said. Bertram Phillips and Margaret Bridges will be here in a few minutes. They want to talk more about withdrawal. Then you have to meet with your National Security Advisor. And finally, we have scheduled a press conference, because we have received hundreds of inquires regarding the decision of Congress."

Fields merely grunted and nodded.

Thor made himself and his companion visible as soon as Jack Brill left. "But first you must talk to me, Mr. President," he said.

"You! Fields shouted! How the hell did you get in here again?"

"Well you know, I simply walked in, Mr. President."

"What do you want, Berksten? And who's that with you? He looks familiar."

"He should, Mr. President. He is your exact double. We know him as Damien Moss, Captain, Techna Force 20. But from now on you will call him Howard Fields, President."

"Preposterous. No one can take my place. It would violate the Constitution."

"No one will know the difference. It will be a seamless transition. He has been your understudy for some time and is ready to take your place. Ask your wife."

"What are you talking about, Berksten?"

"Ask her. Ask her right now."

Fields glared at Thor. His jaw was clinched. His eyes grew very hard. "You're godammed right I will, " he said and flew out of his chair and out the door.

He found his wife alone in her private office. She looked up from her work, surprised to see him. He came into the room and put his arms around her shoulders from behind. "Howard, what on earth are you doing? Surely you don't want to make love again. You just left here twenty minutes ago." She took his hands in hers. "Wasn't that enough for one day? I must say, though, dear, it was the most wonderful love-making we have ever had together, but twice in a day? That is very new to me."

The President stiffened perceptibly, for Mildred's response confirmed his worst fears. He did not know what to say. The realization that he had been cuckolded was enough to send him—any man for that matter—over the edge, but the thought that the man who did it to him was about to replace him, not just as President, but also as the man in Mildred's life, was almost more than he could bear. Thor Berksten had told the truth. Fields hurried out of his wife's office without another word and rushed back to the Oval Office, where Thor and his double were still waiting.

"As he came in, Thor asked, "Satisfied, Mr. President?

There was a look of sheer rage on Field's face "I'll kill you for this, Berksten. Where is Jack Brill?"

"I don't know, Mr. President. He left without telling me," Thor replied.

Fields grabbed the phone on his desk. "Get the secret service in here. I'm being accosted by agents from Techna Planet again," he said, to whoever answered.

Within seconds the two secret service agents now familiar to Thor appeared. "Yes, Mr. President?"

"I want you to arrest these two men immediately. They are threatening my life."

The agents scanned the room, then looked at Fields quizzically. What two men, Mr. President? We see only you in here." They were growing a bit tired of this game the President seemed to be playing.

"There, you fools," Fields shouted, as he swung around in his chair to point to where Thor and Damien were supposed to be. There, right in front of ..... Hell, what happened to them? They were here a minute ago."

"Well, they are gone now, Sir. Call us if you see them again."

"When the agents were out of sight, Thor said, "Mr. President, it is over. You are no longer President. You are now going to Prison Planet, from which you will never return." He pointed his left arm at Fields, and sent a laser dart that paralyzed him and made him invisible. Two additional TF20 agents then appeared and took Howard Fields away. Thor turned to his companion. "Damien, or should I say, Mr. President, it is now up to you."

"Thank you, Commander. I will do my very best, beginning with notifying my Cabinet of my decision on withdrawal."

"When will you announce that decision, Mr. President?"

"Right now," the new Howard Fields said, and called Jack Brill back into the Oval Office.

"Yes, Mr. President?"

"Assemble the full Cabinet as soon as possible."

"Very well, Howard. What is the subject?"

"Withdrawal from Iraq."

Brill nodded and left.

*   *   *

Thor's next stop that day was to the office of Bertram Phillips, Secretary of Defense, located in the huge pentagon complex. It took him some time to locate a directory of the building, but once he found one it gave clear directions to the Secretary's suite. Not knowing what to expect, he kept himself in I-Mode and walked directly into Phillip's office, thus bypassing a fleet of secretaries and assistants.

Luckily, he caught Phillips alone, seated at his great mahogany desk. He placed himself directly in front of the desk and said, "Good morning Mr. Secretary," just as he made himself visible. His sudden appearance startled Phillips, who was obviously deep in thought, and his shoulders jerked sharply upward.

"What? Oh, Good morning Commander," he responded, recovering quickly. "What brings you out here so early in the day?"

"The need to talk to you privately, Mr. Secretary. Let me be the first to inform you that President Fields will announce later today that he is withdrawing from Iraq."

"When?"

"When is he going to announce it, or when is he going to withdraw?"

"When is he going to announce his decision, is my question."

"Mr. Secretary, he has asked Jack Brill to arrange a Cabinet meeting as soon as possible, and he will say then that he is ordering immediate withdrawal."

"I won't ask how you know this."

"Thank you, Sir."

"So. Why are you telling me, when he will do it then?"

"Because I want to offer you the help of Techna Force 20 in bringing the soldiers and equipment home. I am putting five starships at your disposal. They are much faster than anything you have; they can carry 500 fully equipped soldiers at a time, and make a round trip from Baghdad to the United States in about two hours. You see, Secretary Phillips, I want your armies out of there as quickly as possible, and my starships are the best way to accomplish that."

"I see, and you want me to suggest that to the President, is that it?"

"Yes."

"You know how he feels about TF20, of course. What makes you think he will accept your offer?"

"I don't know that he will, " Thor lied. "But if it comes from you he might be more receptive."

Phillips stared hard at Thor for several seconds. "Very well. I will suggest it. When will your starships be available?"

"Immediately, Sir. Just let me know."

At that moment, Phillip's secretary stuck her head in the office door. When she spotted Thor she let out a gasp and her hands went to her face. "Oh, Mr. Secretary, I am so sorry. I don't know how he got past me."

"It's alright, Mary. Please don't worry. Incidentally, this is Commander Thor Berksten from Planet Techna. I am sure you have heard of him."

"Yes, of course," Mary responded, giving Thor a long, hard look from top to bottom. How do you do, Commander.?"

"Fine, thank you, Mary. It is nice to meet you."

"Mary," Secretary Phillips, said. "He is friendly, and is welcome here. Now, what did you want to see me about?"

"Oh, yes. I am to inform you that a Cabinet meeting has been called for two p.m. today."

"Thank you. Inform the White House that I will attend," Phillips said. Then he turned to face Thor. "Now, what I'd like to know is how you arranged this change of mind on the President's part?"

"How do you know I did?"

"Just a hunch. A very strong hunch."

"Well, Mr. Secretary, let's just say TF20 is a very powerful organization."

"That's it?"

Thor smiled and shrugged his shoulders, then left the office.

*   *   *

It has been said that the best imitation is one no person recognizes as an imitation. If that is the case, the new President Fields passed the toughest of exams: exposure to a Cabinet composed of 13 people who had worked with and been in close proximity with, his predecessor, for none of them saw any difference in appearance, mannerisms, voice or thought processes.

The only apparent change was in his opinion of the war in Iraq, an opinion that was now diametrically opposite to what had been expressed so many times before, and as recently as two days ago. But they attributed that change in opinion to the arguments they had presented at that time to convince him of the need to take a different direction, and they were pleased to see that he had heeded their advice.

Bertram Phillips was first to speak. "Mr. President, I applaud you for recognizing that the time has come to end this war. This decision will do much to alter the world's image of our country."

"Well," Pierce Clemons, Secretary of Homeland Security, said. " I don't agree. I think this decision will weaken our position in the eyes of the world's people, not strengthen it, and we can expect even more terrorist attacks like 9/11."

His comment started a heated discussion that consumed more than twenty minutes, but in the end, the nine Cabinet members who had raised their hands in favor of withdrawal won the day.

"Mr. President, have you thought about how we will disengage?" Phillips asked. "I mean, how we will get out troops back here quickly?"

Bertram, I think that will have to be left to the military leaders, but it seems to me we won't do it overnight."

"Well, Sir, what would you think of asking Techna Force 20 for help? I understand their starships are extremely fast and can move many people at a time."

"I don't know about that, Bertram. They are our enemy."

"Sir, I think they are not so much our enemy. Rather, I see them as being more concerned about protecting their own planet, and being very tough negotiators."

"Yes, I see your point. Still, it is a tricky question, but if their Commander were to offer, I would certainly consider that option"

"Mr. President, the man you speak of, their Commander, is almost certainly in this room as we speak, Margaret Bridges said. I am betting you will get just such an offer from him momentarily."

"We will see, Margaret. In the meantime, I will announce this decision in a press conference today, then I want you, Bertram, to begin the withdrawal planning process immediately. Now, if there are no other comments, this Cabinet meeting is hereby adjourned."

* * *

The new President completed his first press conference in a flawless manner. If any of the attending reporters noticed a difference in the President it did not show on their faces. He fielded dozens of questions more lucidly than his predecessor ever did, but in a deliberately, stumbling way, much as the old President would have done, and he even incorporated the colloquial slang that was so apparent before. At the conclusion of the press conference, he walked swiftly back to the Oval Office.

"How do you think it went, Jack?" he asked Brill."

"Excellent, Howard. I think you did your best work in there. And it seemed to me that most of them were genuinely pleased at the news of withdrawal. In fact, I didn't see one frown on any face, and that bunch includes a lot of hawks, as you well know."

"Yes. I am pleased with it too. But now we have much work to do. Will you get Bertram Phillips over here as soon as you can. He and I need to start working out the details."

"Sure thing, Mr. President." Jack said, as he stood to leave. I'll get right on it."

When he was safely out of the room, Thor made himself visible. "Excellent work, Mr. President," he said. You fooled them all. I am very proud of you."

"Thank you, Commander. Is it true you offered to let us use Techna starships to transport the troops home?"

"It is true, yes. I have arranged for five additional ships to be delivered immediately. Each was outfitted to carry 500 fully equipped soldiers. They left two days ago, and should arrive next Monday, March 29.

"Very good, Commander, but how are we going to handle this? Techna Force 20 is viewed as the enemy of America—even as a terrorist group. Won't it seem strange if we now ask that enemy for help?"

"Yes, I have considered that problem, too. If I were you, I would go before the people on national television and tell them the truth. I would tell them right out that the United States believes it has done all it can to bring peace to the Middle East. Point to the removal of Saddam Hussein."

"Then I would tell them you are now conceding that the Muslim way of governing, which has been a tradition for thousands of years, is best for Arabic-speaking peoples, and that you will no longer try to force them to accept a democratic form of Government."

"Finally, I would tell them the United States understands the hard feelings that have been present toward it, England and France, because of the joint decision these three countries made long ago to partition Palestine so that Israel would have a land of its own, but that you continue to believe the decision was appropriate. I would offer to provide substantial financial aid to Palestine, to help it become a stronger, more self-sufficient nation. That third point—helping Palestine financially—should go a long way toward healing bad blood and, after all, it is just, for you have poured billions of dollars into Israel, and almost nothing into Palestine."

"Then," Thor said, "I would conclude the address with the news that you are bringing American soldiers home immediately, and that you will guarantee them employment at government expense until they succeed in finding work in the civilian sector."

"Lastly, I would tell them that you are accepting an offer from Techna Force 20 to provide its starships, so the troops get home as fast as possible, and that TF20 has never been an enemy of the United States, only of some of its policies."

"That sounds wonderful, Commander. Perhaps you should deliver this address."

"You jest, of course, but I cannot. It must come from you, and it must be done quickly, for the press already has the news. Tonight is much more preferable than tomorrow night."

"Very well, I will have my Press Secretary arrange it immediately."

Thor nodded, very pleased with his choice of a replacement for Fields, then left the Oval Office.

*   *   *

As soon as he was out of the White House, Thor called Sam Fischer and gave him the news. "Sam," he said, "the President will address the nation on television tonight. I am not sure of the time—probably early."

"How the hell did you pull that off, Commander."

"Sam, I may never be able to answer that question to your satisfaction. Have a great day."

*   *   *

The President's television address, which took place at 8:00 p.m. Eastern time, was a huge success, and left people everywhere dancing in the streets with happiness. Their sons and daughters, brothers and sisters, fathers and mothers, were coming home at last, after eight long years of misery, poverty and war. Not since the end of WWII had people felt such exhilaration. And no one who had come in contact with the new President Fields, including his Cabinet members, and the press had detected that the change in their leader was far deeper than they could ever know. No one except Jack Brill, that is.

*   *   *

Thor returned to Sardine Mountain on the afternoon of Thursday, March 25, because several Group Captains wanted to discuss their projects. He decided to call a general staff meeting so everyone could be updated, and had Manta arrange it for 9:00 a.m., Friday.

Then he called Sarah. She did not answer her phone at home so he called her at work.

"CTS *Sunday Review*," came her familiar voice. "How may I direct your call?"

"I can listen to you say that all day long, angel. Will you say it again, please?"

"Oh, Thor, how good to hear *your voice*. Are you anyplace nearby?"

"Sorry, but no. I am at Sardine Mountain. Needed to have a staff meeting. Now I have a question for you."

"What is that, may I ask?"

"How would you like to get away from that terrible old winter blizzard up there and spend this weekend with me under the palm trees in warm, sunny San Diego?"

"I would just love it, Thor. When do we leave?"

"Can you be packed by seven tomorrow evening?"

"I'll be ready. Do you think your transporter can land in this snow storm?"

"Honey, it would have to be a hundred feet deep to keep me from getting there. See you at seven or thereabouts. And Sarah?"

"Yes?"

"Bring something nice to wear; two events, both evening."

"In our room, or in public?"

"Well, now that you ask, both places. Bye for now."

Sarah giggled then said goodbye to him.

*   *   *

Thor went to the commissary where he had a very light dinner, then returned to his stateroom. It was time for reflections. Reflections on what he had accomplished since coming to Planet Earth. Reflections on where Techna Force 20 should go next. Reflections on his personal relationship with Sarah Malloy.

With respect to the first item, he was pleased with progress. In just forty-two days, counting from February 11, 2010, the day he wrote to CTS, he and Techna Force 20 had won their primary objective, which was to force U.S troops to withdraw from Iraq. It had not happened yet, but he was certain withdrawal would commence very soon.

With respect to where TF20 should go next, the die had been cast, essentially; they would take on America's huge corporations, the massive illegal drug problem and the televangelists who were robbing the poor to feed their own greed. And, as he well recognized, there were many more opportunities to excel on Planet Earth.

With respect to his personal life, he was finding that he needed to be with Sarah Malloy much more frequently, even though they had known each other just since February 11. Thinking about it, he realized that he had fallen in love with her on that very day, but just had not realized it before. Though he was very disciplined and would not let personal matters interfere with his work, any spare moment not given to work was given to thoughts of Sarah. She was now as much a part of him as any part of his own body, and he chafed at not having her with him more often. But, of course, how could he be with her more when his work demanded so much of him, he mused. How much time is a man expected to spend with the woman in his life? he wondered. He did not know how other men would answer that question, but he knew that, in his case, he should be with her at evening time of every day, most days, and would want to be, anyway. The most obvious questions then was, how best to arrange that? He thought he knew the answer, but realized he was not yet prepared to vocalize it.

*   *   *

"It is good to see all of you again," he said, opening the meeting the next morning. "Our work takes us far and wide, so it is not often we can be here together. Let me begin with some very good news: The United States Government has finally seen the light and is going to withdraw from Iraq. That decision is effective immediately. Thus, we are finally about to reach one of our primary goals. So there are no secrets here among us, I will tell you that we had to replace the President to accomplish this mission, and we did that by substituting a double. We also had to replace 75 members of Congress with doubles for the same reason, and will soon replace 35 more because they promised to vote for withdrawal, then reneged when the vote came up. As you know, we do not tolerate broken promises."

"Great news, Commander," the assembled Group Captains said, almost in unison.

"Thanks. We have to give much of the credit to Truls Heyerdahl. He played a major part in the effort. Good work, Truls."

Heyerdahl smiled and nodded. "My pleasure, Commander."

"On that same subject, we have offered the new President the use of five of our starships, so he can get the Iraq troops home as soon as possible. I have arranged for five new units, all without staterooms, but equipped to transport 500 soldiers with full gear at a time. They should reach Earth on Monday or Tuesday and will be based at Andrews Air Force Base, Washington."

"Now, let's get started. Assim, what do you have?"

"Commander, we are tracking the largest drug shipment ever—it is worth more than one hundred twenty million on the street—and is expected to arrive at the United States border. We have agents traveling with the shipment, and are also shadowing it with transporters. As you all know, our drug extermination program has made it very difficult for manufacturers of illicit drugs to distribute their deadly products north of the border. So far they have not been able to ship a single load since we started the intercept process. They are hurting for money, and are very angry. Because they fear another interception, they have divided this shipment into five drops, all to different State-side locations. So we have had to borrow more agents from Guri's reserve forces in order to stay on top of every shipment. Our plan is the same: we intercept as soon as the transfer is made, confiscate the money, then destroy the drugs. I predict there will definitely be some killings over this—some pretty big corporate names."

"Very good work, Assim. Please express that to your people. Tell them also how important it is to stamp out illegal drugs entirely. Also, tell them to be extra careful."

"I will, Commander."

"Siran?"

"Yes, Commander," Siran reported. "We now know the names of all the corporate executives that have been appointed to high government positions. We also know how those men have interpreted—or even changed laws, rules, and so forth—to benefit their corporations who, by the way, continue to pay them full salary. Double dipping at its finest, let me tell you," she added. Then she continued, "Truls has been very instrumental in this effort, as well, because of his inside knowledge. The second way they control government is through their lobbyists, who are also highly paid by their various corporations. We have their names and their relationships to those corporations. The third way they control is by buying Congressmen—paying them thousands more than what they receive from the Government--even powerful committee chairmen are not immune to bribes, it seems, so they will decide committee agenda items in favor of the payer corporation. The entire system is rampant with fraud and graft. I am recommending today that we make our research public through CTS *Sunday Review*. It is either that or start an eradication process of our own, and I believe public exposure is the more effective way. I assure you, Sir, every claim we make is backed up by irrefutable written proof; we have a mountain of research on this."

"Siran, I agree. CTS is the answer on this one. Are you willing to meet with Sam Fischer, if I set it up with him, and go on national television if he asked you to go?"

"Absolutely, Commander."

"Good. I will talk to Sam. Arne, what is going on in your Group?"

"Commander, Group 3's research into the operations of televangelists has also been completed. As with Siran, we have a huge amount of backup detail, including video footage and still photos, on about a dozen of the largest televangelist operations, plus similar data on many more smaller organizations, and we are also ready to expose these scumbags. I have never seen so many Rolex watches, so much fine furniture, and so many extremely ostentatious homes, in my life. I mean these people are nothing more than common thieves. Not all of them, I hasten to point out; there are some who are sincere in their efforts to bring religion to people and do not care to increase their wealth But the others

146

are just thieves. If CTS is willing to do an expose' on them that would be the best way to go, in my opinion, and that is my recommendation."

"Arne, you say you are ready to go on this?"

"Yes, Commander."

"Then I ask you the same question I asked Siran. Are you will to meet with Sam Fischer?"

"Definitely. The sooner the better. And I, too will tell the story on television if he wants."

"Consider it done, Arne. Sam has already expressed an interest—in both the corporate graft and televangelist projects."

"Now, another matter: It is time for my annual report to the Prime Minister. As you know, I am required to make that report in person, so I will leave here April 16, returning May 6. Truls Heyerdahl will be in charge, as the Senior Group Captain. Since

I do not want any secrets between us, I tell you that I will take a friend—someone who is not from Techna Planet—with me on the journey. She is someone I met here; someone very special."

"Commander," Siran said, "We all know about Sarah, and are very happy for you. Can we go with you?"

"Yes, If you feel your assignments will stay on track for three weeks without you."

Siran laughed. I was just kidding, Commander. I cannot speak for the others here but now would not be a good time for me to leave. Perhaps later?"

"Absolutely," Thor said. Anyone else want to go on this trip?"

In answer to that question, both Assim and Arne said they wanted to stay to watch over their projects as well, but would like to visit family sometime in the future. Other members of the staff felt the same way.

"Good," Thor said. Just let me know when you would like leave and I will arrange it for you. I should also remind you that you are free to return to Techna permanently as soon as you complete your assignments here. It looks like that could happen very soon for you, Siran, and you Arne. For Assim it might be longer. But whether you do so is completely up to you."

"Sir," Siran said. I was not thinking about going home. I love my country very much, but there is nothing there for me right now. It would be nice to meet someone here, if that is permissible."

"Of course, Siran. You have the same rights I have. There is no double standard. All of you have that right. I understand that you have private lives. You know the conditions: do not discuss Techna secrets with an outsider, however close to you that person may be. That is the only thing you must remember. Otherwise, you are free to choose. And if you choose to remain on Planet Earth for an extended period—even permanently—we will provide you with living accommodations—a home of your very own, for example, at no expense to you. You even have the right to become a citizen of some country on Planet Earth, if allowed, and still keep your Techna citizenship. The one condition is that you never abuse your ability to become invisible. Our law is very specific on that, as you know."

"Commander, there have been questions on the subject of making a permanent home on Planet Earth," said Assim. "It is good to hear you confirm that we have that option. We appreciate your honesty."

"Assim, I will go even further. I can see the day when we will get into problems at the local level on Planet Earth, problems with local government and other quasi-government bodies, such as home owner associations, which are the common way to self-govern here, but lead to many problems because of the lack of expertise. If we go there we will actually want to place agents in those communities so they can vote as members. That could be another way for a Techna agent to have his or her own home on Earth, one that would be paid for by Techna, of course. Something to think about. Now, are there any other reports or problems? If not, our business here today is concluded. You have all done a splendid job. May I suggest that you take the week-end off and do some much deserved relaxing?"

"Thank you, Commander," Arne said, as Thor stood, signaling the end of the meeting.

CHAPTER SEVEN

A Surprise for Sarah

Jens Petersen came to Thor's flagship office late Friday afternoon, March 26, to discuss their flight to New York. "Commander, " he said, "Because of the heavy weather there we should leave early. May I suggest 6 p.m. instead of 6:30?"

"Sure, Jens. I'll be ready."

"Also, Commander, I anticipate heavy cloud cover over Central Park, so we will use our hovering and vertical take off and landing capability (VTOL), once we arrive there. That way we can settle straight down gradually through the muck to the ground without hitting anything, like buildings."

"Good plan, Jens. I'll fly right seat and take care of the CAS while you monitor GPS." (CAS stands for Crash Avoidance System, a sophisticated electronic aide which monitors aircraft location relative to surrounding obstacles).

"I appreciate that, Commander. It is good to have an extra pair of hands and eyes in this kind of weather, especially when they belong to a highly experienced pilot, as you are."

Thor nodded. "Yes, my friend. You would do the same for me, I am sure."

*   *   *

The first part of their flight was in clear weather at 50,000 feet, and went smoothly. As usual, they arrived over Central Park in thirty minutes, having descended to an altitude of 12,000 feet. The thick cloud cover lay just below the little transporter, as Jens had predicted. When the GPS guidance system told him they were exactly over their desired Central Park landing point, Jens called out to Thor, "Going VTOL. Ready for CAS, Commander."

"Roger, Jens. CAS activated. Commence descent."

The transporter began a steady decent at 500 feet per minute, with Thor calling out CAS readings every few seconds. Though strong wind gusts blew them off their planned decent line several times, Jens was able to move the ship quickly back on line by using its powerful side thrusters, and they settled onto the soft snow, without major problems, in 25 minutes.

Thor trudged through the snow which was, as Sarah had said, about 12 inches deep, and reached her apartment just about on schedule. When she opened the door he swept her into his arms and kissed her passionately, then held her away from him saying, "Let me look at you, angel. It seems like months since I last set eyes on you, and I might say, you look absolutely stunning."

"You *might* say, Sir?"

"Correction. I do say. You are even more beautiful than I remember. Hi."

"Hi. As you can see," she said, pointing to her suitcase which was right inside the door, "I am packed and ready for any adventure."

"Amazing. No other woman could accomplish that."

"Thank you, dear man."

Thor picked up the suitcase and took her by the arm, and they made their way down the stairs and out onto the street, which was covered with dirty slush. They crossed the street, trying to avoid being clobbered by the wet, messy stuff as it was splashed up with each passing car, but they soon reached the safety of the transporter. As was his custom, Jens bowed to Sarah and said "Good evening Miss Sarah. It is nice to see you again." He took her arm and helped her board the ship, then stowed her luggage.

Once inside, Thor said, "Sarah, I will help Jens in the cockpit until we get safely off the ground and through the cloud cover. Then I will rejoin you in the cabin. It should only be a few minutes."

"That's fine, Thor. I didn't know you could fly."

Jens, who was about to enter the cockpit, turned and smiled. "Miss Sarah, the Commander is an exceptionally fine pilot. I would trust him at the controls anytime."

"Jens, it is nice to know I am served by two great pilots tonight, " she responded.

* * *

Their ascent followed the earlier descent procedure in reverse: straight up until they were above the clouds. When Thor returned to the cabin Sarah asked, "How was it, Thor? Was it difficult?"

"Oh, no, my dear. In fact it was quite easy. It is just that two heads are better than one in bad weather flying. We are above the clouds now and should have a smooth flight. We will be there in about an hour. Are you hungry?"

"Famished!"

"Sorry. We'll take care of that in San Diego. I have selected a very special restaurant called Anthony's Star of the Sea Room. It is right on the bay. Ever been there?"

"No. I've never been to San Diego, in fact."

"It is a beautiful city, angel. I always thought I might like to live there some day. I think you will like it, too. We will be staying at a very old, very nice downtown hotel called the Sophia. It is close to everything—Horton Plaza, The Embarcadero, fine restaurants"

"Did you take someone else there, Thor?"

He turned to meet her questioning eyes. "No, my love. There has only been one other woman in my life, as I said on our first date, and she never came to Planet Earth, at least not with me, nor with anyone I know."

Sarah was silent for several seconds, then said. "That was catty of me, Thor. I am sorry."

Thor put his arm around her and kissed her. "It is alright, Sarah. I do not mind. There is nothing I will ever hide from you, except possibly secrets about my work I am not at liberty to divulge to anyone. Otherwise I will always be open and above board with you."

She snuggled close to him but said nothing.

* * *

Later in the flight, Thor picked up the intercom phone connected to the cockpit, and said. "How is it going, Jens?"

"Fine, Commander. We should be landing in about ten minutes. Sophia Hotel, correct?"

"Yes, that is correct. And Jens, then you get the weekend off—at least until you pick us up again Sunday night. We will be scooting all over the San Diego area day and night, and I do not want you to be chauffeuring us around. I have hired a limousine for that."

"I appreciate the time off, Commander, but you did not need to do that."

"Glad to, old friend."

* * *

Thor and Sarah checked into the Sophia Hotel. Their room was in the southwest corner of the fourth floor and overlooked the Old Town section of the city's downtown area, as well as the harbor beyond. It was a spacious room decorated in pastel cream and sand colors, with dark walnut furniture. It consisted of a sitting area, a large dressing area/bath combination and a bedroom. Thor, who wore a dark grey business suit on the flight, and shed his overcoat and rubber overshoes upon entering the transporter, changed to a white dress shirt and touched up his dark and already showing beard while waiting for Sarah to dress. Then he sat down to wait for her.

Sarah emerged from the shower and donned only black panties, bra and garter belt, at first. From where he was seated he could not see her directly, though he could see her image in a full length mirror on the partly open door to the dressing area. Having watched her dress during their Palm Springs outing at her invitation, he had no plans to do so now. Yet, so fascinated was he by the natural beauty of this lovely woman who had entered his life, and so eager to learn everything about her, that he could not stop watching.

He knew the process would take some time and involve a carefully orchestrated series of steps, but did not care how long it took. First she did her hair, which was easy, since it merely involved several passes of a brush through short, bobbed locks, then she applied a small amount of facial makeup with the greatest care, and added perfume or cologne, though he was not sure which. Next she donned dark-colored nylons and attached them to the garter belt. The stockings were followed by a full length black slip, and a form-fitting black knee-length dress with scooped neck line. She placed a simple gold chain and pendant around her elegant neck, stepped into black leather shoes with medium heels, wrapped a dark grey shawl around her shoulders, and made her entrance to the bedroom. "How do I look, Thor?" she asked.

"Fabulous, Sarah. Simply beautiful. You are so beautiful to me normally, that I would not have believed you could improve on that. But you have. However, my darling, something is missing."

"Oh, no, Thor. What did I miss?"

"This," he said, and opened a small velvet box previously concealed in his hand. In it was a beautiful gold engagement ring with a two caret' diamond in the center, surrounded by a circle of 14 small diamonds. The circle, in turn, was flanked on opposite sides by 1.5 caret' diamonds. Sarah's eyes grew big as saucers and her jaw dropped. "Oh my God, it is beautiful, Thor," she gasped. "But wh...."

"Angel, it means I would like you to be my wife. It means I fell in love with you the moment I first saw you. It means that I love you more than I can find words to describe that love, and that I want you in my life for all time. How do you feel about it?"

Sarah felt her knees grow weak so she moved slightly to her left and sat down, never taking her eyes off his face. "Thor, dearest Thor, I can't believe this is happening, It is a dream come true, but are you sure, darling? I mean, we have only known one another such a short time."

"I have never been more sure of anything, Sarah." He took both of her hands in his and helped her stand again. "The question is, will you accept me as your husband? It may not be easy being married to someone from another planet."

"Oh, Thor!" she exclaimed. "Yes, yes, yes! I will—I do-- accept your proposal. And I don't care what anyone says about you. I love you—I have loved you, too, from that first day."

Thor swept her into his arms and held her close for a very long time. Then he kissed her passionately, not once but several times, still holding her close. "I must confess, angel, all this is new to me."

She pulled away just far enough to look into his eyes. "It is new for us both, Thor. It will be our life adventure together."

"And continue for at least a 100 years after the wedding," he responded, then held her close again.

*   *   *

They left the hotel hand in hand, and walked the short distance to the Embarcadero, then a little farther to Anthony's Star of The Sea Room on San Diego bay. Sarah was unusually quiet during the walk, prompting Thor to ask her if anything was wrong. In answer she squeezed his hand and said, "Oh, no, Thor. I am just in a daze, that's all. I never expected this. I guess I need time to get used to the idea."

"Second thoughts?"

"None whatsoever."

By that time they reached the restaurant. Thor introduced himself to the Maitre-d, who immediately recognized the name and escorted them to a reserved table overlooking the bay. Their waiter, whose name was Ramon, appeared immediately.

"Ramon, are you serving abalone tonight, by any chance?" Thor asked.

"As a matter of fact, we are, Sir. And it is quite good—the best we have seen in a long time."

Thor thanked him and ordered a bottle of Pinot Grigio. While waiting for him to return with the wine, he said, "Honey, I urge you to try the abalone. There is nothing quite like it in the entire world; it is very rare and the taste is magnificent."

Sarah smiled and nodded. "Sounds fine to me, Thor. I have never tasted it, but your recommendation is good enough for me."

*   *   *

All through dinner Sarah could not stop looking first at her new ring, then at her husband-to-be. And the smile on her face when she looked at him warmed Thor's heart. It was the smile of a very happy woman, and he hoped he could keep it on her lovely face forever.

"A penny for your thoughts, my love," he said at one point.

"Well, sir, I am thinking how lucky I am to have a man like you, and how very much I want to make you happy. And, as you have probably guessed, I am beginning to make wedding plans. It just dawned on me how much there is to do. Do you mind if we have the ceremony in Brookline? So many members of my family live there or near there. Friends, too!"

"Of course not, Sarah. It is traditional to have the wedding in the bride's home town, is it not?"

"Yes, dear man, but I don't want to be making all the decisions. I want you to know that you are as much a part of these plans as I am. That's the way I feel, anyway. Do you?"

"Yes, I do, Sarah, and Brookline is no problem, I assure you. Besides, my people—those who will come—can go there as easily as they can go anywhere in the States. By the way, the tradition of my country says we need to have another ceremony on Techna Planet. Do you mind that?"

"Oh, Thor, of course I don't mind. In fact I am looking forward to it." She laid her hand on his. "Right now, I am walking on cloud nine. You have no idea how happy you have made me today."

"I am glad for you, honey. And I am glad for myself. You talk about being lucky. Let me tell you how lucky I feel. Before I walked into CTS back in February, I was reconciled to never finding the right life partner. And there you were, the most beautiful woman I had ever seen and not even married yet. I fell for you and you fell for me. Now, no man ever gets more than one chance to meet someone like you. That is what I call luck. You are my lucky charm."

Sarah squeezed his hand. "You are so very sweet."

* * *

After dinner, which Sarah said she enjoyed very much, Thor had planned to visit Mr. A's further north of the downtown area, for after dinner drinks. But when he mentioned that to Sarah, she asked if they could return to the hotel instead. "I think the excitement of events tonight have finally caught up with me, " she explained. "Besides, I just want to curl up in your arms and stay there all night."

"I like your plan better, Sarah, Thor replied, and put his arm around her shoulders as they strolled back to the Sophia.

*   *   *

Thor woke up at his usual time, 5 a.m., feeling more rested than at any time he could remember. He made a cup of tea then sat in one of the easy chairs and just watched Sarah, who was still sound asleep. She is the most beautiful thing I have ever seen, He mused. I know marriage to her will change my life, but I also know it will be a good change. Then he began to think about where they would live. He did not want it to be in his starship; that would be convenient, though not very appropriate. She should have a home of her own, he reasoned, and I should live in that home with her. Perhaps we will have to live in Roswell until such time as I know what the future holds. Perhaps I can resolve that question when we return to Techna Planet in April. He made a mental note to follow up on that subject later, then went back to watching his new bride-to-be.

Sarah began to stir sometime round 8:00 o'clock. She had fallen asleep on her right side after they made love, and slept that way all night so she could occasionally watch her man as he slept beside her. Now she rolled onto her back, stretched and yawned several times, then locked her fingers behind her head and stared at the ceiling for several minutes, not yet aware that her every move was being watched. Then she spotted Thor who was walking toward the bed, and held out her arms to him. He came to her willingly and lay down next to her. "Good morning future Mrs. Berksten," he said. I hope you slept well."

"With my prince charming in bed beside me, how could I not sleep well, Sir?" Then she smothered his mouth with kisses until he was gasping for air.

"I do not remember anything, my love," he responded when he finally caught his breath.

"Nothing at all?"

"Well, now that you mention it, I seem to recall ravishing a fair young maiden. Was that you, by any chance?"

"Who else?"

Thor raised himself on one elbow and searched the room. "No. no, I do not see any one else. It must have been you. Did I really treat you badly?"

"It was definitely me, Sir, and no you did not, and yes I would like you to do it again."

*   *   *

At noon they boarded the *Mystic Star*, a beautiful sloop, for brunch, while cruising the harbor under full sail. It was a two hour cruise during which they ate ravenously while taking in the sights and sounds of San Diego's beautiful but busy harbor. The temperature was a balmy 72 degrees, which made the cruise even more enjoyable.

After that, they walked to Horton Plaza, the block-square, two-story shopping mall in the middle of the downtown district, They had intended only to stroll along and window shop, just to digest all the food they had consumed on the cruise, but soon found themselves entering stores offering home decorating accessories and furniture. Thor smiled to himself as he watched Sarah, for she suddenly had the determined look of a woman on a mission. Although he had never done any serious shopping with a woman before, he sensed that his bride-to-be was in the initial stage of planning her nest. She did not ask him to buy anything; she was simply trying to get ideas as to what would work for her and what those things would cost. She asked him many questions, such as, "Do you like this table, or this chair, or this set of dishes?" as they wandered through the various shops, and he patiently answered each and every one as best he could, knowing it was just a planning exercise, not a purchasing expedition. Besides, it was fun just watching her because she was so obviously adept at taking charge of such a vital part of setting up housekeeping.

For over two hours he followed her from store to store, and at the end of that time he could almost visualize how their home would look, if they had one, based on the items that seemed to interest her the most, and he liked what he imagined that home to be. However, this 'shopping trip' proved exhausting for both of them so, with Sarah talking a mile a minute, they strode back to the Sophia for a bit of rest.

* * *

So far, they had not used the limousine service Thor had arranged for at all. He was on the verge of cancelling it until an idea came to him that could lead to covering a lot of territory on Sunday. Originally, he had planned to take Sarah to Balboa Park to see the many amateur performing acts that had been a tradition in the Park's lovely promenade for years of Sundays. But after watching Sarah in the Horton Plaza shops, he thought she might now enjoy an entirely different type of outing that could be even more entertaining for her, as well as informative, and began to formulate a plan.

* * *

Around 5:00 p.m. they began to dress again, this time for dinner at the highly rated Currant American Brasserie, a restaurant just off the Sophia Hotel lobby. After dinner they would enjoy the American Ballet Theatre performance of *Giselle*, the beautiful romantic ballet, Thor's favorite. He was looking forward to seeing it again, with Sarah, because she had said it was her favorite, as well. "I saw it performed by Ballet Ruse De Monte Carlo, The Kirov, and the New York City Ballet Company," she said. "But I have not had the pleasure of seeing the American Ballet Theater Company performance. I understand it is far superior because of that company's artistic capabilities."

At the restaurant, they chose the roast chicken and found it to be as excellent as their waiter claimed. During the meal, Sarah mentioned how much she had enjoyed the sailing cruise, and commented on the delicious food they were having at the moment. But she dwelled more on their shopping tour of Horton Plaza than on the cruise or the Currant America Brasserie, which made it clear to Thor where her current thoughts were.

"What style of furniture do you like, dear?" she asked at one point. "I still don't know."

Sensing that a minefield lay dead ahead, he responded that style was not too important to him; he thought quality and serviceability should be deciding factors. "I believe in having furnishings that last a long time, Sarah," he said. 'Do you not agree?"

":Sure, Thor, along with comfort, too. I don't go for any particular style, either, though I would probably choose pieces that do not have lines that are too stiff and formal—something more...."

"Livable, more welcoming, perhaps?"

"Exactly."

"Then that is what you shall have, angel."

* * *

Their theater seats were in the very center of the first row of the loge where, as Thor explained, "we can see the various dance segments unfold in all their grace and beauty."

"Thor, it is amazing how much we think alike. I would have chosen precisely these two seats for the same reason you mentioned." She squeezed his hand and snuggled just a bit closer. "The wonder of it all is how we found each other. Someone is surely looking out for us."

"I am eternally grateful to that someone, my darling," he replied. "I have never accepted the concept of Guardian Angels, but finding you could make me a believer. Ah, the music has started. I hope you enjoy the performance."

"Thor, I am certain I will. This has been such a wonderful weekend. I know I will never forget it."

He took her hand and put it to his lips. "Nor will I, Sarah. Nor will I."

* * *

The presentation of *Giselle* was the finest either of them had ever seen. As Sarah said as they were leaving the theater, "No other ballet has its grace and sheer beauty, and the hauntingly beautiful music is a perfect fit to the magical choreography. And this version was a masterpiece. It was just wonderful, Thor," she repeated several times. "Absolutely wonderful."

"I could not agree more, honey. I loved every moment of it—always have--but if I had to single out specific highlights I would choose the opening scene, when Giselle opens the door of the house to Hilarion's knock and finds Prince Albrecht there in- stead. The little dance of gaiety she performs at that moment is magic for me. But the most wonderful part comes in act II, when she and Albrecht dance the hauntingly beautiful *pas de deux* of death in the forest glade. I could watch that for hours—and have."

"Thor, I do believe you are an incurable romantic."

"Yes, dear heart, I suppose I am. Is that a weakness in my character.?"

"Not in the least. It is a sign of gentleness and feeling."

He put his arm around her shoulder and they walked back to the Sophia.

* * *

Early Sunday morning, while Sarah was still sound asleep, Thor stole quietly out of their room and went down to the hotel lobby in search of a Sunday newspaper. He found one at the desk and reached for money to pay for it. The desk clerk shook his head and said, "There is no charge, Commander."

Thor thanked him and asked, "What time is breakfast served?"

"In the Brasserie they start serving at 6:30 a.m., Sir—in about 20 minutes."

"Thanks, that's a bit early. We will not be ready until 8:30 or 9:00."

" I will make a reservation for you at 8:30, if you wish."

"Yes, that will be fine," Thor said, and turned to walk back to the elevator.

* * *

He was half way through the thick *San Diego Sunday Tribune* when Sarah began to stir. As she did the day before, she rolled onto her back and placed both hands behind her head, as if contemplating what lay in store for her today. She remained that way for several minutes before sitting up and taking stock of her surroundings. It was then that she spotted Thor, who was watching her intently.

"Good morning, Sarah, " he said. "I hope you slept well."

"Very well, thank you. Did you?"

"Yes, as you Americans say, I slept like a baby."

She managed a little laugh through her sleepiness. "And what do you have planned for this day, my love?"

"First a little breakfast. Our reservation is for 8:30, I might add. Then...."

"But isn't that kind of early? I'm not even awake yet."

"Early for you, perhaps. But I wanted to get an early start."

"On what, may I ask?"

"Oh, I thought you might like to look at some homes in this area, and...."

Before he finished his sentence she had bounded out of bed and was sitting on his lap. "Oh, Thor, do you mean it?"

"Yes, love."

"Oh, that will be wonderful! But can we afford a home here? I mean, it seems like a very expensive place to live."

"'I do not know, angel. At any rate, we are just looking, trying to get an idea of what kind of home we want, old style, new style, big yard, small yard, and so forth. This will not be a buying trip; just an educational one. We will have the limousine driver take us up the coast, to La Jolla, Del Mar and Solana Beach, three areas I have heard of where demand for homes is high. And perhaps we can talk to a real estate agent or two who can give us some idea as to the cost of property in those areas. I would like to stay under a million dollars."

Sarah's eyes grew big as saucers. "Did you say one million dollars? That seems like a lot of money for a house. How will we ever manage?"

"Maybe we will not have to. Maybe we can find a little house for less. Do we really need a big house? I am not sure, are you? One thing in our favor is that the market for homes is not so good right now. People who can no longer afford to make their house payments are losing their homes to foreclosure. Bank-owned properties can generally be purchased for less. Anyway, it's just a thought. We are here, and it does not hurt to look. What do you say? Want to go check them out, or shall we stick to the original plan and just visit Balboa Park?"

"No, no, Thor. I would love to explore homes in this area."

"Great. Now please get dressed my love, before I starve to death."

Sarah was out of his arms in a flash. She showered and dressed in an amazingly short time, and said, "I am ready, master. Have you arranged for the limo?"

"I have. You look absolutely gorgeous."

*   *   *

Thor scanned the house-for-sale ads in the newspaper as they ate, after apologizing to Sarah for being rude and reading at the table. "This is something I was taught never to do by my father," he said. "But I did not think you would mind this morning. This way, if I see something interesting I can call on the way."

Sarah smiled. "You are forgiven this time, my dear man. See anything we can afford?"

"Maybe a couple in Del Mar. But you have to inspect them to really know. I don't find anything under 5 million in La Jolla, and Solana Beach does not look too promising , either."

*   *   *

The limousine driver took the Coast Highway which paralleled the Pacific Ocean, though it was not often visible while they were going through the village of La Jolla. However once they left that quaint little enclave and had passed through the Torrey Pines section of Highway 101 they began to see the ocean. It was at its most picturesque as they proceeded North down the highway grade from the Torrey Pines heights toward the

Del Mar beach area. Sarah, who was quite used to seeing ocean, raved about this picture of the Pacific, saying she had never seen anything quite so beautiful.

On the way, Thor talked to two real estate agents, one in Del Mar and another in Solana Beach, the next city north of Delmar. The Solana Beach agent said he had nothing under two million dollars, which ended the matter with Thor.

The Del Mar agent was a woman, whose name was Carla Longstreet. She said she might have a couple of homes that could fill their requirements. When they arrived at her office, she showed them to seats next to her office desk and arranged for them to be served refreshments. Sarah chose coffee, while Thor asked for tea. "Now," she said, "I understand that you are looking to buy here, is that correct?"

"Well, not exactly, Carla. We are just beginning the process of determining where we want to live, and since we were in San Diego this weekend, we thought it might be good to see what is available. Let me emphasize that this is an exploratory trip. We will also want to investigate the Boston area, where Sarah grew up, and perhaps Connecticut, which is close to her work in New York, or even the Washington D.C. area, where I spend a great deal of my time. So I do not want to leave you with the impression that Del Mar is it for us."

"I understand, Mr. Berksten, and I appreciate you candor. Can you be a bit more specific about what you are looking for, size, age, lot size, price, you know, that kind of information?"

"Certainly. We would like to stay under one million dollars. A smaller home, perhaps one that is older, might be acceptable. We would even consider one that needs work—maybe even a foreclosure. But we really desire one with an ocean view."

"Hmmm. Yes, I think that might be doable. I have just two homes under one million. Both are small, older homes. One needs a lot of repairs; the other just needs TLC."

"TLC? What is that, TLC,? Sarah asked.

Carla laughed. "I see you are not from California. TLC means Tender Loving Care. It's a euphemism for homes that could strand some repair work. You know, painting and so forth."

Sarah and Thor exchanged glances. "Yes, we would certainly consider something like that," Thor said.

"Good. Will you require financing? Real estate loans can be difficult to come by right now."

"No," Thor responded. "We will pay cash."

Carla's eyebrows went up. "Gee," she said, "That makes it a lot easier. Why don't we take my car and have a look?"

"We have a limousine; there is plenty of room for all of us."

"Thank you, Mr. Berksten, but I think it would be better to leave the limo here. Might give the seller ideas, you know?"

Thor nodded in agreement. "Yes, I see your point."

*   *   *

The first house they looked at was not at all acceptable, and Thor said so. "This one needs much more than TLC, Carla; it needs to be torn down, in my opinion. Besides, there is no ocean view. I think it is overpriced at $560,000, even for this area."

Carla was not offended, and said she thought they would really like the next house. As they were driving to its location she explained, "This one has a fantastic view of the Pacific because it sits high on the hill above downtown Del Mar. It is an older craftsman design of 1500 square feet with three bedrooms and two baths. It is a foreclosure that definitely needs some TLC, but the possibilities are endless. And the price is right, at $625,900, plus, the bank might take less."

"What does foreclosure mean?" Sarah wanted to know.

"Foreclosure means the house is bank-owned, usually because the people who bought it could not make their payments. We are seeing a lot of that right now. Sometimes we find a property that has been almost destroyed by angry owners just trying to get even with the lender. They take everything they can, including the stove, dishwasher, sinks—you name it. That makes a property very hard to sell. But this house has not been damaged in that way at all. It just suffers from neglect."

As they were pulling into the home's driveway, and she caught her first sight of the house, which sat well back on the lot, Sarah tightened her grip on Thor's hand to get his attention. When he looked at her face she was smiling broadly, and he knew she was thrilled with what she saw.

The home's front door was sheltered by a wide covered porch that stretched the width of the building. Standing there, waiting for the agent to unlock the door, they both turned to look back the way they had come. The ocean view was, indeed, awesome and encompassed nearly 180 degrees from South to North. 'You will have beautiful sunsets here every evening, folks," Carla told them.

Upon entering, they found themselves in the living room. Beyond that was the dining area, then the kitchen, all in a row. To their left, through a door off the living room, were the three bedrooms and the two bathrooms. All the rooms were small, and all needed painting at the very least. But the kitchen and baths showed a great deal of wear and needed complete remodeling.

Thor left the two women and went out to inspect the exterior of the house, and the grounds. When he was out of earshot. Carla said, "Well, what do you think, Mrs. Berksten? Would this house work for you?"

"Please call me Sarah, Carla. And I am not Mrs. Berksten yet." She held out her left hand to show her engagement ring. "It just happened Friday. We haven't even set a wedding date. But I hope it will be sometime later this year."

Carla looked at the ring for some time. "It's gorgeous, Sarah. Congratulations."

"Thank you. Yes, this house has definite possibilities, and I love the location. But, as Thor said, we don't know if California will be our home. Maybe we should stay in the East, closer to family and work He would be willing to commute from here, I know, if I choose to live here, but I don't know if I want him to do that. Commuting can be awfully stressful."

"I understand. Fortunately, San Diego has many daily flights to the East, which should help."

"Oh, that isn't the problem; he has his own plane and pilot, you see. Still, it's stressful."

"Yes, I suppose it would be," the agent replied, though it was hard for her to comprehend how flying in one's own airplane could be stressful, especially when you had a personal pilot. He must be someone pretty important—and wealthy, she surmised. At any rate, Sarah, whose last name Carla had not yet captured, and Thor Berksten seemed to be the most qualified clients she had seen in six months. The woman likes this house, and that is a real plus, she thought. Maybe I can finagle a sale after all. God, that would be a life saver. The bill collectors are growing more impatient by the day.

"Listen, Sarah," she said. "If the price is a problem I could talk to the lender. I would be willing to do that, you know, since it is obvious you really like this house, and I think you could do wonders with it. For Del Mar, which I know you will enjoy, this is still a bargain. Almost every listing we have is well over a million dollars. You certainly would not go wrong buying this house, because it will surely appreciate."

"Yes, Carla, I do like it, and I can see ways to make it into an adorable and cozy home for us. But Thor has a major say in the decision. And, as I explained, we don't know if this area is for us or not. I promise you, though, I will let him know how I feel. Then we will see."

"Well Sarah, I do understand. But I wouldn't wait too long, if I were you. This one won't last long."

At that point, Thor returned from his inspection tour. "How is it going, ladies?" he asked.

"It's a lovely old house, Thor," Sarah said, excitedly. "It is plain and drab now, but as I was just telling Carla, I see ways to make it a wonderful cozy home for us. What did you find outside?"

"Honey, it seems solid enough. No signs of rot. No settling. The roof looks to be fairly new, which is a plus. Beyond that I can not tell. I would, of course want a licensed architect and an engineer to inspect it before we make our final decision. The ocean view is fabulous though, isn't it?"

"Yes. As Carla says, we should have gorgeous sunsets every evening. Wouldn't that be wonderful? We could have an old fashioned swing on the porch and sit there and watch the sun go down."

Thor smiled, and looked at Carla. "Well, it looks like this one has definite possibilities. But for reasons I have already expressed we will have to let you know. I really appreciate you taking the time to show us around."

"Glad to do it, Mr. Berksten. Here's my card. Call me anytime." She had heard those words so many times that she was able to hide her disappointment without much difficulty. And who knows? They may still be buyers at some future time.

*   *   *

After Del Mar, they went to Solana Beach which bordered it, and drove slowly through the older sections overlooking the ocean. There were many for sale signs but, as Thor had learned from the agent he talked to on the phone, none of them were in his price range. Besides, the area seemed more run down than Del Mar, and he wasn't sure they would even be interested in living there. They did take time to have an early dinner there, in a small Mexican restaurant called Fidel's. The food was served on over-sized platters and was excellent. It was nearly 4:00 p.m. when they finished the meal, and Jens would be picking them up in an hour, so they had to rush back to the Sophia to check out. On the way, Thor asked Sarah if she was disappointed because they did not buy "her house."

"Oh, no, dear man. I am most certainly not disappointed. I never expected to buy one today, but it was a good idea to look. I am glad you suggested that, because it started me thinking about what I really want in a home, and where it should be."

"Yes, I feel the same way, "Thor replied.

"Do you feel that we should live in California, Thor?"

"Well, the weather is great, but it is very crowded and expensive, and a long way from Boston, New York and Washington. So, all in all, my choice would be the East coast someplace. I'll bet there are older homes in those areas just like the one we saw today. How do you feel about it?"

"The same way. I don't even like it that you must commute from Roswell, and Del Mar is much farther. Plus, as I told you on our first date, my family is very close. I would be happier, and so would they, if we lived close to Boston."

"Then, angel, I see no reason to live anywhere else. Boston it is."

Sarah snuggled closer to him. "You know, don't you, that all these things you are doing just make me love you more and more."

"Hummm. I will have to be more careful, lest I spoil you."

167

"Too late, Sir. I am half Jewish and half Catholic remember? I am already spoiled and I rather like it. Now you must keep up the tradition."

"I do not know if I am up to it, honey, but I'll try. Speaking of your parents, I should have asked your father for your hand the very first thing. I think we should start over. Maybe he will say no."

"Foolish man, this is 2010. That is hardly ever done anymore. Besides, if he did refuse I would come to you anyway. I will tell them right away, of course, and I do so want you to meet them soon. When can you come to Brookline?"

"How about next weekend? I expect that meeting to be difficult, and I prefer to handle difficult tasks as soon as possible."

Sarah looked up at him, pouting a bit. "Why difficult, Thor? I have already told them we are dating, so it won't come as a complete surprise."

"Do they know I am a little green man with one eye in the middle of my forehead?"

"Well, no. And you are not, silly. You are Technian, and a beautiful one at that."

"But they do not know that."

"That is true."

"Then it will be difficult. No matter. I will charm them into accepting me."

"Then I must prepare the way."

"No, little one. I do not hide behind a woman's skirts."

"I am not just any woman, sir. I am your wife, almost."

"Hummm, I do not know. I will have to think about that."

Sarah snuggled even closer, thinking, You can think about it all you want, dearest one, but my duty is clear.

*   *   *

They arrived at the Sophia just at 4:30 p.m. Thor paid the limousine driver in cash, including a large tip, and they rushed up to their room. Fifteen minutes later they had collected all their belongings and were on the elevator back to the lobby. As Thor was paying the bill he heard Sarah say, "Hello, Jens. It is good to see you. And you are always so prompt."

"Thank you, dear lady. Did you have a pleasant weekend?"

"Yes, Jens, it was wonderful; most wonderful."

"Then I am glad for you," he responded.

At that point, Thor turned away from the cashier's counter, and shook hands with Jens. "Right on time, old friend. I hope you rested."

"I did, Commander," Jens replied, then picked up both suitcases and led the way out to the parking lot where the transporter was waiting, and in a matter of minutes they were in the air heading for New York.

En route, Thor received a call. It was from Truls Heyerdahl, to let him know that the five new starships had arrived at Andrews Air Force Base. "Good news," Thor replied. I want to meet the crews individually in the morning. Please have them assembled in their ships at 7:00 a. m. "

"Very well, Commander. I will see to it."

Thor replaced his smart phone in its holster on his belt. then turned to Sarah. " The five new starships I ordered have arrived from Techna Planet. We are loaning them to the United States Government."

"Why, Thor?" Sarah asked.

"They are to be used to bring U.S troops home from Iraq, immediately, angel. Nothing more."

"Has the President agreed?"

"Yes, he has."

"Thor, that is wonderful news. But how in the world did you accomplish it?"

"Honey, it was easier than even I thought possible, once we found the right levers."

"I don't suppose you can tell me what those levers are."

"Sorry, but I cannot. As I have said, the methods used by Techna Force 20 are top secret, which means I cannot talk about them to anyone who is not a direct member of the force. I hope you understand. It is nothing personal, I assure you."

"Very well, Thor. As much as I want to know about everything in your life, I do understand and trust you. I will try hard not to be too nosey."

Thor put his arms around her. "Thanks, angel. Please know that I will always tell you as much about my work as I can. By the way, in case I have not told you lately, I love you more than anything in the world, and I will do everything in my power to make you happy. This weekend was the most wonderful I have ever had, thanks to you."

"Yes, it was wonderful. Surprises always are, and I have never had one like the one you gave me Friday night. Will I hear from you soon?"

"I hope so. Actually, you owe me a call about coming to Boston next weekend."

"I have not forgotten. I will let you know as soon as I talk to my parents."

* * *

Jens voice cracked over the cabin intercom. 'Commander, we are over Central Park, where the weather is clear and the ceiling is 15,000 feet. Please prepare for landing."

"Thanks, Jens. We are ready."

------///------

CHAPTER EIGHT

Many Challenges for TF20

Thor arrived at Andrews Air Force Base in his transporter a few minutes before 7:00 a.m., Monday , March 29, 2010. Using a secret Techna homing signal, Jens was able to locate the five invisible starships with no trouble. Also in I-mode, he landed just in front of the lead ship, where Truls stood waiting.

"Good morning, Commander," Truls said as Thor walked toward him. "Everything is ready, as you requested. But before we go in, I want to tell you that you were on CTS *Sunday Review* last night; you probably didn't see the program because you were in the air. It was a rerun of your earlier appearance, updated to disclose news about withdrawal from Iraq, and the part Techna Force 20 played. I thought CTS put a very positive spin on us being involved, though some Government officials, notably military officers, they interviewed, seemed very angry."

"Yes, I anticipated that, Captain," he said, as they made their way to the row of starships. "We are still considered invaders, and in a sense we are, but they do not understand that we are trying to help the United States, not destroy it. I am pleased that CTS supports us." He and Truls entered the first starship to find its crew standing at attention.

Thor greeted the crew warmly, then said "It is good to see all of you looking so well after your long flight. Your mission is a worthy one: bring American military forces home from Iraq. We have worked hard to make this eventful day a reality. Having succeeded in that effort, we must now help this country get its soldiers out of there as rapidly as possible. You will be transporting people, not equipment. Your starships have been outfitted to carry 500 fully equipped military personnel. I cannot tell you to what bases you will carry them, because they are almost certainly going to be disbursed to many bases in the United States. Each time you return to Iraq you will receive destination instructions from an American officer. Just do your usual fine job and I am certain this mission will turn out successfully. Then you can return to Techna. That should happen in about two weeks. While you are on Planet Earth you will be part of Captain Heyerdahl's Group 1. Good luck and safe flying."

He saluted the crew who returned the salute snappily. Then he moved on to the next starship and gave an identical speech. When he finished number five he returned to the transporter and instructed Jens to take him to the White House.

*   *   *

The new President Fields was already at work in the Oval Office, even though it was just 8:00 a.m. Seeing him there made Thor smile to himself, for he had never seen the original Fields there so early. Though he entered the office in I-mode, the President saw him immediately. "Come in, come in, Commander," Fields said warmly, as Thor changed to visible mode. "I have been expecting you."

"How are you, Mr. President? Do you need my help with any problems?"

"Well, yes, Commander, I do. I am ready to commence troop withdrawal from Iraq."

"Good. That is why I am here. The five starships I promised you have arrived. They are parked at Andrews presently and await your instructions. I just briefed the crews on their mission, And made them part of Truls Heyerdahl's Group."

"I am grateful for your help, Commander. This mission will be managed by the Secretary of Defense, Bertram Phillips, who has already received my orders. May I have him contact Captain Heyerdahl directly, or should he go through you?"

"Mr. President," Thor responded, handing the President a card containing Trul's smart-phone number, "we have always taught that the shortest chain of command works best. Please have Secretary Phillips contact Captain Heyerdahl directly, at this number."

"Very well. I will tell him. By the way, I am going to adopt your suggestion regarding soldiers who will be returning without civilian jobs. It is unfair to simply dump them back into civilian life to fend for themselves. After all, we forced them into active duty in the first place—and sent many of them back to Iraq a second, even a third time. So, they will have the option of serving as guards along our border with Mexico until they find new civilian jobs. That will at least give them income with which to care for their families."

"That is good news, Mr. President. What would be even better is if you would provide their families with decent portable housing and other necessary facilities close to where the soldiers are serving as guards. Then they will be truly reunited with their families."

"A splendid idea, Commander. We have thousands of new travel trailers stored in Mississippi that were intended for Hurricane Katrina survivors, but were never used. Perhaps we can make use of them until we can provide something better."

"Yes. They are better than nothing, Mr. President. One caution on this plan, though."

"What is that, Commander?"

"You will face a great deal of opposition to this worthy plan from American businessmen who use cheap Mexican labor to increase their own profits. They will fight you."

"Yes, I understand. They will fight, but they will not win. The days when this Government is run by powerful corporations to suit their own interests are over. I know that is another of your goals; it is also one of mine."

"Then we are truly on the same page, Mr. President. I am pleased. Siran Missirian, who heads Group 2, which is responsible for reforming corporations, will be pleased as well. I will ask her to work closely with whomever you appoint to act for you in that matter. Siran is, as you know, very capable."

"She will be a great asset to me, Commander. There is one other problem I would like your help on."

"What is that, Mr. President?"

"Afghanistan. I am greatly concerned that we are about to trade one quagmire, Iraq, for another named Afghanistan. We seem to be following in the footsteps of Great Britain and Russia in this regard. They both failed, and we are failing, as well. What are your thoughts on this thorny issue?"

Mr. President, I happen to agree with you completely. Afghanistan is an entirely different problem because of Al Qaeda's control there. They are a disorganized band of renegades whose head we do not see. Sending more and more soldiers there is only a guarantee of more and more deaths, not greater success of the mission. I would prefer to deal with this problem by sending a very small, highly skilled force in there to find Osama Bin Laden, or whoever is leading that gang, and bring him to justice."

"Commander, if you are suggesting that I send in Techna Force 20, I am afraid I do not have that authority."

"Yes, I understand, old friend, but I am not bound by such constraints. In fact, I have asked Truls Heyerdahl to organize just such a force, and he has made great progress. The most difficult task has been to learn the language of Afghanistan. But now we have over two hundred agents who are fluent in both Dari and Farsi, the two dominant Persian language versions in use there. That ability to communicate in their tongue, coupled with our great power to move about unseen makes us the best choice for such a mission. So we will undertake it. Will we be successful? Right now, I cannot give you a guarantee of success. I can only tell you we will do our very best. Incidentally, there must not be any publicity on this. But, of course, you do not know anything about this plan, anyway."

"That is true. I do not. I cannot be involved directly. However I will be eternally grateful for whatever success you have ."

"We have had an excellent meeting today, Mr. President. Putting you in this job was one of my better decisions."

"Thank you, Commander. By the way, I think Jack Brill suspects something."

"Well, I would not be surprised. He worked for your predecessor a long time, and knew him well. Do you think he will cause problems for you?"

"I am not sure. He has been watching me very closely of late. The big question is whether he agrees with my handling of matters or not. If he does, I don't expect him to bolt. But if he does not, he could quickly blow my cover."

"He could try, but would anyone believe him? For now, I would suggest that we just keep an eye on him. There will be plenty of time to deal with him if he is against you."

"Yes, I think that is a good plan."

"Is there anything else I can do for you Mr. President?"

"No, except that my new wife is driving me to drink with her demands for attention."

The two men laughed, and Thor said, "Well, if she becomes too much for you we can always do to her what we did to her husband: send in a substitute."

The new President smiled broadly. "Except that then I fear I would be even more tired."

"Then I assume the First Lady has no inkling of what we have done."

"Correct. She just thinks her husband has found renewed interest, and she is quite content. "

"Then, perhaps she could become a valuable asset later on. "I hope you will try to keep her content."

"I will, Commander. Have a good day."

*   *   *

Jack Brill had worked with Howard Fields many years and figured he knew Fields better than anyone else. Thus, he found the changes that had come over the President recently to be most troubling. It was not like Fields to change his mind once it was made up, even if he recognized that his choice of action was dead wrong. Yet, he had completely reversed course now and had issued orders to withdraw from Iraq. That pleased Brill, but reversal was so uncharacteristic of Fields that Jack was convinced someone must have taken the Mafia approach and made him an offer he could not refuse. He didn't see how the change could have happened, otherwise. Then, too, there was the matter of Field's relationship with his wife, Mildred. Jack knew her almost as well as he knew Howard, who, in private she called that 'old son of a bitch.' In other words, as close as Brill could see, she hated her husband, and stayed with him only because of the scandal leaving him would cause. Yet, she now seemed to have reversed her opinion, and in their private quarters she could not keep her hands off him. That, too, was totally uncharacteristic.

So troubled was Jack by the behavior of Howard and Mildred Fields that he set about to find the cause. He began by paying much closer attention to the President, hoping to discover something different about him that would explain what had happened. He found nothing different; Fields still acted stubbornly on most issues, at least in Jack's presence, except that something had made him much more amenable on matters dealing with the war. Jack vowed to find out what that something was.

*   *   *

After his meeting with the new President, Thor called CTS to talk to Sam Fischer, and was pleased when Sarah answered the phone. "Good morning, angel," he said. "Are you well?"

"I am very well, thank you, Thor. If this were not a company phone I would tell you just how well I am."

"Then I must call you tonight to get at the bottom of this. Better still, I could pick you up for dinner around seven, if you so desire."

"Oh, please do. That would be wonderful. Now, how may I help you?"

"Well you can let me talk to Mr. Fischer, if he is available."

"Let me check with his secretary," Sarah responded, then came back on the line. "Yes, Sir he is in. I will connect you. Have a great day."

Almost immediately, Sam came on the line. "Hey Thor, how are you? Mark and I were just talking about you. What's happening?"

"Sam, I met with my Group Captains last Friday, and am pleased to inform you that we are ready to meet with you on two matters: Corporate higher-ups working for the Government, and the televangelist problem, and I have a proposal for you: What would you think of interviewing the two Techna Force 20 Group Captains, who have worked so hard to put these reports together, on the air so they can tell their stories first hand? I can be there too, if you wish. The thing is, though, they might not be ready at the same time."

"Thor, I really like that idea. Could we meet them ahead of time to get acquainted and preview the programs?"

"Certainly. I will arrange it and call you back," Thor said and hung up.

*   *   *

Thor's next stop was Andrews Air Force Base, where he met briefly with Truls Heyerdahl in the latter's starship. During that meeting he asked how preparations for the Afghanistan mission were going.

"Very well, Commander. I think we can commence this coming Monday, if you agree. That would be April four."

"Excellent. I have informed the President of our intent to help him with this matter, and he is anxious to start. What is your plan?"

"I think one starship manned by the 200 agents who now speak the two dominate languages, and six B series transporters should be sufficient. We will insert agents equipped with our private communications devices in Al Qaeda units, in the hope that one of them will get a link to Bin Laden's location. Of course our people will never be visible."

Thor nodded in agreement. "Good. Let's hope we can bring this to a successful conclusion quickly. By the way, using the B series transporters is a good idea. They are larger and have sleeping spaces. That way our agents will have comfortable quarters."

"Yes, Commander. That is my thinking, too. Do you have time for another matter?"

"Certainly."

"It is about the congressmen who reneged on their agreement to vote for withdrawal."

"Ah, yes. There were 35 of them, as I recall."

"Your memory is excellent, Commander, and all of them have now been replaced by doubles. We now have 110 agents in the House of Representatives."

"I call that justice, Captain. They broke their promise. Now, may I use one of your offices for a while? I need to talk to Siran and Arne."

"By all means, Sir. Use mine."

Thor thanked him and said, "How are the new crews doing?"

"Fine, Commander. Anxious to get going, of course."

"Yes, I am sure they are. They will get their wish very soon, possibly as early as Monday, right?" Then he left for Truls' office, where, in quick succession, he talked to Siran Missirian and Arne Klein about their pending appearances on CTS *Sunday Review*.

As it turned out, they were both ready and eager to tell their stories. He promised to let Sam Fischer know immediately, and to give both agents specific schedules for the introductory meeting with CTS, and for the actual program taping. Then he called CTS again. Sarah was on her break, but the receptionist on duty put him through to Sam's office right away.

"Sam Fischer here."

"Good afternoon, Sam. I am calling to let you know Group Captains, Siran Missirian and Arne Klein are ready to meet whenever you are ready. And I would like to bring Assim Agassi along, as well. He is in charge of stamping out illegal drugs in your country. I think you might also be interested in that story."

"Beautiful, Commander. How does Wednesday morning at 10 a.m. sound? That will be March 31."

"Fine, Sam. See you then."

*   *   *

Thor worked on planning in his transporter for the rest of the afternoon. He needed to prepare for the meeting between Sam Fischer, of CTS *Sunday Review*, Siran Missirian, Arne Klein and Assim Agassi, and on Friday he planned to brief the new President Fields on the problem of overcharges in Iraq by private American contractors. On the following Monday, programs to bring American troops home from Iraq and to solve the Afghanistan problem were finally going to begin and he wanted to be on hand for those historic events. He also wanted to be ready for his meeting with

Sarah's parents on Saturday. Then, too, there was the visit to Techna Planet which would take place for Sarah and himself in just two weeks. So, as usual, he found himself juggling many balls simultaneously. As was his long-standing practice, he took these tasks from their imaginary pigeon holes in his mind one at a time and dealt with each of them individually. When he felt he had done everything he could on one, he put it back and selected another. It was a method he learned from his father, who had told him when he was just a small boy that it was the system Chinese people had used to deal with their problems for centuries. It had worked for his father, and it worked for him.

At ten minutes to seven p.m., he told Jens he was ready to go to New York to meet Sarah, and at five minutes to seven the transporter touched down on the soft grass of Central Park.

Thor was about to knock on Sarah's door when she opened it. "Oh, Thor," she said, smiling up at him. "I just had a feeling you were here. Please, come in."

He stepped inside and immediately took her in his arms. "My dearest," he whispered into her ear, "I have missed you so very much. Is everything alright with you?"

"It is now, dear man. My life is complete only when I am with you."

"Yes, I know. It is the same with me. Do you suppose we should consider marriage?"

She held up her left hand to show him her ring. "Does this mean we have already done that?"

"Oh, yes, I forgot," he said with a sly smile. "But then, I gave you that such a long time ago."

"Hmmm. If my memory serves me correctly, my love, that long time ago was just three days ago, right?"

"True enough. Where does the time go?"

She smiled and held him close. "I think you need to take me to dinner before I decide my hunger is for something else."

"Well, if you insist. How does the Coonamessett Inn sound? We have not been there for a while. I have reservations for eight p.m."

"It sounds wonderful. I'll get my coat."

*   *   *

179

They dined on Maine lobster while chatting non-stop. Sarah wanted to know what he had been doing all day and he told her as much as he could, including the news that American soldiers would start coming home in one week, and that he would be seeing her boss, Sam Fischer, on Wednesday.

* * *

"That is wonderful news, about getting out of Iraq, I mean," she said. "What a waste of life. Is that why you are coming to CTS?"

"No. That visit is to lay the ground work for a program on several other projects we are working on, My Love. But I cannot tell you more."

"I understand, Thor. Now, are we still going to Brookline this coming weekend?"

"Definitely. I am really looking forward to it."

"So are my parents. Actually, they can't believe I am going to marry a little green man with one eye in the middle of his forehead, and are in a state of complete shock."

Sarah and Thor had a good laugh over this bit of news. Then Thor asked, "Are they really upset?"

"Upset is not the word I would use, Thor. It is more like disbelief. Neither of them ever believed the stories out of Roswell about aliens, you know. Now their precious daughter is going to marry one. You are going to have to put on your best performance to convince them that you are worthy of me, my prince. My mother is Jewish and my father is a lawyer, remember? They will have you on the stand for hours, and of the two, I think my mother is the better interrogator. She will be merciless."

"That is fine, Sarah. I understand, and do not mind."

"But just how will you deal with them?"

"Oh, I have a plan, but actually, that plan is to just be myself and play it by ear. I'll just charm them to pieces, honey."

"Well you are quite good at that, dear man. It should be a very interesting weekend, indeed."

"Yes, it should. When are they expecting us?"

"Late morning would be good. They don't get up too early on weekends."

"Very well, I will pick you up at 9:30 a.m., if that is alright, but we will need to identify a landing place for the transporter."

"No problem. My parent's home is just across Lee St. from the Brookline Country Club. There is a good sized grassy area between that street and the first green of the golf course that would be a perfect landing area. It's not for aircraft, of course, but since no one will see the transporter, why worry? From there we could walk to their house. But I have a better plan: Why don't you stay over at my house Friday night? I'll fix us breakfast, then we can fly to Brookline and walk to their house."

"Fine, I like that even better. There is just one thing, though: as much as I love snuggling with you in bed, it might be prudent to have separate bedrooms at your parent's home, if available, or, I could always sleep on the couch."

"A wise suggestion, Thor. They have plenty of bedrooms."

* * *

Thor awakened at his usual early hour of 5:00 a.m. to find Sarah cuddled next to him and still sound asleep. The feeling of her warm body next to his was something he was certain he would never tire of. He lay there for a few minutes, listening to her soft, measured breathing and watching her beautiful face. Then, reluctantly, he slid out from under the covers very carefully so as not to disturb her, dressed quickly, and made a cup of hot tea. Then he wrote a little note which ended by telling her how much harder leaving her each time was becoming. He placed the note on the kitchen counter where she would be sure to find it, crept softly back to the bedroom and kissed her lightly on the cheek, then left her apartment without a sound. He made the short walk across Central Park West to where the transporter rested in its usual place, with Jens waiting beside the open door.

"Good morning to you, Commander," he said cheerfully. "There is tea and a breakfast snack in the cabin. Where to today?"

"Back to Sardine Mountain, old friend. Then tomorrow morning we must be back here for a 10:00 a.m. meeting with CTS. Siran, Arne and Assim will join us on that flight."

"Very well, Sir. I will prepare the transporter for an early departure."

"Good, Jens. My work would be nearly impossible without your help, and I appreciate all that you do."

"Thank you, Commander."

* * *

On the brief flight, Thor checked his laptop for messages. There were several from his Group Captains, including one from Assim Agassi. It contained an update on Assim's latest attack on the illegal drug trade, stating that the attack was the most successful to date, since it caused the destruction of five drug cartel planes, each loaded with nearly a ton of cocaine, and the deposit into Techna Force 20's treasury of seventy-five million dollars. At the end of his report, Assim said, "I cannot say that we have ended the illegal drug problem, Commander. The drug lords are a tenacious, greedy and treacherous bunch of evil men. But I do know this latest raid hit then especially hard. The South American jungles are full of angry messages vowing to kill whoever took their money. You and I know they have no clue who they are up against, and I promise you we will continue the pressure for as long as it takes to totally eradicate this terrible cancer that is threatening Planet Earth." Thor re-read the email, then smiled, pleased with the results of the action, and very pleased with Group Captain Assim Agassi.

There was another message on his computer. It was from Manta Sames, and presented a detailed itinerary for his forthcoming trip to Techna Planet with Sarah. It made him realize that, in the rush of day to day events, he had given that journey short shift. He made a mental note to begin serious trip preparations for himself —and Sarah, especially for her, for there were many things she needed to know about his home planet.

* * *

Not feeling Thor's body next to hers, Sarah wandered into the kitchen to find him. But he was not there, or in the living room or the bathroom. She was disappointed that he had left without saying goodbye, but then she found his hand-written note and picked it up to read it.

> *My darling Sarah:*
> *The temptation to remain with you today was very, very strong—in fact, it grows stronger each time we are together. I do not know what special force brought us together, but I am eternally grateful. I want you to know, dear heart, that one minute with you is more precious than any other experience I might have, however long. Until we meet again, and may that moment come soon, I love you.*
>
> *Thor*

Sarah clutched the note to her heart as tears of happiness welled in her eyes.

*   *   *

"Please prepare for landing, Commander," Jens said over the intercom, and minutes later the transporter descended and glided through the giant doors to the vast underground hanger.

Thor made a brief stop for breakfast in the starship's commissary. Siran Missirian was there, sitting by herself at a table along one bulkhead. He took his tray of food and walked over to her. "Good morning, Siran," he said. May I join you?"

"By all means, Commander."

He took a seat across from her and said, "How is everything with you? Well, I hope."

"Yes, Sir. Very well. I am glad you chose to sit with me because there is something I want to discuss with you in private.

"And what might that be, Siran? We Techna agents have no secrets from each other, as you know."

"Yes, of course. I do know, and it is not a secret, just a matter I am not sure how to handle."

"I will be glad to help, Siran."

"Very well. A man I met—an American—lives in Southern California, in a community called The High Desert Club. It is managed by one of those home owner associations that seem to be so common in this country as a form of government. He mentioned in one of our meetings that he was troubled by rumors circulating in his community concerning missing association funds. According to what he was hearing the amount was quite large for such a small community. I listened, but did not disclose that I am a member of Techna Force 20. He does not know who we are or what we do. Nor did I offer to look into the problem that concerned him. But later, it began to trouble me that someone might be absconding with the association's money. Compared to the many other problems we are trying to solve in America, this one is almost infinitesimal—yet it is, potentially at least, just another sign of the lack of morality that exists here. So I sent an agent to investigate, in I-mode, of course. She was there for two weeks; enough time to check the books and attend two board meetings, and based on what she found she confirmed my friend's suspicions: a few members of the association's board of directors are actively engaged in embezzling funds through the mechanism of kick-backs from several contractors. The amount they have taken to date is slightly more than five hundred thousand dollars. These board members have covered the theft by keeping two sets of books—we have learned that this is known as "cooking the books," in this country—which is easy for them to do since they are responsible for how the association's funds are spent. Now that the theft has been confirmed to me, I feel I must do something about it."

"And I think you should, Siran."

"It does not bother you that this is a small problem in the overall scheme of things, when we have so much to do?"

"No, Siran. It does not. Dishonesty is dishonesty, regardless of the extent of it, and we have a duty to end it wherever we find it. As you said, it is symptomatic of the overall situation here. Small, perhaps, but just as significant. You were absolutely right in investigating. Now the question is, what do you recommend we do about it?"

"I want to expose these men to the association membership, first of all. Then, ordinarily, I would recommend that they be turned over to the local authorities. But if I do that, nothing will come of it because the locals have so many of these crimes on their plate that it may take them years to prosecute, if they ever do. In all likelihood the culprits will escape without penalty. Therefore, I am considering sending them to Prison Planet. No one will know what happened to them; they will simply disappear. The problem with doing that is two-fold: first it does nothing to replace the embezzled funds, and second, as rotten as these men are, they still have families to support."

"Yes, I see your point. And I think I see where you are going with this. You want us to cover the loss and care for the families, yes?"

"Yes, Sir, I do."

"Siran, I would agree with you entirely but for one important fact: the association must have what is called 'Errors and Omissions Insurance' on their board members, and that insurance should cover the funds lost through board member embezzlement. Therefore, I do not agree that we should reimburse the association. However I will agree to establish a fund to provide for the families. They have no such safety net, and presumably are not at fault. Is that a correct assumption?"

"Yes, Commander. according to my agent the families were unaware of what was going on."

"Then the thieves get the publicity they deserve before going to Prison Planet, and we will set up the support fund for their families. Good work, Siran. Bring this up in our meeting today, then I will instruct Manta to make all the arrangements."

"Thank you, Commander. It is very difficult to know what the correct course of action is at times. I really appreciate your help."

"Siran, we all face such uncertainty once in a while, no matter how long we have been engaged in this work. In this case, I suspect that your agent would have discovered the existence of the insurance coverage given a little more time. In my opinion, you handled this one hundred percent correctly, and I am proud of you."

*   *   *

Thor began the staff meeting with the news that withdrawal from Iraq would begin the following Monday, April 5. "Many of the returning soldiers lost their civilian jobs after being called to active duty," he said. "So they will be assigned to do guard duty along the border with Mexico. That will serve two purposes: First, it should help reduce the massive influx of illegal aliens. Second, it gives those soldiers income they desperately need. I believe I mentioned this plan before, but just wanted to reiterate it today."

"Also, we are going to assume a major role in Afghanistan starting Monday. I would like you, Truls to give them the details on this."

Truls nodded and said, "We are sending two hundred agents to Afghanistan to infiltrate Taliban and Al Qaeda forces, in the hope that we can locate and capture Osama Bin Laden. Our agents have undergone extensive training in the Dari and Farsi dialects of the Persian language, and will operate totally in I-mode. They will be equipped with one starship and five large transporters, as well as our secret communications gear. I will keep all of you posted on developments."

"Very good, Truls, "Thor said. "Next I would like all of you to hear from Siran Missirian concerning a problem she recently encountered."

"Thank you, Commander," Siran responded. Then she told the same story she had discussed with Thor earlier.

"Manta," Thor said, "Will you set up the family support fund for those people?"

"Yes, I will, Commander.. Do you have a number in mind?"

"Whatever is reasonable according to the standard of living they have enjoyed, Manta."

"Very well, Sir."

"Siran was concerned that this type of project might be too small for us. I just want you all to know that, as I said to her, anything that helps re-establish the morality that is so lacking in this country is important, no matter how small or seemingly insignificant. Now, Siran, let's hear about your plans for dealing with corporate control of government in this country."

"Yes, Sir. I have gone over this in my own mind countless times. The Federal Government has long followed the practice of hiring government officials needed to head key agencies from the very corporations that are supposed to be regulated by those agencies. FDA, for example will look to major pharmaceutical companies, food processors and major farmers for people. FAA looks at aircraft manufacturers and airlines. SEC goes after high-powered stock brokers and finance managers. The thinking has always been that these people are best equipped by experience and education to manage the vast Government regulatory agencies. But what has happened is that the corporations giving up their key employees to the Government have signed secret, very profitable contracts with the departing employees which require them to provide preferential treatment to their former employers. The result is, in effect, no regulation."

"I think the only way to cure this mess and restore much needed regulation of industry is to replace those corporate moles —that is what they are, in my opinion—with people who have no personal interest in the field to be regulated. Unfortunately, there is a huge shortage of honest individuals who are willing to take on such responsibility. Thus, I conclude that we—Techna Force 20—must fill that void, and I propose to do it using the doubles system we have employed in other parts of the U.S. Government. I think most of you know about that practice. We used it in both the Legislative and Executive Branches, and it has worked exceptionally well. I am convinced it will work in the agencies as well."

Thor nodded and said, "Thank you, Siran. I am interested in how you intend to present that to CTS. It will not be tomorrow, by the way; that meeting is so that Sam Fischer, the producer of CTS, can meet all of you prior to the time they plan to put us on the program."

"Sir, I plan to say only that Techna Force 20 will assume control of the regulatory agencies. I do not intend to tell CTS about the doubles plan."

"A wise decision, I think. That is a tool we must keep secret. That was a good report. Thank you. Arne, what about your plans?"

"Commander. I plan to show CTS—through video and audio clips—the behind-the-scenes reality of evangelistic television. I see no need for Techna Force 20 to take over the industry since, in my opinion, seeing how their money is really spent will turn most people off completely, and they will simply stop donating. That should be enough to put these leaches out of business."

"Arne, you are banking on us being able to prove how the televangelists spend donations. Do you think that is enough?"

"Yes, Sir. I do. Our presentation will be very graphic. I have seen it and as hardened as I am, the Sodom and Gomorrah aspect turns my stomach instantly."

"Very well. Assim, I think the Group Captains would like to hear about your latest success."

"Certainly," Assim responded, then he reported on the latest cocaine bust and the related collection of seventy-five million dollars. All the Group Captains clapped in approval. Then he continued, "but we are still a long way from a total solution. Drugs are pouring across the Texas border at many locations. We must find a way to plug those holes."

"Assim," Truls said. "As I reported earlier, soldiers returning from Iraq without jobs will be assigned to patrol the border with Mexico. Could they not help you with this problem?"

"Absolutely. They could be the answer we need. Will they be armed?"

"Yes," Truls said. "It will be for them as it was in Iraq. I have not heard whether they will be ordered to shoot to kill, but they will be armed and ready."

"They will have orders to shoot to kill if in their judgment the situation warrants," Thor interjected. "

"Even women?" Erika Varda wanted to know.

"Unfortunately, yes, Erika, if they try to run. Women—and children-- are often used as drug 'mules,' just because authorities might think they are innocent. We cannot assume that."

"What a terrible world this is."

"Erika, it is a terrible world," Thor said. "And we must all do our best to make it better. I know it seems an insurmountable challenge, but we will prevail. We must prevail. How is your work to help the middle class progressing?"

"Commander, it goes slow at the moment, but I believe we are making progress. People in the middle class have been hardest hit by the current recession. Many have lost their jobs and cannot find new ones. Without jobs most end up with no medical coverage for their families. We keep hearing about a stimulus plan coming out of Washington, but so far it has not materialized. Furthermore, Republicans in Congress are fighting against any proposal that spends government money; they will only agree to tax reductions and argue that such reductions will do more than handouts. But what good are lower taxes to people who are out of work and no longer pay taxes? The answer is clear; it will do no good. That idea has been tried and it failed. Thus, I believe we will have to lean hard on Republican Congressional members to change their position."

"I agree, Erika," Truls responded. "And now we can. Remember, we have eliminated 110 of those negative votes by inserting doubles into congress. The Republican Party no longer has any teeth. It is weak and powerless, and we intend to keep it that way."

"Good point, Truls," Thor said. " Erika, I will follow up on this problem with the Congressional leaders and the President. There must be a strong stimulus package, particularly for the middle class. Private industry will not help them, so the government must. They are the ones who spend the money that keeps the U.S. economy running on all cylinders. We must see that they have the funds to do that. Now, about tomorrow: Siran, Arne, and Assim, we will leave here in my transporter at 9:15 a.m. for New York. This was a good meeting. It was informative and productive. Thank you all for coming."

*   *   *

The three group captains assembled for the trip to New York with their commander the next morning, as scheduled. Thor was not very comfortable with having so many key people fly in one transporter anywhere, notwithstanding the safety record of this aircraft type. But landing space on the roof of the CTS building was very limited so he made an exception this time. Fortunately, the flight was uneventful and at 9:45 a.m., he, Assim, Siran and Arne made the long walk from the elevators to the reception desk, where Sarah waited and watched. She had already been briefed on the pending visit by the Techna Force 20 contingent.

"Good morning, Commander Berksten," she said. "We have been expecting you. How was your flight?"

"Good morning to you Sarah," Thor replied. "It went quite well, thank you. As you can see, I brought reinforcements with me this time. Do you remember them?"

"Of course, Commander. Welcome, Assim, Siran, Arne, on behalf of CTS *Sunday Review.* We are honored to have you as our guests. I will ring Mr. Fischer's office now." She spoke into the tiny microphone wand extending from some hidden place beneath her hair to a point just behind the left corner of her mouth. Then, looking directly at Thor she smiled and said. "Your party may go in now, Sir. Do you remember the way?"

"I do, Sarah," Thor replied and motioned to his agents to follow him.

Margie Peterson met them at the door and escorted them to Sam Fischer's office, where Sam and Mark Haddon were waiting. The two CTS men stood as they approached and greeted Thor with broad smiles and handshakes. "Good to see you again, Commander, " Sam said. We have been looking forward to this meeting with eager anticipation.."

"Well, Sam, Mark, I think you will find it very interesting." Then he began introductions by saying, "This is Siran Missirian, Captain of Group 2, Arne Klein, Captain of Group 3, and Assim Agassi, Captain of Group 4. Siran is responsible for reducing corporate influence over your Government. Arne has similar duties with respect to religion. And Assim is responsible for correcting problems in your legal system. You mentioned to me that you might be interested in including their work on a forthcoming CTS *Sunday Review* program, so they are here to get acquainted with you and Mark. With that, I will turn the meeting over to you."

"Great, Commander. Siran, let's begin with you. I know a little about your work, and you certainly have an important task, in trying to prevent our huge corporations from taking over the Federal Government. It is truly wonderful to find someone so young in such a responsible position. What would you say to our American Television audience to convince them of the need to get corporations out of Washington's hair?"

"I would tell them the truth, Mr. Fischer. I would show them how putting a high-powered corporate executive in charge of a Government agency helps the corporation that provided the executive far more than it helps the American public. And I would present a plan to rid the Government of this problem. It is my understanding that we are not here today to review that plan in detail, but I brought a copy of my plan for each of you to review at your convenience." She handed each of them a thick blue folder. "I think you will find answers to most questions in it, and I will be happy to fill in any missing details later. As you know from dealing with Commander Berksten, Techna Force 20 makes the difficult decisions that must be made to solve problems. My solution for ending corporate control of Government may shock American citizens, but I believe they are savvy enough to understand that it is the only solution. Of course, I am prepared to name names and provide explicit examples. These folders also include a 15 minute DVD summary."

Sam and Mark exchanged knowing looks as they thumbed through the folders. Finally Mark said, "Very impressive, Siran. Sam, I will have to study this proposal, but at first glance I think it is a perfect subject for *Sunday Review*."

"Okay, Mark," Sam replied. "It looks good to me, too. Let me know as soon as you can. Now, Arne of Group 3, what do you have for us?"

"Sir, my area is religion, and my current project is to expose many televangelists for what they are: thieves. I am not against religion. What I am against is using it for personal gain, as many televangelists have been doing for years. We have been working on this for some time now, from the inside. To clarify, my agents and I burrowed into various televangelist organizations without detection, using our powerful ability to work in I-mode, and given that vantage point we have uncovered shocking proof of how these organizations spend the donations they receive—most of which come from very poor people. Our goal is to stamp out this thievery once and for all. We will give you graphic evidence, in the form of videos and audio recordings of behind-the-scenes conversations, as well as intimate views of life in typical televangelist homes and offices. These people live and work like kings and queens, and virtually none of those donations benefit the truly needy. "

"Another perfect fit, for us, Sam," Mark said excitedly. "Arne, when can you be ready to go on the air ?"

"I am ready now," Arne answered, handing Mark a DVD. "Here is a preview of the full story. I would like you and Sam to review it. Let me know if you think it needs more work. But as far as I am concerned this expose' is ready for prime time, as you say in your business."

Mark and Sam laughed simultaneously. Then Sam said, 'We will go though the DVD right away, Arne. There is no question that this is a story America needs to see." He turned to look at Assim. "Group 4, right, Captain?"

"Yes, Sam. That is correct."

"Sam," Assim said, "My Group is currently operating on two fronts, so to speak. One of our primary goals is to stamp out the illicit drug trade. Another is to make the American legal system work as it should."

"So far we have prevented import of more than three hundred million dollars worth of drugs into the United States, not only confiscating and destroying the product, but also destroying the entire supply line, from growers to much of the distribution network. However, the most important part of drug distribution—the buyers—is still alive and well. What may not be understood is that the people who buy this stuff now are no longer just your ordinary corner drug dealers; some pretty big, apparently legitimate, corporations have discovered that lots of money can be made here and they have piles of ready cash to spend. They also have their very own dealer network on the streets. I am sure you both know that the profit in drugs is huge. That has brought some big names into the game, and some of those names might surprise you. We are going after them and will eventually expose them. I believe exposing what we know at this point would drive our prey underground; it would be better to wait until we gather the necessary proof."

"Agreed, Assim," Sam said. We are very interested in this subject and are prepared to help whenever you say the word. What about the Texas problem, though? We are hearing that drugs are flooding across that state's borders."

"They are, Sam. The Federal Government's new fence has not helped at all. The drug lords just hire workers to dig tunnels under it, and there are plenty of eager hands in Mexico who are more than willing to take on this task. There are also plenty of hands in Texas ready to risk all to distribute the drugs once they cross the border. So Texas is a big problem right now, which is another reason to wait. We have a plan underway to stop this influx of drugs but need more time to perfect it."

The two CTS men nodded in agreement, and Sam said, "Right, just let us know when you are ready, Assim. Anything else you would care to tell us?"

"Well, we are tracking a huge marijuana problem in California's Mendocino County, that the local authorities seem unable to deal with. It looks like we will have to get involved in that very soon. I am sure Commander Berksten will keep you posted on our progress there. Also, as I am sure you are aware we were responsible for the recent execution of a large number of death row prisoners, and we will soon undertake a similar program with respect to so-called 'life without parole' prisoners. This might be too sensitive to put on the air, though."

"Yes, it is sensitive. However the people have a right to know, and you might be surprised at how many approve, " Sam responded. "We might want to do a story on it, but let me give it some thought." Then he turned to Thor. "Commander, there is no question about the corporation and televangelist projects or, for that matter the illegal drug problem. Mark and I have already agreed that we want to do them as soon as possible. We need a little time to put the stories together, but I am thinking we can do that in two weeks. Mark, what do you think?"

"No problem, Sam."

Sam studied the calendar on his desk for a moment, then said, "Good. Let's set them up for the 18th of April. Does that work for everybody?"

"Sam, I will not be here on that date," Thor answered. "I will be on my way back to Techna Planet then, with Sarah, as you may recall. We leave on the 16th of April, and will be gone for three weeks. However, I think you should go ahead without me—but only on the corporation and televangelist stories, since Assim believes we should wait on the illegal drug issue. Siran and Arne will do just fine, and the sooner we get these problems in front of the American public the better, My being here is not really necessary."

"Very well, it's a deal. We go on the 18th, excluding drugs. Mark, you've got the ball."

"Right, Sam. I think this is going to be one of our best efforts. Siran, Arne and Assim, my sincere congratulations. You have all done a fantastic job. Commander, I congratulate you, too, for bringing Techna Force 20 to Planet Earth. I predict that what appeared to many people as a fearful invasion will turn out to be a blessing for this country."

"Thank you, Mark. But please do not underestimate the contribution you and Sam have made to this effort. Without CTS *Sunday Review,* TF20 would in fact, be treated as a bunch of ruthless alien invaders, I think. This has been a solid joint effort and, as you people say, the best is yet to come."

* * *

On Friday, April 2ⁿᵈ, Thor returned to Washington to meet with the new President regarding serious over-charges by private contractors hired by the U.S. Government to perform various non-combatant duties. Such over-charges were adding many millions of dollars to the cost of war in Iraq, and he wanted to make certain the President was aware of the problem. Former President Fields had been briefed several times on this, but did nothing to stop the practice. The meeting, which lasted about an hour, pleased Thor very much, for the new President was not only aware of the problem; he had already ordered it stopped. In addition, the contractors in question had been ordered to reimburse the Government for the over-charges, under threat of being disqualified from future contract bidding. It was, Thor, thought, an order with large and very sharp teeth.

The President also informed Thor that most of the military equipment sent to Iraq for the war was being returned to the United States. "I imagine that subject was on your agenda for today, Commander, so I thought I would ease your mind a bit."

"Yes, it has been on my mind, Mr. President. I am glad to hear that nothing of consequence will be left behind over there. Otherwise, as I am sure you realize, some very sophisticated equipment could—probably would—fall into the wrong hands."

"Quite so, Commander. We are not going to let that happen again."

* * *

Siran Missirian returned to California on Thursday, April 1, 2010, to take care of the embezzlement problem at High Desert Club. She timed her return so as to be present at the Club's monthly open board meeting, scheduled for 7:00 p.m. that evening. The meeting room was already full when she entered at five minutes to seven, with approximately 200 members milling around, laughing and talking with one another. Techna Force 20 agent, Katrina Meintz, whom she had sent to investigate the allegations earlier, joined her, and the two women, dressed in perfectly tailored uniforms, took seats in the front row of the room and waited for meeting to commence.

At exactly seven p.m. all seven members of the Club's board of directors appeared, and took their seats at the dais. They were joined by a white haired woman who Katrina identified as the Club's General Manager. Caroline Crawford-Smith, board president, called the meeting to order and, in accordance with tradition, asked for comments from the floor. Siran was the first in line, waiting at the microphone-equipped podium, for her turn to speak. Mark Harshfeld, the man who had originally told her about his suspicions regarding fund shortages, happened to be standing next in line behind her.

"I am Siran Missirian, a member of High Desert Club. My home is located on Manzanita Terrace. I am here to inform you of a serious financial problem in this community." Speaking in measured tones loud enough for the assembled members to hear, she addressed the board, and began by explaining her position with TF20. "Madam President, I am here tonight because another High Desert member told me of his concerns regarding possible shortages in this Association's funds. I sent TF20 agent Katrina Meintz, who is here with me tonight, to investigate his concerns. She is also a member of High Desert Club, and is highly skilled in financial analysis. She subsequently confirmed that more than $525 thousand dollars has been taken from your treasury through the medium of contract kick backs, by four members of your board of directors. Those board members are, John Henderson, Samuel Bromstein, Erik Krause, and Peter Kasperian, all of whom are present here tonight. We have absolute, indisputable, proof of their embezzlement, and they should all be in jail right now. Unfortunately, the District Attorney says his office cannot get to this for at least six months, which is unacceptable to us. So, by the power I have as a Senior agent of Techna Force 20, I shall prosecute them here and now." She raised her right arm as a signal, and immediately a TF20 agent appeared behind each of the accused men. "Take them away, agents," she ordered, and the four men plus their guards vanished from the dais.

There was a collective gasp from the assembled audience, and screams from the men's spouses seated among them.

"What have you done with them?" Board President, Caroline Crawford-Smith asked in a demanding voice.

"They are on their way to TF20's penitentiary, on Prison Planet, millions of miles from here. As a warning to anyone who might be similarly tempted, these men will serve sentences of at least ten years at hard labor, before they are eligible to return to Earth."

"What about the money they stole from this association? Who is going to pay us back?"

"We know you have Errors and Omissions insurance for that. Look to your insurer for recovery."

"And what about us?" yelled a woman in the audience in a loud voice. "We are their families. What are we to do now?"

"The families will be taken care of," Siran responded, turning to face the questioner. "TF20 will see to that. You will all receive a stipend equal to the income formerly provided by your husbands. Thus, financially, you will feel no difference."

"Yes, but you have taken our beloved husbands away. How can you be so cruel?"

"They are criminals, madam," Siran said. "They took money that rightfully belonged to all members of this community. "Pretend they are dead. Make a new life for yourself and your children. I am sorry that you must suffer this, but they did this to you, not me," and with that she and Katrina disappeared.

Their sudden departure set off a cacophony of chatter so loud and disorderly that the President was forced to gavel the meeting back to order, and even that took some effort. But finally, the man who had been standing in line behind Siran, raised his hands for quiet. That worked.

"Madam President," he said. "I am Mark Harshfeld, Special Agent, FBI, and a member of The High Desert Club. I have two points to make: First, It was I who told Miss Missirian about my suspicions regarding the fund shortages, though I did not know she was an agent of Techna Force 20 at the time. Second point:

The Bureau has known about Techna Force 20 for some time. Their leader is Commander Thor Berksten, and they have become an extremely powerful force in our country. They are solely responsible for ending the war in Iraq, and executing more than 3500 death row prisoners. Officially, we must try to stop them; they ignore our laws and use harsh, take-no-prisoners tactics. You have just seen how effective those tactics are."

"While I cannot officially condone the way TF20 operates, they have helped the U.S. with some pretty difficult problems. Tonight they brought swift justice to four thieving scoundrels, a job that would have taken our system years to accomplish. The problem is, they had no legal right to take that action."

"So, why didn't you arrest her and her accomplice?" someone in the audience yelled.

"Because we can't catch them, that's why. No one can. They have that formidable power to vanish into thin air when danger threatens, and neither the bureau nor any other agency knows how to corral them. That gives all of us a huge headache. So, while I secretly applaud her for helping The High Desert Club tonight, and for all the other help TF20 has given the United States, tomorrow morning I must renew efforts to try to capture her. Sorry. I've talked too much. Thanks for giving me time."

"Thank you for that explanation, Mr. Harshfeld," President Crawford-Smith said. "How would you like to become one of our board members? It seems we suddenly have four openings."

"Sorry. It's against the Bureau rules. But if I were to lose my job over what I just said, which could happen, I might consider. How is the pay?"

"Not very good, I am afraid."

"Well I think you have some pretty competent people in this community, and some honest ones. I am sure a few will come forward."

CHAPTER NINE

Thor Meets Sarah's Family

On Friday, April 2, Thor appeared at Sarah's apartment door with an armful of red roses. As had happened before, Sarah opened the door just as he was about to knock. "Good evening, my love. How did you know I was here?" he asked.

"Oh, Thor, I am a woman, you see," she answered, a smile lighting up her face. "I felt your closeness, even through the door. Call it feminine intuition."

He held her in one arm and offered the roses.

"They are beautiful, Thor," she said, stepping aside to let him enter. "Would you believe they are the first roses anyone has given me?"

"No, I would not believe it, my love. You must have received dozens and dozens."

"Not even one rose, dear man. You are the very first."

"Then I am surprised and deeply honored to be first."

"Did you have a good day?"

"Yes, I did, Sarah. We are operating on many fronts now, so I need a day from time to time to evaluate our progress on them all, and to plan our next moves, of course. That is what I did today; I did not leave my office in Roswell until Jens announced it was time to come to New York. In fact, Manta had to pack for me, which is quite unusual. How about you?"

"First, let's discuss packing for your trips; you see, I expect to be doing that once we are married."

"Of course, dear. Manta will not mind; she grumbles about doing it even the few times she has been given the chore. And I will not mind. Your packing is sure to be quite an improvement over mine."

"Good, then it is settled. I will be your chief packer. Now, my day? Well, to tell the truth, it was the longest day of my life."

"Oh? Why, dear heart?"

"I suppose I was excited about you being here today, first of all, then about this week-end. I have no idea what to expect from my parents. Guess I am just edgy about that mostly."

"Please do not worry your pretty head, Sarah. From what you have told me about them I would say your parents sound like very level-headed people. Their concern is for your welfare and happiness. When they see I am not a little green man with one eye, that I have a good steady job, and that I love you with every fiber in my being, I think they will welcome me with open arms."

Sarah busied herself with putting the roses in a vase filled with water as Thor talked. When he paused, she turned to him and put her arms around his waist. 'Dearest Thor, I do so want this to work out for us and at times I become afraid it is only a dream."

"It is no dream, darling, which reminds me, I think it is about time we set a date for the wedding, yes? Can we work on that this weekend? I hear nothing cures a girl's uncertainty like planning the details of her wedding, and you have two to plan, remember?"

"Yes, I remember. And I did not realize until this moment just how wise you are."

They held each other close for several moments, then Sarah said, "Are you hungry? I am famished. I had planned to have dinner here tonight, but in the press of the day I could not manage to put anything together."

"No problem. How about the little Italian place in the lobby? Would that work for you?"

"It would, indeed."

* * *

Angelino's had just six tables—booths, actually—along one wall, plus a long table between the booths and the bar, in case a large group showed up. The decorations were typical of small, family owned Italian restaurants, with lattice on the ceiling and empty Chianti bottles hung from the lattice amidst artificial grape clusters. Italian music played softly in the background.

When Thor and Sarah entered, only one other couple was in the restaurant, seated at the booth closest to the street-side single large window. Thor asked for, and was given, the booth at the rear of the room. He ordered a chilled bottle of Chianti and while they waited for it to arrive they studied the menu. When their waiter, who Sarah said was also the owner and the chef, returned with the wine, they ordered the house specialty, Cannelloni. It proved to be a superb choice, and neither of them could stop complimenting the waiter-chef-owner, who hovered near their table throughout the meal, smiling from ear to ear. Other than their exchanges with Angelino, their conversation centered mostly around the trip to Brookline the next day, and about a wedding date. On the latter subject, they agreed in principle that both of them wanted an autumn ceremony. though the exact date was not determined. "It will have to be on a Saturday," Sarah said. "Catholic weddings traditionally take place on Saturday."

"But I am not Catholic, " Thor responded. "How will that effect things?"

"Your religion no longer matters, dear man. There was a time when a Catholic could not have a traditional wedding in the church if she or he was marrying a non-Catholic. But that rule fell by the wayside years ago."

"So all we really need to decide is the date—the Saturday date—and go from there. I think I will leave that up to you and work my business schedule around what you decide, if that is alright."

"It is perfectly alright with me. I'll let you know as soon as I can. I need to check with family to see when everybody can fit it into their schedule."

"Of course, dear. Then perhaps we could have the service on Techna Planet a few weeks later?"

"I don't see why not, but let me plug that into my family inquiry, as well."

*   *   *

As Sarah had promised, she made breakfast for them the next morning. With Thor watching from a bar stool at the kitchen counter, she expertly and quickly assembled a meal of Eggs Benedict, fruit compote and tea, all of which he enjoyed very much, and said so accompanied by a kiss afterwards. Then they did the dishes and cleaned her little kitchen together. Afterwards, they prepared for the adventure that awaited them.

*   *   *

The flight to Brookline took just minutes, since the distance from New York to Boston is only 215 miles by ground transportation, and considerably less by air. Based on information Thor had given him regarding their landing spot adjacent to the first hole of Brookline golf course, Jens plotted his course using GPS, then hit that spot exactly. When they touched down it was exactly 10:00 a.m. From there, Sarah and Thor walked across Lee Street toward a large white Colonial Sarah pointed out as belonging to her parents. They walked the short distance from street to house via a lovely curving brick walk edged on both sides with perfectly manicured flower beds.

Lush green grass bordered the beds. The home's exterior was in near-new condition, which showed Thor how proud the Malloys were of their property. As they climbed the three steps to the front porch, which was enclosed by screens on three sides, the front door opened and Thor and his future in-laws saw each other for the first time. Rose Malloy, whose eyes and hair were dark brown, was at least a head shorter than her husband and a bit on the plump side, but for all that she moved with surprising speed from the doorway to her daughter's side and wrapped her in ample arms. Then she stepped back, with her arms still on Sarah's shoulders, and said, "How wonderful to see you, darling. I have missed you so very much."

"And I have missed you, Mama. You look wonderful."

While Mother and daughter were greeting one another, Thor stepped forward and said, "Hello, Mr. Malloy. This is a moment I have been looking forward to for quite a while." The two men shook hands, eyeing each other all the time, and Kenneth Malloy said, "Welcome to our home, Commander. I, too have been waiting for this moment. Sarah has not given us much information about you so I have many questions."

"Fine, Sir. I am ready, but please, call me Thor."

"Good by me, and you can call me Ken. Let's go in. Sarah and her mother will probably linger on the porch for a while. Would you like some coffee? I just made a fresh pot."

"Ken, I hate to be a bother, but I do not drink coffee; only tea."

"No Problem. We have that as well. Please take a seat here in the living room while I get it."

While he waited, Thor wandered around the room looking at the many photos that adorned it, and at the room's furnishings, which were tasteful and obviously of very high quality. In a few minutes his host reappeared with a cup in each hand. "Would you like cream and sugar?" he asked.

"No, black is fine."

"Okay," he said, and handed one cup of steaming tea to Thor. He pointed to a pair of chairs flanking a round table in front of a window. "Let's sit here, shall we? I want to know everything about you. Frankly, I have had some concerns about Sarah's choice of a husband. It isn't everyday a man's daughter marries someone from another planet, you know."

Thor looked up at his about-to-be father in law. He was a good looking man Thor judged to be about his own height, in his sixties, with neatly cut white hair and blue eyes. "Yes, I agree, Ken, and I understand your concerns. My own father shares your feelings."

"Ah, yes. He is Prime Minister, I believe Sarah said. And he is concerned, you say?"

"He was, until we talked it out. My argument was that the people of Planet Earth and the people of Techna Planet are not very different from one another."

"Well, Thor, from what little Sarah has disclosed to us about you it seems there are a lot of differences. For example, your...." He paused as Sarah and her mother entered the room. "Hey, you two, Thor and I were just getting acquainted. Rose you've not met him officially, but here he is, and a fine specimen of a man he is , I might add. Thor, this is my wife, Rose."

Thor stood and took Rose's outstretched hand. "I am pleased to meet you, Mrs. Malloy, and I hope we can have a long and wonderful family relationship."

"Thank you, Thor. I too want that. Please call me Rose. Ken, if you will please bring more chairs over, Sarah and I would like to join in this extraordinary first meeting."

Thor left with Ken and each returned with a chair from the adjacent dining room. Then they all sat down, and Ken picked up where he had left off. "I was just telling Thor that there seem to be a lot of differences between people from Techna Planet and Earth. Thor, how do you respond to that?"

"Well, what I was trying to say is that our two peoples are not so very different. I am referring to physical appearance, manner of dress, that sort of thing, Ken. I am not sure what your reference point is, but I judge us to be quite different in terms of ethics and morality from Americans in general and, of course we Technians have defensive powers not found anywhere on Earth. Is that your point?"

"Thor, I tend to look at things through the eyes of a lawyer. I guess it comes naturally after all my years of law practice. Sarah has told us something about your efforts to stop the war in Iraq. Rose and I applaud you for that work; it is an unnecessary war that has cost us untold thousands of lives and billions of dollars. What concerns me are your methods. To put it bluntly, you do not fool around, do you? According to the papers, you gave President Fields an ultimatum: Get out of Iraq or else. When he refused, you blew up the Green Zone, our new Embassy and one of our finest aircraft carriers, the Ronald Reagan. That seems a bit extreme, don't you think?"

"Sir, that is our way. It may seem extreme to you, but the methods we use are very effective. I did give the President an ultimatum. His response was to try to have me arrested on the spot for even being in the White House. Furthermore, I gave him time to evacuate not only civilians but military personnel from the three assets you mentioned. He agreed to my request as far as civilians were concerned, but refused to remove the military."

"So you did destroy those facilities."

"Yes, yet he still refused to end the war."

"But eventually he did agree. How did you manage that?

"Ken, there are things I cannot tell you about Techna operations, but I will tell you we did it by convincing the Congress to end the war. The vote was virtually unanimous."

"Why was ending that war any business of yours in the first place?"

"Actually, it wasn't part of our original plan when we came to your Planet. Our original objective was to keep the United States from locating Techna and either destroying it or taking it over. But, as I told Sarah, we found such great dishonesty and lack of ethics in your Government that we decided to step in—in many of its agencies. As part of that move we discovered the lies published by the Executive branch concerning weapons of mass destruction in Iraq. It simply was not true that Saddam had such weapons; President Fields was fully cognizant of that fact. He went ahead with the war, anyway."

"Well, Thor, what you did was commendable, but how you did it violated our laws."

"We are not bound by your laws, Ken."

"Yes, I gather that. However, being an attorney makes me an officer of the court and I have to report such violations or risk losing my license."

Sarah gasped. "Daddy! I think you are judging Thor too harshly."

"Honey, perhaps I am. But the law is the law."

"Ken, I think you should report it, notwithstanding the fact that the United State's invasion of Iraq was itself illegal, or that the invasion has killed 5,000 Americans and more than 30,000 Iraq citizens, to say nothing about the more than one trillion dollars squandered by President Fields on the war. Notwithstanding all of that," Thor said. "It is your duty as a lawyer, as you say. In fact, I would not think kindly of you if you did not report it."

"Oh, Thor, please don't say that. They will put you in prison, and that would break my heart."

Thor got up and went to Sarah and put his arm around her. "Do not worry, my dearest. They will not be able to do that, I promise."

"Wait a minute, Thor. Don't make promises you can't keep," Ken said. "You can and will be put in jail, I assure you."

"Sir , I can make that promise because it is true. The only person who can incarcerate me is my father. No one in your country has that power over anyone from Techna Planet. For example, if you were to put a gun to my head right now and threaten to kill me if I did not turn myself in, then in the microsecond between the time you pulled the trigger and the departure of the bullet from the muzzle, I would enter I-mode and become invisible. The bullet would pass harmlessly through the space I vacated by doing so. Such is the power a Technian possesses. Your authorities cannot even arrest one of us, for any attempt to do so will simple make the subject of the arrest disappear into the safety of I-mode. Therefore, what I say is true. No prison on Planet Earth can contain a citizen of Techna. The ability to become invisible is a major defensive mechanism we all possess. We lose that power only when we are convicted by an appropriate Techna official of violating a Techna law, or certain Earth laws. So I do not fear being reported by you to your authorities. Turn me in. It will not lead to my going to prison, but it will get you off the hook, so to speak."

"Are you really that powerful?"

"Yes. Ask President Fields. In addition to trying to arrest me in the White House, he sent a squadron of F-22 Raptors to destroy our secret base. They had the exact location of that base, but when they arrived at the target neither we, nor our equipment could be found. Their mission failed. It is precisely because of that great power that we are able to accomplish what no one in your country can. I have agents in many high-level Government offices at this moment. No one sees them, but they are there, observing, recording, reporting. They are in Congress and the White House. They are in the Departments of Defense and State. In short, they are everywhere."

Ken looked his son-in-law-to-be straight in the eye and said, "Thor, I had no idea, but I see now. If only I had such power as a lawyer. I would win every case."

"You do not, Sir. But I will help you win anytime you deserve to win."

"You would do that?"

"Of course. We are always ready to help right an injustice."

"My goodness," Rose said. "All this heavy talk is making me hungry. Kenny why don't you stop picking on this poor boy? Let's all go to the dining room and have lunch. There we can talk about something nice for a change, like Sarah's and Thor's wedding."

"Sorry, Mother, guess I just got carried away," Ken responded, as he rose to lead the way.

Rose took Thor's arm. "I am so glad we finally have a chance to meet. Sarah thinks you are wonderful, and I can see why. But, please, don't take her to some far off place so we will never see her again. Promise?"

"I cannot promise it will never happen, Rose. But I will promise you this: No matter where we are, you and Ken will always be welcome, and I will see that you have proper transportation to get there."

"Oh, good. I hear you have fantastic airplanes."

Thor laughed. "Yes we do. Say the word and I will whisk you away to Techna Planet from Brookline in about five days. Or, if you prefer Palm Springs in winter, it is but a thirty minute ride by transporter."

She patted his arm. "Listen, Palm Springs I would love, let me tell you."

Thor hugged his future mother in law, and said, "Any time you are ready."

* * *

When they were all seated in the dining room, Rose said, "Normally I do all the cooking in this house, but today, in honor of Sarah and you, Thor, and so we can all sit together and talk without me running back and forth to the kitchen, we will be served a catered luncheon that was brought in from outside. Enjoy. Now, Sarah and Thor, have you decided on a wedding date?"

"Yes, Mama, and Daddy, Thor and I have decided that an autumn wedding would be nice. What do you think? Would that fit into your schedule?"

"Darling, we will make it fit," Rose answered. "I will talk to your sisters and your brother about it when they arrive today. Do you have a specific date?"

Sarah glanced at Thor. "How about October 2nd? It's a Saturday."

"Fine," her mother said. "We will make all the arrangements. But Thor, what about your family? Can they make that date? And isn't there to be a second ceremony on Techna Planet?"

"Yes, Rose. I have already checked with my family and they assure me they can be here. As for the second ceremony, it is mandatory according to our tradition, but the timing of it is flexible. Sarah and I are thinking a few weeks later, if that is alright with all of you. We will provide transportation, of course. But as Sarah may have told you, it takes about five days to travel to Techna and another five to return to Earth. So you must allow at least three weeks time for the trip."

"Techna Planet!" Ken exclaimed. I am still having trouble comprehending that there is another planet in the universe, Thor. What is it like there?"

"Ken, Sarah had the same question when we first met. I will describe it to you the way I described it to her: Think about St. Augustine, Florida, which I understand your family has visited, and you have a fairly good idea of what Techna Planet is like, at least in terms of architecture. We are 613 years older than Planet Earth, however, so our buildings and homes tend to reflect that age difference, even though our people take great pride in them and keep them in good repair. Where you will see a big difference is in technology. We have a vast underground subway system that serves virtually every section of our city/state, so you rarely see above ground transportation other than an occasional bicycle. No cars or trucks on the streets. A few people do own private transporters, but they are certainly not the norm. What you will see are many more pedestrians, especially in the shopping areas. Our people love to walk and window shop, not unlike New Yorkers, I might add. You should also know, by the way, that there are at least four other inhabited planets besides Earth and Techna, but their civilizations are nowhere near as advanced."

"Amazing," Ken said. "And we thought we were the only ones. Are you certain there are not more than just the six inhabited planets, including yours, Thor?"

"No, I am not sure. Four are what we have discovered as we travel through space. I would be very surprised if there are not many more out there, actually."

"Thor, where do your people get their food?" Rose wanted to know.

"We grow all of it, Rose. A great deal of open farm land surrounds the city. It is owned by private farmers and ranchers whose job it is to provide food of all types."

"How many cities are there on Techna Planet?"

"Only one major city, Ken. There are many small villages, of course, but we are essentially a single city/state/country, on a planet roughly one-tenth the size of Earth."

"What about religion?" Rose asked.

"There is no formal religion as yet, therefore no churches. We do not prohibit religion; it just seems there has never been a need. Our people are taught ethics and high moral standards from a very early age, and most of them respect each other's rights and property. Thus, while crime is not at zero level, there is very little of it. Citizens who do break one of our laws soon find themselves before the Commander of their district—or perhaps even the Prime Minister. If found guilty, they are stripped of all rights and sent to Prison Planet, usually for life."

"But didn't you say, a few minutes ago, that no one can incarcerate a Techna citizen?" Ken asked.

"No, Sir. I said no one *from your country could incarcerate a Techna citizen*. And that is true; only a high Techna official can do it and, incidentally, that official—me for example—can levy punishment on a Technian for breaking one of your laws, if it is a law we support."

"Ah, there's the catch, Commander. It seems to me that you support very few of our laws."

"Forgive me, Counselor but I must take issue with that claim. It is true we do not support your right to wage war on another country, such as Iraq, without cause. But I think we have great respect for your laws."

"Can you be more specific?"

"Well, laws covering fraud, illegal drug sales, murder, rape, interference with the work of a Government agency by corporations, abuse of power by Government officials, to name a few. There are many more. The major difference, in my view, is that we carry out penalties much more swiftly and with greater finality. As a case in point, your Government imposed death penalties in more than 3,500 capital crimes, yet executed very few—even allowing many death row convicts to languish in prison for up to fifteen years. Your way is not justice in our minds. And it is certainly not at all effective. You cannot have true justice, or force compliance with laws, without certain, timely enforcement. We have applied the same philosophy to eradication of illicit drug activity. We find the guilty parties and take them out. As you put it, we do not fool around. We have taken immediate action in all of the law violations I just mentioned, and will continue to do so."

"Ummm. I see your point, Commander. As I said earlier, I would love to have the power and the enforcement freedom you have."

"Sir, I can understand your frustration. I, too, wish for that. There are simply too many obstacles to law enforcement in your system. It needs to be simplified; we believe that can be accomplished in time. Now, I want to thank you and Rose for a wonderful lunch and the chance to get acquainted and, since my beautiful future wife has offered to show me the rest of your lovely home and your back yard garden, I ask for a brief recess to spend time with her."

"Oh, of course, Thor," Rose said. "When you return we will have a little dessert, and perhaps you can meet Sarah's brother and sisters."

* * *

Sarah and Thor walked arm in arm from room to room, and Thor was very impressed. The furnishings in every one were exquisite and expensive, though done in an understated way, but the thing that impressed him the most was how immaculate the house was. At one point in the tour, Sarah paused at the doorway to one of the second floor bedrooms. "This was my room, dear man," she said. "Do you like it? It could be our room tonight."

"I would love it," he responded, taking her in his arms, "just as I love you. He kissed her passionately. But, as we discussed earlier, it would be better if we did not sleep together here. I know I would be more comfortable with that arrangement."

"I've already discussed that with my mother. She is not keen on the idea but gave her permission."

"Thank you, honey, but I really think we should respect your parent's traditions and wait. But you know what?"

"What?"

"I think I will marry you. I love your parents, and you are not so bad yourself."

She held him tight and looked up at him smiling. "Who are you kidding, dear man? Break our engagement and I will have my father sue you for breach of contract and affection. As you can see, he is a very mean lawyer. There is no way you are going to escape."

Thor laughed. "Not to worry, Sarah. There is no escape for you, either. By the way, your father was only doing his duty to protect you. I liked that very much, and your mother....She is nothing like I expected. She is really a very sweet person."

"Yes, she is. But did you see how she watched you when you were talking to Daddy? She simply let him do the dirty work of checking you out. Fortunately for you she liked everything you said, otherwise, I wouldn't give a nickel for what was left of you. She can be a real tigress. Shall we have a look at the back yard?"

"I would love to get you alone in the back yard."

"No chance, dear. I think my brother and sisters are waiting to give you the once-over. I just heard their voices. We just have time for one quick look at the garden, then we must return to the inquisition."

Thor feigned disappointment. "Well, alright, but I would rather just be alone with you."

* * *

When they returned to the dining room after their brief walk in the garden, Thor met six additional members of the Malloy family for the first time. There was James, the Malloy's only son, and his wife, Carol; Celia Malloy Brightmann, Sarah's sister, and her husband, Kurt Brightmann; and Ellen Malloy Miller, also Sarah's sister, and her husband, Peter Miller. Ken made the introductions, and said, "just so you know, Thor, James is the oldest in our family and a partner of my law firm. He and Carol have three kids, Mark, Adam and Melissa, whom you will meet eventually. Celia came next. She and Kurt own a very successful Mercedes automobile dealership here in Brookline, But no children so far. They are hoping and so are we. Last but not least is Ellen, who is two years older than Sarah. She and Pete have two girls, Hannah, who is the oldest at six, and Elle who just turned four. Pete is also a partner in our firm, which specializes in corporate law, almost exclusively."

"Guys, Rose and I have had a wonderful session with Thor and approve of him one hundred percent. As you all know, he is from another Planet, as incredible as that sounds. I find him to be well educated and extremely sharp. He, and the large contingent of agents he commands, have caused quite a stir in our world, primarily in Washington, which certainly needs stirring. While some of his methods are questionable under our laws, no one can argue with his success. We wish him and our beloved Sarah great happiness, and welcome him into our family. Hope you all will do the same. Thor, anything you care to add?"

"Ken, I would just say to everyone assembled that discovering Sarah was the most wonderful event in my life. I would have been happy just with her because she is so very special. But today I find that she comes with a beautiful dowry called family. I truly look forward to getting to know all of you much better than is possible in just this one short first meeting. Beyond that, I thank all of you for allowing me to share in your lives. Ken has had me on the witness stand for several hours and can fill you in on details about me. However I will happily answer as many of your questions as I can."

Everyone laughed at his characterization of the gathering, having been exposed to Ken's inquisitions themselves many times.

"Thor, please don't feel that you have been singled out," James said. "I work for him and get this all the time. Welcome to the family."

"Right," said Celia. "But if anything he picks on his daughters more."

"Celia! How can you say that?" Ken responded, feigning hurt feelings.

"Because it is true, Daddy. But we all love you just the same."

"Now, shush, all of you," Rose interjected, signaling the caterers to start serving, "before this becomes a big argument. let's all enjoy some nice dessert, alright?"

As they all waded into the pies and cakes that quickly appeared on the table, Thor and Sarah were bombarded with questions. Where would they live? Would it be on Planet Earth or on Techna Planet? When could they see Thor's transporter and his starships? When could they go for a ride in them? How was he able to accomplish so much in so short a time? Dozens and dozens of questions, and the time simply flew by. Ken tried to intercept some of the questions on more sensitive issues by saying that Thor could not discuss many aspects of his work. But his two law partners pressed on anyway, until Thor finally reiterated what he told Ken earlier: namely that there were aspects of his work he could not discuss with anyone. That seemed to satisfy them, and the questioning ended.

"I have just one more, Thor. As I understand it, You are next in line to be Prime Minister of Techna Planet. When do you take over that position?"

"Upon my father's death, James. However he is only sixty years old and is in very good health. Therefore, I anticipate it will be many more years before I must face that eventuality. One never knows, of course, but my father comes from a family noted for very long lives; his own father was 92 when he passed on."

"I see. But when the time comes, you will have no choice but to accept the mantle?"

"No, I do have a choice, but if I decide not to accept the challenge I would break a tradition several hundred years old. It would take some very unusual circumstances to make me do that."

"Yes, that is quite understandable, Thor. One more question: What is your formal education?"

"James, I have a Level One degree in Business Administration from Techna University. That corresponds to a Bachelor degree here. I also have a Level Two degree in Aeronautical Engineering, and a Level Three degree, or Doctorate, in Government Science. Finally, I hold type certificates to fly all aircraft in Techna's fleet, including the largest starships."

"Wow, that is very impressive, Thor. Very impressive, indeed."

"Thank you, James. But it is not unusual. While most agents do not fly, many hold similar degrees. To carry out our mission we must be schooled in many disciplines."

"Does the prosecution rest?" Sarah wanted to know. "You have been grilling my poor husband-to-be for hours. Maybe he has some questions for all of you."

"Very well, my daughter. the prosecution rests. Thor, I am impressed by your knowledge of our country's problems, and by your willingness to make a concerted effort to solve them. I am sure I do not need to tell you the magnitude of that challenge. And then, too, I understand that you are about to take on corporate involvement in Government affairs, as well as the greatest ponzi scheme in this country: televangelism, not to mention illegal drugs. My God, Man, you are either a superman or you have a huge army of agents. I don't see how else you can accomplish all that you have set course to accomplish."

"Counselor, I do not think of myself as being a superman, as you put it. But please do not under-estimate the powers I have or the latitude I have in handing out punishment. Those powers allow me to operate very effectively, with a staff of only 2000 agents. I am confident we will accomplish all our goals here."

"Yes, I believe you will, and I welcome you to our family. Your goals are very worthy, and our problems have been so long in need of change."

"Thank you all. I am proud to be given the opportunity to join your fine family. I love Sarah more than you may ever realize. She has accepted me for what I am and for what I have to do. She is truly an amazing young woman, and I am incredibly fortunate to have found her. I will never do anything to hurt her, and now I see clearly where her beauty and brains come from."

"Well put, Thor," Rose said. "We love all our children, but Sarah is our baby girl, so we can readily understand why you chose her. But I warn you, we probably spoiled her too much. She can be very demanding at times."

"Mama, Please!" Sarah objected. "You are embarrassing me."

"Honey, it's true. Girls should be spoiled because they have such great responsibility in life, what with the burden of running the home, bearing children and raising them, and all. To me it is a compliment, not a criticism. I think we spoiled Celia and Ellen just as much as you."

* * *

Sarah was a long time getting to sleep. She loved feeling Thor beside her in bed and was disappointed that he was not with her on this night. She understood his reasons for choosing a separate room. Most American men his age would have jumped at the chance to sleep with "their woman," even under their parent's roof. Thor was different, very different, and she loved him for it. The pillow talk she had planned, much of which centered around her curiosity concerning how he felt about her family, would keep. With that realization her eyes finally closed and she fell into deep slumber.

But around 4:00 a.m. she was awake again, thinking about him, knowing he was just in the next room, wanting to be with him. Unable to stand it any longer, she left her bed and padded out of her room, in her nightgown, on bare feet, and in seconds she lay beside him. He did not stir. Nor did she detect any change in his breathing, which was deep and soft. But then he rolled over and was practically nose to nose with her, and his eyes were wide open. "Oh, Thor," she whispered. "I didn't mean to wake you; I just had to be next to you."

"That is alright, honey. I was awake, just thinking about how wonderful your mother and father are, and your sisters! Wow! I never saw two more beautiful women. They are simply stunning, and so feminine. Maybe I chose the wro...."

"Before he could finish the sentence Sarah's hand was over his mouth. "What is this? What did you just say? Thor, please, you can't mean that!" She tried to wiggle out of his grasp but he held her very tight. And then she realized his body was shaking with uncontrollable laughter, and she began to pummel him with her tiny fists. The only way he could stop her was to put his mouth on hers until he felt her relax in his grip.

"That was really bad, Thor. I mean really bad. How could you?"

"Sarah, I am sorry. I just could not resist. I know you were probably wondering what I thought of your family, so I decided to play a little joke. Do you not yet know there could never be anyone else but you in my life? I love you and only you, angel."

"Are you sure, Thor, really sure?"

"Absolutely positive," he answered then kissed her again, long and passionately, and finally they fell asleep, locked in each others arms.

*   *   *

Thor awoke early as usual, to find Sarah gone from the room. Thinking that perhaps she was still a bit agitated by his prank, he quickly showered, shaved and dressed, then went looking for her. Much to his relief he found her in the kitchen with her mother, two sisters and her sister-in-law. They were busy as could be preparing breakfast, and all the while they were chattering and giggling like little girls. When Sarah saw him she stopped what she was doing and came to him. "Hi," she said. "Did you miss me?"

"Yes, I did, honey. I thought maybe you were still upset about last night."

"Oh, silly, of course not. I'm over that. Want some tea?"

"I would love some, thank you."

She handed a steaming cup and said, "The guys are in the den, waiting for you. Breakfast will be ready soon."

"Thank you, Sarah. You look beautiful this morning," Thor said, then walked away to find the Malloy men.

When he was out of earshot, Sarah asked, "Well ladies, I have to know. What do you think of my man?"

Carol was first to answer. "Sarah, I think he is the most beautiful man I have ever seen. I looked at his tightly curled hair and steel grey eyes and just melted right down into my shoes. God, but he is gorgeous, and I am soooo envious."

"Would you trade James for him, Carol?"

"Never, Sarah. I chose James. I still choose him."

Next to answer was Celia. "Sarah, he is one scary dude, if you ask me. He has so much power—such awesome power. One wonders whether he will use it for good, or will it go to evil causes. Would he be too much for one woman to handle? I don't know, but I agree with Carol; he is very, very handsome—a Greek God almost. I am very happy for you, but he is not my type at all."

"Ellen, what do you think?"

"Sarah, I can see why you fell for him. A powerful man is super exciting to most women, including me. Yet he seems gentle and caring, and there is no question he is madly in love with you. I think he will make a very good husband and, if you are lucky enough to have his children, a wonderful father. I don't agree that he might dominate your marriage; he will want you to be truly an equal partner. My one question is how you will deal with his work. From what you have said, he does not talk much about it. My guess is he can't share much about it with anyone, including his wife. That would be a huge problem for me, but I gather you are comfortable with such an arrangement. Correct?"

"Yes, Ellen. It is. I know he is extremely powerful, but I believe he will always use his power for good, not evil. And when we are together, it is so wonderful. Not knowing what he did all day concerns me not one bit. What matters is how much we enjoy each other's company."

"Mama, what do you think? "

"He is a fine man, honey. A beautiful, fine man. He will always be good to you, provide for you and love you. I pity any one who crosses him, but believe strongly that that will never apply to you. With you he is putty in your hands. Let him do his job without your interference. Take care of his every need in your home. The rest of your life together will flow just fine."

"I thank you all for your opinions," Sarah said. "They mean a lot." What she did not tell them was how relieved she was that none of the women would be a real threat to her. After Thor's playful little prank last night she had been feeling a bit insecure.

*   *   *

Thor used the breakfast time to study members of the Malloy family, while simultaneously joining in the lively discussion of a whole variety of subjects, from politics to raising children. James Malloy was a carbon copy of his father, not only in looks, but in how he thought and acted. He was most vocal when the subject concerned some point of law, but said very little otherwise.

His beautiful wife, Carol, was a tall platinum blonde with green eyes and a lovely body that gave no evidence to having given birth to three children. Whereas James was the quiet one, she was bubbly and very vocal on many subjects.

Sarah's older sister, Celia, was no less beautiful than Carol. She had brown eyes and dark brown hair which she wore long. She was dressed to the nines in a very expensive emerald-green gown, and wore an over abundance of gold and diamond jewelry around her neck, on both wrists and virtually every finger of both hands. Her husband, Kurt, appeared to be perhaps ten years older than his wife. He had blonde hair and watery blue eyes that seemed hard to Thor. He was dressed in Black: black slacks, black shirt open wide at the neck, polished black loafers with tassels, and he, too, had adorned himself with gold around his neck and on both wrists. Thor thought them both much too flashy for a family breakfast gathering.

Sarah's sister, Ellen, two years her senior, was virtually a twin to Sarah. She had the same auburn hair and wore it short like Sarah, and the same lovely blue eyes. She did not possess the lovely body of Carol or Celia, yet there was about her the epitome of feminine loveliness. As with Carol, there was no sign she had borne two children. Her husband, Peter, had black hair that was slightly receding at the temples, and brown eyes. Thor judged him to be about thirty-five, yet the tips of his sideburns were already tinged with grey. There was a warm and friendly demeanor about him, and a ready smile that Thor found pleasant.

All in all, they seem to be a class family, he thought, though he had already decided to withhold further judgment until he had an opportunity to talk to each of them one on one.

After breakfast, everyone pitched in to clean up and put things away. Following that, the Brightmanns, Millers and James

Malloys said their goodbyes and left to return to their own homes. Sarah disappeared with her mother, and Thor and Ken wandered back to the living room. "So, Thor, I hope we did not overwhelm you with all the questions we threw at you."

"Not at all, Sir. I would have done the same if the situation had been reversed. You have a fine family, I think, and I enjoyed meeting all of them, including you and Rose, of course."

"Good. Sarah tells us you would like to take us to the Cape for dinner at the Coonamessett Inn today. I gather you mean to fly us down there?"

"Yes. I understand it is one of your favorite restaurants, and it is certainly one of mine."

"True enough. We don't get there often enough anymore because of the driving time. So we accept your gracious offer and are really looking forward to it."

"Wonderful. I thought we would board the transporter about six-thirty p.m., if that is alright. Our reservations are for seven o'clock.

"Isn't that cutting it kind of close? Falmouth is eighty-five miles from here, you know."

"Yes, I know. We will be fine."

Ken nodded and said, "I am sure you're a better judge of this than I. We will be ready."

*   *   *

At a few minutes before their departure time the four of them left the Malloy house and strolled across Lee Street to the golf course. When they were a few feet from the transporter landing site, the little aircraft suddenly returned to V-mode, with Jens standing in his normal location beside the open hatch.

He bowed to Thor and said, "Good evening, Commander, Sarah. I trust you have had a most relaxing week-end."

"We have, Jens. I want you to meet Sarah's parents, Ken and Rose Malloy. Ken and Rose, Jens has been my personal pilot for more years than I can remember. I would be lost without him."

After the introductions Jens said, "the ship is ready for boarding, Commander."

Sarah led the way into the cabin and helped her parents into forward-facing seats, then with their seat belts. Then she and Thor took seats across the table from them as the cabin hatch closed silently. Thor explained that the transporter would take off vertically very, very fast, and asked his guests not to be afraid. Then he gave his customary, "Ready when you are Jens."

"Very well, Commander," came the prompt reply, and they were instantly airborne.

"Holy Mackerel!" exclaimed Ken and Rose almost at the same instant, and their eyes were wide with wonder as they gripped their armrests tightly. Then Rose said, "is this remarkable or what? What an experience!"

"How long will this flight take, Thor?" Ken wanted to know.

Thor was about to answer when Jen's voice came over the intercom. "Prepare for landing in one minute, Commander."

Thor looked at Ken, held out both arms and smiled warmly. "I think the total flight time will be about two minutes," he said.

"I am beginning to understand how you get so much work done, Commander. This is an amazing aircraft."

*   *   *

The Coonamessett Maitre d' took them to the same table Thor and Sarah had on their first date. It was not a coincidence, actually; Thor had requested it specifically when he made reservations.

"Oh, Thor, darling, look, they have given us *our table.* Isn't this romantic?"

He smiled and gave her a loving hug.

When their waiter came, Ken insisted on treating with champagne in honor of Thor and Sarah's engagement, and ordered a bottle of Dom Perignon. Thor ordered little neck clams in a broth of roasted garlic butter, chourico, leeks, roasted tomatoes, fresh herbs and a crisp Frei Brothers chardonnay for all. When the champagne had been poured, Ken raised his glass and said, "To our little Sarah. May her life be filled with joy. And to her fiancé, Thor Berksten: If I were to have picked a mate for Sarah it would have been Thor. Rose and I wish you both great happiness."

While they enjoyed the champagne and clams, and were waiting on their entrees—baked Chatham Scrod for Sarah and her mother and Lobster for Ken and Thor--the conversation turned to where Thor and Sarah would make their home.

"Daddy, we did look at some property in Southern California when we visited San Diego, but nothing appealed to me. My heart is in the East, and I think Thor's is, too. So I think we have pretty much decided to live in the Boston area—maybe even Brookline, if we find something affordable. Actually, New York would be better for me as long as I am working—we could even stay in the apartment you gave me, for that matter."

"What do you say to that, Thor?" Ken wanted to know.

"It really does not matter to me, Ken, as long as Sarah is happy, and I think she would be happier in Boston , if and when she decides to give up her CTS career. But upon reflection, life would be a bit simpler if we had a place to keep the transporter, which is like my shoes to me—indispensible, so maybe someplace in the country, perhaps Connecticut, would be good. We will just have to check out all the possibilities."

"That's the way to do it, Thor," Rose said. "Make a list of what's important and be guided by it."

"Thanks, Rose. That makes good sense. We would love a home similar to yours, a lovely, solid older home would be perfect. Above all, it has to be affordable because we will pay cash."

"Well," Rose said, "We will keep our eyes out for one in Brookline. Having you close by would be wonderful."

"Thank you, Mama," Sarah said. "We think that would be nice, too."

"Thor, you mentioned the transporter, " Ken said. "I can see how much you depend on it. Just how fast is it?"

"Well, you do not get a feel for its speed on short trips like the one we just took, but it is capable of 5000 miles an hour, as Sarah knows. When we flew from New York to San Diego—a flight of just under 2900 miles—it took just thirty minutes."

"Amazing. Plus, you don't need to check into airports and go through that hassle."

"Correct."

"Now, I've been meaning to ask when the troop withdrawal from Iraq begins."

"Tomorrow morning, in fact. We have loaned the President five new Techna starships for use in transporting military personnel. Each ship has capacity for 500 soldiers with full battle gear, and will make the round trip from here to Iraq and back—about 12,000 miles—in a little less than two hours, cruising at an altitude of 100,000 feet."

"Wow. That means 2500 guys and gals get home every two hours," Ken exclaimed.

"Yes, and since each starship has three complete flight crews on board we are prepared to operate 24 hours a day until the mission is accomplished."

"So what does that mean? That is, how long to get them all home?"

"Well, I am told there are 160,000 soldiers over there, plus an additional 125,000 civilian contractor employees, so probably about ten days."

"Man, that is really something. Thor. The President has predicted it would take months. But where will you put them?"

"The U.S. military commander will call the shots on that. The troops will be disbursed to various bases around the U.S. Where we take them will be at his discretion. "

"Daddy, as you know, the really sad thing is that few of them will have jobs waiting," Sarah added.

"That is right. If you just turn them loose to get along as best they can—at a time when there are so few jobs anyway, I think that is a terrible injustice. So I have recommended to the President that any soldiers without a civilian job to come home to be kept on duty as border guards along the Mexico/U.S. border, at full military pay, of course. He has agreed, and even intends to provide temporary housing for them so they can be with their families down there."

"Smart move, " Ken said. "That way, we accomplish two goals: give the soldiers paid work, and protect our borders."

"I have a question, Thor, if it not too personal."

"Of course, Rose. What is it?"

"How do you support yourself and your agents? Do you receive money from your father?"

"Well, indirectly, yes. He cannot fund our operation using Techna money, because it has no value here. So we had to find ways to raise our own funds."

"I see. And just how do you do that, Thor?"

"Well, one of our programs here is to stamp out illegal drugs, and we have been quite successful. Whenever we intercept a drug shipment we destroy the drugs and confiscate the money. So far we have confiscated more than three hundred million dollars worth of drugs at street value, along with more than one hundred million dollars in cash. That money is sent to a bank account controlled by my father as Prime Minister on Techna Planet. He distributes it back to us on an as needed basis."

"But isn't that stealing, honey?" Sarah asked.

"In a sense, yes, but money is the life blood of the drug cartels. We are convinced that if they do not get it they will eventually go out of business, which is exactly our goal."

"Well, that does make sense, Thor," Ken said. "It is almost a Robin Hood story. Take from the rich to help those in need."

"Yes, Sir. That is how we see it."

Ken looked at his watch. "Oh, boy, ten o'clock. I didn't realize it was so late. I am sorry Thor for asking so many questions. It's just that I find your life very fascinating. I could go on all night, actually. Rose and I have thoroughly enjoyed this time alone with you and Sarah, but I guess it's about time we headed back to the house."

"Sure, Ken. By the way, I really do not mind the questions. You have a right to know as much about me and my work as I am at liberty to tell you." He motioned to the waiter for the check, paid it, and they left the Coonamessett's dining room.

*　*　*

It was well after midnight when they returned to Sarah's Park Avenue apartment. The Malloy's had insisted they come in for coffee (tea for Thor) before leaving Brookline, and that led to more conversation—almost all of it centered around Thor's work, this time his plans to rid Government of corporate involvement. That had been the one subject not previously covered. Thor explained as best he could, without divulging too much, what he planned to do to solve this problem, and discovered, much to his surprise, that his future father-in-law, whose entire law practice had to do with corporations, agreed with him. Now in the comfort of Sarah's home he settled into a large lounge chair in her living room.

Sarah sat on the chair's arm and put her arm around his shoulders. "Are you tired, dear man?" She wanted to know.

"Yes, a little, honey. But it is a pleasant tiredness—a relieved tiredness."

"Relieved? Were you uptight over the visit to my parents?"

"Not exactly uptight. Just a bit uncertain about how they would feel about me. But they were wonderful. I really like them a lot. Glad we went."

"I am too. And I thought you were pretty wonderful, yourself. So many questions, some pretty stupid, if I do say so, yet you handled all of them calmly and without showing any impatience. I was very proud of you."

Thor took her hand in his. "Thank you, my love. You know, I really feel sorry for Kurt and Peter."

"Oh, why?"

"Because neither of them chose the most beautiful Malloy daughter. But then, that is my great good fortune."

Sarah rested her head against his and was quiet for a long time. Then she kissed him on the forehead and said. "Ready for bed?"

"Yes, dear heart. More than ready."

CHAPTER TEN

Going Home

Withdrawal from Iraq commenced on Monday, April 5, 2010, as planned. American military personnel on the ground there had previously been divided into groups according to the U.S. Base to which they would be sent. One group, numbering about 50,000 soldiers, did not go to a holding barracks, however. It went directly to Afghanistan to beef up military strength there. Those soldiers were not at all happy, but what could they do but follow orders? The other groups—consisting of 110,000 military personnel plus 50,000 civilian contractor employees waited anxiously in their assigned barracks at the Baghdad airfield for transportation home. They had not been told what form that transportation would take.

At 0700 hours, five large, very strange looking aircraft settled silently onto the tarmac of the airfield, and there was an announcement over the base intercom for the first 2,500 soldiers to assemble on the field. There was no need to make the announcement a second time.

When that first contingent caught sight of the huge black aircraft, it did not take long for some one in line to identify them. "Those are starships!" Someone said in an excited voice.

"Yeah," said another. "Techna Planet starships. I've read about them."

"Wow, we're going home in spaceships!"

"Yeah? How do you know? Maybe they're sending us to another planet."

"Nah, man. We're going home. I know it!"

*   *   *

Following directions from military police officers stationed at strategic locations, the long line of waiting soldiers soon divided into five lines of 500 each, and each sub-group moved swiftly toward the boarding stairs located underneath and at the center of their starship. At the top of the stairs, another MP directed arriving soldiers to their seats, saying, "Fasten seatbelts immediately, we take off the minute the last man boards."

Weary young male soldiers, soon caught sight of a beautiful, dark haired woman who waited patiently at the front of the starship's cabin, and whistles and catcalls echoed loudly through the ship. She smiled and waved, and when the last passenger took his seat, held up her arms to get the attention of everyone on board. "Good morning and congratulations," she said. "You are finally going home." Her next words were drowned out by the loud roar that went up from the happy soldiers. She waited patiently for them to quiet down again, smiling all the while. When the gleeful roar subsided she continued, "I know you are all anxious to be on your way but can anyone tell me how long this trip will take?"

A hundred voices tried to answer her question at once. One soldier said, "I think it will take about twelve hours—that's how long it took to get over here."

Another man said, "naw, this ship is faster. I can tell. I say ten hours max."

"Six hours is my guess," said another, and so it went for several minutes.

"Well, those are great answers," their hostess said. "But would you believe just one hour.? Yes, that is right. One hour. As you can see, this is no ordinary airplane. This is what we call a starship, a very fast vehicle designed for travel through space.

My Government has loaned your Government five of these starships just so you will get home in the absolute shortest amount of time. You must buckle your seatbelts and keep them fastened throughout the flight, but then, I am pleased to say, you will have just one more hour to wait before you are back in the United States.

In a moment we will lift off vertically with a thrust that will drive all of you deep into your seats. Do not be afraid. This is our normal takeoff method. Now, please sit back, relax and enjoy your journey, and my best to all of you." She raised a mobile phone to her mouth and spoke, and instantly they were airborne. The four other starships lifted off at exactly the same moment.

*   *   *

Late in the afternoon of April 12, Thor sat patiently in the White House Oval Office until new President Fields said goodbye to his last official visitor of the day, Senate Majority Leader, Edward Reynolds. While he waited unseen he listened as Reynolds described progress on the President's most urgent project: national health care for all Americans. The news on this vital program was not good, and the President's displeasure showed clearly on his face. As soon as the Majority Leader left, Thor stood and made himself visible.

"Ah, Commander. Good of you to wait. I noticed you there, but Reynolds' report was rather urgent to me. Sorry."

"Not a problem, Mr. President. Forgive me for being nosey, but you are not getting much cooperation from the Republican side of Congress, are you?"

"None at all on this matter. It is obvious that they see the possible failure of my healthcare program as my personal downfall. And they are getting a lot of help from conservative, 'blue dog,' Democrats. I expected more cooperation from them. We really need their vote to stop a Republican filibuster."

"Yes, Sir, I know, but, of course, corporations who provide private health care are behind all of this. They stand to lose billions if you succeed in getting a public option passed. I am sure it is no secret to you that they finance Republican political campaigns, or that they have the money to fight you to the death."

"So true, Thor. So very true. It is, as we say, a predicament."

"A predicament, but not an impossible one, Mr. President."

"Then I take it you see a spot of blue in this otherwise dismal gray sky."

"I see several, Sir."

"I am listening."

"Well, for one, have you considered pulling a President Truman on them—nationalize the healthcare industry, in other words?"

"He didn't do that, Thor. He took over the railroads when their union threatened to strike, and then later he did the same thing with the coal miners. But how are those examples relevant?"

"They are relevant because they show that you have the power to do the same thing with health care. They constitute precedents, Mr. President."

"Humm. Yes I see your point. That might just work. But that's only one idea. You claim to have others."

"Two more, Sir. First, get some laws passed to deprive those corporations of many of their most profitable tax deductions. Corporations have become much too powerful because of tax advantages, and need to be taken down several notches. They have far more privileges than your average American anyway. This is a step you can take that applies to all businesses, not just to those involved in healthcare."

"Yes, Thor, that is a good option, and I will consider it seriously. And your third idea?"

"Let Techna Force 20 deal with the recalcitrant Republican congress—and the Blue Dog Democrats. Just say the word and I can assure you of a 100% vote in favor of your health plan."

"Now that one is very tempting, Commander. Very tempting, indeed. Let me give all of your suggestions some serious thought. I promise to get back to you very soon. Now, was healthcare your real reason for being here today?"

"No, Mr. President. I came to give you a report on troop withdrawal from Iraq."

"How is that project coming, Thor? I could use some good news today."

"Sir, I am pleased to report that the mission has been accomplished. Counting the time needed to load five hundred soldiers and their gear, plus the time to disembark that number of troops in the U.S., each of the five starships completed one round trip between the United States and Baghdad, and lifted off with another load of returnees every three hours. Thus, during each twenty-four hours of operation, our fleet brought 20,000 American soldiers home. The entire operation air-lifted all civilian contractor workers, plus 110,000 happy service men and women out of Iraq in just eight days. That is the good news. The not- so- good news is that many thousands of those soldiers lost their civilian jobs and will soon have no means of support, as you and I have previously discussed."

"And your suggestion was to send them to the Mexican border as guards, Thor. Do you still recommend that?"

"Yes, I do, Sir, and provide housing there for their families."

"Then that is what we will do." He arose from his chair, walked around the huge desk and shook Thor's hand. "Great job, Commander. Thank you for taking it on and for completing it in such a timely manner."

"You are welcome. Mr. President. I hope to bring you similar good news on Afghanistan very soon."

"Have you located Bin Laden? If so, that would be great news indeed."

"No, not exactly. But we have narrowed the search to a very small section, so it will not be long."

"Well, Commander, I do not need to remind you that Afghanistan is a greater worry to me than Iraq ever was. I long for the day when we can bring our troops home from there as well. I was not involved then but I know it is a far worse place in which to fight an enemy than Iraq. From what I have read, it is a lot like Vietnam, where we almost never saw our enemy either, where our men could be surrounded without knowing it. I understand we must go from cave to cave in those impossible Afghan mountains. That must be terrible for our soldiers. "

"I understand, Mr. President. It is a terrible place, so difficult to travel in and establish communication and supply lines, plus al Qaeda fighters hide behind every rock. But we are gaining ground on them every day, leaving fewer and fewer places for them to conceal themselves. I think we will corner Bin Laden very soon. Then you shall have your wish come true."

"Good. Now, when do you and your lovely fiancé leave for Techna?"

"In just four days, Sir, the 16th. Truls Heyerdahl will be in charge while I am away."

"Yes, you told me. He is an excellent leader and will do well, I think."

"Agreed. If you decide to call on TF20 for help with the health care problem, or anything else, in my absence please contact him through Manta. He is prepared for that assignment."

"Thank you. I will do that."

*   *   *

After leaving the White House, Thor flew immediately to Sardine Mountain. During the flight he contacted Truls Heyerdahl and Siran Missirian and arranged for them to meet him there. Their transporters and his arrived within minutes of one another. He and the two Group Captains went directly to the conference room.

"Good to see you both again," he said. "Sorry to intrude on your busy schedules, but I believe President Fields will ask for our help with the healthcare issue, and I want you to be prepared. Siran, I know you have been very active on this. What do you see as the primary roadblocks to passage of the program?"

"Commander, there is no question in my mind: the six huge health care corporations are the biggest problem. They have marshaled an army of well-financed lobbyists whose sole responsibility is to block every congressional move toward passage, and so far they are succeeding ."

Truls nodded in agreement. "There is a good chance they will lose billions of dollars if a public option becomes law, " he said. "Profit is their god, you know. They are not going to give up one cent without a fight."

"Yes, Truls, I agree. But in my opinion, human suffering should never be a source of profit for any business. Have you two gone into this problem far enough to have a plan?"

Siran and Truls exchanged knowing glances. "Yes, Sir," Siran responded. "We propose a three-pronged approach. The first prong will be to replace every member of congress who votes 'NO' on all democratic bills, with a double who really participates in deliberations. The second prong will be to do whatever it takes to neutralize powerful health care lobbyists."

"And the third prong?" Thor asked.

"The third prong will be for TF 20 to take control of the six health care corporations."

"Why should we do that, Siran?"

"Because, Commander, we are motivated by a desire to see that Americans get the health care they need, not by greed."

"Why not let the federal government run them?"

"Sir, the federal government has a very poor track record where business management is concerned. They are good at making laws, but terrible at administering them; they are even worse at managing businesses."

"I agree with Siran, Commander," said Truls. Replace the top thirty or forty executives in one of those companies and the effect should alter thinking at every level of the business."

"No doubt, Captain. But once we start taking over American corporations where do we stop?"

"Sir," Siran responded, "I think I can answer that question. We know the Federal Government is controlled by the energy industry, with its four major players; the health care industry, with six; and the banking and finance industry, with four. So if my math is correct we would need to take over just fourteen corporations to wrest control of Government from corporations and return it to the people, where it belongs. There are many other corporations, to be sure, but they lack the power their larger brothers can bring to bear on Government—even acting collectively."

"So you want TF20 to take control of all of those corporations, not just the health care sector?"

"Not right away, Commander. I think we will have to eventually, but my thrust at this time is gaining control of the health care industry. The need there is great for the American people. We can give them much better medical coverage at about the same amount the Government is paying now through Medicare. For one thing, those six health care insurance companies spend billions on personnel compensation and other administrative costs, whereas our costs for those items are much, much lower. I will have more precise figures when you return from Techna, but I believe the savings will help pay for greater health care coverage."

"I will be interested in your figures, Siran, but what you say makes sense, and it puts us in a much stronger position to protect Techna Planet."

"Right, Commander."

"Very well. Good work, both of you. I would like to review a detail plan when I return. Is that possible?"

"Definitely, Sir," they answered in unison. "We will be ready."

*   *   *

After the meeting, Thor returned to his office and called Sarah at her home. She answered immediately with a simple "Hello."

"Hello to you, dear Sarah. Are you well?"

"Oh, Thor," She said. "What a wonderful surprise. I walked in the door just this minute, and you cannot imagine how much it means to me to be greeted by your voice."

"It is the same with me, Sarah. Days are very long without you, and this has been one of the longest."

"You sound a bit tired, Thor."

"A little. We started the task of bringing all the troops back from Iraq on Monday, as you know. It went very well and they are safely home now. But there has been much criticism."

"Yes, my love, I heard. It has been all over the news. But don't worry, the critics are mainly a few conservative talking heads; they are against everything that doesn't originate with some Republican. Will this interfere with our trip to Techna?"

"No, no, dear heart. Not at all. In fact I am calling to see if you are ready to go."

"Almost. Just a few more things to pack. It's hard to know what to take and what not."

"Yes, I suppose so. Afraid I have almost no experience helping with that chore, but I am sure you will do just fine. I am thinking of coming for you tomorrow evening. We can have a going away bite to eat in that little Italian place in your building, then fly back to Roswell. Will that work for you?"

"It will, Thor. And I am so excited."

"As am I, my love. See you tomorrow."

*   *   *

Jens Petersen entered Thor's office just as he completed his call to Sarah. "Good afternoon, Commander," he said. "I came to tell you all is ready for the flight to Techna Friday morning."

"Good, Jens. Including the special precautions we discussed?"

"Yes, Sir. Our course and speed will never be displayed on navigation monitors. We will use our scrambled audio system on this journey; only you and I will have access to that."

"Well done, old friend. I do not expect any problems, but we must always be very careful never to disclose the location of Techna. It is just that, for the very first time, we will have a non-Technian on board one of our starships. Sarah is the last person I would suspect, and I really hate having to do this, but we must always act prudently. By the way, we will go to New York at six p.m. on the 15th, to pick her up."

"Very well, Commander. I will be ready."

*   *   *

Jens had no sooner left Thor's office when Truls Heyerdahl called. "Afternoon, Commander," he said. "We captured Osama Bin Laden and a hundred al Qaeda militia members in a blind canyon just north of Peshawar, Pakistan. From the looks of things they have had a base camp there for some time, which seems unbelievable. There is only one access to that canyon and we blocked it. The canyon walls are far too steep to climb so there was no way he and his band could escape. We have them all in custody now and are waiting for your instructions."

"Great news, Truls. I will notify President Fields. immediately. Stand by."

"Very well, Commander."

Thor put the phone down and walked swiftly to Manta's desk. "Tell Jens there is a change in plans, and to get the transporter ready immediately, please. I have to talk to the President right away."

*   *   *

Thirty minutes later he walked into the Oval Office, hoping the President would still be there. He was, and Jack Brill was with him. Thor made himself visible just as he entered, which startled the two men. "Sorry to intrude, Mr. President," he said, "but I have something that needs your urgent attention."

"Very well, Commander. What is it?"

"We have captured Osama Bin Laden. He and about one hundred of his al Qaeda fighters are in our custody in northeast Pakistan. What would you like us to do with them?"

"Commander, that is the best news I have had in ages. Is there an American army unit in that area, do you know?"

"Yes, Sir, there is. A battalion of the First Marine Division is about two miles from our location. Shall we turn our prisoners over to them?"

"That will work. Jack, please call Secretary Phillips, will you? I want him to handle this."

"Certainly, Mr. President."

Bertram Phillips came on the line quickly. "Bert, good news. We have Bin Laden. What? Yes, that's right, a unit of Techna Force 20 has him in custody. I am told there is a battalion of the First Marine Division there, and I'd like you to arrange for transfer of custody to them, okay? Yes, it is good news. Actually it's great news. When can you do this?"

"Right now, Mr. President. Is it alright with you if I have them sent to Guantanimo?"

"Yes, until we decide how to proceed."

"Very well, Sir."

While the President was talking to his Secretary of Defense, Thor stepped outside the Oval Office and informed Truls Heyerdahl of the prisoner turn-over plan by cell phone.

"Commander, it is too bad we can not deal with Bin Laden in our way. The American legal system is too slow and cumbersome, and may well put Bin Laden in some fancy prison for life. That is not justice."

"Yes, Truls, I agree. Keep in mind that no decision has yet been made on his punishment. He is simply being incarcerated until he can be dealt with appropriately. I intend to see that we are involved and that he pays a dear price."

"I like the sound of that, Commander. We will turn him and his al-Qaeda bunch over to the marines as ordered."

*   *   *

Jack Brill had to fight to conceal his astonishment over the obviously warm and friendly relationship between the President and Thor Berksten. The meeting had answered all his questions concerning the great change that had recently come over Fields, for he was absolutely certain now that the man seated in the President's chair was not Howard Fields at all. He had been suspicious immediately because Field's behavior changed so uncharacteristically and so suddenly. No man goes from obstinate and stupid to cooperative and intelligent that quickly without reason. He had worked many years for Fields, and had never found him to be reasonable on any matter. But suddenly he had become another person entirely, mild, even-tempered—even smart. Jack knew Howard Fields was not smart. He had always been an oil industry puppet, bought and paid for, and they controlled his every action and word by pulling his strings.

But though Brill had tried very hard to uncover the reason for Field's magic transformation, it continued to elude him... until tonight, that is. Tonight, in this first meeting between the President and Berksten that Jack had attended, the reason became clear. Here was Thor Berksten, in the same room with Fields, and they were communicating like old friends. Before, Fields had gone ballistic at the very sight of Berksten. Here was Berksten suggesting that Bin Laden be sent to Guantanimo, and Fields agreeing to that without an argument. Berksten must be behind this, he reasoned. He has either put the fear of God in Fields, or has replaced him with someone who looks like Fields. Troubling as all this was, Jack had to agree that what he saw was a very pleasant change in Fields demeanor and behavior, changes he believed he would never see.

He was pleased yet troubled at the same time. Technically, an imposter was now in the White House, and no one knew who he really was, or where he came from. Was he even an American?

Or was he a Techna agent from outer space? Jack's first impulse was to report what he now knew to the Secret Service. The presence of an imposter in the highest office in the land was probably the most serious violation of the laws of the land that he could imagine.

On the other hand, much good had been accomplished since this 'new' President came on the scene. That, plus the change in Congress, the execution of all death-row prisoners, the withdrawal of troops from Iraq, and now the capture of Bin Laden—these were great accomplishments far beyond old Field's ability. He would never have succeeded in completing any of them if, in fact, he even wanted to. This change in Presidents has done no harm—only good, so why reverse it? Jack thought. Perhaps the country needed just such a shake-up. After all, it had been the cash cow of huge corporations who controlled it—and old Fields—for years. If Thor Berksten could eliminate that problem he could be the greatest hero America ever had.

I think he will do just that, Brill concluded, and he decided to keep what he had just discovered to himself. These could be the most exciting years I have ever spent in Washington, he said to himself.

* * *

As soon as he left the Oval Office, Thor called Sarah, hoping she had Sam Fischer's home phone number. She did and quickly found it for him.

"Is anything wrong, dear?"

"No, darling. In fact things are great. We captured Bin Laden in Pakistan today, and I just left the Oval Office where I gave the President the good news. Now I want Sam to know."

"That is wonderful news, Thor. I am so proud of you. Does this mean you will be coming here tonight?"

"You know, angel, that is a very exciting thought. But you have to work tomorrow and so do I. Will you not be too tired?"

"My dear man, you might be too tired, but I will not. Please spend the night with me."

"I would love to. I will be there as soon as I talk to Sam."

* * *

"Hello, Sam. This is Thor Berksten. Hope I am not disturbing you."

"No, Thor, not at all. What's up?"

"I wanted you to be the first to know, after the President, that is, that we captured Osama Bin Laden a few hours ago in Pakistan, along with about one hundred al-Qaeda fighters."

"Wow! Thor, this is a real scoop. Thanks so much for letting me know. But is it for real? I mean, do you actually have that bastard in custody?"

"Yes. We actually have him. We are in the process of turning him over to a nearby unit of the First Marine Division, and the President has ordered them to transfer him and his thugs to Guantanimo immediately."

"Fantastic. Can I go with the story?"

"Sure, Sam. But you did not hear it from me."

"Understood, my friend. Understood."

"One more thing, Sam. Do you have any time tomorrow? There is another matter I want to bring you up to date on. It should only take a few minutes."

"I'll make time, Commander. How does 9:00 a.m. sound?"

"Perfect. See you then."

*   *   *

Going to Sarah's apartment was, Thor imagined, a bit like going home from work at the end of the day, and he longed for the time when doing so could happen with far more regularity. He had not seen her since their visit with her family in Boston, almost two weeks past. Throughout their short relationship, days, even weeks, often passed between meetings and Thor was becoming a bit impatient with such gaps. Being with Sarah was always such a highlight and pleasure that he wanted to be with her every day. Thus were his thoughts as he put his hand out to press her door bell. But, as had happened several times, the door opened before he could announce his presence. He smiled at the sight of her and said, "How did you know it was me, dear heart?"

"Oh, Thor, you always ask me that," Sarah answered, holding out her arms, "And I always say it's because I am a woman and we sense when our men are close at hand. I am so happy you are here. Please come in."

They stayed locked in each others arms for several long moments. Then Sarah asked, "Have you eaten?"

"No dear, I have been on the go constantly since leaving Roswell this afternoon, and have not given much thought to eating. Now that you mention it, I am famished, but do we have to waste time on food?"

"Why, Thor, what a bad boy you are,." Sarah said, blushing.

"Sorry, angel. It is just that I miss you so much and see you so seldom. I have grown accustomed to your smile, your laugh, your beautiful face."

"Ah, I believe there is a song that goes something like that. It was written long before my time, but is still one of my favorites. I think it might have been composed for a movie called *My Fair Lady*." Not sure, though."

"Surely whoever wrote it must have had you in mind, Sarah."

"Well, I don't know about that, but thank you, just the same. Now, please come into my kitchen. I think feeding you is the number one priority. Have you ever had pizza? That is what I had for dinner tonight."

"No, I do not believe I have. What is it?"

Sarah described the dish for him.

"Oh, yes. That sounds interesting."

Sarah warmed up the left-over pizza and placed it before him, then sat down next to him at the bar and watched as he ate. He finished the meal in minutes, then said, "That was really great, honey. I did not realize how hungry I was. By the way, you look gorgeous tonight. How could I have been so fortunate to find you?"

She touched his hand, and said, "I think it was destiny, Thor. My mother always told me that's how it happens. 'Your prince will appear suddenly, Sarah, when you least expect it,' she would say."

"And I would express doubt, not believing. But Mom's response was always the same: You will know, my child. You will know. And I did know. I knew the moment I first saw you walking from the elevator toward my reception station."

"How very strange. I knew then, too, but I also feared."

"What did you fear, Thor. Me?"

"No, my love. I was afraid you would reject me once you discovered my origins."

"You never told me that, or even let on. And for the record, I already knew, and knowing made no difference. My prince had come."

"Ah, I see. That must be a woman thing—I mean, to dream and plan for the day you will meet your man. At least, I do not recall my mother ever telling me things like that . My father talked to me about such subjects, not my mother; and he stressed treating women gently and with kindness. I remember him telling me how much more complex women are than men, and that I should never try to understand them. I later came to realize the truth of his warning."

"Do you really think that about women, Thor?"

"Yes, dear heart, but only in terms of respect for your gender. Your role in life is much different than mine; your destiny is to create and nurture life, whereas mine seems always to be to destroy it."

"Oh, Thor, what a terrible burden that must be. But I will always be your safe harbor. When you need comfort, I will be there."

Thor took her in his arms and kissed her gently, then said, "darling, I shall always need you, as I need you now."

* * *

Just prior to 9:00 a.m., he made the now familiar walk from the elevator in the CTS building to where the woman he had just left sat waiting. She smiled as he approached and he paused to take her hand in his. "Good morning, again, my darling," he whispered. This is how every day should begin."

Sarah blushed. "Thank you, Commander Berksten. I have already announced you. You may go right in. Mr. Fischer is expecting you."

Thor squeezed her hand and smiled knowingly, then walked toward the door to Sam's office. His assistant, Margie Peterson, was waiting and greeted him warmly. "Good morning, Commander," she said with a smile. "You look well. Tea as usual?"

"Thank you. So do you, Margie. Tea will do just fine."

"Please have a seat. Sam is around here somewhere. I'll page him then bring your tea."

*   *   *

Sam appeared a few minutes later. The two men shook hands and Thor said, "I appreciate the time this morning, Sam. I know you are very busy so I will get right to the point."

"No problem, Thor. You wouldn't be here if it were not important, and I always want to hear what you are up to. How in the hell did you find Bin Laden so fast?"

"It was not as simple as you might think. We knew that if we could identify his key lieutenants one of them might lead us to his hiding place. But identifying them was not easy; his officers do not look any different than their soldiers. Eventually we found one by putting invisible Techna agents in every group of of al Qaeda fighters we encountered. One of them finally led us directly to Bin Laden. He had foolishly built a permanent camp in what you Americans call a box canyon, a deep canyon with only one access; easy to defend, but impossible to escape from, as Bin Laden discovered. He tried without success to scale the nearly vertical rock walls of the canyon to get away from us."

"Fantastic. I hope he gets swift and fitting punishment."

"Yes, Sam. We hope so too."

"So, what brings you here today, Commander?"

"Well, I want to give you a heads up on 'what we are up to now,' as you put it. You are current on the health care battle being waged in Washington, I presume."

"I am, Thor, and it is a sorry state of affairs, if I do say so. The problem is those huge health insurance corporations who, along with oil industry and banking giants, control our Federal Government. Somehow we've got to put a stop to that."

"I am rather surprised to hear you say that, Sam, since the corporation you work for is a giant in its own right."

Sam nodded. "Yes, we are big in our industry, but it is one that believes in absolute separation of business and state, as well as church and state. We don't meddle in Government business we simply report what Washington is doing. They don't like it most

239

of the time, which puts us in the cat bird seat, and we have had offers. We just don't take them. It's much better this way."

"Then what would you say if I told you we might take over six of those health care insurance companies, if the President does not get his public option?"

"And do what? Run them, you mean?"

"Yes my two Group Captains who are following the progress of this fight, are advocating that. You see, Sam, it is our philosophy that the welfare of people should not be a source of corporate profit, and we doubt that these six corporations will ever be willing to become non-profit. Furthermore, our agents are paid far less than the thirty or forty officers of each of those insurance companies. If we replace their top people with our own agents, billions more can be used for actual health care.

Furthermore, we *will* insure that every American is covered fully."

"Are you going ahead with this, Thor?"

"I have broached the subject to the President in general terms. If he wants us involved we are prepared to help. I am waiting for his reply."

"Do you want to know what I think?"

"Yes, Sam. Your opinion is important to me."

"Very well, I think it is a damn good concept. It takes politics completely out of the equation, presuming, of course, that your people do not become politically motivated."

"No Technian will stoop to that, Sam. It is beneath our moral and ethical codes, and would never be tolerated."

"Then I would support the idea fully, and I think my superiors at CTS would support it, as well. Maybe you should extend this plan to include oil and banking, Thor."

"As a matter of fact, we have discussed that. But please do not jump the gun on any of this, Sam, including health care. It is up to the President, you see. We will not proceed without his authorization. I must ask that you keep this secret for now."

"Certainly, but you will let me know if it becomes a reality, right?"

"Absolutely. I will let you know the minute I know."

"Wow. This could change the entire complexion of our Government system—for the better, I mean. I am very excited, Thor. Hope you get the go ahead from Fields."

"So do I, my friend. Now I must go. Sarah and I leave for Techna Planet tomorrow, and we will be gone three weeks."

"Yes, wish I were going too. What a story that would make."

"Sam I must go every six months. Come with me next time."

"It's a deal, Commander. Take care and safe journey."

CHAPTER ELEVEN
Journey To Techna Planet

After his meeting with Sam Fischer, Thor returned to Sardine Mountain, to put the final touches on his report to his father, the Prime Minister of Techna Planet. Later he met with Guri Kohn, Captain of Group Six, Reserve Forces. He advised Guri that he might return with special agents to serve as doubles in Congress, and asked him to begin contingency plans for their training. "I will let you know soon, Guri," he said.

Next, he talked to Manta Sames about looking after Sarah during those periods when he would be occupied with the Prime Minister and other officials while on Techna.

"Thor, I will be happy to do that," Manta responded. "But I was not aware I would be going on this trip."

"I know. I considered leaving you here to help Truls, but after some further consideration I decided that would not be necessary. Sorry for the short notice, Manta, but I really need your help. Without you I could not accomplish much."

Manta smiled. "Thank you, Thor. It will be wonderful to see my family again."

*   *   *

When he arrived at Sarah's New York apartment on the 15th,, Thor had to summon Jens, waiting at the transporter for him , to help carry her three large suitcases. He and Jens fought hard to conceal their amusement, knowing that she was probably bringing far too many clothes, when anything she might need would be readily available on Techna. But of course, as they both knew, she would not understand that.

* * *

Manta was waiting on the landing apron inside Sardine Mountain when Thor and Sarah returned from New York. After warm greetings, the two women left for Sarah's stateroom to empty her suitcases.

* * *

Thor was going through progress reports in his office late in the evening of April 15 when Truls Heyerdahl called from Afghanistan. "Sorry to bother you at this hour, Commander, but we have a problem."

"Oh? What is that, Truls?"

"Republican Senator Virgil Perkins, of Arkansas is holding up confirmations on 55 presidential appointees until he gets approval of a pet project for his state that will cost taxpayers 50 million dollars, a large portion of which will go directly to his pockets. Democrats classify this project as nothing more than 'pork barrel appropriations', and are blocking approval."

"Truls that sounds like business as usual to me. It is a practice that is wrong and, as we both know, must be fixed. What concerns you about this case more than any others?"

"It concerns me, Commander, because Perkins is a Techna agent—one we inserted as a double for the real Perkins."

"Ah, I see. Yes, that is very serious. It means he broke his Techna ethics and morality oath. What is your recommendation, Truls?"

"Sir, I am recommending maximum punishment, and have arranged for Guri to provide a replacement double from our reserves."

"Agreed. Do you want me to handle this personally?"

"No, Commander. I will leave for Washington immediately to deal with him."

"Fine. Good catch, by the way."

"Thank you, Commander. I hope your trip to Techna goes well."

*   *   *

It was nearly midnight when Truls and agent Andor Deme entered the Washington D.C. apartment of Senator Perkins and found him fast asleep. Agent Deme stood by in I-mode as Truls strode to the head of the bed and shook the sleeping man.

Perkins bolted upright and there was an instant look of recognition on his face. "What are you doing here?" he demanded.

"You have broken moral and ethical rules all Technians must follow; now you must answer for that."

"But I am not Technian anymore, you made me an American. Get out of here before I call security!"

"Wrong, Perkins. You will always be a Techna agent, and will always be subject to Techna laws."

"Go to hell. Since I am Technian, as you claim, what can you do to me? I have the same powers you have."

"Have you forgotten? When you violated your Techna oath you forfeited all the protection and powers granted to you as a Techna citizen; your personal security shield is gone, and you know the penalty."

A momentary look of terror crossed Perkin's face as he scrambled out of bed and rushed toward the bedroom door. But before he could reach it, Truls fired a massive laser beam directly at him. He was instantly vaporized, leaving not a trace of evidence that he had ever lived. Agent Deme made himself visible at that moment.

"I am sorry you had to witness that," Truls said. "It is only the third time in more than ten years that I have had to do this, and I take no pleasure in doing so."

"Do not worry, Captain. I am neither offended nor shocked. He knew the rules, and received the punishment he deserved. Greed tempted him. It is all around us here, you know. You did your duty. The news of this will remind all agents of our sacred vow, and perhaps others will not be so tempted."

"Is the temptation so strong, Andor? Do we not compensate all agents fairly?" Truls responded. "Surely you and the others have not lost sight of our reason for being here on Earth."

"The temptation is very strong, Captain, especially in this city, where we are exposed to powerful men and women whose only goal is to increase their personal wealth. I think it is truly amazing that only one agent has strayed."

"Are you certain we have lost only one?"

"No, Captain, not certain. But the 'grapevine' among Techna agents is every bit as effective as any in America. If others have been compromised we would have heard, and the problem would have been reported.

Truls nodded in agreement. "Very good, Agent Deme. Are you prepared to take on this assignment and carry it out faithfully?"

"I am, Captain. As the new Senator Perkins I will end objection to those appointments. "

"Good. I will leave you then."

*   *   *

On his way back to Afghanistan Truls advised Thor that the Senator Perkins problem had been resolved, and that a new double for him was in place.

"Thank you, Truls. I know it was not an easy task. By the way, how many Republicans are in the House and Senate at this time?

"Commander, there are still 55 American Republicans in the House and 30 Americans in the Senate."

"Good. Do you have any questions before I leave for Techna?

"No, Sir."

*   *   *

Early on the morning of April 16, Thor's starship, and two of the five specially fitted ships loaned to the U.S government for the purpose of bringing American service personnel home from

Iraq lifted swiftly off the landing pad outside Sardine Mountain. Aboard each of the ferry starships were four hundred Techna agents who were being rotated back to their home Planet for a well deserved rest. Thor's flagship carried one very excited young American lady on her first starship voyage, and another 200 agents on their way home. The ferry starships would return to Planet Earth with 800 replacements for them at the end of Thor's visit to Techna.

In minutes the three huge starships escaped the pull of Earth's gravity. They accelerated to their cruising speed of 50,000 miles per hour and turned to the flight course pre-programmed into their sophisticated Galaxy Positioning System by Jens Petersen just prior to lift-off. Ahead lay a five million mile journey.

Sarah, standing next to Thor as the starship hurdled into space, held tightly to his arm and said, "Oh, my God!"

"It is alright, honey," Thor responded gently. "Everyone goes through that the first time. I think you handled it very well."

"Do you, really, Thor? It is such an amazing experience, nothing like flying on your transporter. I thought that was fast, but this ship is unbelievably fast."

"Yes, well, the transporter can reach the same speeds given enough time; it is just that, in it, we are never in the air long enough."

"How fast are we going, Thor?"

"Right at 50,000 miles per hour. But after we have been traveling for two or three days you may wish we were going faster. It can tend to get boring because there is not much to see out the windows. Rather like being on a cruise ship in the middle of the ocean, I would say."

"Oh? I would have thought there would be much to see— other planets, stars, maybe an old discarded rocket or two."

Thor laughed. "You would think so, angel, but most space objects are much further out than we imagine, and even if we did encounter one it would be just a blur at the speed we are going."

"So, my dear leader, how do we spend our time? Would this be a good time to talk over wedding plans?"

"A perfect time, Sarah. And about our dream home, as well. These five days will go very fast. But fortunately, I cannot go off and fight some political fire in Washington. Nor will there be meetings to interrupt us. The telephone will be about the only interruption, and hopefully there will not be many calls. I have already prepared my report to the Prime Minister, so there you have it. Most of my time is yours until we get to Techna.

"Ummm, " Sarah said, nestling against him. "I love the sound of that."

"Good. Shall we have a cup of tea and get started on us?"

"Tea for you, coffee for me, and I would love to."

They walked hand in hand to Thor's office complex, where Manta was busy as usual. "Ah, you two. I was just coming to look for you," she said with a smile. "Thor, I have a fresh pot of tea for you, and a fresh batch of coffee for you, Sarah."

Thor smiled. "I see you have been reading my mind again, Manta. We will be in the conference room, where I plan to convince my future bride of the house I want."

Sarah looked up at her husband-to-be and smiled. "Don't you mean the house we want, my darling? Besides, we should talk about getting married first, don't you think?"

"I will bring your drinks in a moment, and it sounds like maybe I should sit in as a referee."

"Good idea, Manta," Sarah responded, with an impish look. "Besides, what do men know about weddings and houses? I wouldn't mind reinforcements."

Thor looked serious. "Sarah, you do not need reinforcements with me. Manta is my first choice to help with our wedding. I want it to be a very special occasion, and know that she will be a great help. I want to be deeply involved in the planning, but as you know, I am certainly no expert. You two can be my teachers and I will try to be a good student."

"Oh Thor," Sarah said and touched his cheek gently with her hand. "I am so sorry. I didn't mean to hurt your feelings."

"No, no, dear heart, I am the one who should be sorry—for being so touchy. Shall we begin?"

*   *   *

The wedding planning session lasted over two hours, and Thor tried to remain involved the entire time. He discovered just how complicated preparing to get married was on Planet Earth.

He was amazed that Sarah knew so much about the process in spite of her young age, and very thankful for Manta's help.

After the wedding discussion, the two women listened as he described the home he was thinking of building on Cape Cod.

"I do not know how you feel, Sarah, but I am most intrigued with the design often called *Cape Cod Cottage*, with its covered porches, dormer windows set into a steep roof, and bedrooms on the second floor."

Sarah smiled and said, "Thor, that style is my favorite, too, and I could be very happy in such a home. I do think we should put the master bedroom suite on the first floor—in preparation for our old age, you see."

"Ah, yes, I see your point, dear heart. You are planning far, far ahead."

Sarah nodded. "Yes. I think of it as the only nest I will ever have—on Earth, that is. And I would hope we could build the exact same home on Techna when the time comes. Which reminds me: Shouldn't we plan for a garage for your transporter?"

"I was coming to that. Yes, we will need a building parcel large enough and secluded enough for a hanger and landing pad."

"Thor," Manta said, "Sarah is familiar with Cape Cod. I think you should let her find the perfect location."

"Good idea, Manta. Would you be willing to take that on, honey?"

"Of course, Thor. I would love to."

"Great. I will arrange for Jens to provide a personal transporter and pilot for your use."

*   *   *

On starship voyages, all meals were served in the main dining room, and everyone on the flight except the duty flight crew manning the ship's bridge at that moment ate at the same time. The dining room was laid out with round tables for eight, and everyone on board was expected to sit at a different table each meal. Thor never dined with the same people twice, for these journeys gave him an opportunity to get to know hundreds of members of his force he seldom encountered otherwise.

Sarah accompanied him sometimes, but more often than not made her own separate rounds of the tables.   Her beauty and warmth, plus her dual status as an American as well as the fiancé of their commander made her a hit at every table.   In fact, she was a hit wherever she went on the starship, because she was always eager to stop and talk, and seemed genuinely interested in learning about her new country and its people. They, of course, were just as eager to learn as much as possible about her. It is safe to say every one of them fell in love with Sarah Malloy, a fact that pleased Thor immensely.

*   *   *

For Thor, who had made so many other trips to Techna, This one was very special. It was special because Sarah was with him and would be introduced to all of Techna Planet as his bride-to-be. How would they receive her, the first foreigner ever to be allowed in their world? By now the news of her pending arrival had spread throughout Techna, and its citizens knew that the wife of their next leader would be from a different world. How would they react? How would his father react? And his sisters, and their families?

This visit was also special because he had so much to tell his father, the Prime Minister, about problems in the United States, and about proposed solutions that would guarantee the protection of his beloved Techna Planet, while giving Techna agents a greater say in operation of the American government at the same time—a step that would probably alter Techna's status in the Universe forever, and in ways even he could not foresee. He knew his father might be a hard sell on that idea, but that the very future of his country depended on his ability to convince the Prime Minister of its merit.

Such were his thoughts on this first day of probably the most significant visit to Techna ever. And at that moment he felt Sarah's soft body next to him as she slid under the covers of his bed, and all thoughts of country and destiny vanished from his mind.

*   *   *

The balance of the journey was fairly routine, much as Thor said it would be; a bit like traveling on an ocean-going cruise ship, in that the passengers were confined to this vessel, where everything was done for them. Their meals—always exquisite— were served by white uniformed staff members, their staterooms were cleaned and maintained just as they would be on a cruise liner, and each evening there was professional entertainment for their enjoyment-- mostly music.

Not that time dragged on. It did not, in fact, at least for Sarah. Manta was there for her and the two talked for hours about life on Techna, and made plans to go shopping and sight-seeing. From her Sarah learned that life on Techna was much simpler, and moved at a much slower pace. Also, it quickly became apparent to Sarah that Techna's people enjoyed greater freedom from Government interference and laws than did the people of the United States. There was no taxation whatsoever; no vehicle traffic, therefore no traffic laws; no crime, therefore no criminal law, or courts, judges and police. It seemed, from what Manta told her, that Techna people just got along better and were more free. That was news that surprised her, for she and Thor had never discussed the subject, and she, being so conditioned to controlled life in the States, just assumed any other civilization must be worse.

Thor made a point of spending as much time as possible with her every day. Some of the interludes were short because he had other obligations, but most, including meals, were long and joy-filled for Sarah. She had never seen him as relaxed as he was on this voyage, compared to their times together on Earth, which were usually relatively short intervals. Here they were together in the same time capsule so to speak, never as far apart as Roswell and New York, and she almost always had ready access to him. It was an arrangement she much preferred, for by now she vacillated between wonder at how she ever got along without him, and terror at the thought of losing him to an accident or worse: another woman. She was not by nature a jealous woman; it was just that she was now so in love with him that she could not bear the thought of life without him.

And so the five days seemed to fly by much too swiftly for Sarah, who had reached a point where she wished this experience would go on forever. When, at dinner on the fourth day, Jens announced that they would land on Techna around noon the next day, she experienced a sense of momentary panic: uncertain of what lay ahead. She gripped Thor's arm and he looked at her. His eyes told her he understood and for her not to be afraid.

*   *   *

Techna Planet was everything she had been led to expect. Their starship settled noiselessly onto the tarmac of the airpark, which was, itself far different in that there were no runways, just patterns and arrays of circular-shaped landing pads, many occupied by similar starships. Their flight was met by what appeared to be a train of many interconnected, streamlined carriages, though Thor called it a monorail. "We have these throughout the city," he explained. "There are no cars or trucks here, just subways and monorails like this one, but of varying length, depending on the load to be met. It will take us to the Prime Minister's home, where we will be staying, and then deliver the other passengers to wherever they choose to go."

They rode the monorail, which was elevated above the roof tops through the narrow, well-maintained streets of what Sarah assumed was the original section of the city—actually the city/state—for Techna Planet had but one main city, as Thor had explained. The buildings that lined the streets were obviously very old, judging by their architectural style. They were of brick and stone construction primarily, two and three stories tall, and every one was in splendid, almost new, condition. As at the air terminal, there were no cars to be seen, yet Sarah saw many people walking, biking, or stopping to chat with one another, or simply window shopping. They were generally neatly dressed. Most of the women she saw wore dresses, though some wore slacks and blouses, or what appeared to be business suits. The men wore clothing that would not make them stand out in any American town or city.

From time to time she would clutch Thor's arm, and direct his attention to something of particular interest, saying, "Oh isn't that beautiful," or "look at those beautiful flowers in the window box, Thor. I feel at home already." At one point she exclaimed, This really is a beautiful city, my love. And it is so much like St Augustine, Florida, just as you said it would be."

"I am pleased that you find it so, Sarah."

Eventually they left the area of shops and found themselves on a slightly wider street—perhaps boulevard would be a better description—lined with large stately homes separated from the street by wide expanses of green lawn. They passed block after block of these fine homes, causing Sarah to say, "Thor we must be in the wealthy section of the city now, am I correct?"

"No, my love. These homes are typical of the type of housing everyone owns here."

"But they look so expensive, Thor. The people must be paid well."

"Everyone is paid about the same, Sarah. We are not a class conscious society, and the state—Techna—covers so much of the cost of living for all citizens. Remember, there is no income tax here, and many things people need, such as transportation, health care, and so forth are free. Also, these homes were constructed many, many years ago, when costs were even lower than they are now, so they are less expensive to buy even today, and the interest on home loans is very low, as well."

"What a wonderful system, Thor. I am so impressed."

Finally, the train stopped in front of a large white brick home not much different than others they had passed. "We are here, Sarah. This is the Prime Minister's residence. Let's go in, shall we? Our luggage will be brought in for us."

They left the monorail and strode along the wide red brick walk lined with beautiful roses of all colors. As they approached the home's entry, the front door opened and a man wearing the familiar blue/grey uniform of a Techna agent was waiting. "Welcome home, Commander," he said, and held out his hand. May I presume this is the Lady Sarah we have heard so much about?"

"Yes, you may. Sarah, this is Dirk Shultes, my father's long time aide. Dirk, I am pleased to introduce Sarah Malloy. Is she not beautiful?"

"Indeed she is, Commander. And I would say you are a very fortunate man. Please. Come in. The Prime Minister is anxious to see you and meet your lovely fiancé."

*   *   *

Sarah had never seen a photograph of Karl Berksten, Thor's father, but she would have recognized him nevertheless, for except that his tightly curled hair was more white than black, he was an identical copy of Thor. Same height and build, same handsome face, same intense grey eyes. He walked briskly toward her now, just as Thor had done that first day and, as he approached, his face lit up with a broad smile. He took her hands in his and said, "You must be Sarah, whom I have heard so much about. How very beautiful you are, my dear. Welcome to our Planet."

"Thank you, Mister Prime Minister. This is a very special day for me."

"And for Techna. You are our very first foreign visitor, in over 600 years, you know. We must celebrate this occasion, and we will, I assure you. By the way, please call me Karl." He turned then to Thor. "And Thor, my son, your burden on Planet Earth seems not to have changed you at all. You look quite well to me. It seems we have a lot to discuss."

"I am well, Father. I thank Sarah for that, and yes, there is much to go over."

"I am anxious to hear all about your work and plans, Thor, but not today. Today we visit and catch up. We will work tomorrow."

"That will do just fine, Father."

*   *   *

Dirk took their bags and led them up to rooms prepared for them on the second floor of the house. "Commander, we were not sure whether you preferred one room or two, so you have a choice."

Thor looked at Sarah, whose eyes answered his silent question. "We will only require one, Dirk. Thank you."

Dirk bowed. "Dinner will be at 7:00 p.m., Sir. Just the family. Casual, you know."

"Very well, Dirk."

*   *   *

The room was large and airy, with windows that looked out on the street below. It was furnished simply, with a large bed, a dressing table/mirror combination, a tall chest of drawers, and two upholstered lounge chairs in front of the windows with a small round table between them. All of the furniture was finished in dark red mahogany , and looked to be very expensive.

Thor took Sarah in his arms and whispered, "Welcome to my world , honey. I am so happy you decided to come, and though it will be a short visit, I will do my best to make it enjoyable for you."

"Oh, Thor, I am already having a wonderful time. How could it be any better?"

*   *   *

Later, when they returned to the main floor "public rooms" a few minutes before seven, Thor's sisters and their husbands were waiting to greet them. "Sarah Malloy, this is my youngest sister, Dana, and her husband, Soren Ibsen. Next is Erika, and her husband, Jean Bonnet. This is Birgit, and her husband, Krause Unger, and last but by no means least, Kirsten, and her husband, Ivan Tesler. He then embraced each member of each couple. "I am so pleased to see all of you again. But tell me, where are the little ones. You did not bring them? "

"No, Thor," Kirsten, who was the oldest said. "We decided to use this visit to get acquainted with your bride-to-be, and she is very lovely. Already we see that you chose well indeed. But the children are dying to see their Uncle Thor, so you must make time for them."

"I will, Kirsten. I Promise. Sarah, these four prolific ladies have given me seven beautiful nieces and three handsome nephews, as I told you on our first date."

"Thank you for your kind words, Kirsten," Sarah said. I hope we will have a chance to talk soon. I do so want to get to know all of you personally, and meet your children. Hopefully Thor and I will add more nieces and nephews some day."

There was a great deal of laughter, and Birgit said, "Ah, do not worry, Sarah, you will. By the way, we have made big plans for you tomorrow. Manta will join us then. Six of us on a shopping spree. I believe you call it 'woman power?"

"Yes, that sounds wonderful. I can't wait."

*   *   *

The next day, Wednesday, the 21st of April, Thor and his father had a very long meeting. The first question the Prime Minister asked was, "My son, how is it going on Planet Earth. Do you think we can be protected from the Americans?"

"Not without some major changes in their political system, Sir."

"Such as?"

"Such as revolutionizing their two party legislative system. Right now those two parties—Republicans and Democrats fight constantly. The party out of power does everything it can to destroy the party in power. This goes on endlessly for at least four years or until the balance of power changes. The result is that nothing of substance ever gets done. Universal Health Care is a case in point.."

"But is it not true that there are members of each party in control at any given time?"

"Not exactly, father. There is a mix of Republican and Democratic members at any one time, but one or the other party will usually hold a majority. And in their system of congressional procedures, the minority still wields some power to thwart—or even stop—the passage of a bill."

"So, Thor, what do you suggest?"

"Sir, as far as helping the American people, the Democrats do a much better job; it is the Republicans—who favor large corporations more than common citizens-- who are always trying to block Bills that aid those citizens. In my opinion, congress should always be working to make the life of the people better, not large corporations. Their Government needs to do as we here on Techna do: Give the people help they cannot give themselves. To do that we will need to neutralize the Republican party. "

"And how do you propose to do that?"

"By doing what we had to do to end the war in Iraq; we replaced over a hundred Republican members of Congress with doubles; one hundred and ten, to be exact."

"Doubles? I am not familiar with that term."

"I know, Sir. It is a new technique we developed. It amounts to sending in a Techna agent disguised as, and trained as, a specific member of the Government--an exact double for that member— if you will, except that the double will always give Congress a Democratic majority, and will always vote with that majority, thus neutralizing Republican impact on every bill."

"What do you do with the original member, the one you replaced?"

"That depends. If the original member is very evil we might terminate his life. If he is not evil but is simply being obstinate to break the majority party, then we send him to Prison Planet for life, though we leave open the opportunity for 'retraining'. "

"Is that what you did with Howard Fields, their President, send him to Prison Planet?"

"Yes, Sir. But in his case it was a close call. He was evil, just not to the point where we draw the line."

"I see. Rather harsh, but effective. And now you want to do that on a larger scale. Will that not require a great many more Techna agents?"

"Sir, if we had to replace every member of Congress I would require another 535 agents. But I do not think we need to go to that extreme. Most of the Democrats, who are now in power, vote the majority party line. It is the Republican minority we need to neutralize, and that number stands at 85 currently—45 men and 10 women in the House, 30 men in the Senate. We already control the executive branch. With the Republicans under our control our power would be enormous. Nothing happens in America without Executive or Congressional approval. "

"Hmmm, yes, a most interesting concept."

"And most productive. It is important to remember that it is these same Republicans who would vote to have their military try to locate and destroy Techna Planet, if they were in power, not the Democrats. "

"You are certain of that, my son?"

"Without a single doubt, Father. The Americans know we have invaded their country, and they are furious. Right now, they cannot touch us. Their space vehicles are crude machines next to ours—little more than rockets—but they are a gifted people when it comes to science and engineering, and are quite capable of swift movement when it comes to developing tools of war, notwithstanding the fact that they have allowed much of their manufacturing capability to escape to other countries. I predict that they will eventually develop space ships equal to or better than ours. Of course, they have no idea how we make ourselves and our equipment invisible, or how we make part of a human a laser weapon—not yet, anyway, but I think they could discover those secrets at some point, given enough time. We must never give them that time."

The Prime Minister was silent for several minutes, then said, "In your last report, you mentioned being concerned about how to deal with several large corporations engaged in providing health care coverage for the people. Is it your plan to use this doubles method to solve that problem?"

"You are very wise, Father. Yes, we are working on such a plan. It would replace the 30 or 40 top officials of those health care corporations-- and there are actually six—to change their operating philosophy. We may also want to use this technique in other business fields, such as petroleum and finance. I have Group Captains Truls Heyerdahl and Siran Missirian working on that now, and will review their recommendations when I return."

"Two very fine agents, Thor. Very fine. I will be anxious to read your proposal. Right now I can tell you I have no problem with how you plan to handle the American Congress. I think there is no other alternative. In fact, I can not express my pleasure concerning your management of this entire mission in strong enough terms. You have done a fantastic job, my son."

"Thank you, Sir."

"And as for your choice of a wife, I must say well done again. Sarah is the perfect mate for you. At first I had reservations about you taking a foreign wife, because you will become Prime Minister some day, and I still harbor the hope that you will return to Techna Planet when that day comes, but after being with her last night at dinner and hearing her say that she would be happy here if called upon to be here, I withdraw my reservations. She is a thoroughly delightful young woman, and wise beyond her years. Your mother would be very pleased as well."

"Father, I think I knew she was the right one the very first time I saw her there in the CTS office. I am so very glad you approve."

"On another subject, you have not said anything about the Afghanistan situation. How is that mess going?"

"It is still a mess, Father. But we did capture Osama Bin Laden just before I left to come here. Sorry I failed to report that. But at any rate, there is little reason to continue that war and I believe the new President Fields will agree. He and I will talk when I return."

"Good. I have just one other question. Do you have adequate funds for your operation? I hear you have not requested Techna funds from our treasury."

"Father, captured drug money is more than enough. Illegal drug traffic is a huge business in America. The drugs are produced in South America, and then smuggled into the United States. Because there is so much money to be made, greedy American companies have gotten in on the action. They do not seem to care that what they are doing is illegal, or that it does terrible things to citizens. Our goal is to stop the inflow of illegal drugs. We have a long, long way to go, but have had some success. To date we have captured and destroyed about twenty thousand pounds of marijuana and cocaine, and have confiscated nearly one hundred million of dollars. That is the money that pays our way."

"What about the people involved in that drug trade? What do you do with them?"

"If the seller and buyer do not kill each other, which often happens, then we execute them, Father. They are evil men beyond reform. Their products destroy innocent lives."

"Remarkable, my son. Remarkable that you can accomplish so much with so few agents. What other aspects of American life are you involved in?"

"Well, Sir, the long answer is that we will pursue any government or business activity that has a negative impact on American people, or might endanger Techna Planet. But the only other aspect of life there that we are investigating right now is a form of religion called televangelism."

"Which is...?"

"Which is another form of big business, that uses religion to play on the emotions of people in the hope of extracting money from them. Televangelists receive millions of dollars in contributions, and use virtually every cent to finance their own opulent lifestyles. They are a batch of sickening vultures. Our investigation on this matter is still on-going, but I would not be surprised if we end up exterminating some, if not all of them."

"How is it that one planet can have so many problems?"

"Greed, Father. But it is not the entire planet. As usual, only a few countries are involved, and the ring leader at this time is America."

"My son, you have given me a great deal to think about. I am sorry you must endure this, but I am eternally thankful that you are in charge. Thank you for your fine work, and please continue to keep me informed, as you always do."

"Certainly, Father."

*   *   *

Beginning Monday, April 19, Truls Heyerdahl and Siran Missirian met daily to finalize the proposal they would make to Thor upon his return from Techna Planet. The first order of business was to review the research Siran's agents had compiled on how the six health care insurance companies did their work, and how their financial structure worked. Siran was so well prepared that she made the first part of the presentation without notes. When she came to the financial structure segment she did use charts and graphs to illustrate the huge sums of money that flowed into all of those the companies—much of it from the U.S. Government—and how those funds flowed once received.

"It is even worse than we thought, Siran," Truls said when she finished her presentation. "Those firms make, on average, 80 billion dollars a year each, yet it appears that only ten percent of that ever gets to the ill people who need the medical help."

"Yes, Truls, The system is literally upside down. And you should see how those executives live, their incredibly plush offices, three thousand dollar suits, and hundred thousand dollar cars. Plus, they really do not have to work hard for the money they bring to their company; most of it comes through the Federal Medicare system which is extremely lax on oversight. Basically, whatever a hospital charges—whether it is the actual costs for that patient, or, more often than not, some highly padded figure-- Medicare just approves it and pays the insurance company."

"So, our problem is not just with the insurances companies; we have to change the way Medicare does business as well."

"Correct."

"And you have a plan to resolve this entire travesty of justice?"

"I do, Truls," Siran responded, and with that she began a step by step explanation of the most elaborately detailed action proposal Truls had ever seen. When she had finished he said,

"Siran, this is absolutely brilliant. It is so perfect there is nothing I can think of to add. You have done a masterful job, and it is clear to me that you have a thorough grasp of this entire problem. Very good work. I think Commander Berksten will be very impressed."

"Thank you, Truls. I hope so. There is so much more we can do for those poor people in need."

*   *   *

On Wednesday, while Thor and his father were meeting, his four sisters took Manta, and Sarah on an all day tour of Techna Planet's only city. Shopping and sightseeing were the objectives given, but all understood that the main reason to be together was to get to know Sarah.

They boarded the monorail in front of the Prime Minister's residence and rode it all around the beautiful old city, with Manta, Kirsten, Birgit, Erika and Dana all acting as tour guides. At times, as one or the other of them pointed to some special sight, they were all talking at once, and that in itself, brought frequent laughter to all.

As the train proceeded above what appeared to Sarah to be a main street, Dana spotted a restaurant she visited often. "I think we should stop here for lunch," she said. "The food is wonderful, and they have a large table in a quiet corner where we can talk in privacy." Everyone agreed, so they left the train and followed Dana into the building. Fortunately, the large round table was available, and they gathered around it.

When they were seated, Sarah said, " This appears to be a German restaurant. How is that so on Techna Planet?"

"Sarah," Erika answered, "We have all wondered about that—not just this facility, or just Germany, but all European countries seem to have representation here, and no one seems to know why. To our knowledge, we have never had visitors from there, so it is a mystery."

Sarah nodded. "Yes, I have noticed that you have all married men with names from different countries."

"And you are about to marry a man with a Norwegian name, dear girl," Dana answered, which brought laughter to the group. "Thor was born here, as were all of us Berkstens, and our mother and father were born here, so how is it that we have such a foreign name? No one knows."

"Yes, Sarah," Kirsten said. "We are told you are from Boston, in the state of Massachusetts, yet you have an Irish name: Malloy. Were you born in Ireland?"

"No, and neither were my parents, but my father's forefathers came from there many years ago. "

"And your mother, Rose?" Birgit asked.

"She is Jewish, and her family came from Europe long ago to settle in New York. You see, America was the destination for many people from Europe. They came to escape poverty and religious persecution, mostly. That explains how we Americans can have so many different surnames. It must be the reason all of you have different names, but how did those people get here? That is the curious question. "

"Well," said Kirsten. "There must be a logical answer. Perhaps we will discover it some day. Sarah, I heard you tell my father last night that you would be willing to live here. Were you really serious? You would be so far from your family."

"Very serious, Kirsten. It would be a difficult adjustment, but I believe a woman must be with her husband. If Thor had to return to Techna permanently I would not hesitate to come with him. He is my life now."

"Well said, Sarah. I think we all feel that way. It is the only way, the proper way. But Darien Lachsa could not accept being away from her family. You know about her, I suppose?"

"Yes, I know. Manta told me. I would support Darien for sticking to her principles, but not for being so rigid. Anyway, her loss is my gain. I believe I got the better part of the bargain. Thor is everything I ever dreamed of in a husband. I would follow him anywhere."

"Well, in any event, you will probably meet Darien at the reception Friday night. As a senior Government official she will be invited and will probably attend. By the way, are you prepared for the reception?"

"Yes, I suppose I am, except that I am not sure what to wear."

"A long gown is traditional, Sarah," Manta said. Did you bring one?"

"Manta, I am afraid that is about the only garment I did not bring."

"Not a problem, dear girl," Manta replied, looking around the table. "All it means is that our next stop must be Marcus Brothers. "

"Oh, yes, " said Dana. "They will probably have the perfect gown for you, Sarah. They make every one they sell. Great quality and reasonable prices."

"That sounds fine, Dana."

"Good. What do you say, girls. Shall we take Sarah shopping after we eat?"

"I have a better idea, Dana," Erika said. "Let's all go shopping . Why should Sarah have all the fun?"

*   *   *

Lunch took much longer than anticipated, mainly because they were all having so much fun exploring Sarah's background, as well as answering her many, many questions about Techna Planet. Thus, it was mid afternoon before they left the restaurant, and much later before they completed what turned out to be a most successful shopping spree. It had been a very long time since Sarah had spent that much time with women friends, especially women she liked as much as she liked Manta and the Berksten sisters.

* * *

On Friday, Thor finished dressing for the formal reception, And then wisely left the bedroom to spend quiet time with his father while Sarah dressed, after promising to return to escort her down stairs.

He found his father in his study just off the main public rooms. He knocked softly on the open door to get the Prime Minister's attention.

"Ah, my son, please come in, come in. I am glad you are here because there is something we need to discuss."

"What is that, Sir?"

"Your wedding, Thor. I assume you will have a ceremony in Brookline, where Sarah's parents live; Sarah will want that. But I would like you to be married in a Techna ceremony as well. It is a long standing tradition, you know."

"Of course, father. We understand that, and plan on having one here, with all of Sarah's family in attendance. But before that we both want very much to have you, as well as the girls and their families at the Brookline ceremony. "

"An excellent idea, my son. That way we can meet our new in-laws in their own environment."

"I am glad you agree, father. While you are there I hope you will have a little extra time. I would like you to meet the New President Fields, and perhaps see how the new Congress is doing."

"I would like that very much, Thor."

"Good. Then we will plan on it. I will send you information on dates and so forth." They heard voices outside the study which caused Thor to look at his watch. "Ah, I see it is seven p.m. I must go , Father. Sarah will be waiting."

"Certainly, but if I may suggest, wait about ten minutes until all the guests have arrived, then bring her down."

* * *

When Thor returned to their room, Sarah had just finished dressing. She was standing in front of a full-length mirror, checking every detail. Her gown, the hem of which just touched the floor, was of brilliant burgundy silk with a straight skirt, gently scooped neckline and three-quarter sleeves. Around her neck was a single strand of pearls, and one tiny pearl adorned each earlobe. Sensing his presence, she turned to face him. He paused in the doorway for one brief moment to let her incredible beauty wash over him, then advanced toward her with arms outstretched. Sarah said, "How do I look, Thor? I do so want to please everyone."

"Honey, I can honestly say I have never seen you look more beautiful. You will give Techna women some real competition tonight, I think."

"Really, Thor? I do value your opinion. I just want to look good for your sake."

"Sarah, I could not ask for more than I see before me at this moment."

Notwithstanding his comments of approval, she spent a few more minutes in front of the mirror, then finally announced that she was ready.

Thor offered her his left arm and said, " Shall we go?"

They left the room and walked slowly to the top of the wide, gracefully curved staircase leading to the spacious foyer below. It was filled with men in formal black, and women in long gowns of every description and color. As if on signal, all heads turned to watch Thor and Sarah make their way down the stairs,

And a collective murmur of appreciation and wonder drifted up to them.

"Thor, please don't let go of my arm," Sarah whispered, as they started down. "My legs are trembling so much I fear I might trip and fall."

Thor placed his right hand gently on Sarah's arm. "Do not be afraid, angel. I will never let that happen."

"Thank you, my love. I don't think I have ever felt such stress."

"You are doing just fine. Only a few more steps."

* * *

The Prime Minister was waiting at the foot of the stairs as Thor and Sarah arrived. Thor, well schooled in reception protocol, guided Sarah to a position just behind his Father, then took his place just behind her. Next came the Prime Minister's six cabinet members, each preceded by his or her spouse.

The moment the receiving line was in place, people began to advance toward it. Sarah noticed a tall statuesque woman with blond hair, who was in line third from the front. The woman had been staring at her since she took her place in the reception line.

As was the custom, each guest bowed to the Prime Minister, and was then introduced by him to Sarah, as the guest of honor. Sarah felt the eyes of each of the 60 invited guests, including the blond woman, on her as they approached. Each of them welcomed her to Techna Planet and congratulated her on her engagement to Thor, then took just a moment to add a personal comment. Sarah responded gracefully to each of them, before they moved on to Thor, the next person in line.

When the blond woman reached the Prime Minister, he said, "Hello Darien," and gave her a big hug, then turned to introduce her to Sarah.

"So, Sarah," she said. "I have heard so much about you."

"All good, I hope. I have heard much about you as well."

"Yes, I am sure you have." Then she glanced toward Thor and smiled. "Did he tell you?"

"No. When we first met I asked him if he was married. He said no, but that there was someone before me. He did not elaborate. I t was Manta who gave me the details."

"Ah, I see," Darien said, as a look of sadness crossed her face. "Thor was my big mistake, you know."

Sarah looked perplexed and said, "Really?"

"Yes. You see, he asked me to be his wife and I refused."

"Because you did not like being so far away from your family?" Sarah offered.

"Correct. That was the mistake I am referring to, for I have yet to find someone to share my life with. But that is not your problem, is it? Thor is a wonderful man. He will take care of all your needs, I assure you, and I am very happy for you. I am also here for you if you ever need anything."

"Thank you, Darien," Sarah said, and the two women embraced.

Darien then advanced one step to Thor's position. "You look well, Commander. Is it because you thrive on your work on Planet Earth, or, is Miss Malloy responsible? Congratulations, by the way. I am very happy for you both."

"But not very happy with your own life right now, I think. Sorry, I could not help overhearing your conversation with Sarah."

"No, I am not very happy. But that is not your fault, of course. You offered a good life for me, but I could not accept the conditions. I should have said yes instead of no."

"Darien, I do not think you should worry. You have not lost your beauty at all. Some man is sure to discover you soon."

"Perhaps. But will it be in time?"

"I do not understand."

"My biological clock, Thor. You should remember how much I want children. I am getting closer and closer to the deadline. You know, age thirty-five? Not being able to conceive would be the most severe punishment for declining your proposal that I can imagine."

Thor did not respond. Darien smiled faintly and moved on, and he turned to find Sarah looking at him. It was a look that told him he had better talk to her again about Darien, and soon.

Manta and Jens were next in line. She looked wonderful in her gorgeous emerald green gown, and Jens, always handsome and debonair' seemed even more so in his black tuxedo.

"Why, Sarah, you look utterly fantastic," Manta said. "What did you think of Darien? Some blond, right?"

"Yes, but such a sad case, Manta. I will tell you all about it later."

* * *

After going through the receiving line the guests proceeded to the grand ballroom, where they helped themselves to an abundant selection of hors d'oeuvres, including pickled herring, liver pate', various cheeses, cold ham, roast beef, and chicken, and petit-fours, plus every form of desert imaginable. A huge crystal punch bowl occupied one end of the long table. Next to it were dozens of glasses filled with champagne. Large coffee and tea urns completed the refreshment menu. There were no alcoholic beverages anywhere in the room.

Thor and Sarah mingled freely, and were stopped again and again by guests wanting to know more about Sarah, with whom there was an obvious strong fascination. Most people seemed genuinely surprised that she was little different from themselves. The men were so taken with her beauty that they could not keep their eyes off her. And, as Thor had predicted, the women were also mindful of her beauty and kept sharp eyes on their husbands.

Though few couples danced, soft semi-classical music playing in the background prompted Thor to guide Sarah to a less crowded area of the room and expertly execute a waltz with her in his arms. "Do you remember the last time we danced, dear heart?"

"Oh, yes, Thor. It was during that beautiful weekend in Palm Springs, California. How could I ever forget?"

"Are you having a good time tonight?"

"It's wonderful. I was so frightened at first, but thanks to you I got over that. And I really love your father and sisters—your whole family, in fact. They have made me feel right at home here."

"I am glad, honey. They all love you, too. They want to spend more time with us, which I guess will probably consume the three days we have left."

"I know. The time has gone so fast, and leaving is going to be really sad."

"I understand, but remember, we can return anytime you want—and of course, we must return for our wedding."

"That's fine, Thor, but I meant this first visit was very special and I hate to see it end. Besides I have not seen as much of your city as I would like. Do you think we can see more? "

"Certainly, my dear, We will find a way."

"Good. I would like that very much."

"What did you think of Darien, Sarah? You seemed a bit out of sorts after talking to her."

Sarah gave him a look that said danger, and said, "Darling, it was just a momentary fit of jealousy. She is so beautiful and almost had you in her grasp once. For a second I feared she might try again—and succeed."

"Not in a million years, angel. It could never have worked. She is too much into herself—too selfish. You never have to worry about Darien—or any other woman, for that matter. Things work out. My destiny was to discover you, and I am indescribably happy I did. Now you will never escape my evil spell."

Sarah snuggled against him. "Darn," she said. "I guess I will just have to accept my fate."

*   *   *

On Saturday afternoon, the day after the formal reception, the entire Berksten family—Thor and Sarah, the Prime Minister, plus Kirsten, Birgit, Erika and Dana, with their husbands and children, boarded a monorail train for a picnic beside a beautiful lake at the edge of the city, where the Prime Minister kept a small rustic cabin. The Prime Minister's aide, Dirk, was there, and he brought baskets of food and drink.

During the train ride to the park, Thor was the center of attraction among the very young, all of whom wanted to sit on his lap at once. But he succeeded in convincing them that one at a time was better. Little Karla Ibsen, one year old, was first. She was a tiny, beautiful image of her mother, Dana, and was only three months old the last time Thor saw her. After a minute or so he handed Karla to Sarah, who had joy written all over her face as she held the baby girl. Karla looked at Sarah and smiled, and almost instantly the two females began communicating verbally. It was a magical moment.

Next came Desiree Bennet, Erika's one year old, who had dark brown hair and was no less beautiful than Karla. She, too, insisted on sitting on Sarah's lap. Sarah was beside herself with happiness.

And so it went. In no particular order, the children spent a minute or two with Uncle Thor, who then introduced them to Sarah. There were Erika's two other children, Jean, Jr., age 5, and Chantel, age 3; Brigit's son, Anton, age 9, and daughter, Lisette, age 7, Kirsten's oldest daughter, Duci, age 8, followed by her sisters, Kristina, age 4, and Gisella, age 6. Last to visit his uncle was Karsa Tessler, age 10, but when Sarah asked him a question about school he blushed shyly, turned red in the face and walked away. Sarah laughed and said to Thor, "Don't worry, dear, I will win him over."

"I know you will, angel. You have a way with men. I am living proof. And you have a wonderful, loving way with children, it is clear. I find that so beautiful to watch."

"Thank you, dear man. I am practicing for our own, you know."

"And how many will that be?"

"As many as you want, Thor. As many as you can provide for."

"Then we must enlarge our house plans considerably, I should think."

Sarah laughed, but said nothing.

When the group reached the park, which Sarah found as beautiful as any she had ever seen, with tall pine trees everywhere, shrubs just beginning to develop leaves after the winter cold, and the lovely, shimmering lake just beyond, next to Karl's cabin, she thought it was a picture-perfect painting, not unlike others she had seen in New England, and loved so much.

She got off the train and just stood there, breathing deeply and taking it all in. Then she turned to help unload all the picnic baskets and carry them to a nearby table. Thor worked right beside her all the while.

While the women were laying the table, the older children made a dash for the lake shore, and were now amusing themselves by trying to skip pebbles across the surface of the water. Thor walked over and joined in. His few throwing attempts showed that he had had a lot of experience at this game, for each pebble skipped at least three or four times, and one even skipped six times! He soon found himself surrounded with eager students of the sport and kept them all busy for quite a spell, until picnic lunch was announced, at which time he joined the other men at their end of the table.

The segregation of sexes did not go unnoticed by Sarah; rather, it reminded her of her own family gatherings in Brookline, and she found no fault in the practice. This was a time for women to exchange news and ideas of interest to them, while their men were off doing the same on more masculine matters. Actually, she was pleased to find the same tradition on Techna Planet as on Planet Earth, for it was just one more indication of how alike the two worlds were.

The men gathered around Thor to learn about his experiences on Earth. There were many questions and he freely answered all of them, among which were many dealing with government, and business. One question in particular, put to him by Birgit's husband, Krause Unger, concerned acceptance of Techna Force 20 by Americans.

"Krause, we have had little contact so far with the average American, not because we try to avoid each other, but because our work puts us in contact almost exclusively with Government officials. I do not know how the citizens will react when they are exposed to our agents, but I can tell you that most of the Government officials hate us and would have us executed if they could."

"Why is that so, Thor?" Ivan Tesler want to know.

"Because we are making them do things they need to do but do not want to do. We made them stop a terrible war in Iraq because it was never justified and was killing thousands of their soldiers. At first their President resisted strongly, so much so that I found it necessary to destroy some major buildings put there by the Americans, as well as one of their newest aircraft carriers, to get his attention. Unfortunately, some American lives were lost before he gave in, but in the end, the people were happy to have their sons, husbands and fathers back home safe. However, businessmen—and some members of Government, all of whom were making a financial killing on the war, that is, huge profits, were very angry with us. They still are."

"But you did them a favor, Commander. I do not understand."

"I know, Ivan. But war is big business on Earth, and sadly—very sadly--business is god to them. One of the prior Presidents explained it best, when he said: *The business of America is business.* That country is materialistic beyond belief, which is why it is in such terrible financial shape today. All the profits—and they are typically huge—go to the people who run large corporations and rarely trickle down to the general public. Consequently, where there were once three classes in their society—wealthy, middle and poor, there are now only two: wealthy and lower middle class, and the gap between widens every day. Nations do not survive when they allow a very small percentage of the population to 'earn'—using that term loosely—50 million or more dollars a year each , when the average wage of middle class workers is about 40 thousand dollars. Therein lies the problem. I truly believe America will face a major revolution if the situation does not change soon."

"And according to Karl, you are about to force major changes in their health care system," said Soren Ibsen. "Will that not add fuel to the fire?"

"Yes, Soren, it will, but I think only temporarily. Our plan, which I cannot discuss yet, will eventually make American citizens understand that we are good , honest people who really are concerned about their welfare. When that happens I believe they will not only accept us but welcome us."

"What about them trying to destroy our little planet, Thor?" Jean Bonnet asked. Is that rumor or fact?"

"It is fact, Jean. Their scientists are working very hard to find us—and their objective is to neutralize us if they succeed. I can assure you, we will never let that happen."

"How can you stop them, Thor?"

"Easy. I have agents in every one of their space research facilities. Those agents have authority to destroy equipment— even entire plants-- if necessary."

Throughout this exchange between his son and sons-in-law, the Prime Minister listened carefully but said nothing, though he was very pleased with how Thor handled the many questions. Now, in a lull in the conversation, he said, "Well gentlemen, these are problems we could spend all day and night discussing, I think it is time to rejoin our women and children, Yes?"

*　　*　　*

By this time the sun was beginning to settle lower on the horizon, and there was a distinct chill in the air. At the Prime Minister's suggestion, everyone walked the short distance to the cabin. It was indeed rustic, with timber walls, and roof trusses of large peeled logs. A stone fireplace was centered on one end wall, and there were old but comfortable chairs surrounding a huge pine coffee table that showed signs of heavy use. One of the men made a fire in the fireplace, while two others brought the coffee and tea urns in from the picnic table. An old upright piano stood against the wall opposite the fireplace, and to Sarah's surprise, Thor began to play a hauntingly beautiful composition she did not recognize, so she asked Karl if he knew.

"Yes, Sarah. It is the National Anthem of Luxembourg. Thor was there once, and fell in love with that melody. It is beautiful, Yes?"

"Very beautiful, and he plays so well."

"Forgive a father's pride, my dear, but you will find that he does many things quite well—things other than his work, I mean. When he is interested in anything he tackles it with gusto. Playing the piano is just one example."

While Sarah and Karl were talking, all of Thor's nieces and nephews gathered around their uncle, and he began to play a game with them—kind of a take off on can you name that tune, except that his question was, can you sing that tune? He would play a few bars of something then challenge his young audience to join in. The older children knew quite a few of them, and pretty soon all the kids were singing whether they knew the song or not. Then Thor's sisters joined in, and all of them, including Uncle Thor began to laugh and have a great time. Sarah thought it was one of the most wonderful moments she had ever witnessed.

But, as the saying goes, all good things must come to an end. The hour was growing late and it was time to gather up their belongings and head back to the Prime Minister's house. Inspired by the songs they had been singing, all of the children hummed or sang the entire trip.

* * *

On Sunday, April 25, Thor and Sarah slept in until almost nine a.m., for their Saturday night did not end with the picnic in the park. Thor woke up first, and lay there watching the beautiful woman who lay beside him. Her face was the picture of pure contentment, and he still could not believe his good fortune.

After a few moments, and as had happened several times before, she stirred, as if sensing his presence. Her eyes opened just a bit, then even wider, and she smiled and moved closer to him.

"Good morning, my princess. Did you sleep well?"

"I did, Thor, but how wonderful to wake up and find you here."

"Well, this is my room, you know."

She propped herself up on one elbow and said, "It is, really?"

"Really. I grew up in this very room. Of course it had more toys then—I mean, toys much less interesting than are here now, and not nearly as beautiful."

Sarah bent to kiss him, then responded, "I hope to bring you all the toys you will ever need."

"Umm. I cannot wait. Now, what do you say to a long ride in the country today? "

"Oh, Thor, that would be wonderful. When do we leave?"

"Well, we can go right now, but it might be better to put some clothes on first, Yes?"

"Silly man. I meant after we dress. Could we have breakfast in some tiny country place?"

"Why, I think that can be arranged. We will leave as soon as you are dressed."

*   *   *

They boarded the sleek monorail in front of the Prime Minister's residence just after 10:00 a.m., and were soon speeding through the tall pine forest near the clearing where they had the picnic the day before, then along the lake front for several miles, before stopping at a long building of rustic, weathered wood.

"We are here, honey," Thor said as he reached for Sarah's hand to help her off the train. "This is one of the oldest inns on Techna Planet. It may not look like much, but it has a very good restaurant. I think you will enjoy the food."

They chose a light breakfast of assorted cheeses, thinly sliced ham, and toasted raisin bread, with coffee for Sarah and Thor's usual cup of tea, and watched the diving, soaring sea gulls from their table by a large window as they ate.

"This is beautiful, Thor. What is the name of this place?"

"It is called *The Inn At North Shore,* My Love. It has been a favorite meal stop for my family for as long as I can remember. The Inn is frequently visited by newly married, honeymooning couples."

"I can see why. It is so peaceful and quiet, and the lake is lovely. What is it called?"

"*Lake Of The Forest.* We have no oceans on Techna Planet, just this single lake, but it is quite large—about the size of your Lake Michigan, if I remember correctly, and it is fresh water, not salt."

Sarah gazed out the window, then said, "Oh, Thor, look, there is even a boat—a large boat—way off in the distance."

"Yes. That is a ferry boat and it connects a number of small lake front villages with one another and with Techna City."

*   *   *

After breakfast they boarded the monorail again and journeyed along the lake shore, past many small farms. Some seemed to hug the steep, grass covered slopes, while others were sheltered in long valleys that ran at right angles to the shore. Sarah saw farm animals everywhere—chickens, cows, pigs and other species—that were no different from animals on the farms of Earth. And everywhere there were neat vegetable gardens with their rows and rows of crops. The scenes that zipped by the speeding train's windows reminded her of her beloved New England as well as the parts of Europe—especially Germany— where she had visited.

At one point, she and Thor left the monorail and hiked along a steeply rising trail through the beautiful forest. Along that route she saw more incredible sights: lovely spring flowers in yellow, gold, blue , lavender and many hues of red; birds of various species familiar on Earth, including robins, sparrows, jays—even ravens; and most incredible of all, a pair of small deer which stood quietly near the trail and watched them unafraid as they passed. When they finally reached the end of the trail, near the crest of the hill, they found a small sparkling stream that seemed to be singing as its waters rushed around the rocks and down the slope. They sat there, on a large stone for some time, holding hands, saying nothing, just taking in the beauty before their eyes. It was there that Sarah remembered those occasional gatherings of friends, before Thor came into her life, when they all scoffed at the notion of life on other Planets in the Universe, and in particular, intelligent human life. Now with her own eyes she had witnessed the truth, and had made sure her trusty little digital camera, on which she clicked away as they rolled or walked along, would display that truth for all to see back on Earth. At times she found it hard to believe she was not on Earth, so similar were the Techna scenes.

After a time they walked back down the trail, and boarded another train going in the same direction. Eventually they came to one of the little villages Thor had mentioned, and left that train to explore it. This village was composed of perhaps a dozen or so buildings, all of wood, lining a single road paved in cobblestones of various earth tones. The little town, which Thor called _Charlot,_ prompted her to ask why it had that French-sounding name. "I am not sure, angel," He replied. "But my guess would be that it is named after one or more families with that name that live here. It is quite common, you see. A man moves to an area like this, builds a house and starts a little farm. Eventually he finds a wife and they have children, and the children grow up and start their own farms in the same place, and the place becomes known by their family name. It is much the same as on Planet Earth, yes?"

"Yes, dear man. I agree. That must be how it happens. Anyway, I find it all so very beautiful."

"I am glad, Sarah, for I had hoped you would like my home Planet."

"Oh, Thor, I don't like it, I love it. I truly love it—all of it."

He squeezed her hand and smiled. "Let us go into this store, shall we?" He said, pointing to a small shop with an open door.

The shop sold baskets and pottery, as well as original paintings and other works of art. A tiny, frail-looking, woman with silver hair, greeted them warmly, saying, "Good afternoon, Commander Berksten."

Her greeting startled Thor. "How is it you know who I am?" He asked, "And what is your name?"

The old woman smiled. "You came here once with your mother and father when you were just a small boy. Your father bought a pair of gold earrings for your mother. That is when I learned the family name, and I have followed your career ever since. I am a member of the *Charlot* family, and we are very proud of what you have become, Sir. But this beautiful young lady, I do not recognize."

"Her name is Sarah, Mrs. Charlot."

The woman nodded. "Yes, now I remember. She is from Planet Earth, and is to become your wife." She took Sarah's hands in hers. "I am so happy for you, child, and wish you much joy. Are all Americans so lovely?"

Sarah blushed. "Mrs. Charlot, I think all people are lovely."

"Wisely put, Child." She looked at Thor and said, "Sarah will make a fine mate for our next Prime Minister."

"Madam, I did not come to your shop for compliments, but thank you very much."

"If not compliments, what can I offer you, Commander?"

"Well, how about something nice for my lady?"

"Of course, and I have the perfect gift. Come, Sarah. Let me show it to you." She led Sarah to the rear of the shop and pointed to a white gown hanging there. "This is the traditional gown for a wedding on Techna Planet. It was to be my wedding dress, but I never married. For years I have kept it, and everything else a woman needs for her most special day, in the trousseau chest you see there on the floor. It should fit you very well, and I want you to have it—all of it."

"I am overjoyed, Mrs. Charlot. The dress is so beautiful; it has such simple but elegant lines. Are you sure?"

"Yes."

"What is the price, Madam?" Thor wanted to know.

"Ah, the price," She responded sadly. "There can be no price for something like this, but an invitation to your wedding would be wonderful."

"Do you like it, my love?"

"Oh, yes, Thor. I adore it."

"Then, Mrs. Charlot, " Thor said, "You shall have a very special place at our wedding. Can you keep this here until then?"

"I could, Commander, but I would rather send it to your father's home."

*   *   *

After their visit to the little shop in Charlot, Thor and Sarah boarded a monorail for their return to Techna City, for the daylight was fading fast, leaving little time for additional sightseeing. Sarah could not stop talking about her gift, or the wonderful woman who owned the shop. Thor simply listened and offered an occasional comment, while he savored the ecstasy of being in the company of a woman who was becoming more wonderful to him with each passing moment, and all too soon they arrived at the Prime Minister's residence.

*   *   *

Early the next day, which was Monday, April 26, Jens took Thor to the Techna Security Base, located about 100 miles from the city, by transporter. The Security Base was the home of all Techna agents not otherwise assigned, and Thor was to meet the base commander to finalize transfer of 950 agents from the Security base to his staff on Planet Earth. He was primarily interested in the dossiers of the 85 agents he had requested or duty as doubles, and spent most of the morning studying them. The agents selected for him by the base commander pleased him greatly, for they met all the qualifications he had specified.

The base commander told him the 800 agents who were replacing those who came home from Earth with Thor for rest and recreation, would board starships at the Security Base early the following morning, Tuesday, April 27. Thor advised him that the 85 specially trained doubles agents would travel to Earth on his flag starship, which would arrive at the base at 9:00 a.m. to pick them up. "You have prepared them well," he told the base commander, "but I want every available moment to impress upon them the magnitude of their assignments. They are going to face very difficult challenges as members of the American Congress."

* * *

That evening, all members of the Berksten family, as well as Manta Sames and Jens Petersen, gathered at the Prime Minister's residence for a last farewell dinner. They had had many similar gatherings before, but never with someone from another planet in their midst, especially someone like Sarah. She had won the hearts of all of them.

After dinner they lingered around the table long into the night, talking about many things. There were, as usual, many questions about Planet Earth. The Prime Minister had been there several times, but only for brief periods. Thor, Jens and Manta, had been working there the longest and had learned a great deal about it and its people. But Sarah was from there, and was regarded by the Berksten women as the real expert on subjects that mattered most to them: family life, children, food, clothes and husbands. They seemed to have an insatiable desire to learn every detail about life in America. Sarah happily gave them all the information she could, but on the question of husbands she had to admit that she did not have one of those yet. That brought much twitter from the females present. "We just want to know if they are any more difficult to understand than ours, Sarah," Dana said.

Sarah smiled and replied, "Sorry, Dana, but I just don't know. My guess would be that men are men, no matter where they are from." She put her hand on Thor's. I can tell you, this man is wonderful to me, and that is all I care about."

Thor thanked her and said, "I read something in an American magazine once—no author was listed--that went something like this: *To be happy with a man you must love him a little and understand him a lot. To be happy with a woman you must love her a lot and not try to understand her at all.* I believe that sums it up fairly well, ladies."

"Well put, " His father said. "Now, before we end this night, I must tell you how pleased I am to have us all together again, to have Thor back even for a short time, and to meet his lovely bride- to-be. I only wish his mother could be here with us. She would love Sarah, I am sure. But time moves swiftly,

278

and it will be but a short wait until we all meet again in Boston, Massachusetts, for what can only be described as the wedding of centuries, for it is not only the wedding of two people, it is also the wedding of two planets. Then, soon after that, Thor and Sarah will return to Techna, and bring her family, for our traditional marriage ceremony. In the meantime I urge every one of you to remember why our son and brother must be so far away, on Planet Earth; the very security of Techna Planet depends on his work there against the forces of evil."

* * *

On April 27, Thor's starship lifted off from Techna Airpark, with Jens as pilot in charge, and set course for Planet Earth. Just before 9:00 a.m., he had flown it to the Security Base, to board the new special agents. As he approached, he saw them far below, waiting next to the landing ramp in one long row, two abreast, standing at attention in perfect formation, holding their duffle bags in a vertical position by their left side. By the time the starship touched down they had formed a single line, ready to board as soon as the stairs descended. Once on board, they moved quickly along the curving corridor in search of the stateroom that had been assigned to them, and were soon busy unpacking. All of them had been on short starship flights during training, but none had ever been outside the airspace of their own planet, let alone to Planet Earth, so, while there had been no talking in ranks, they now talked excitedly about their coming adventure.

* * *

Elsewhere in the ship, Manta and Sarah were busy stowing clothes and other travel paraphernalia in their own staterooms, chattering all the while about the visit to Techna Planet. Thor was in his office going over notes for the talk he would give the special agents at 11:00 a.m.

* * *

At the appointed time, he entered the ship's main lounge. The Group Captain in charge of this agent contingent announced him and instantly the agents rose to stand at attention.

"Good morning to all of you, and please be seated," Thor said pleasantly. " I am here to welcome you aboard my starship, which is at this moment streaking through space, destination, Planet Earth! I know you have been briefed on your mission, and I want to extend my personal thank you for accepting this very large and very important challenge. When we arrive at our secret base in Roswell, New Mexico, Group Captain Guri Kohn will be responsible for the final training details you will need to embark on your assignment. So I am not going to steal his thunder now. He gets pretty angry when I try to do his job, and besides, he is a lot better at it. But while we are on this five day journey to Earth, I will try to answer any questions or concerns you may have about the United States, or its people, or its traditions, rules and so forth, or anything else that is bothering you. I will make myself available here, in this lounge, every day at 8:00 a.m. If something is on your mind, do not be afraid to come forward. Again, thank you, and I will see you tomorrow morning." He turned to leave the room and all of the agents stood at attention and saluted.

*　　*　　*

Thor returned to his office to find Sarah and Manta waiting.

"Hi, my dear," Sarah said. "How did your meeting go?"

"It went fine, Sarah. But it was just a welcome meeting to introduce myself, and let them know that I am here for them if they want to talk. I told them Guri will conduct their mission training when we reach Sardine Mountain. I think they will do well."

" Good." Manta said. "How about some lunch? We brought it to the conference room because the dining room is very crowded. Hope that is alright with you, Thor."

"Not a problem, Manta. It will be a good time to talk about our visit to Techna. Sarah, I feel I neglected you while we were there, and I am sorry for that."

"Oh, Thor, I didn't feel that way at all. I knew you would have a lot to talk to your father about. Besides I really had a wonderful time with your sisters and their families, and Manta, I actually don't know what I would have done without you. Thank you so much."

Manta smiled and patted Sarah's hand. "I loved the time we had together. We went to places I have not visited in years, and saw things I had completely forgotten. And it was just fun to watch you as you took it all in."

"Well, Techna Planet is just such a fabulous place. You two had told me all about it, but seeing it really pulls everything together. I can't wait for my father and mother and the rest of my family to see it. They are going to be so amazed."

"I am glad you enjoyed yourself, honey. I had some pangs of anxiety, I admit."

"Why, Thor?"

"Oh, you know, concerns that you might be uncomfortable."

"Really, my dear, I never felt that at all. In fact, what was so amazing was that Techna City could be almost any place on Planet Earth—and you were right: It really is like Saint Augustine. That was a perfect analogy."

"What about the people of Techna?"

"There were no surprises for me there, Thor. Knowing you, and Manta, Jens, and all the agents I have met—I just assumed everyone on your Planet would be as you all are. And that assumption was correct. When can we go back?"

Thor and Manta laughed, and he said, "Do not worry, honey, in time you will see much of Techna Planet."

*   *   *

After that first day of the return trip to Earth, they all fell into a daily routine. They shared breakfast together, usually in the dining room among all the special agents, then Thor moved to his daily post in the lounge for two hours, to field questions from those same agents, and there were many questions, mostly about life in America. There were also questions about their mission, but he dodged those skillfully by reminding the agents that Guri would be in charge of their training. They did not press him after the second day.

After his daily visit with the agents, he made it a point to spend several hours with Sarah, often over lunch. They talked about their wedding—actually two weddings—and about the design of their Cape Cod home, and the fact that Thor planned to ask Sarah's father to help them find land for the house as well as an architect and a builder, an idea that gave her great joy. And they talked at great length about Thor's family, and it was clear that Sarah was not just pretending to like them—she really did.

Thor also made time to organize his thoughts in preparation for a meeting he intended to have with New President Fields. That meeting would be his first order of business when they reached Earth, for it concerned probable corporation take-over, as well as dealing with the Congress. After that, he would meet with Truls and Siran to hear their proposals on those two subjects. Then, too, there were other unfinished tasks, such as dealing with life-without-parole prisoners, televangelists, and illicit drug traffic. So, if all went as he expected, he could see that Techna Force 20 would get very busy indeed.

These matters and other problems left him with virtually no spare time, and before he realized it, Jens was announcing their landing at Sardine Mountain.

------///------

CHAPTER TWELVE
Death of the Party of "No"

Very early on Monday, May 3, Thor left Sardine Mountain for the White House. Sarah was with him. He stopped at the CTS building, in New York and walked with her to the reception desk, where he kissed her goodbye. Less than a half hour later he entered the Oval Office in I-Mode. New President Fields and his chief of staff, Jack Brill, came in a few minutes later, and Thor realized from their conversation that he was witnessing a regular morning briefing that started even before the President and Brill walked through the door. Brill was red-faced and visibly agitated over something, and that something was soon identified. "Mr. President," he exclaimed loudly, "Republicans in Congress are members of your own party. Why in hell they refuse to support your National Health Care proposal is something I will never understand. It's a very good proposal—even better since you gave up on having a public option in it, and it could give the Party some much needed points. It just makes no sense to me."

"Jack, I understand how you feel. Their actions are very frustrating. Furthermore, that applies to every other program I want for the people, not just health care. I can only conclude that they do it to make the Democrat members look bad, but in the process they make this administration look terrible."

"Well, Sir, I sure think it's a bad situation. Can't you do something? Maybe you should get those Congressional leaders over here and talk to them like a Dutch uncle."

"Yes, that is an idea. Let me think about it. Anything else?"

"Nothing that can't wait, Sir. This health care mess is the most important item on our plate right now."

"Very well, Jack . Thanks for your concern."

As soon as his Chief of Staff was out of the room, the President came around his desk to greet Thor just as he made himself visible. "How good to see you again, Commander. Did you have a relaxing trip?"

"Yes, Sir, but it is good to be back, and it looks like we have work to do ."

"Ah, yes, you must have heard my conversation just now. Jack is right. The Republicans are far more of a hindrance than a help right now. Simply put, they are no longer a relevant part of Government. Any suggestions?"

"I offered to take care of that problem for you when I was here on April 12. My offer still stands, Sir."

"I thought we were discussing the health care industry then."

"That was part of the discussion, Sir, but I believe I made an offer concerning Congress as well.

"How were you going to do that, Commander? I am afraid I do not remember."

"Little wonder, Mr. President. You have much on your mind. But, to answer your question, it is better that you do not know my methods. There will just be a seamless transition that will make your impossible task of reforming health care much less impossible."

"Commander, if it was anyone but you making this offer, I would reject it out of hand. But I have faith that you will do what is right, and I grant you permission."

"Good, Mr. President. I think you will be pleased with the result. By the way, how is Mrs. Fields?

"She is still very happy, but I do not get much sleep."

Thor smiled knowingly, but said nothing, The two men shook hands and he left.

* * *

284

From Washington, Thor flew directly to Sardine Mountain, to attend a meeting with Siran Missirian and Truls Heyerdahl to review their proposal concerning the health care corporations and Congress. "Good to see both of you again," He said. "And you, Guri. I am afraid we are going to overload you with work, old friend. You now have almost 300 replacement agents to get up to speed."

"We will deal with it, Commander."

"Good. Siran and Truls, I have asked Guri to sit in today, so he can be in the information loop right from the start. Manta is here for the same reason. Now, for openers, the trip to Techna was very successful. The Prime Minister likes our work here, and our progress. I talked to him at length regarding problems with Congress and the health care corporations, and gave him a general outline of what we propose to do about those problems, based on what I know from previous talks with you, Siran, and you Truls. He has given his approval to proceed. Now, so we are all on the same page, it is time to look at your plan, which I gather you are ready to present, is that correct?"

"Yes, Commander," Truls responded. "We are ready. Siran and I worked many hours on it while you were away, and are convinced it is the best solution, under the circumstances. Siran, would you like to start?"

"Certainly. Let's begin with Congress. A major change is needed there. As you all know, it consists of two political groups, Republican and Democrat, with a few Independents thrown in. They should all work together for the good of the American people, but they do not. Virtually all of their energy is spent fighting one another, leaving no time to work for the people." She went on to explain that Republicans consider big business their constituents, whereas Democrats try to work for the people. She gave numerous examples in support of her claims, and covered the consequences of Congressional members not working in a unified manner. Her main point was that the constant infighting made achievement of their purpose for being impossible. She concluded by saying, "There is no longer a need for the two party system, if in fact there was ever a need. There is enough disagreement—healthy disagreement—within either

285

party to guarantee a good outcome. The question is, which party should be eliminated? Truls and I struggled with this question a long time, only to conclude that the party to keep was the party that works for the good of American people, not American corporations, who are big enough, powerful enough, to look after themselves. Thus, we propose eliminating the Republicans. We will insert doubles for them, and send them to Prison Planet, where they will have to fight hard just to stay alive. If we leave them on Planet Earth the fact that we have put aliens in Congress, which is illegal, will soon come to light, and will have a massive negative effect on our efforts. I think that is a good place to stop. Are there any questions?"

"Well done, Siran and Truls," Thor said. "I agree with your evaluation. The U.S. Congress reminds me of a large family whose members are constantly criticizing each other, sniping, shouting, and exploding in fits of anger. Such families do not live in harmony. They live in a world filled with animosity and misery. Furthermore, their neighbors, and perhaps some family members not engaged in their petty disputes, are left miserable as well, to say nothing of feeling as if no concrete progress is ever going to happen. That is Congress, and left to its own devices it will never change. So, for the good of the American people we must change it. I like your proposed plan to do that. Using the doubles approach will bring much needed change immediately, and the people will accept it as simply another flip flop from their crazy Government system, not Techna Force 20. Therefore, I approve the plan, and urge quick implementation."

"Guri, 85 of the new agents we brought to Earth on this trip have been hand picked and partially prepared to serve as doubles for this assignment. I took dossiers on all Republican members of Congress with me to Techna. Those dossiers were given to agents on a best fit basis, and the agents were instructed to study them in great detail. Hopefully they have done that. If not, your burden is even greater. I have copies of all the dossiers for you, as well. Now we must indoctrinate the doubles in the workings of Congress, and in adjusting to the American way of life, so that they slip into their new roles in an absolutely seamless fashion. Yet, we must never let them forget that they are Techna agents and are bound by Techna rules of ethics and morality. That is your job, and I cannot stress its importance enough."

"Commander, I understand and will do my very best."

"I know you will, Guri. We will need a time line so we can schedule implementation."

"Yes, Sir."

"Now, shall we move on to your presentation on health care, Truls and Siran?"

Truls nodded in agreement then said, "Commander I will set the stage by reviewing the state of health care as it is presently. Then Siran who, with her fine staff, has done all of the necessary research, will give you our recommendations. "

"Very well, Truls."

"Sir, we all know about the tremendous struggle that went on in Congress over health care reform, before it was finally approved. Unfortunately, it was approved without inclusion of the so-called public option, which would have given the Federal Government an opportunity to offer the people, the alternative of choosing a government sponsored health care package. That plan was defeated largely by Republican members of Congress, with the help of a few, 'Blue Dog Democrats.' The result was that health insurance companies were left in almost the same powerful position they were in before the vote."

"Siran and I consider that an unacceptable solution, because, while it provides health care for a significantly larger number of Americans, it does so without adequate cost and premium limits. Therefore, insurance companies will, in all probability, become even richer than they are today. Siran?"

"Yes, thank you, Truls. Our first thought was to nationalize the health insurance companies—let them be government run, in other words. But, as we all know, governments do a terrible job of running businesses, which invariably leads to more inefficiencies and greater costs. So we dropped that idea, leaving us with just one alternative: let the insurance companies continue to run their businesses as before, but the down side to that approach was, to us, prohibitive. Let me explain. There are ten huge health care insurance companies. They each average annual gross revenue of $80 billion dollars each year. Roughly half of that revenue comes from Medicare payments for services they render to patients; the other half comes from corporations whose employees they provide health care services for. Of the total revenue these ten companies receive, barely 20 percent ever gets to patient care. The remaining 80 percent goes to pay operating expenses of the company and its affiliates—salaries, bonuses, administrative costs, dividends and, of course, profit. Executive compensation chews up a huge portion of the salary/bonus budget; the top 30 people in each company receive incredible amounts, with the CEO's averaging $30 million dollars a year each. In our view, no person is worth that kind of money. In short, this is big business at work."

"The system is upside down, and we propose to right it. How? By making operation of those ten companies the responsibility of Techna Force 20. By doing that we send $64 billion dollars per company to patient care instead of $16 billion, each year, leaving $16 billion instead of $64 billion for administrative expenses, including the much more reasonable salaries of Techna agents managing at the top. We reverse the division of money, in other words."

"Furthermore, we propose to merge all ten companies into a single, non-profit corporation with regional operations, which will produce even greater benefits. Once we have weeded out all the redundancy and duplication of effort, our analysis and calculations indicate that we can manage the larger single company with $32 billion dollars a year. That provides a further increase of funds going directly to patient care in the amount of $12.8 billion per company. The Internal Revenue Service of the United States has agreed to this plan in principle. Thus, the amount of money going to patient care will increase to $768 billion per year, from $106 billion, an increase of six hundred percent. We will be able to provide care for virtually all Americans, and the quality of care for each patient will be much higher. So far we have only talked about the ten large corporations. Bear in mind that there are also more than seventy smaller companies in this field, companies with gross revenue in the $10 billion or less category. They operate the same as their larger brothers, but serve fewer patients. However their ratio of patient care costs to administrative costs, and their bottom lines are amazingly similar to the huge health insurance providers. What they do is worsen the fragmentation effect in the industry, and that makes the situation an even larger problem. We propose to bring all of these smaller companies into our overall plan to have a single health care umbrella in the United States, but that phase will have to be done more gradually. So there you have it, Commander. That is the proposed plan."

In a rare show of emotion, Thor clapped his hands repeatedly and said, "Bravo, bravo! That is fantastic. Siran, Truls, my congratulations on your outstanding work. I have just one question, and then a general comment. First the question: How many agents will you need?"

"Sir, on average each of the ten target companies has 30 to 40 top executives. Our agents would replace those people when they leave Planet Earth for Prison Planet. So if nothing else changed, we would need approximately 400 agents. However, since we propose to merge the ten companies, we will eventually need only about 80 agents. Please bear in mind that those 400 temporary doubles must still be in place, in I-Mode, before we make any announcement of the take-over. In addition, we will need to assign agents to vulnerable people before the announcement."

"Why, Siran?"

"Well, Sir, we think you should go on CTS Sunday Review to announce this project, and when the top executives of those companies get the news we expect them to go ballistic. They are capable of anything, including kidnapping—even murder. They will discover that they cannot get to any Techna agents because of our personal security system, so they will go after others— people like Sarah, her family, CTS personnel, Sam Fischer, Mark Haddon. Agents need to be in position 24/7 before we announce to protect them. Also, having agents in place within the health care companies gives us the added advantage of time to learn their operating systems beforehand. The sooner we do this, the smoother the transition will be. "

Thor nodded in agreement. "Yes, I see your point, Siran. I am amazed at the depth of your research."

"Thank you Sir. It could not have been accomplished without Trul's help."

"Guri, What do you think?

"I think we can handle it, Commander. We will need lots of information on personnel to be replaced by doubles, but having our agents in place beforehand will make that task a lot easier."

"Manta, any comments?"

"Yes. Sarah will be the primary kidnap target. Have you given any thought to providing I-Mode security for her?"

"No. That is a great idea. I will take care of it immediately."

"Commander, what do we do with people who do attempt kidnapping? "

"We take them out, Truls, and we take out the person or persons giving such orders. Those people will not be going to Prison Planet. By the way, do you have a time line for this?"

"Sir, Siran and I believe it all hinges on how much time Guri and his staff will need for training. We can go as soon as the doubles are ready."

"Guri, if my numbers are correct you will need to train about 385 agents quickly for these two projects. Can you do that?"

"Yes, Sir., When you gave me the heads up before you left for Techna, I put together a sizeable training team. I also contacted the 25 doubles agents we put in congress previously, and they are providing valuable insight into Congressional operations. Couple that with the knowledge we will gain from the doubles to be inserted in advance in the health insurance companies, and I would be willing to commit to a six week training schedule."

"Guri," Truls said, "That would put insertion of agents at June 15, for the health care project. Give them a month to learn operation details and we could complete the take-over about July 15. I suggest Monday, July 12. Agree, Siran?"

"I think those are realistic goals for health care," Siran responded. "However, I think we should implement the Congress insertion no later than May 31, if possible."

Guri studied the note pad in front of him for several moments, then said, "Yes, I can make that work. So we will prepare the Congressional doubles by May 31, and the health care doubles by June 15. Agreed?"

Thor looked at Truls and Siran. What do you think?"

The two Group Captains nodded in the affirmative.

"Then we work toward those dates. Let's all stay in contact on this. It is very important. Keep in mind that we may be doing the same thing with respect to other industries in this country. We need to use what we learn here so we do not have redundant effort. Good work, all of you. Meeting adjourned."

* * *

After the meeting, which ended at 3:00 p.m., Thor went back to his office. Manta was with him, and he said, "Please try to reach Sam Fischer at CTS. I know it is late in New York, but maybe he is still at his office."

"Sure, Thor, but after that I would like to talk to you."

Thor nodded and strode into his office. He had no sooner settled into his chair when Manta stuck her head in the door and said, "He is on the line."

"Hello, Sam. You are working late, but glad I caught you. How are you?"

"I am okay, Commander, and working late is how it is around here. What's up?"

"Well, I would like to pay you a visit tomorrow if possible—give you an update on our work on health care."

"Great, I sure could use something interesting. When, tomorrow?"

"Your call, Sam."

"Okay, how about eight a.m.? It's quiet around here then."

"Perfect."

"Should Mark be here?"

"That would definitely be a good idea."

"Done. See you then. Margie will have the coffee on."

"Tea for me, please."

"Yeah, right. I forgot."

Thor hung the phone up and walked out to Manta's desk. "Please tell Jens I need to be in New York by 7:45 a.m. tomorrow," He said. "Now, you wanted to talk?"

"Yes, Thor. I am really worried about Sarah. She is very precious, and very vulnerable. I would die if anything happened to her."

"I understand how you feel, Manta. I am going to give her I-Mode capability right away. I gather you think more should be done."

"Yes I do. I think you should assign agents to her at all times—around the clock—except when you are with her personally."

"Hmmm. Maybe you are right. It seems prudent and certainly cannot hurt. But she must not know."

"I agree, and she will not. I will ask Group Captain Erika Varda to set it up."

"Tell you what, Manta, have Erika set up security on everyone who could be in harms way. Sarah, her family, the CTS people, everyone of them, and Manta?"

"Sir?"

"Good catch. Thank you very much. I really appreciate it."

* * *

At exactly 7:45 a.m. the next morning, the 4th of May, Thor's transporter settled silently onto the CTS rooftop helicopter pad. Once again he took the elevator down to the 60th floor and walked briskly through the long corridor toward the reception desk. As she had done the first time she saw him, Sarah watched him every second as he approached." Good morning, Commander. You are up very early," She said warmly.

"As are you, my dear. And what a wonderful surprise it is to see you. This is a treat I did not expect."

"Thank you, Sir, you may go in. They are waiting for you." That is what she said, but what she was thinking and did not say was, *I shall have many treats for you, dear man.*

Thor smiled at her and disappeared through the now familiar door. Margie was waiting for him with a steaming cup of tea in her hand. "Welcome, again, Commander. Good to see you. Here's your tea. Sam and Mark beat you here this time."

"Thank you, Margie," Thor said, taking the cup from her. "Good to see you, too. By the way, they should beat me, right? After all, they both live here."

"Commander, that is truer than you might think. They are always here."

Thor nodded and made his way to Sam's office. "Good morning Sam, Mark," He said, shaking their outstretched hands. "Thanks for giving me the time on such short notice."

"No problem, Commander," Sam said with a smile. "I am betting we will be richly rewarded. Have a seat, have a seat."

"Well, I certainly hope so. I am here to tell you what we intend to do about the U. S. health care situation, and to ask for your help. We have received Presidential approval to proceed."

"Okay, Commander," Sam said. "Lay it on us."

"Sam and Mark, this has to be extremely confidential for now, but our intent is for Techna Force 20 to take control of the health care industry, gradually, of course, because of its gargantuan size. We will begin by inserting Techna agents, who are very experienced in running large corporations, into the operations of the ten largest health care insurance companies on June 15. They will operate in I-Mode until July 12. Then they will become visible and take over management of the companies."

"What year are you talking about, Commander?" Mark wanted to know.

"This year, Mark. 2010."

"Wow, this is huge. What happens to the existing corporate officers?"

"They will take a one way five million mile trip to Prison Planet."

"Commander, you have not said what happens to the spouses and children of present officers. Do they go to Prison Planet, too?"

"No, Sam, and that is the tricky part of all of this. Our agents for such assignments as this—who are called *Doubles*--become those officers. They are made to look like the person they are replacing, talk the same way, dress the same, eat the same food. We already have dossiers on every officer and each related spouse and child in every health care corporation. Usually, the spouses are very pleased with the attention given them by their new/old mates. It sounds outlandish, I know, but we have had very good success with this approach."

Thor's explanation brought roars of laughter from Sam and Mark. Sam said, "Incredible. Absolutely incredible," and Mark exclaimed, "Jesus, Gawd Almighty! "So your guys just slip into another guys clothes and go from there. Is that it?"

"Basically, yes, Mark. Of course there is much detail in the preparation of such a plan, and in picking the agents."

"So, Commander," Sam said, "How does CTS Sunday Review fit into this plan?"

"Sam, I would like to announce it on your program."

"I see. But tell me first, how will your taking over health care benefit the United States?"

"Sam, we believe services your people depend on—such as national security, energy, and health care, should not be the responsibility of private, profit-motivated corporations. Putting such services in their hands jacks up the cost tremendously, while reducing the effectiveness of the service. You have seen this in your military's efforts to use private contractors for some of its work. The cost goes up over time, while the quality goes down. That is the natural evolution for profit-oriented companies."

"Techna Force 20 is not profit oriented. Our goal is to give your people—all of your people--the best health care at little or no cost to them, including a public option if they choose. We can do it better because our agents do not make anything near what health care corporation executives make, and because we will change these corporations to non-profit status, have no stockholders, and therefore no dividends to pay, eliminate much of the overhead by merging the separate businesses, and pay no income taxes. Under the present system, only about 20% of the gross revenue of these companies ever goes to patient care. The rest goes to cover drastically inflated operating costs. We will reverse that situation. We will send 80% or more to patient care, and only 20% to operating costs, thus increasing the amount of money available for patient care by about six times"

"Commander, that does sound like a very significant improvement," Mark commented. "And God knows we need it. But why announce it on *Sunday Review?* Why not just do it? You have the power."

"Because we want the people to get our reasons for stepping in directly from us—not from the health insurance companies. They will make us look like very bad guys to save themselves. American citizens trust *Sunday Review.* If you put us on, they will be more comfortable with this change."

"Commander, you know, of course that if we put you on we will have to offer insurance company representatives equal time—in order to provide a balance."

"Yes, Sam, we understand that and are willing to take our chances."

Sam and Mark exchanged glances, and Sam said, "Mark, what do you think?"

"I say we do it. It will be an incredible story. It is good for the country, it's good for the people, and it's perfect for us."

"Sam and Mark, I have to tell you, there is great risk in doing this. Health insurance company leaders will go ballistic when they hear about it. They will try to come after Techna Force 20, but will fail. So they will probably come after you and anyone else they can identify as allies of Techna Force 20. However, we have anticipated that and have taken steps to protect you."

"Commander, how can you guarantee our safety?"

"By taking you under our protective wings until the dust settles, and putting Techna doubles in your places. You will still have total control of your operation, of course, but your faces, which everyone knows, will be on our doubles. They cannot be harmed."

"Okay, Commander. It's a deal. We will do it," Sam said. "When would you like to go on our show?"

Just before July 12, Sam. That will be a Monday, so could we do it on Sunday, the 11th?"

Sam and Mark exchanged glances, and Mark said, "That would work, Boss. We only have some tentative subjects for that show, but nothing firm yet. I vote yes."

"Then we go, Commander. Do you have something we can use to develop a script—notes—that sort of thing?"

"Yes, Sam," Thor responded, and handed a sheaf of papers to each CTS man. If you need anything else let me know."

They all stood and shook hands, and Mark exclaimed, ":Commander, I'll say one damned thing: You don't do nothing small. I thought our first program with you was big, but I think this one is going to be huge. It will shake Wall Street *and* the Government to their very roots."

"Well, I hope it does, Gentlemen. Somehow, the Government leaders of your Country must be awakened to the fact that your people are hurting, and that most corporations—especially the largest ones—could not care less. I am pleased that Techna Force 20 can be a part of this effort."

* * *

On his way out of the CTS offices, Thor stopped at Sarah's reception station. "Honey, what would you say to spending all day Saturday with me? I have a surprise for you. It just seems like ages since we have been together and I miss you so much."

"Oh, Thor, that would be wonderful. What is the surprise?"

"No, dear heart, I cannot tell you now, but I think you will be pleased."

Sarah pretended to pout, then said, "Oh, all right. I will be patient."

"That is my lovely girl. Suppose I pick you up at nine a.m. We will have breakfast on the Cape, lunch on the Cape, and yes, dinner on the Cape."

"I'll be ready, Thor, though I have no idea how I am going to get through the rest of the week."

He reached across the reception counter and took her hand in his. "Until Saturday, dear lady. I do love you so very much."

* * *

Thor returned to Sardine Mountain directly from the CTS building in New York. When he reached his office suite, Manta was there as usual. "Manta, are you doing anything special on Saturday?"

"No, Thor, nothing special. I might go to Roswell and do some shopping. Why?"

"Because I have a better idea."

She looked up at him warily. "Such as?"

"Such as accompanying Sarah and me to Cape Cod for the day—with Jens, of course. Breakfast, lunch and dinner all on me. What do you think?"

"I think you want something."

"Humm, yes, I rather thought you might have that reaction, but, actually, I am planning a little surprise for Sarah and I thought you might like to be a part of it. And it is beautiful country."

"So I hear. Yes, I would love to come along."

"Great. Will you let Jens know, please?"

*   *   *

Thor, Manta and Jens arrived at Central Park West a few minutes before nine, on Saturday morning, and Thor went to pick up Sarah. When he returned with her and she saw Manta her eyes lit up with joy. The two women hugged and Sarah said, "Oh, Thor, is Manta your surprise? If so, she is a wonderful one."

"She is but your first surprise, my love. Ready, Jens?"

"Ready, Commander."

The flight from Central Park West to Barnstable, Cape Cod took just over five minutes. Their first stop was at Mashpee Commons, where Jens landed the transporter on a small grassy area adjacent to the town's main shopping center. From there they walked about one city block to the *Barnstable Cafe*, and enjoyed a leisurely breakfast. They emerged from the restaurant to find a long black limousine waiting at the curb. Its driver, dressed in a black suit, white shirt and black tie was standing by the car's open rear door.

"Ah, good, I see the car has arrived," Thor said "I thought this would be a better way to see the Cape today, Let's get in, shall we?"

They drove through Barnstable for some time before coming to a road shaded by huge maple trees. They drove along that road a few miles, until the driver turned left, through an open pair of ornate wrought iron gates. He drove slowly up a gracefully curving gravel drive, before finally coming to a stop in front of a stately home. The home's exterior was of weathered cedar shingles that were now nearly black from years and years of exposure to Cape Cod's harsh winters. There were three dormer windows on the equally weathered wood shingle roof, and all the trim pieces— windows, doors, fascia—were painted white. It was the classic Cape Cod style home, and Sarah thought it the most beautiful example of that style she had ever seen.

When the driver opened their door, Thor said, "Alright, everyone, this is something you must see." They walked about 30 feet to the home's front door, and he tapped the brass knocker several times. It was opened immediately by Sarah's father. She put both hands up to cover her mouth, which, like her lovely blue eyes, was wide open in absolute disbelief. "Father!, what are you doing here? Is Mom here, too? What in the world is going on? I'm so confused" She turned to look at Thor who was standing beside her, and saw a broad grin on his face. "Thor, please tell me what this is all about. We could have gone to Brookline, if it was just to see Mom and Dad."

"Easy, easy, darling. Let's go inside. Your father has something to tell you. But first, Manta, this is Ken and Rose Malloy, Sarah's parents."

Manta received hugs from both parents, and told them how much she had been looking forward to meeting them.

Next, Thor said, "Ken, the floor is yours"

"Sarah, this is your new home," he announced. "If you like it, that is. "

She gave Thor an angry look and said, "honey, I know we talked about this, and that you planned to ask Dad for help, but I thought we would look together. And here you have already bought it?"

"No, angel. Let me explain. I did ask a local realtor to begin looking for property here on the Cape, fully expecting that we would look at whatever she found together. A day or two later she called to tell me about this home. Your father checked it out and said he thought you would like it very much, but that the price was way above our range. He discovered that it had been on the market for almost three years, and did some hard negotiating. As a result, he was able to drive the price down to just under half the asking price, fully furnished. It has everything you and I talked about having in a home; five bedrooms, four bathrooms, plus plenty of room to add more of each; a huge yard for our children to explore and enjoy—14 acres, to be exact—a beautiful ocean front location, and traditional Cape Cod styling. I have not bought this home, or any other, dear heart. I would never do that without you being fully involved; In this case, I simply signed a letter of intent to buy it, contingent on your complete approval, just to guarantee that you would have time to inspect it at your leisure. If it is not what you want, we will move on to something else. I would like you and your Mother and Manta to take a tour—take all the time you want. Your father, Jens and I will await your decision."

Sarah came to him, put her arms around his waist and looked up at him. "Oh, my darling, you are upset with me," She said. "I am sorry."

"No, if I am upset it is with myself for not handling this better. I wanted it to be a very special moment for you, and it is not."

"Honey," Sarah's mother said, "The Commander asked your father and me about making this a surprise. We thought it was a wonderful idea. He told us then that he would not buy any house unless you were with him at the time. Just bringing you to see the house, that was to be the surprise."

"Yes, Sarah," Manta said. "I know Thor. He was only trying to please you. Come," she said, looking first at Sarah and then at her mother. "Let's go exploring, shall we?"

"In a moment, Manta. Thor, from what I have seen so far, it is a beautiful house. I am honored that you want it for me. And I adore you even more for wanting it to be a surprise. It was such an enormous surprise that it overwhelmed me. But I am alright now, and I can't wait to see the rest of the house—But I want you to see it with me. Why don't we all take the tour together?"

* * *

The Barnstable house, had originally been constructed in 1890, but was in like-new condition due to the constant attention of highly skilled craftsmen. It was very large, with twelve rooms, a basement, garages, storage rooms above the garages, patios, sun porch, and screened porch. Sarah and her entourage toured every one of those spaces, carefully inspecting each one and any furnishings in it, as they progressed. Manta and Rose found something wonderful to talk about everywhere they went, and made many well-intended suggestions about furniture placement, decorating, and so forth. Sarah listened and nodded from time to time, but said very little. Yet it was clear to everyone that her mind was taking mental photographs of every detail, no doubt to replace the camera she would have brought had she been better prepared. Thor watched her with amazement in his eyes, knowing full well that this beautiful young lady who had taken control of his heart would probably be able to replay those photographs in great detail at any future time.

When they had completed inspection of the inside of the home, they toured the expansive, beautifully manicured grounds from the front gates to the ocean beach at the rear of the property, and from the left side to the right side. It was not lost on either Thor or Ken Malloy that someone was also maintaining the landscaping meticulously, even though the home had not been lived in for some years. Nor was it lost on Thor that there were several perfect places to locate a combination office/hanger for the two transporters—one for Sarah, and one for him—and along the way, he and Jens made mental sketches of their own on design and placement of such a building.

The group's last stop was the boat dock which was anchored securely at the end of a long catwalk. Several slatted benches, facing out to sea, were positioned along the rear side of the dock, and all six members of the entourage took this opportunity to sit and relax and listen to the gentle rustling of the waves. Sarah and Thor sat close together on one bench, holding hands, not saying a single word. There was no need, and in fact doing so would have intruded on the majestic beauty of the place.

None of them wanted to leave the dock, but eventually it was time to return to the house, where they hoped to hear Sarah's decision.

Once back in the spacious great room, they all found seats and waited for her to speak. They did not wait long. When she saw that everyone was comfortable she walked to Thor's side, looked up into his eyes, and said, "My dearest Thor, this home is absolutely everything I could ever want. I just love it. But will it work for you?"

"Angel, first of all, I think it will be a wonderful place to raise our family. Additionally, I want it to be a sort of home away from home for your family, and my family, including Jens and Manta. Will it work for my business? Yes. As Jens and I were saying a bit ago, we will need to build a hanger for the transporters, apartments for the pilots of those ships, and an office. Otherwise, it is perfect for me, too. So, what do you say, shall I tell the realtor we will take it?"

"Oh, yes, Thor. How will I ever thank you?"

"You already have, My Love, by agreeing to be my wife. Without you this would just be another building."

*   *   *

From their soon-to-be new home, Thor and Sarah went with her parents, Manta and Jens, in the limousine to the Coonamessett Inn in the village of Falmouth, Cape Cod, the same place where Thor and Sarah had their first date; as well as a subsequent dinner, and a long-time favorite of Ken and Rose Malloy. Ken announced that he was treating on this occasion, to celebrate the home purchase decision, and suggested white wine and New England lobster for everyone. The vote was unanimous. While they waited for their meal to be served, there was much excited conversation about the house and the pending wedding. When Rose said she could not wait to meet Thor's family, Sarah said, "Momma, you will love them. They are super people and, of course, they will be here for the wedding."

"At five million miles, that will be the longest trip to attend a wedding on record," Ken said. "And I can't wait to meet them, either. Nor can I wait to visit Techna Planet, Thor. Will you fly us there, personally?"

"No, Ken. Any more, I leave flying to the experts. Jens is my expert. I would be lost without him, and I am afraid I burden him too many times with sudden special flights."

"The Commander is too kind, and much too modest. He is a fine pilot in his own right, and I have the best job in the universe."

"Mr. and Mrs. Malloy, all of us from Techna Planet are very pleased that our favorite leader, Thor, discovered Sarah, and through her you and your extended family," Manta said. "We are about to witness not just a wedding of two people in love, but a wedding of two planets in the universe. What a momentous occasion that will be."

Ken held his wine glass high and said, "Here, here! I second that, and from what little our Sarah tells us about your plans, Commander, I would say we Americans are about to get the better of that union. I am all for it, frankly."

301

"Thanks, Ken," Thor responded. "We hope it will be a mutually beneficial proposition. There is so much good we can do together."

At that moment the lobsters arrived and conversation about the house and the wedding took a back seat to a discussion on the proper way to consume New England lobsters. Fortunately, they were guided by expert New Englanders and dug in with great enthusiasm.

It was a fine meal and a wonderful ending to a very special day. Sarah had a look on her face that said everything about her feelings at that moment: Contentment. Bliss. Wonder at her good fortune. She was at peace. She was a woman for whom dreams of a child were becoming the reality of a woman. She looked lovingly at the man who would soon be her husband, a quiet man with awesome powerful, wisdom beyond his years, yet possessed of great tenderness and understanding. It was nothing she had planned; she had never once expected to meet a man from outer space, let alone become his wife. Nor had she ever considered that other Planets existed in the vast Universe, let alone travel to one of them. Nor had she ever expected to live in a house so beautiful, in a place so dear to her heart. Yet, all of these things had happened, and in much less than one year. Under the table, where no one could see, she took Thor's hand in hers and squeezed ever so gently. It was a gesture that said so very much in absolutely no spoken words.

*   *   *

Later that day, or rather that night, for it was now quite late, the limousine driver dropped Sarah's parents off at their own car, then delivered her, and Thor and Manta and Jens to Mashpee's Towne Centre parking lot where, after he left, they boarded the transporter for their return trip. But they would not be stopping in New York to drop her off, for she would be spending the night in a stateroom, in a starship, in Sardine Mountain, in New Mexico, with a man: a very special man.

*   *   *

-

Guri Kohn went to work on the preparation of doubles agents for Congress immediately after the meeting with Thor, Siran and Truls. Using the dossiers given to him by Thor, he rechecked the agent match for each Congressman and, finding no problem with any of the 85 matches, he made the tentative final mission assignments. Next, he called a meeting of his staff of instructors in order to get the training process started. He knew that nothing he was responsible for was as complicated or as important as getting 85 agents ready to step into the shoes of Congressman. It was not simply a matter of teaching them the ways of Congress; that was the easy part. The greater difficulty lay in making them look, act, talk and think like the House or Senate members they were to replace, and it would be even more difficult to bring about the metamorphosis needed to fool their new wives, children, other family members and friends. The doubles agents had been chosen and matched very well, but still needed a great deal of polishing.

Guri chose to work backwards, that is, to tackle the immense challenge of giving 85 wives a new husband and their children a new father, without the family realizing it, before completing the training to turn the agents into Congressmen. The doubles agents already knew the name they would adopt, as well as the names of their new family members, from studying their dossiers, so Guri ordered his instructors to build on that knowledge. They began by sending each doubles agent to his soon to be new home, in I-Mode, for at least a week to observe life in that household first hand. That proved to be a very wise approach, for the agents learned much more about their new life, in much less time than expected. When they returned to the training base in Guri's starship they already knew what changes they would need to undergo, in areas such as appearance, voice, mannerisms and dress, to fit into their new life. Each also knew a great deal about his new wife; her choice of clothes, jewelry and perfume; what she thought about; who she confided in; what she told others about her husband; even very private moments a woman save just for herself, and of course, they saw how she interacted with her children. They shared all of this knowledge with their instructors in great detail. The instructors fleshed out and elaborated on each bit of information thus obtained, added some important do's and don'ts along the way, then fed the expanded, modified information back.. Through such a repetitious routine the students completed a very complicated part of their education in an amazingly short time.

Changing agent appearances came next. It was accomplished with deft precision and amazing accuracy by expert TF20 plastic surgeons who had been called upon to perform such work countless times, always under very tight deadlines.

Voice and mannerism training, the final steps necessary to giving these agents a new life, followed quickly, as did learning to be U.S. Congressmen, and on May 31, as scheduled, all of them stood quietly and unseen in the Capitol Rotunda, waiting for the signal to take their place as America's new Republican Members of Congress.

* * *

At 7:30 p.m., of that same day in 2010, TF20's Prison Planet starship settled soundlessly and in I-Mode onto a parking lot adjacent to the United States Capitol for the second time in less than two months, and began to take on passengers. The passenger list included 30 members of the Senate, and 55 members of the House—85 powerful members of Congress in all--everyone a Republican. Many of them had been here before.

They appeared at the top of the boarding ladder one by one, groggy and shaky from the tranquilizer administered to each at the moment of being taken into custody, shielding their eyes against the bright lights inside the starship with their hands, and instantly angry at the sight of Truls Heyerdahl, who many remembered from their last visit, and who, in his quiet way, directed each of them to move along and take a seat. Those who had encountered him before shouted invectives and demanded to know why they were here, again as they passed. When the last person was seated, Truls began to speak. "I will not welcome you to this starship," he said, "because you are not going to find this a pleasant experience. Many of you were here on March 20, because you refused to cooperate with our plan to end the war in Iraq. I told you then that unless you did cooperate we would replace you with others more reasonable. You responded positively to that threat then and it was my hope that perhaps you would reform permanently. Unfortunately, much to my sadness, you have not."

John Raider, Senate Minority Leader, rose from his front row position, and said, "I told you before, and I tell you now, we don't answer to you, whoever you are."

"Yes, Senator Raider, I recall you saying that last time and, as I told you then, I do not answer to you or to your Government, either. I answer to a far greater power, and have enough power of my own to annihilate all of you here and now. Would you prefer that choice?"

"No. I would like you to release us, now, immediately. In fact, I demand it."

"That option is not available to you. Please take your seat, before it is too late."

Senator Raider hesitated a moment, then sat down.

Truls looked at him hard and nodded. "As I was about to say, tonight, as you were assembling here, I heard many of you ask again why you are here. I will tell you why. You are here because your motivation is all wrong. You are supposed to be representing the citizens who elected you. That is especially true of you Members of the House, but it is also true of you Senators, as well. Your responsibility is to them, not to big corporations. Your constituents—the people—need help with services they cannot provide for themselves—protection from foreign enemies, adequate health care, low cost energy, and protection from unscrupulous bankers—these are but a few of their daily needs. It is within your power to give them such services, but you do not. Instead, you shill for the huge corporate manufacturers whose only interest in national security is the money they stand to make from production of military material. You also shill for powerful healthcare insurance companies whose motivation is profit, not better health care; the petroleum industry which, likewise, is driven by constant efforts to increase profits; and by greedy bankers with the same motivation: profit, profit, profit. At this moment you Members of Congress are in great demand, only because you hold the enviable position of being able to feed the profit hunger of these corporations. But mark my words: the day will surely come when you, like any corporate asset that no longer contributes to the bottom line, will be discarded—thrown out with all the other non-productive garbage, by the very corporations you now so willingly help. The leaders of those businesses will just as quickly, just as callously, throw out the entire U.S. Government, if it stops serving their selfish appetite for profit."

"Rubbish, " said House Minority Whip, Murray Rosenthal, who was seated next to Raider. "We are here because you want to stop us from preventing the Democrats from giving all the Government's money to people who are too lazy to work for a living."

"An interesting claim, Congressman Murray, but untrue. We do not support malingering in any form. If you would bother to study the history of your Government you would learn that Republicans distribute far greater amounts of Government revenue than do Democrats. The difference is, they distribute to wealthy people, and even more to wealthy corporations, who do not need it, but take it out of sheer greed. Since 2003, you Republicans have distributed $3.5 trillion dollars just to the Iraq and Afghanistan war efforts. $3.5 trillion! The Democrats do not come close to matching your willingness to distribute such horrendous sums. It took a while to discover your reasons for doing this. But we now know it is to satisfy your very own insatiable thirst for wealth."

"Let me remind you that the vast majority of Government revenue comes from the middle class and the poor. Your policy of redistributing that wealth to your wealthy friends, in the hope that much of it will trickle down to you, is despicable. You do not want those poor taxed-to-death people to get even a single penny from their tax investment."

"That is why you are on this starship tonight. We no longer believe you can be reformed; you are simply too indebted to your corporate masters. You are here because you have no intention of working with the Democrats to overcome the many serious problems facing your country and its people. You are locked into a situation created by those same masters, who could not care less about the welfare of American people, or the country, unless there is huge profit in such caring—which is not the case. Bipartisan effort is of no interest to them, because they understand the Democrat's motivation, and detest it. Big corporations cannot tolerate a philosophy that makes common people the beneficiary of Government largess, rather than themselves; since you are their shills, the Democrat position cannot be of interest to you, either."

"Furthermore, you have as your secondary objective, the destruction of the Democrat Party because of its humanitarian philosophy, in the apparent belief that your Republican philosophy serves the greater good in the world. We believe that fragmentation of your country's managers into two parties, Democrat and Republican, though never provided for in your Constitution, has in fact been responsible for diluting your ability to concentrate on the country's real responsibilities: the needs of its people.

We also believe you made a serious mistake by classifying corporations as people, then giving them the same rights as real people. They are Corporations, not people. They are businesses run by people whose goals are avoidance of taxation, litigation, and anything else that cuts into profits. Those rights, coupled with their great wealth, makes them your masters and dictators of Government policies. So you have trapped yourselves. Whether wittingly or unwitting, you have put the greatest Country on Planet Earth on a path to destruction."

"Your masters have so corrupted you that, even if Democrats were saints, which they certainly are not, you would never be able to work with them, even for the good of the country. You have sold your ethics and morality, yea, even your souls, for money and power. Sadly, you have not yet discovered your master's thirst for profit is virtually insatiable."

"You might be forgiven for siding with them against middle and lower class citizens if, in the day to day battles on Capitol Hill, you actually offered some intelligent, sincere alternative proposals. But you do not do that, either. You simply say , 'No.' You have become the party of NO."

"For these reasons, and our deep-seated conviction that the people must be served first, rather than last or never, we are, tonight, taking a page from the corporate play book and removing you from the game."

"You will not like where we are sending you. It is a terrible place where you will have to fight constantly for every morsel of food, every warm blanket, every bit of shelter from the elements. Your situation will be made worse by the realization that you will probably never leave there. Do I feel sympathy for you? No. As you sow so shall you reap, so goes the saying. You have made this bed of your own choosing. You broke your promise to the people, because, like your masters, you thirst for wealth and power."

"None of you will be going home tonight, or any other night. The people of the States you represent need a voice in Congress. Sadly, unless they earn at least $200 thousand dollars a year you do not represent them. That situation ends tonight."

Truls paused and scanned the assembled faces. "Your places have already been taken by people who *will look after* the welfare of all American people. Those same people have already assumed responsibility for the care, protection and nurturing of your families, as well. We regret the need for such drastic action, but you have brought this on yourselves."

He turned to TF20 Captain, Karl Russo, the officer in charge of the Prison Planet starship, who was standing by his side, and said, "Captain, I release these prisoners to your care. Please see that they get to their destination."

"Very well, Sir."

At that point, John Raider and Murray Rosenthal stood again.

"Gentlemen," Truls asked, "Are you standing because you want to switch parties?"

"No," Senator Raider responded. "We want to know what it will take for you to end this foolish adventure and release us?"

"It will take the signatures of all of you on the Change Of Party form I hold in my hand, nothing less."

The two Congressional members conferred briefly in whispered tones, and Rosenthal said, "We will need time to present that ultimatum to our members."

"Very well. You have one hour." Truls looked at his watch and said, "It is now 8:30 p.m. I will expect your answer promptly at 9:30." He nodded to Captain Russo, who gave the order to post guards at all exits, then he left the room.

Approximately ten minutes later, Captain Russo, who remained in the lounge in I-Mode, sent a text message telling Truls the Congressmen were plotting an escape and had no intention of signing the document. He asked Truls to return immediately. Truls walked in to find the congressmen facing off with fifty Techna agents.

"So," He said. "Your request for time was nothing but a ploy, just another lie."

"You're correct, by God," Rosenthal said. "We are getting out of here now. You have neither the right nor the power to hold us."

"Congressman, if you take one step toward the exit ladder, it will be your last."

"I don't believe you," Rosenthal responded, and moved a step forward.

Instantly, an agent standing directly in front of him fired his laser. Rosenthal dropped like a stone, and was dead before his head hit the floor. The room filled with angry shouts, but they were soon replaced by shocked silence.

Truls turned to Captain Russo, and said, "Captain, prepare to get under way. I suggest you confine all of these men to locked cells immediately. They can no longer be trusted."

"Very good, Sir."

Truls then left the starship and returned to his own ship, where he immediately contacted Group Captain Guri Kohn to inform him of the execution of Rosenthal. Then he said, "But we will still need his double, Guri." Next, he called Commander Berksten to let him know that the Congress mission had been completed as planned, in spite of the escape effort, and the death of Murray Rosenthal.

"Good work, Truls. Please extend my gratitude to your agents. What will you do about Rosenthal?"

"Commander, we have already sent his double to congress."

"Fine. Very good thinking."

"Sir, I only hope we see positive progress now in Congress. New Republican candidates will continue to try for election to Congress, of course, but to make certain unity does occur, we have put procedures in place to prevent them from ever taking the oath of office. The Republican Political Party is effectively dead as of tonight."

"Right, Captain. We gave them a chance to act like responsible adults, but they insisted on acting like children so we had no choice but to send them to their rooms."

Truls laughed. "That is a good way to put it, Commander; we sent them to their rooms."

"We will see, my friend," Thor responded. "We will see. I fear we will have to do much more of that before the Americans truly unite to achieve their common goals." He almost told his second in command that he knew nothing really concrete would be achieved by Congress until both parties, Democrat as well as Republican, no longer dominated American politics, but he decided to save that for later.

* * *

The take-over of the Republican Party contingent in Congress became a reality with hardly a ripple. A few Democrats noticed that many Republicans were suddenly voting with them on key issues for the first time, and that much more legislation was being passed much quicker. They did not understand why, of course, but were very pleased. No longer did they face the animosity of the past—the ridicule, the harassment—there was genuine cooperation for a change, with disagreement at times, yes, but with sincere intent to conclude the matter successfully.

* * *

The giants of industry had quite a different reaction. It did not take them long to realize that their relationships with members of Congress were no longer as they had been. For many years—since just after the end of World War II, in fact—the CEO of a corporation had only to crook his little finger at 'his' Congressman or Congresswoman, stuff a few hundred thousand dollars in his or her pocket, or to his or her favorite cause, to get done whatever favor he wanted done. That was the way the system worked, and because of it, millions upon millions of dollars in orders for goods and services had flowed to those corporations who preferred to play that game, whether the goods or services in question were essential to Government programs or not; in fact they were often non-essential, and therefore an outright waste of tax-payer money.

But after the May 31, 2010, Republican purge, Corporate CEO's found more and more Congressional doors closed to them, if not actually slammed in their faces, and they were very angry. Having to win Government contracts the old fashioned way, through competitive bidding, was a lot more difficult and time consuming, to say nothing of the fact that there was no longer any guarantee they would get whatever contract it was they wanted, or that they expected to get more for their 'donations.' "

Faced with such a great loss it should surprise no one that these powerful men would use every tool in their bag of weapons to regain control of such a valuable asset as   Congress, or that they would act swiftly. So it was that a dozen powerful men, constituting a Steering Committee, gathered in the conference room of a posh resort hotel on Hilton Head Island, a few days after the loss occurred. The group included CEO's from big oil, health care insurance, banking, manufacturing, and agriculture, among other industries. They brought with them the legal authority to act for all corporations, and their objective was to find the cause of Republican defection, and stamp it out. They would stop at nothing, so important were the Washington contacts to their bottom lines.

The first two days of the gathering were dedicated to strategy. They knew what had happened, but needed to know why. Finding out was made the first step. Next, they needed to find a way to restore their control over Congress. Determining the why and the how turned those two days into marathons, but by midnight of the second day, the consensus was that they had answers to both questions. At that point, disregarding the lateness of the hour, calls were placed to the Minority members of Congress, John Raider, and Murray Rosenthal. There was no mistaking the tone of the calls; they were, in effect, non-negotiable summons to meet the CEO's at Hilton Head.

The Techna doubles masquerading as Raider and Rosenthal decided to play along, so they appeared early the next morning, as ordered. They listened patiently to the charges against their Party for over an hour, at which time Perry Spatz, CEO of Coastal Oil and Gas, and acting Chairman of the Steering Committee, said, "We need to know from you Congressional leaders, what you intend to do to get our good relationship back on track. The business community has been very generous with support for your party for many years, as I am sure you realize. We would not like to see that good relationship end."

New-John Raider stood to respond. "Mr. Chairman, let me point out that the relationship has been mutually profitable. Yes, business has been generous, but Government has been generous in return, perhaps much more so. It seems to me that we have looked the other way too many times, when we knew that your bids were far higher than justified, an oversight failure that has often resulted in gross waste of Government funds. Furthermore, speaking of oversight, all of the corporate fields of endeavor represented here—and many not represented--have successfully lobbied for and been the recipients of drastically reduced Government oversight. Such reductions have not been at all favorable to the American public."

"Yes," the Committee Chairman responded. "I see your point. So it's more money you are after. We can fix that, you know. Everything is negotiable."

"I am afraid that won't work, any longer, Mr. Chairman," New-Murray Rosenthal said. "We are taking a great deal of heat from Democrats on just the subject of excessive contract costs, forget oversight. They are accusing us of fixing bids, and are demanding return to honest, open competitive bidding."

"Come, come, now, Murray, let's be realistic. We can't make it in the market place--American or World--any other way. You know that."

"If you mean you can't make it and achieve the same level of profits that way, I'd say you're probably right. But we all know your profit margins are huge—beyond huge, in fact. Something has to give."

"What has to give here is Congress, Murray. You guys made a deal. You need to honor it."

"Whoa, hold it a minute, Mr. Chairman," John Raider said. "There is a limit to what Congress can do for business. We have already pushed that limit beyond stretching point. There is no more give to give."

The Chairman turned to face his corporate colleagues and said, "Gentlemen, I think we should find Congressmen who are more cooperative. What do you think?"

There was a chorus of affirmative responses, after which the Chairman said, "John, Murray, thanks for coming. You will be hearing from us, I assure you."

"That's fine, Perry. Just don't expect business as usual. The days of doing business this way are over."

"We will see about that, John."

* * *

After the Congressmen left the conference room, Chairman Spatz called the meeting to order again. "Gentlemen, " he said, "We have a problem. I don't know what is going on here, but something sure as hell is. Rosenthal has been like putty in our hands for years. He has always seen to it that our interests were taken care of in the House. Raider, while not as flexible, has done good work for us in the Senate. The millions we have paid those two has been money well spent. Now, I am not so sure about either of them. It's as if they are different men, though I don't know how that could be. It's pretty clear, to me at least, that we have lost their support. I will entertain a motion to replace those two minority leaders with more supportive people. That motion was quickly made and seconded. Then a search sub-committee was formed to carry out the necessary research, and the meeting was adjourned.

* * *

When John Raider and Murray Rosenthal left the Steering Committee meeting, it was to go immediately to a meeting with Commander Thor Berksten, who had, himself, attended the Steering Committee meeting in I-Mode. "Good morning John and Murray. What do you think?"

"It went about as expected, Commander," Murray said. "They feel as if we broke a bargain, and are very angry. Also, you could see the look in their eyes. They are very confused by the sudden change in Congressional attitude, after so many years of getting their way. I am certain they will try to replace John and me."

"No doubt," Thor responded. "But that attempt will fail, of course. Every Republican member of Congress they might try to buy is a Techna agent who cannot be bought. We need not concern ourselves with what they are going to do. We must move ahead to the next step: reinstalling effective corporate oversight in all major business areas. How are those bills progressing?"

"Commander, drafting of key oversight Bills for the petroleum, health care, banking/finance, agriculture and transportation industries is well along in the House," Murray said. "Democrats have tried to get them reinstated for years, but were always stymied by balky Republicans. Now they see that our positions have come full circle and closely match their goals, and that pleases them very much. There is strong support for corporate oversight on both sides of the aisle now. I think we will see a successful vote as soon as the end of June."

"How about the Senate, John?" Thor asked.

"Same situation, Commander. Senate Democrats have long advocated greater oversight. These Bills could pass with a huge margin when the House sends them over to our chamber. I foresee only moderate problems in reconciliation, and anticipate passage by the 15th of July. I also agree that the corporate kingpins will fail in any effort to find support for defeating oversight—in either house, and in either party. Democrats have little use for their greedy ways, and no new Republican candidate to whom they give support will survive long enough to even take the oath of office. We definitely have them boxed in. Actually, American people have had quite enough of corporate greed. They have long believed we were selling the Country to big business, and will have no sympathy for them."

"Very good work, Gentlemen. Now we can move on to our next objective, which is taking control of key business entities, without having to concern ourselves with negative political intervention."

"Commander, are you referring to the health care industry, by any chance?"

"Yes, John. Health care will be our first target. We need to give the people a health care system that is much better than the one Congress passed. It needs to be managed by a non-profit , non-government organization, for maximum efficiency and greatest coverage."

"Sir," Murray Rosenthal said, "You can now count on the full support of the House wherever you need it for that venture."

"Right," John Raider said. "And of the Senate. The Party of 'NO' is now the party of 'YES'. Government is no longer the enemy of the people."

------///------

315

CHAPTER THIRTEEN

TF20 Versus Big Corporations

Thanks to the hard work and dedication of Guri Kohn and his staff of expert instructors, one group of 30 doubles agents took its place as invisible observers inside each of the six major health insurance companies on June 15, 2010, as planned.

In the first phase of training, which was allotted just one month, doubles agents learned to handle the business responsibilities of the specific corporate officer each was to replace. During a part of each day every doubles agent spent time with his or her 'target officer' in the latter's corporate office, in I-Mode.

In the second training phase, doubles spent time in the homes of the corporate officers they were going to replace, during the time their 'target' would be at home, in order to learn everything possible about his or her personal life, as well as time in a classroom environment in the starship during each day.

Thus, on July 12, the takeover date, they were all fully capable of assuming their 'target' officer's complete identity, and did so seamlessly.

*   *   *

Assim Agassi was committed to another kind of success: the end of illicit drug cartels. In the few short months he and his agents had been assigned to their mission, they had intercepted and destroyed 12 huge drug shipments from South American countries. Aside from preventing significant quantities of drugs from reaching U.S. markets, Assim's Group had added more than $500 million dollars to the income of Techna Force 20. While the acquisition of money was certainly not the primary reason for going after drug cartels, it did have the collateral benefit of financing good programs for the American people, rather than bad.

Now Assim's Group Four was on the verge of ending the largest drug operation ever uncovered, one with a projected street value of more than $15 billion dollars. Techna agents had been tracking it for weeks, and every element, from fields and factories deep in South American jungles, to the vast transportation network in Mexico, to the sophisticated, nation-wide American distribution system with outlets in all large U.S. cities, was identified on detailed charts and maps, along with names and photos of the key players. The lists of names and the number of photos ran to thousands. Some of the players held the highest positions possible in some of America's largest corporations. Many more were top-level Federal Government officials.

Group Four agents, in I-Mode, were imbedded at every key position. They were on full alert, ready to strike at a moment's notice on Assim's command.

The command came just after midnight on June 15, 2010, the date and time set by cartel leaders for 25 simultaneous drug shipments to cross United States' borders at various points in California, Arizona, New Mexico and Texas. The shipments came by every conceivable conveyance--cars, semi-trailer trucks, boats, airplanes, and in the backpacks and clothing of poor peasants desperate for money. The drug lords figured that, with so many shipments moving north, drug enforcement agents would simply be overwhelmed and confused, and many shipments would get past them. But of course they did not reckon with the power of TF20, which intercepted and burned every one of the 25 shipments. Every bag, box, suitcase, carload and truck load of cash was seized. Every drug lord, under-boss, and worker with anything to do with the operation at any level was promptly executed, and every drug crop field was burned or plowed under.

On the buyer side of the transaction, numerous powerful, and very successful corporations found that key officers and employees had suffered violent deaths. They tried to cover up the deaths as "accidents," but those efforts failed because

Techna agents published detailed dossiers linking every guilty male and female employee—and through them the corporations themselves--to illicit drug activity. It became shockingly clear that they were successful corporations only because of involvement in drugs, not because of the products they manufactured or the services they provided. One by one those corporations filed for bankruptcy protection and would no longer be a factor in the American business arena.

Likewise, many high-level Government employees went missing, never to be found. No small number of law enforcement agencies suddenly found themselves short handed, and hundreds upon hundreds of drug distributors were found dead on the streets, in allies and scruffy hotel rooms, and in vehicles, all along the U.S. Border. Had it been within their power to comprehend who was responsible, DEA agents would have only needed to check with Assim Agassi. For all the executions were carried out on his orders, with the full approval of Commander Thor Berksten. At the final count, TF20 was richer by the actual sum of $17.5 billion dollars. The illicit drug trade might attempt a comeback, but its efforts would be spasmodic at best, and it would never flourish again in the United States. But in the off-chance it did rise again, Techna Force 20 would be waiting.

*   *   *

Among the buyers waiting to profit from this drug operation were ten televangelists who had already acquired great wealth through virtual extortion of donations from gullible people, yet still wanted more. Arne Klein was very familiar with these ten men who, collectively, were the dregs of that religious element, and had destroyed the good reputation of dozens more televangelists through their greed.

So, on the morning of June 15, 2010, when those ten received news that drugs they had ordered, and paid for in advance, had been 'lost' along with the aggregate $50 million dollars they had pooled to make the buy, and were in great shock, Arne was secretly thankful. By selling their portion of the drugs, they expected to gain a sizeable return on their money--something on the order of fifty percent profit--to be squirreled away to help continue their extravagant personal life styles if donations dried up. Instead they had nothing. Now they would have to go back to their congregations and beg for more donations, 'because costs had gone up more than expected, making it impossible to help the poor.'

But their flocks were no longer gullible. This time their congregations were not just hearing phony sob stories from their pastors; they were also getting reports, backed by facts, from clean-cut, well-dressed Techna Force 20 agents, who were appearing all over television, telling quite a different story about what happened to the money. Their leader, Captain Arne Klein, made many of the TF20 speeches, and he was especially believable.

As a result, televangelists suddenly found it virtually impossible to raise funds. One by one, they went out of business. One by one, their opulent mansions, once the centers for lavish gatherings, went on the auction block, along with all their expensive furnishings, as bankers sought to recover whatever they could from the disaster. One by one, their sophisticated television production studios were dismantled and sold piecemeal by the finance companies that had funded them.

Some televangelists, a resourceful bunch, to be sure, tried to start new churches in run-down buildings in older sections of the cities, but failed. Others returned to their roots as used car salesmen, or found work as carnival hucksters, selling kitchen utensils, jewelry, computers and other goods. None of them showed any remorse for the people whose money they had lavished on themselves for so long, and would do so again given the chance.

Their complete absence of feelings, unwillingness to repent and readiness to resume the fleecing of their flocks, all in the name of religion, did not go unnoticed by Captain Klein. Convinced that another chance was not in the best interest of American people, he ordered Prison Planet sentences for all guilty televangelists, as well as other unscrupulous religious ministers using their churches exclusively for personal gain. Religious denominations such as Catholic, Baptist, Episcopalian and Lutheran, were given the benefit of doubt and escaped his directive, but he assigned Techna agents to them and to all other religious denominations, with instructions to keep watch and report. In particular, agents were to investigate every charge, past and present, of child molestation by Catholic Priests; charges that had fallen on deaf ears far too long.

* * *

Around this time, Thor asked Erika Varda to accept an additional assignment. When they met at Sardine Mountain, he said, "Erika, there is one area of American life we are not covering adequately"

"Oh, what area is that, Sir?"

"Crime. Erika. Capital crime, to be precise. I refer to all the convicts in prisons who have no possibility of parole, as well as current capital cases being tried in U.S. Courts as we speak."

"Yes, I see, but does that area not fall within Group Captain Agassi's responsibility?"

"Yes, it does. However, as you know, he is very busy right now with the illicit drug problem, and asked to be relieved of the crime issue because he does not feel he can do it justice. He recommended you for that assignment, and I believe you are the best choice."

"I am honored, Commander. My work load is not heavy at this time. How can I help?"

"Erika, there are two parts to this assignment. The first has to do with righting an inhumane situation wherein people convicted of capital crimes, such as murder and rape, are essentially warehoused for life without the possibility of parole. As you know, we warehouse bad people ourselves, on Prison Planet, but we never put people in cages as is the practice here. Instead, we put them in an environment where they must fight to survive. They pay a huge penalty because the life is hard, but they retain a modicum of dignity by having to fight for every bite of food, every rag of clothing, every bit of meager shelter."

"Sir, that system is not possible here?"

"It is possible, Erika, and it might work, I think. But Americans are soft touches. They disagree with our thinking, Notwithstanding the fact that their way does not reduce the number of heinous crimes. On the other hand, People of Techna know that fear of death is the most effective deterrent to crime.

Americans who kill, or rape have no such fear; they know they will simply spend time in a warm cell, with food and clothing provided for life. We must stop the warehousing of capital criminals. "

"Releasing them is certainly not an option."

"Correct."

"So....I am to execute them?"

"Yes, Erika. That is your assignment. But please understand: these prisoners should have been executed originally—right after their trials and a reasonable appeal process. The legal system did not let that happen, and still does not. People convicted of capital crimes are given endless opportunities to appeal. Unreasonably long appeals are the norm. Appeals go on for years, just as they did for death penalty prisoners, and the cost escalates and escalates, most of it going to the legal profession. Ultimately, the government simply caves in on trying to execute people, because it actually costs more to execute someone than it does to warehouse them for life. No one in America is going to override that fact—at least no one who stands to enrich themselves because of it. If it is to be overridden, we must do it, because we are not beholden to the American legal system. So. will you accept this assignment?

"I will, Commander. Those poor devils rotting in prison might not agree, but death for them is the lesser of two evils, assuming, of course, that they have had an opportunity to exhaust their reasonable appeal rights. Furthermore, it is the punishment they would have expected in the first place."

"Quite so, Erika. It is the correct punishment, and yes, they have had ample opportunity for appeal, and we will make certain convicted prisoners have it in future cases, before we execute. Now, would you like to hear the second part of the assignment?"

"Yes, Sir, but just one comment first: The statement you just made implies that we will be handling capital punishment long term. Do I understand that to be the case?"

Thor nodded in the affirmative, and then said, "I am pleased that you accept this difficult task. If there is anything I can do to help, you have only to ask. Now, the second part, which also deals with people convicted of capital crimes. Currently, the practice in capital crime cases is to give judges great sentencing latitude. —those involving murder, rape, incest, fraud, and so forth—but the system is not working. Judges are using their latitude much

321

too liberally, and much too frequently. The maximum penalty for a capital crime is death. Yet judges are routinely handing down sentences of as little as five years in prison. Remember, judges must stand for re-election every few years. They do not want to face constituents who are against capital punishment. It is no wonder U.S. prisons are bursting at the seams, or that crime rates are going up instead of coming down. We must put their legal system back on track, and the only way to do that is to enforce the death penalty beginning now."

"How, Commander?"

"By sending our agents into every court in the land that is handling capital crimes, and by giving those agents authority to carry out the death sentence then and there, when judges fail to do it themselves."

"Yes, Commander, I understand, though it seems to me that this part of the assignment is really no different than the first part. "

"Quite so, Erika. Will you accept both parts of the assignment?"

"Yes, Sir, and I will do my very best. These people are getting away with hideous crimes virtually unscathed, and that is wrong."

"I am pleased. Sorry to burden you with this, but pleased that you are willing to take it on. It is a very important issue."

* * *

Erika wasted no time. On June 15, 2010, she dispatched agents to all state prisons, to begin executions of the approximately 30,000 members of the life without parole prison population. As they had done in the extermination of all death row prisoners earlier, her agents worked so efficiently and so swiftly that the task was completed almost before the press got wind of what was happening. When they did publish the news, there was a huge collective cry that "innocent people had been cruelly murdered without cause." But those cries did not come from ordinary citizens, for they were relieved that real justice was finally being done. No, they came from prison guards who lost high-paying jobs because there were no prisoners to guard, from the heads of large corporations with fat government contracts to run prison sections that now stood empty, from law firms growing wealthy processing lengthy appeals, and finally, from civil rights groups that had never supported the death penalty in the past, and would never support it in the future, regardless of how heinous the crime.

The first part of her execution campaign was completed in just one week. Newspapers and television stations covered the story for one week more, then moved on to other news, for by then it was old news.

Also on June 15, 2010, Erika dispatched agents to monitor capital crime trials in process in courtrooms around the country.

In Los Angeles, California, a man accused of raping and murdering a twelve year-old girl was on trial. He was found guilty on all counts by the jury. After that phase of the trial, Erika visited the judge in his chambers, entering in I-Mode, then making herself visible as she stood before the judge's massive desk. His response was predictable: "Who the hell are you, and how did you get in here?" he demanded.

Erika calmly introduced herself, and said she represented Techna Force 20. then got right to the point of her visit: "Your Honor, you just completed a trial in a capital crime case. The jury found the defendant guilty. The proper punishment for this crime under the circumstances involved, is death. I am here to strongly urge you to make that your sentence."

"Young lady, what makes you think I have to do what you suggest? I know all about your Techna Force 20 bunch. You have no authority here. You are just a bunch of bullies, throwing your weight around. But that won't work with me. Now, get out of here before I call my marshals and have you thrown out."

"Very well, Your Honor. But if you do not give this criminal the death penalty, we will. Then I will be back to visit you again, and you will not like that experience."

"That sounds like a threat to me," The Judge responded, reaching for the phone on his desk.

"It is no threat, Your Honor, it is a promise," Erika said, and disappeared.

One week later, the judge handed down his sentence: 25 years to life, a very light sentence considering. Upon hearing the judge's decision, the Techna agent on site, operating in I-Mode, handed down his own death sentence, and carried out the execution with one swift laser shot. Erika was waiting for the judge when he retreated hastily to his chambers, and this time she was not in I-Mode.

"You!" He yelled, as he grabbed at the phone frantically.

"Yes, Your Honor. I am here to make good on my promise." And with that she raised her left arm and fired her laser directly at him.

*   *   *

In Detroit, Michigan, a man was on trial for murdering two convenience store employees during an armed robbery. Three witnesses saw him commit the crime, but his sharp Defense Counsel argued that his client was legally insane. The jury did not agree and found the accused guilty, then recommended the death penalty. Again, Erika followed the judge into his chambers and made herself visible as she stood in front of his desk. His reaction was the same as that of the Los Angeles judge, but as she had done in that prior case, Erika calmly introduced herself, then called the judge's attention to what had transpired in Los Angeles. Then she pointed out the proper penalty for the jury verdict just handed down, just as she had done before, and said, "Your duty is clear, Your Honor. We merely ask that you act accordingly."

"Or what? You will kill me, too?"

"No. We will execute the defendant, but you get another chance, provided you change your thinking on capital punishment, and agree to work to convince your fellow judges to do the same. If you fail, I will kill you, and those other judges as well. Your duty is to see that justice is done. You do so by handing down sentences that fit the crime. When someone commits a capital crime, justice demands maximum punishment.

Hand down a lesser sentence and you as judge are not doing your job. That makes you surplus in our view, and we do not let surplus people live. This time you are safe. But if any future case you hear calls for the death sentence, and you hand down a lesser sentence, I will personally kill you. I hope you understand that, Your Honor."

This judge seemed unafraid, and not intimidated. There was a firm set to his jaw as he stared up at this beautiful young woman in a blue gray uniform, with cold blue eyes. "Madam, " he said, after several seconds, "I will not allow you to tell me how to run my court, first of all. And second, I am having you arrested right now for threatening a United States judge." With that he raised the phone and called for his marshals. When the two uniformed guards arrived, though, the only other person in the room was the judge.

His decision came down three days later: Life in prison, making it possible for the convicted killer to be released in 25 years.

Within two minutes after the decision was handed down, it did not matter, for the killer lay dead on the courtroom floor, the victim of a single laser shot. The judge quickly retired to chambers, where he waited for Erika to reappear. When she did not, he went about his work with her admonition ringing in his ears. *Change your thinking on capital punishment or die,* she had warned. He had seen the determined look in her eyes, and knew she was very serious. Not wanting to die, he made the decision to follow the law, and encourage other judges to do the same.

* * *

In Saint Louis, Missouri, two men and one woman were on trial for stealing 20 million dollars from gullible senior citizens in a blatant ponzi scheme, which left the old people destitute. The evidence against them was strong and all three were convicted, yet in spite of that, their long history of similar crimes, and the warning the judge received from his colleague in Detroit, they were each sentenced to just ten years in prison. As soon as the judge handed down his decision, spectators began to whisper among themselves and to look around expectantly, for the raft of recent court room executions was by now well known to just about everyone. Seconds later these courtroom attendees witnessed three hissing, bright green laser shots that seemed not to have been fired by anyone, but rather, to originate in mid-air. The hissing flashes were followed by the thud, thud, thud of three dead bodies hitting the floor. Seconds later, that judge, fearing for his life, literally fled to the supposed safety of his chambers, but once there he came face to face with a young woman in a finely tailored blue/gray uniform. "I am Erika Varda, Group Captain, Techna Force 20," She said. "I know you received a call from a judge in Detroit. You should have listened to him, Your Honor. Now it is too late." With that, she pointed her left arm at the cowering man and fired. It was over for him in a second.

* * *

And so it went throughout the rest of June and all of July, 2010. In courtroom after courtroom, across the United States, dozens of capital crime trials were held, and criminals were convicted. But now, more often than not, judges handed down death sentences and were themselves spared. The people they sentenced were given a maximum of 90 days in which to complete their appeal, thanks to a new law just enacted by Congress. A few convicts won their appeals, which did result in reduced sentences. Those who lost on appeal, died immediately. Those judges who persisted in the practice of handing down lesser sentences watched helplessly as their prisoners were executed in the court room, and then lost their own lives in chambers at the hands of Erika Varda.

Suddenly the game had changed. Prisoners awaiting trial were now terrified of what lay in store for them in court, for they could see that easy sentences was no longer a sure thing.

Newspapers, television news rooms, and the many talking heads on television were now chattering non-stop about this sudden quick solution to capital crime, and the tiny five-feet-two beauty with short auburn hair who was the chief executioner. At first, they were uniformly in favor of catching her and giving her a taste of her own medicine. But as time passed, and the crime rate dropped drastically, and the general public voiced their approval of now safer cities and towns, the brave girl, Erika, who made it all happen, caused them to change their opinion from hatred of her to great admiration for doing what no one else in the Country had intestinal fortitude to tackle.

Thor, who had always been convinced that the only way to stop heinous crimes against society was to use maximum force, was very pleased that his predictions had come true; and he considered Erika's performance nothing short of magnificent. She was the youngest Group Captain on his staff, and the most untested in battle. But she had certainly showed her mettle in this assignment.

* * *

Meanwhile, the education process for 180 Techna agents destined to serve as doubles in six giant health care corporations was progressing very well in lavish offices around the country. Doubles agents were attending meetings in I-Mode at all levels, flying unseen with corporate representatives on visits to groups of Primary Care Physicians and hospitals all over the country, where the health care corporation's rules were explained and enforced. In short, they "were working" side by side with health care officials on a daily basis, in every aspect of the business. Keeping copious, detailed notes, plus copies of letters, policies, procedures, and minutes of high-level meetings was part of each day's routine.

Also, at the end of each day they returned to "their" soon to be homes and "their" soon to be families, to further the private, but equally important, part of their training. Though never visible, they spent that time, as well as weekends, with those families, and mentally rehearsed how they would play each and every part of being the real head of that family when the time came. This part of their assignment was actually much easier than they expected because, as they quickly discovered, family life in America was very little different than family life on Techna Planet.

* * *

Late in June, 2010, Commander Berksten was in his starship office going over reports from busy Group Captains, when Manta appeared at his office doorway. "The President asks that you stop by the Oval Office the next time you will be in Washington."

"Did he say what it is about, Manta?"

"No."

"Very well, I am going to D.C. tomorrow anyway, so I will see him then."

"Shall I let him know?"

"I think not, Manta. He is accustomed to having me just drop in on him. But ask Jens to prepare for a flight at seven a.m., please."

* * *

Thor arrived in the Oval Office at 7:30 a.m., to find New President Fields already hard at work. Noting that the President was alone, he made himself visible as soon as he entered the room.

"Ah, Commander. Good to see you, but you did not have to make a special trip."

"Not a problem, Mr. President. How may I help you?"

"Well, you can help me understand what has happened to Congress. I cannot believe the cooperation I am getting on oversight legislation—in fact, everything we have wanted for the American people for so long. It is wonderful, and so refreshing."

Thor laughed and said, "That tells me our changes are working, Sir. There are no more Republicans in Congress, actually, at least in terms of political ideology. All of the Republicans are now Techna Agents working as doubles, and they are really Democrats in disguise."

"Ah hah, that explains it. Dare I ask what happened to the real Republicans?"

"Sir, are you asking?"

The President was thoughtful for a moment, and then responded, "No, Commander. I think I had better not ask."

"Mr. President, I will tell you that they are alive and reasonably well. I will also tell you that I have been studying your Constitution on the subject of Congress."

"Oh, why, Commander?"

"To find where it specifies that members of Congress must be members of a specific political party."

"And what did you find, Commander?"

"That there is no mention of political parties in that document at all."

"Yes. Interesting, isn't it?"

"Very."

"And your conclusion, Commander?"

"My conclusion is that an amendment should be written prohibiting membership in any political party. Parties such as the Democrat, Republican, Independent, Tea and others would be allowed to exist and even support candidates for political office. But those candidates would have no allegiance to the political parties whatsoever. All elected members of Congress should work for the American people, not the way it is today, where Republicans work for the wealthy and Democrats work for the middle and lower class. An impartial system would put representation where it belongs: in the hands of the people, and make such representation available to all the people all the time."

"Commander, it amazes me how much you and I think alike. I have had exactly that thought, myself, and I would love to see it happen."

"Then, Mr. President, it will happen."

"You make it sound so simple and easy, Commander. "

"Sir, with the control of Congress that we have now, legislation is much easier to get passed. The thing we must guard against is using that power for the wrong purposes. It must never again be used to satisfy selfish interests."

"Agreed, Commander. That means lobbying must be abolished. Private funding of political campaigns must be abolished. We must establish a government-run campaign system whereby candidate campaigns are funded by the Federal Government, all candidates for a given office receive the same amount, and all television-based campaign advertising will take place on a government run station dedicated to that purpose."

"Absolutely, Mr. President. It will not work, otherwise. But we must also guard against the possibility of political favoritism by the very government that then controls those funds. "

"So how do we accomplish this?"

"Mr. President, I will see to it."

"Please let me know what I can do to help."

"I will, Sir."

"Now, one more thing, Commander."

"Yes?"

"My term will end in another year, as you know. What is to happen to our plans then?"

"They will go forward, Mr. President—with another Techna double. You will be free to go home or, if you prefer, remain here in retirement with your American wife. The decision will be yours, Mr. President."

"Ah, yes, I see your point. It is good that you will provide the next President, and I have a decision to make, correct?"

"Correct. We will always do that, regardless of which candidates win the election. Otherwise, huge corporations would buy the election and we would risk losing control. The only way we can give the American people good government is to insert incorruptible people into all elected political offices. That means Techna people. They will be doubles, of course. That is because we do not find a single United States citizen who cannot be corrupted, sad to say. All have their price."

"Indeed, Commander. It is a sorry state of affairs. Do you have time for a couple more questions?"

"Absolutely, Mr. President."

"Good. I am getting conflicting reports concerning our legal system, first concerning death sentences for convicted felons who have no possibility of parole and, second, the deaths of judges handling capital crimes. Do you know about these matters?"

"I do, Mr. President. With respect to the first part of the question, your legal system has become dominated by anti-death penalty people. They have been very successful in preventing executions of prisoners convicted of some very heinous crimes. As a result, some 30,000 prisoners were clogging your prisons; being fed, clothed, and housed at government expense, and even given medical treatment at government expense."

"Were?"

"Yes, Sir. But they finally received the penalty they should have received in the first place."

"I see. And the second part of my question?"

"Mr. President, that deals with current capital crime cases, and a similar situation, wherein judges pressured by that same anti-execution group have been in the habit of handing down very light sentences. We have corrected the problem, but it took some harsh treatment of prisoners and judges to bring about necessary changes. Now, a person convicted of a capital crime is allowed just one appeal, instead of many, many of them, stretching over years, and just 90 days in which to complete his or her appeal. Concurrently, we convinced the anti-execution people of the great risk associated with continuing their opposition. The system is now back on track and working as intended. A much reduced level of crime, resulting in a much reduced criminal case backlog is ample evidence of that."

The President nodded and said, "As usual, Commander, you make it sound so very simple."

"Sir, it is simple when one does not have to overcome unjustified and unnecessary pressure. People such as this anti-execution group tried to do that, but it never works on Techna Force 20."

*   *   *

Following his hour-long visit with the President, Thor flew to New York for the taping of his *Sunday Review* presentation scheduled for the coming Sunday, July 11, at CTS headquarters. Seeing Sarah as he left the elevator brought him sheer joy and he walked very briskly to her work station.

Sarah smiled and said, "Oh, Thor, how wonderful to see you. They are waiting for you in Mr. Fischer's office."

"Good, honey, but before I go in, what would you say if I asked you to spend the week-end with me?"

"Thor, I would really, really love that."

"Great. I do not know how long this taping will take today, but can you wait for me here?"

"Of course I will wait, dear man."

*   *   *

Thor met with Sam Fischer and Mark Haddon in Sam's office for about fifteen minutes so they could brief him on the show's format. He learned then that health insurance companies had declined to participate. "When I told them what the show would be about they all laughed in my face," Sam said. "As one president put it, 'no one is going to push us out of the healthcare business, period. You can tell your Techna friends that for me.' So, I am just relaying that message, Commander."

"I rather expected such a reaction, Sam. Would you prefer not to go forward with this?"

"Are you kidding? Not on your life. This may be the biggest story we ever do, and it is something really good for the American people. No, I say we go ahead, right, Mark?"

"Absolutely, boss, and to hell with the risk. My bag is packed and I'd love to spend some quality time in Sardine Mountain."

"So is mine," Sam responded.

"Very well. I just need to know when to send my transporter for you, and I suggest that Margie be included. We do not know what to expect. By the way, you will be staying in a place much nicer than a New Mexico mountain."

"Good idea to include Margie. I'll tell her. Now, we are assigned to studio B for taping, Thor. As you probably remember from the last time, we tape today, Friday. The crew works all night to iron out any wrinkles, then we wrap it up tomorrow afternoon—usually around three. If everything goes as planned, we won't need you back here at all. Mark, Margie and I can leave right after the show, which is seven p.m., New York time. We don't do it live anymore, but like to be here for the show, just in case."

"I would like to be here with you on Sunday, Sam, if that is alright. Then we can leave in my transporter from here."

"That will work for us, Commander."

* * * .

The taping session went very well, except that, when Thor announced to the world as he was being interviewed by Mark Haddon, that TF20 agents had already taken over the ten huge health insurance companies, Sam called "CUT!"

"What's wrong, boss?" Mark asked

Sam looked at Thor, and said. "Is that true, Commander? Have you already taken over?"

"No, Sam. But when the program airs Sunday evening, it will be true. Are you worried about your taping crew knowing?"

"Oh, hell no, Commander. I trust these guys one hundred percent. Just wanted to make sure I understood what you said. I see you in a much brighter light now. You are one very sharp guy who never leaves anything to chance. "

Thor nodded, and said, "Sam, we never under-estimate an enemy, if that is what you mean. When *Sunday Review* airs Sunday night, the executives of these ten insurance companies will have all been replaced by Techna agents, and will be powerless against us, and anyone else, for that matter. That was always our plan; but executives of corporations in other fields will be watching, and we must be prepared. We promised to protect you and we will."

"Commander," Mark said, "that comment could be taken to mean you anticipate trouble from other quarters. Am I right? A moment ago you said we would not be going to Sardine Mountain. Is that change part of this?"

"It is, Mark. Your audience Sunday will include some very powerful men in very high places in other corporations. We have reason to believe they will interpret our take-over announcement as a future plan to go after them, and have already set wheels in motion to attack Sardine Mountain. Therefore, we have moved all starships and transporters to other, safer locations. One of them will be your temporary home."

"Okay, I get it now, Commander. I say we finish the taping."

After Sam called the show a wrap for the day, he said to Thor, "Commander, to repeat what I said earlier, this show will rock the world, not just our country. I can't wait to see the reactions. See you Sunday."

Thor said, "Sam, I would not miss it, either. Let us hope the American people take it in a positive way," and left the studio.

* * *

When Thor returned to the reception area, Sarah was just putting her desk in order for the night. "I'll just be a minute, Thor. You finished earlier than I thought."

"Yes, my darling. It went very well, but I failed to mention that I want to be here on Sunday to watch it with Sam and Mark. Do you mind?"

"Oh, certainly not, Thor. There, I am ready," she responded, and stepped out of her cubicle. She took his arm and moved very close to him. She looked up into his eyes and said, "I can't wait to get you home."

*   *   *

When they reached the transporter and were safely strapped in, Thor took a small black velvet box out of his pocket and handed it to her."

"Oh, Thor, what have you done?" she asked breathlessly as she open the tiny box. In side was a gold medallion set with a single one caret' diamond, and inscribed, *"For Your New Home."* When Sarah lifted it out of the box she saw that it was attached to a gold key. There was a momentary look of confusion in her beautiful blue eyes as she stared at Thor, then the light dawned, and her eyes grew larger as a gasp escaped her lips. "For our house? This key is for our house?" she asked.

"Yes, angel. Escrow closed today. And I must tell you, we are not spending this weekend in your New York apartment; we go to the Cape as soon as you get packed. And, furthermore, there will be a surprise waiting for you there."

She unlatched her seatbelt and threw her arms around Thor's neck. "You have no idea how much I love you," she whispered.

*   *   *

When they arrived at their Barnstable, Cape Cod home, the sky had darkened and there were lights in every room. Sarah thought the scene the most beautiful she had ever witnessed.

Jens set the transporter down gently on the rear lawn, and when he opened the hatch she could hear the roar of the surf. He helped her out of the transporter, then Thor joined her, and arm in arm they walked toward the house. As they drew closer they could hear voices and see the shadowy figures of people mingling on the rear patio. Just as they reached the patio, a cheer went up, then the people applauded them and shouted, "Congratulations!," and "Welcome Home!", in unison. Then from somewhere in the house lights for the patio were turned on, and Sarah saw her very first guests. Her mother and father were there. Her sisters and their families were there. Manta was there, now joined by Jens. All of Thor's Group Captains were there. The moment was just too much for Sarah and she could no longer hold back tears of joy. With Thor by her side she moved from group to group, and person to person, hugging and being hugged. In time she regained control of her emotions and invited everyone into the house where, to her dismay, the dining room table was laid out with a catered feast equal to no other. Waiters in white uniforms circulated with bottles of fine champagne, making certain no glass was empty for long, and soft music playing in the background helped create the perfect mood for this very festive occasion.

She took the arm of the man who would soon be her husband and said, "Dearest Thor, how did you ever find time to arrange all this? What a perfectly wonderful surprise."

Thor smiled and said, "It was nothing, angel. Besides I had a lot of help."

At that moment Sarah's mother came up to them and said, "Can I steal her away for a moment Thor?"

"Certainly, Rose. I need to talk to Manta anyway." He left the two women and moved to where Manta was standing with Jens. She smiled at him and said, "Thor, I think you handled this perfectly. Sarah does not suspect a thing. She will be safe here with her family and all of the Techna Captains to protect her. Do you think there will be serious trouble when you make your announcement on television? I see your starship is here. At least Jens and I will not have far to go to be home."

Thor laughed, and responded, "Manta, there should not be any problem with the health care executives, but other corporate people are going to be very angry, so I did not want to take a chance. For one thing, I needed a safe house for the CTS people after the program Sunday night, and having the starship here serves that purpose, too."

"Commander, it is a bit like circling the wagons in the old West, is it not?"

"Yes, Jens. That is a good way to put it. And you have moved all other starships out of Sardine Mountain, I take it?"

"Yes, Sir. They are well dispersed. No one will find them."

"Very good, dear friend."

* * *

The house warming celebration lasted well into the night, and it was past midnight before Thor and Sarah were alone in their new bedroom. As soon as he closed the door behind him, Sarah snuggled close and put her arms around his waist. Then she looked up into his eyes and said, "Darling Thor, are you an angel? You must be an angel, or maybe someone even higher in God's world. There is no other way to explain how wonderful you are—how wonderful you are to me. How do I tell you how much I love you?"

"Sarah, you need not worry about that. I know how you feel about me, because it is exactly the same way I feel about you. I am not of God or from God; I am just me, and my goal is to make you very, very happy so you will give me lots of children."

"Shall we start tonight? I would be willing."

"No, my darling. We must wait. We must wait."

* * *

At exactly seven p.m. July 11, 2010, Mark Haddon welcomed millions of viewers to CTS *Sunday Review,* as he had done thousands of times before, with the simple greeting "Good evening, America." Then he said, "Tonight we are pleased to have as our guest once again, Commander Thor Berksten, the leader of Techna Force 20. Commander Berksten first appeared on our program February 28 of this year, to give us the startling news that planets other than Earth, inhabited by intelligent beings, exist in the vast universe. He comes from one of those planets: Techna Planet."

"Since arriving on Earth, he and the two thousand agents who came with him, have completed a remarkable list of accomplishments. You may think he did all this through smoke and mirrors. But the facts speak volumes. Here is a partial list:"

"Techna Force 20 agents ended the war in Iraq."

"They used their own starships to bring more than two hundred thousand military and civilian personnel home in just ten days."

"They captured Osama Bin Laden in Afghanistan, when we could not even find him."

"They forced Congress to make positive changes in the way it does business."

"They put an end to the illegal drug business, and to televised religion programs that were stealing money from the poor."

"They had the courage to execute almost 35 thousand capital crime inmates who would otherwise be living fairly comfortable lives in prison, at an average cost of $40 thousand dollars per prisoner per year, while the innocent families of their victims mourn in tears."

"Am I for these great accomplishments? Do I applaud Techna Force 20 for making them a reality? Absolutely. They get things done and, in my opinion, the things they get done make our world a better place. Tonight we are pleased to bring you another example of what Techna Force 20 can do. Welcome to *Sunday Review*, Commander."

"Thank you, Mark. It is my pleasure."

"Ladies and gentlemen, tonight, Commander Berksten brings us some very exciting news on health care, a subject of interest to all, but confusing to many. Commander, why are you so interested in our health care system?"

"Well, first of all, Mark, in spite of the changes introduced in the President's new health care system, it is still a for-profit system for a group of powerful insurance companies. These companies sell health care coverage to citizens in return for hefty premiums, most of which are paid for either by the Government's Health, Education and Welfare Agency, or by private businesses. People who are not covered by those two groups of payers either get no health care coverage, or very limited health care coverage. In other words, you have a system that guarantees huge insurance profits and executive salaries, while providing bare minimum coverage. Those companies keep 80% of every dollar they take in, leaving only 20% to cover their insured. We believe it should be the other way around: 20% to the insurance companies, 80% to the insured. Actually, we think health insurance is a field that should be completely non-profit. No company should make money on the health or lack of health of a Country's citizens."

"That sounds like socialism, Commander."

"Mark, some services people need should be provided by the Government. If that is socialism, then it is appropriate socialism. In truth, the money Government uses to provide social services comes from the people—the taxpayers. In our view they get a greater return on their investment in Government than they would from private enterprise."

"Yes, I see your point. So you are advocating Government run health care?"

"No. Our plan will require the Government and private enterprise to fund a national healthcare program, but not manage it. Government does not manage such activities well. We all know that. But we also know letting private insurance companies manage it does not work best for the people."

"So who should do it? Manage health care, I mean?"

"Techna Force 20."

"You?"

"Yes. As executives managing the Nation's health care system, our agents will never be paid more than the President of your country, which is currently $400 thousand dollars per year. That is a fraction of the average $27 million being paid to insurance company CEOs today, in salaries, options and bonuses, and our agents are just as qualified, if not more so. Furthermore, under our control, health insurance companies will become privately held, non-profit, mutual benefit corporations. That eliminates the need for money for profits as well as stock dividends. We will also sell all the corporate jets and eliminate other executive perks that consume vast sums of money. Our goal will be to pay out 80 % of every dollar earned for citizen health care."

"Leaving that 20% for operating income that you mentioned. Can you make that work? It sounds too good to be true, Commander."

"Mark, I cannot give you all the details, but, yes, it will work."

"Who will be covered, Commander?"

"Our program will be available to every U.S. citizen and legal immigrant. We do not support illegal immigration and will not allow such immigrants to be enrolled."

"Is the program mandatory?"

"No. Anyone who chooses to be self-insured may do so. But if they develop a serious illness while self-insured, then decide to opt for our plan so as not to have to foot a huge medical bill themselves, they will be required to pay for treatment of that illness and any related recuperation, anyway."

"That seems very reasonable. By the way, what medical conditions are covered, Commander?"

"Everything is covered. Pre-existing conditions are covered. In fact, there are no exclusions."

"Incredible, Commander. No exclusions, and at no cost.

"To say there is no cost is not exactly true, Mark. People on Medicare, which is part of the Social Security program, will continue to have that monthly deduction to their Social Security payment, and it would be paid to us. By the same token, people who are employees of businesses would continue to pay a portion of the health insurance costs their employer pays to us.

"Yes, I understand. So, what else can you tell us about your proposed health care system?"

"Several things, Mark. For one, U.S. Government employees must be enrolled in this system, instead of in a special system for them alone. Also, we will control all hospitals, clinics, and urgent care facilities. We will end the current practice of limiting the number of doctors that can be graduated each year, and finally, the pay of doctors and other medical professionals will be much higher."

"Commander this sounds like the perfect health care system, but it is a massive undertaking. How long will it take to implement such a huge change?"

"Mark, the change has already been made. When you and I began this program tonight, Techna Force 20 agents started taking control of the six largest health insurance companies. I have just been advised through Techna's communications system that the take-over is complete. There are many smaller health insurers, of course—approximately 80, in fact. But we think they will choose to join *Techna-American Health Care,* as our organization will be called. There will be no financial incentive for them to remain independent. They will simply be unable to compete."

"Commander, I don't quite see how this is any different from Capitalism."

"Mark, the difference is, we are not in it for profit. We are in it to help the American people—to fill a need that has long been unavailable to them: complete health care coverage at the lowest possible cost. That is a far cry from the objectives of present health care insurance corporations. Their motivation is profit; they can always be counted on to do only what will maximize profit."

* * *

One of the millions of U.S. Citizens watching CTS *Sunday Review* on July 11, 2010, was Pierce Morgenthaller, CEO of North American Energy Industries, LTD., the largest petrochemical corporation in the world. As he did every Sunday, Morgenthaller watched the program while seated in his favorite red leather wing chair, in the plush media room of his Houston mansion. But there was another man in Mogenthaller's media room that Sunday, though the oil magnate was not aware of it: He was Techna Force 20 Captain, Truls Heyerdahl.

On a table by Morgenthaller's chair was his ever-present cocktail glass filled with Jack Daniels Bourbon on ice. A white-coated attendant stood nearby, ready to refill the glass whenever its contents dropped to half-full. As Morgenthaller watched, he puffed almost absent-mindedly on a very fat Cuban cigar that protruded from his mouth except when he took a sip of the whiskey. At no time did his eyes leave the huge flat screen television. When he heard Thor's claim regarding constant corporate quests for profit, he nearly bit the fat cigar in two, then removed it and muttered, "That's what we're in business for, you damned idiot." Next he grabbed the phone by his chair and punched in the number for his aide, Donald Glenn. "This is Pierce. Set up a meeting of SABER for eight a.m. Tuesday, the 13th. I asked every member to be sure to watch *Sunday Review* tonight, and I hope they all did that. This is a mandatory meeting, so make sure every member attends. Every member, you got that? I don't give a damn if they say they have other more important matters to attend to; nothing is more urgent than dealing with this crazy bastard, Thor Berksten, and it can't wait."

"Yes, Sir. I'll get on it right now, " the aid responded.

Morgenthaller turned the television set off, took another sip from his whiskey glass and settled deeper into his chair. Establishing SABER, an acronym for Special American Business Executive's Resources, had been his brainchild and one of his best moves as head of North American Energy Industries-ltd. It had only 25 members—all CEO's of various corporations—the most powerful of the powerful-- and they met regularly to deal with matters affecting corporate finances and profits. The beauty of SABER was that it gave CEO's a way to bypass their boards, in direct violation of corporate policies, of course, but an avenue they considered essential to survival. Only after SABER had thoroughly evaluated a proposition and agreed to adopt it did the individual CEOs take the matter up in meetings of their own boards of directors. At that stage such proposals were rarely, if ever, rejected.

*   *   *

After Sam, Mark and Thor finished watching the tape of the show, Sam asked, "Well, Commander, what did you think of it? Did we tell the American people what you wanted them to hear?"

"It was excellent, Sam. You people amaze me, the way you can present such a difficult subject so clearly. I think it was very much to the point and easy to understand."

"Good. Mark, you did your best work tonight. Well done."

"Thanks, Boss. So, where to now, Commander? Do you have a room ready for us in your hotel?"

"I do, Mark. One for you, one for Sam, and one for Margie. There is plenty of room for your families as well. Also, as we agreed, my doubles agents will stand in for you while you are in our protection."

Sam nodded and called out, "Margie, are you ready?"

Margie appeared in Sam's doorway and said. "All set. I already had our bags sent up to the heliport."

"Good work. Commander, I think we are ready. I sent my family out of town for a while. So did Mark. Margie has no family and lives alone."

"They would have been welcome at our hotel, Sam"

"Oh, it's not that, Commander. They just took this opportunity to go visit other family members."

The four of them made their way out of the office, along the marble corridor to the elevators, and in a few moments they were on the roof, where Jens stood in his usual spot by the open door of the transporter. When he saw Margie, he walked quickly to her, took her arm, and helped her board. Knowing she had never been in a Techna transporter before, he said, "Our seatbelt rule is the same as it would be on an airliner, Miss. Peterson." Then he helped her fasten hers. By then every one else was strapped in and ready to go.

*   *   *

The flight to Barnstable, Cape Cod was so short--just five minutes—that Margie barely had time to close her mouth after gasping in wide-eyed wonder at the transporter's rapid lift off. Thor, who was watching, ready to rush to her aid, if necessary, relaxed a bit, realizing she was doing just fine. "Sorry, Margie," he said. "I should have explained how this ship takes off. We forget that others might be caught by surprise."

"That's alright, Commander, but it is more like a rocket launch than a takeoff, wouldn't you say?"

He smiled. "Yes, I suppose it seems that way. You will be ready for it next time."

"Commander, we are on final for Barnstable. Fasten seatbelts, please."

There was laughter in the cabin, for none of them had removed their belts, to begin with.

The transporter settled softly and noiselessly onto the rear lawn of Thor and Sarah's new home, within 20 feet of Thor"s huge starship, which only became visible when the transporter approached. No lights showed from the starship's portholes, but as he led the way under it to the boarding ladder, soft overhead lighting came on sequentially to illuminate their every step to the ladder. When the party reached it, Thor turned to them and said, "This will be you home until we are certain it is safe for you to return to your own. I think you will find our accommodations quite comfortable." Then he led the way up the ladder.

The scene inside was familiar to Sam and Mark, but to Margie, it was like walking into a science fiction movie. She had heard Sam and Mark talk about their visit to this same starship, but had never really comprehended the magic of it until now.

As Margie was staring at the scene before her in wide-eyed wonder, Manta joined the group. "Hello," she said, and introduced herself. "Welcome to our Commander's flagship. It will be my pleasure to see that you are most comfortable, and to serve as your guide around the ship, for the duration of your stay. Let me first say that you are very special guests here, for only one other person from Planet Earth has ever resided in this ship. That was Commander Berksten's fiancé, Sarah Malloy, when they journeyed to Techna Planet a while back. Commander, if you wish, I will take over from here."

"Please do, Manta. Show them to their staterooms and tuck them in. Sam, Mark, Margie, thanks for a great show. You are safe here. Sleep well. I will see you at breakfast tomorrow."

*   *   *

When Thor emerged from his starship, he saw Sarah standing on the rear patio waiting for him. He walked swiftly to her, swept her into his arms and kissed her repeatedly, then they walked inside the house and were out of sight.

*   *   *

The SABER group maintained secret offices in an ordinary-looking building in Alexandria, Virginia, near Washington D.C.'s, Ronald Reagan Airport. The building occupied a full city block and had many entrances, as well as an underground garage. That, plus its proximity to the airport made ingress and egress without detection easy for SABER members.

The 25 members arrived at Reagan by private jet, and then proceeded to the office building in rental cars. They were careful not to use expensive car makes or limousines. Once inside the building, they took elevators to the tenth floor, where SABER offices were located. Inside, they were greeted by attractive SABER hostesses dressed in black uniforms, who guided them to the huge, expensively furnished, conference room. Pierce Morgenthaller, the first member to arrive, was waiting at the door and greeted each arriving member warmly. Six of the members were high-ranking oil company executives; the rest represented various other fields of business. The oil company members were: Kermet Beech, Magellan Oil and Gas; Leonard Boswick, Scanlon-Rogers Oil; Harley Failles, Globe-Pacific Petroleum; Morton Lassiter, Kansas Petroleum Industries; Dean Wallis, Hummer Oil Co.; and Bart Willis, Armbruster Snyder Oil Corp. These six men, Pierce knew, would be the most interested in the subject of today's meeting.

When all 25 were settled in their seats, he called the meeting to order.

"Gentlemen, I requested this meeting because we have a matter of great urgency to deal with; finding a way to stop Techna Force 20—often referred to as TF20--from taking over all of our businesses. If you watched *Sunday Review* this week, you saw them in action. Therefore, today's meeting should be of vital concern to every corporate executive present, and most particularly to those of you in the oil business, because I have reason to believe our industry is next in TF20's sites.

There followed responses such as, "Here, here," and "yes indeed."

Pierce smiled grimly. "I gather from that response that you all watched CTS *Sunday Review*. If so, then you know we have lost the health care industry to TF20 already. It was gobbled up by this monster from outer space without so much as a wimpy complaint. I don't know how they do it, but there is no question about their ability or their record. They ended the Iraq war, thus depriving some of our member companies of huge profits. They have infiltrated the Federal Government to such a point that you can't be sure any member of Congress is in your pocket. They captured Bin Laden, who we thought would keep things stirred up in the Middle East for years, and lead to huge profits in war material for us. Now we have lost that opportunity. They have single-handedly wiped out the lucrative drug trade which, while I condemn it because of the terrible things it does to people—especially kids—has been a major source of revenue for some of our member companies. Now I fear the worst: loss of my own industry—energy—which impacts six other SABER members who are here today. Energy production is the very backbone of American business. If we lose that, we lose everything. If Thor Berksten and his TF20 goon squad take over energy, we will have lost our greatest source of corporate revenue."

"Wait a minute, Pierce," Harley Failles, CEO of Globe/Pacific Oil, said. "Are you claiming TF20 will do away with oil—with energy? How can they do that? The U.S. can't survive without oil."

"No, Harley, I'm not saying that. TF20 never destroys an industry; they simply take it over, eliminate all profit and dividends, and give the American people the product or service at bargain prices. That's what they plan to do with health care—make it available to everyone for virtually nothing. It's great for the people, but a disaster for health care corporations."

"Yes, I heard that Sunday," Morton Lassiter of Kansas Petroleum, said. "But health care is different than oil. Whether they have health care, or no health care, people will survive. But, how will they survive without oil?"

"Maybe I am not making myself clear, Mort. Under TF20, people will still have oil. They will still have gas for their cars. The difference will be that they will pay maybe a dollar a gallon, instead of three or four dollars."

"I don't buy that, Pierce. Why would they practically give the stuff away when they don't have to?" Harley said.

"Simple. TF20's philosophy is, take care of the people, not the corporations. They operate as non-profit closed companies. They eliminate guys like us, who make $25 million a year, and replace us with Techna people who, by their law, cannot make more than our U.S. President--$400,000 a year. They eliminate every perk—our jets, fancy offices, trips to Europe, and so forth—and operate barebones. And you know what? They can do that and still survive. We can't. Or at least we are not willing to do it."

"So you want us to eliminate TF20, is that it?" Kermet Beech of Magellan Oil and Gas, wanted to know.

"Yes, Kermet. That's it. It is either that or go out of business. Which do you prefer?"

"I want to stay in business—we all do, I assume. But from what I saw Sunday, this guy Berksten and his bunch are virtually indestructible. How do you propose to take them out?"

"Kermet," Morton Lassiter said, "no one is indestructible. There has to be a way to get to this guy. We're the most powerful country on Earth, for God's sake. I say we find their base and drop a bomb on them."

"Yeah, an atom bomb," another SABER member suggested. "That should do it."

"Yes, and we know where their base is. It's near Roswell, New Mexico, which has a population of about 46 thousand. Are you willing to wipe out that many people—American people—to resolve this problem?"

"Pierce," Dean Wallis of Hummer Oil Co., said "the whole question is moot. We don't have an atom bomb, or the means to deliver one if we did."

"But if you had one, you would use it, is that your position, Dean?"

"Like I said. The question is moot. I'd like to hear what Bart and Leonard think we should do. We haven't heard from them."

"Pierce," Bart Willis of Armbruster/Snyder said. "I am as concerned about this problem as anybody, and I am willing to take action to preserve our industry—as long as it is within the law. Dropping an atom bomb on innocent people is certainly not within the law, in my book."

"I have to agree with Bart," Leonard Boswick said. "Scanlon/ Rogers would not favor dropping a bomb of any kind on or near Roswell. Nothing would bring the Government down on our heads faster than doing something stupid like that."

"Well, gentlemen, " Pierce Morgenthaller responded, "Let's see a show of hands of all those who favor just giving up and handing our businesses to TF20."

Not one hand went up.

"So we fight. Is that your position?"

"We fight, of course," said Harley Failles. "But that does not mean taking the law into our own hands. There are other ways to fight. We could take away the incentive for TF20 to come after us—lower our profit goals, for example—even become non-profit, at least until this blows over. Or, perhaps we could move our operations off-shore."

Mort Lassiter stood and held up both arms. "Listen," He said. "I was serious. I want to see a show of hands from those favoring bombing the S.O.B.'s into extinction. You won't get anywhere trying to appease them." Still standing, he turned to face the men lining the long polished table. "Am I alone with this line of thinking? If you are with me, please stand."

At once 15 men stood.

Morton Lassiter turned to face Pierce Morgenthaller. "Mr. Chairman, it appears we have a majority in favor of the bomb." Then he sat down.

"So be it, Mort. I need a motion and a second."

Morton made the motion. It was seconded by Kermit Beech, and approved by the 15 supporters constituting a majority.

"Now the question is, where do we get this bomb, and how do we deliver it?"

"Pierce, I will take on that assignment. It will cost each of us a million dollars to buy the bombing."

"Very well, Mort. Now, if there is no other business we are adjourned."

* * *

Truls Heyerdahl left the SABER meeting and immediately contacted Thor to report the group's decision. After laying out the proceedings of the SABER meeting, he said, "They plan to bribe an Air Force general Lassiter knows with 25 million dollars to drop a nuclear bomb; he is in charge of B52 Bomber Command at March Field, and Lassiter thinks he would be willing to do it. Each SABER member will put up a million dollars. They intend to drop that bomb on Sardine Mountain, which will destroy Roswell, of course. As you know, it is very close to our base."

"They can not harm us, Truls. But there is no way we will allow them to kill everyone in Roswell. They must be stopped. How would you handle this?"

"Commander, I think this is another job for Techna doubles. I understand that we are not ready to take over all of America's big corporations, but we can influence the operations of these 25 very large ones, who are SABER members, to a great extent by putting our agents in their CEO positions. Since our next target is the American oil industry anyway, we would not be deviating much from the plan and would just be moving the time table up with respect to their top people."

"Excellent idea, Truls, It gives us a perfect solution to this current problem, and a leg up on the eventual takeover. I like it very much. Please begin the work of putting it into effect."

"Fine, Commander. I will need help from Guri."

"Yes. I will ask him to get started on training right away."

"And I will take care of the general."

"Very good work, my friend."

"Thank you, Commander."

------///------

CHAPTER FOURTEEN

TF20 Spreads Its Wings

Guri Kohn was the perfect choice to lead Group Six. He had an easy-going, roll-with-the-punches attitude that worked very well, considering that, typically, he had very little advance notice of a need for his group's services. Group Six had no other assignment than to manage the hundreds of reserve agents assigned to it, and prepare them for duty when called upon to do so. The problem was, such calls always came with great urgency. That might irritate some people, but not Guri. His way was to expect the unexpected, and handle it as if it was just another routine task. Commander Berksten recognized this trait. The work of TF20 tended to demand sudden action, and sudden action required skilled agents on the line. Guri had never failed to deliver those agents, literally overnight at times, with no complaint or long face, ever.

Now, because his Commander had an urgent need to neutralize SABER, he had asked Guri to train an additional 25 doubles agents. Guri accepted the directive with a smile, and said, "Commander, normally they could be ready in as little as two weeks, but I hear the people these agents will replace are among the shrewdest and most hard-boiled businessmen on Planet Earth. I think we must take additional time to prepare our agents so they appear to have the same toughness while still dealing with their assignments our way. So I must ask for a month to prepare them. Will that be acceptable?"

"That will be fine, Guri. Please select the very best agents to fill the top 25 positions. They will be the key to our success. By the way, I do not tell you often enough how much I appreciate your help, dear friend. "

"Thank you, Commander. My work is my pleasure."

"It shows, Guri. It shows."

* * *

On Thursday, July 15, Thor met briefly with Truls Heyerdahl at the latter's starship, to apprise him of the doubles training schedule he had received from Guri.

"We can live with that, Commander. There is but one pressing issue right now. Morton Lassiter, a SABER member, is to meet with Air Force General Walter Schelhorne, at March Field, in Southern California, Friday, July 23, to discuss the nuclear attack on Sardine Mountain. I will visit March Field tomorrow to have a little talk with the General, myself."

* * *

Truls arrived over March Field a little after eight the next morning, as planned. He asked his pilot to circle the field, and found the B52 bomber base at its Southern end. His transporter landed noiselessly, in I-Mode, near a building identified as "B52HQ" at the edge of that section of the field, and Truls, also in I-Mode, entered the building. One officer and three Air Force enlisted men were working at desks in the "bull pen" area just beyond a counter which served as a barricade. Beyond that area was a door with a name plate that told Truls he had found his General. He passed unseen and noiselessly through the barricade, bull pen and office door, and found himself facing a short, pudgy Air Force Officer with a reddish face and puffy cheeks. On the Officer's desk was a brass name plate reading, "Major General Walter Schelhorne, Commanding Officer," in black letters. On his shirt collar were the two gold stars of his rank. His head was bent forward as he read some document on the desk, giving an indication that his eyesight was not the best. His uniform was wrinkled in a most unmilitary way and, in spite of the name plate and the gold stars, he looked to be anything but an Air Force General. Truls studied the man for several moments, then made himself visible. It took a moment or two for Schelhorne to realize he was no longer alone in his office. He looked up, first over the top of horn-rimmed glasses, then, as danger shown in his dark brown eyes, he stood and tried to make himself seem taller than five feet, eight. He glared at Truls and exclaimed, "Who the hell are you, and how did you get in here?"

"General, I am Truls Heyerdahl, Captain, Techna Force 20."

"Oh yeah, I heard of you bunch of thugs—tryin' to take over the country. You gotta lot of nerve. What you want with me? "

"Do you know a man named Morton Lassiter?"

"Yeah, so what? We served together for a time, before he got out. He's a big shot in the oil business now, I hear."

"Has he contacted you within the last few weeks?"

"No."

"Then he will, General. He will ask you to send a B52 bomber armed with a nuclear warhead to the Roswell, New Mexico area, and use the bomb to destroy Techna Force 20's base near there."

"No way. That would kill thousands of Americans. It ain't gonna happen."

"Good, but what if he offers you $25 million dollars?"

"Me, meaning the Air Force, or me, meaning myself?"

"Yourself."

Schhelhorne's eyes showed renewed interest and he was thoughtful for several seconds. Then he said, "Yeah, it could be arranged. You makin' this offer?"

"Not at all. I am here to tell you not to accept such an offer if it is presented to you."

"You can't tell me what to do."

"True. But I can tell you what I will do if you decide to accept Lassiter's offer."

Schelhorne thrust out his chin defiantly and said, "What do you think you can do, big shot?"

"I can and will kill you, before you ever see one dime of that $25 million dollars. TF20 will not allow blatant murder of 46 thousand innocent Americans. "

"That's a threat, by God."

351

Truls said, "No, General, it is not a threat. It is a promise." Then he disappeared. Schelhorne was still standing, but his cockiness and belligerent look were gone, and in their place was an ashen face and fear-filled eyes.

* * *

After his visit with General Schelhorne, Truls met with Thor to brief him on recent developments. "I believe the General will be unable to resist $25 million dollars, Commander. I predict that he will launch a nuclear attack on Roswell and Sardine Mountain."

"Humm. That is not good, news, Truls. How will you handle it?"

"I left an agent with him. He is authorized to do whatever is necessary to prevent such an attack. So we are covered there. If SABER insists on trying to destroy us they will need to find another way, and I have agents watching them every minute as well, especially their leader, Pierce Morgenthaller."

"Well done, Captain. Morgenthaller is an oil man, is he not?"

"Yes, and SABER includes six other oil company CEO's. In fact, all major oil companies are represented on that very private Commission. Those seven men are the instigators, Commander."

"It appears we must take on the oil industry, much sooner than anticipated—even before we conclude our work on health care."

"Yes, I agree. But the health care transition is progressing very well, and does not require both Siran and I; either of us can manage it at this point. Since she has done so much of the research, and is doing such a fantastic job of coordinating the take-over, I recommend giving her sole responsibility for it. Then, if you wish, I will be free to tackle the oil industry project."

"That makes good sense, Truls. I am very impressed with Siran. She is exceptional in every way. I am also very impressed with Erika Varda, and her work on the capital punishment problem is coming to a close. We must define her next assignment very soon."

"Commander, as you know, the SABER Commission includes the heads of all pharmaceutical corporations as well as banking, two other corporation groups we plan to take over. I ask that you consider giving them to Erika."

"An excellent proposal, Truls. In fact, if Siran and Erika are willing, I will make the assignments as you suggest. Now, there is one other matter troubling me right now."

"What is that, Sir?"

"Your discovery that it was the SABER Commission that engineered and conducted the World Trade Center attack on 9/11, not Osama Bin Laden. SABER simply hired 19 Muslems to do the actual work just to make it appear that Arabs were behind this fiendish scheme."

"I know, Commander. It would be impossible for any Techna agent to comprehend, let alone initiate, such an evil act. I, too, have been unable to get it out of my mind. With your permission, none of the SABER members will survive our take-over of their businesses. That is, none will be sent to Prison Planet."

Thor nodded in agreement. "A fitting solution, my friend. And it must apply to former President Fields, as well. He was very involved in that plot, sad to say. In hindsight, sending him to Prison Planet was too good for him."

*   *   *

On July 19, a week and a day after the Health Care take-over was announced on CTS, Thor contacted doubles agents fronting for Sam Fischer, Mark Haddon, and Margie Peterson, to determine if any threats had been made. None had, so he concluded that TF20, not CTS was the target. From CTS headquarters he flew to Barnstable, Cape Cod, where he gave Sam Fischer the news that he and his staff were free to return to their offices. To all three, he expressed his regrets that they had to be restricted to his starship.

"Hey, Commander," Mark Haddon responded. "Best darn vacation I ever had. I mean, you people really know how to live."

"They all laughed at Mark's comment, and Sam said, "I agree, Commander. We could not have been treated better. And we really appreciate the protection you have provided."

"Thank you, all. Jens will take you back to New York whenever you are ready."

* * *

Thor exited his starship after talking to the CTS crew to find Sarah waiting at the foot of the boarding ladder. "I saw you land, dear husband-to-be, so I thought I would surprise you."

"And what a wonderful surprise it is, my darling. Are you well this morning?"

"I am very well....now that you are here. Can you stay a while?"

"Yes. As a matter of fact, I thought we could work on plans for our weddings—that is, if you have the time."

"Oh, Thor, nothing would please me more. It's not every woman who gets to plan two weddings for herself, instead of one. I have thought a great deal about the one we will have in Brookline, because I am familiar with New England traditions. But I have absolutely no idea where to start on the Techna ceremony."

"Yes, I understand, little one, and I am afraid I know even less than you; it is a male deficiency, I guess. But I am certain Manta will know, and will love to help. Would you like me to ask her?"

"That would be wonderful, Thor."

"Good. I will talk to her right away. By the way, would you mind very much if we did that ceremony first—in September, perhaps? It has nothing to do with Techna tradition, but I may have to go there about that time on business."

"I don't mind, Thor. Let me talk to my parents and siblings, to make sure they could go then. About three weeks, as before?"

Thor nodded his head and said, "Yes, I think we should plan on three weeks, angel, though the trip may require less time. than that."

* * *

After an all-too brief, one day visit with Sarah, Thor caught up with Siran Missirian in the Philadelphia headquarters offices established beforehand for Techna-American Health Care. After discussing progress on this massive project, and learning that Siran had everything under control and running smoothly, he told her about the need to commence take-over work on the American oil industry, his decision to put Truls in charge of that project, and Trul's recommendation that she assume full responsibility for the health care industry. Siran accepted eagerly.

"As soon as you tell me you are comfortable with how Techna-American Health Care is operating, I have another assignment for you, this time dealing with the Federal Government, if you are interested, that is."

"I am very interested, Commander."

"Good, Siran. Then the assignment is yours."

* * *

On Wednesday, July 21, Thor was going over project status reports in his flagship office when he received a message from Assim Agassi. The purpose of Assim's call was to advise Thor of the rapid growth of Mexican drug cartels. "Commander," He said, "They are everywhere along the border, and DEA is losing the battle to contain them. Even with the 200,000 returning Iraq veterans on site, DEA still cannot plug all the holes; it simply does not have the necessary equipment. The cartels cross into the U.S. almost at will, bringing drugs and illegal aliens in, and taking money and sophisticated arms back to Mexico. I think we can help with this problem."

"Do you have a plan, Assim?"

"Yes, Sir, I do."

"Very well, There will be a staff meeting on Friday, the 23rd. I would like you to present your plan to the group then."

* * *

As Group Captain-In-Charge of health care reform, Siran Missirian's days were filled with meetings and strategy sessions. Promptly at eight each morning, she met with the six Techna agents who had been chosen to fill the roles of Corporate Executive Officers, to make sure all of them were on the same page regarding the operating policies being established to guide their new health care companies. This step was essential to ease the eventual transition from six individual companies to one, a change planned from the very beginning. The challenge was to change the long-practiced thinking in six individual companies—thinking that had been practiced for years before Techna Force 20 took over. But the beauty of this venture was that these Techna agents were working as Techna agents always worked: for the good of the task at hand, the common goal in other words, not for individual self interests. So, for all their complexity, the meetings always went smoothly--even pleasantly--at times.

Surprisingly, the thousands of American employees who had been working for these corporations for years, performing tasks according to arcane, boring rules, became energized themselves by the excitement and enthusiasm exuded by their new leaders, and quickly adopted Techna's "can-do" attitude. For them, work became purpose-driven and fun again, even to the point where they were offering their own suggestions on how to make their companies better. To help keep that spirit alive, Siran preached constantly to her Techna agents acting as corporate officers, about the importance of developing team efforts and giving recognition whenever and wherever merited; she also practiced what she preached by frequently appearing in various offices with the TF20 agent in charge. Because of these appearances, she became a familiar sight to hundreds of employees.

Concurrent with the revolution in daily company operations, work was going forward to expand health care coverage to all Americans, as well as to make that coverage cost free, beyond long-established deductions from Social Security checks and employee pay checks. Upon taking charge, Siran immediately established a steering committee to design, plan and implement this much higher level of health care coverage. The steering committee met once each week, and Siran was always in attendance.

On top of all other duties, she was also responsible for keeping Thor current on progress, as well as problems and proposed solutions to them.

Thus, she was busy from sunup to sundown, and often long after sundown, seven days a week, and when she finally returned to her starship home, it was to eat a quick meal prepared for her by one of her aides, then an hour or so of reading reports and other correspondence, and then to bed. Once her head hit the pillow she fell into an immediate and deep sleep, happy in the knowledge that she was filling a necessary role and really helping to make a difference.

*   *   *

On Friday morning, July 23, all group captains assembled in Thor's flagship in Barnstable, Cape Cod. At that meeting he made official, the new project assignments, stating that Siran Missirian would assume full responsibility for completing reformation of the American health care system, freeing up Truls Heyerdahl to commence takeover of the giant U.S. petroleum industry. "We had not planned to do this so quickly," Thor said. "But the leaders of big oil, along with other members of the powerful SABER group have been doing a bit too much 'saber rattling' against TF20 since our health care announcement on CTS. As all of you know, we have scattered our starships and transporters in anticipation of a nuclear attack on Sardine Mountain. Concurrently, I am giving Erika Varda the task of reforming the pharmaceutical industry, another element of SABER, and putting it under Techna's wing and, though I have not discussed this with any of you, Arne Klein will take on the same responsibility in the banking industry arena, which is also a major SABER player."

"I know these are most difficult assignments, but am convinced that all of you have the ability to manage them successfully. Guri, old friend, these projects must begin as soon as possible, and I must call on you to do the impossible once again. In addition to the 25 doubles agents you are already training as CEOs, we will now need to train 750 more--25 sets of 30 doubles agents—one set to fill all executive positions in each SABER company. I have already arranged for that many new agents to be sent from Techna as soon as possible. "

"No problem, Commander. Things have been a bit boring since the health care take-over. We needed some new challenges."

The conference room filled with laughter for several moments, and when it died down, Thor continued with, "Yes, well, here is another one for you. Assim has a proposal I would like all of you to hear. Assim?"

"Thank you, Sir. As I reported to the Commander two days ago, we are losing the battle to keep illegal aliens and drugs out of the U.S. The U.S. border is a sieve; there are entry points about every ten feet at times, or so it seems. DEA has not been able to stop the flood, even with the thousands of returning Iraq veterans assigned to stand guard almost shoulder to shoulder, on our recommendation.

I believe we can help with this problem. My proposal is to divide the 1969 miles of Mexican/ American border into three equal segments, and patrol each segment with one transporter, fitted with our best surveillance equipment, as well as laser armament, 24 hours a day, seven days a week, in I-Mode. This way, we can identify intruders the minute they attempt to enter the U.S., and either alert forces on the ground or handle the matter ourselves. A transporter moving at maximum speed can go from one end of a 656 mile segment in about 2.5 minutes after detection of an intruder. The bad guys cannot cross the rivers and other barriers that fast."

"Assim, I like your plan," Thor said. "But do you have the resources to do this?"

"Sir, I have the transporters, lasers and surveillance equipment; what I lack is the manpower. I will need 27 agents, preferably flight-trained—three agents per transporter per eight hour shift, in other words."

Thor scanned the room with his piercing grey eyes. "Any questions or comments?" He asked.

Erika was the first to speak. "Commander, I think Assim's plan is excellent. I cannot think of anything he might have overlooked."

Her comments were met with a unanimous affirmative nodding of heads."

"Guri?"

"Commander, I, too think it is an excellent plan. As it happens, we already have nine qualified pilots. I see no problem getting 27 agents ready. Assim, can you give me a week?"

"I can, Guri."

"Good," Thor said, "Then we go with this plan as soon as possible.

Assim smiled and said, "Thank you Commander, I will of course keep all of you informed."

After the meeting, Truls stopped by Thor's office and said, "Commander, I am glad you gave banking to Arne. He will do a superb job. I should have suggested him to you myself."

"I am not offended, Truls. You have much on your mind, and Arne was ready for a new assignment, anyway."

*　　*　　*

On Monday, July 26, Truls received a message from the agent assigned to watch General Schelhorne. "Captain," he said, "Lassiter has contacted the General with an offer of $25 million, and the General has accepted. The attack is scheduled for tomorrow morning at daybreak."

"Very well, I will alert Commander Berksten. Let me know if anything changes."

"Yes, Sir, I will."

Truls called Thor immediately. "Commander, the nuclear attack on Sardine Mountain and Roswell is to take place at daybreak tomorrow."

"We proceed as planned, Truls. I am going to give CTS *Sunday Review* a heads up on this. I think it is a major news story they should have."

*　　*　　*

Margie answered the phone instantly, and said, "Sam Fischer's office."

"Good morning, Margie. This is Commander Berksten. I have an urgent message for Sam."

"Certainly, Commander. One moment, please."

"Hey, Commander, what's up?"

"Something you might be interested in, Sam. SABER--you know about them, I believe--is behind an air-borne nuclear attack that will take place tomorrow morning against our Sardine Mountain base. Of course, Roswell, New Mexico, is very close to us and will almost certainly be incinerated. That is 46 thousand people, Sam."

"Jesus, Commander, are you serious?"

"Very serious. We will try to stop them, certainly, but the American people should be told."

"Absolutely. This can't wait for Sunday, but I know our daily news staff will want the story."

" Yes, I thought so, and there is something else, Sam, and this will blow your mind."

"I'm listening."

"It was SABER that engineered the World Trade Center disaster in 2001, not Bin Laden, or any other Muslem group. SABER simply hired 19 Muslem men from the Middle East to do the dirty work—for the glory of Allah-- of course."

"My God. And you have proof, Commander?"

"Will a videotape of that SABER conversation suffice?"

"Perfect. Can you testify, if needed?"

"I was not at that meeting, but Captain Truls Heyerdahl was and he would gladly testify."

"Commander. I will be in touch on this and, thank you so very much. These stories are dynamite. Really appreciate it."

"Glad to help, Sam. Have a great day."

*   *   *

Trul's starship was hovering over March Airbase in I-Mode, on Tuesday, July 27, when a single B52 Bomber lifted off from the airfield. The bomber climbed to its assigned altitude on a heading that would take it directly to Sardine Mountain. As it crossed into Arizona, the starship shadowing it descended to just a few feet above it and became visible. Speaking on the Air Force radio frequency, the starship pilot said, "B52, abort mission immediately. I repeat, abort immediately, and return to base."

The B52 crew could not see the starship pilot, but they could see the giant round black object poised menacingly just above them. "Whoever you are, you are interfering with a U.S. military mission. Break off, or we will shoot you down. That is an order."

The starship pilot responded by moving even closer to the bomber, so close, in fact, that the bottom of its fuselage scraped the bomber's vertical stabilizer with a loud "scrunch."

"Jesus, that crazy bastard is going to wreck us both! " Yelled the bomber pilot into his open microphone. "52 to base, we've got a situation here. An unidentified aircraft is trying to force us down. What are your instructions?"

"Base to B52. We show you on a training mission. Why are you under attack?"

"Negative, base. We are on a destruct mission against enemy targets in New Mexico. Need fighter support, immediately."

"Unauthorized, B52! I say again, unauthorized. You are to break off and return to base now."

"Base, this is General Schelhorne. I am on the B52 mission, and I authorized it."

"General, with due respect, you do not have that authority, and you are in violation of Air Force directives. I must order you to break off and come home."

Schelhorne turned to the B52 pilot beside him and said, "continue this mission. We are ignoring that order."

"Yes, sir, but what do we do about that guy above us?"

"Kill him! He's an enemy of our country! Kill the bastard!"

"But General, we don't have guns on this ship, and we can't reach him with rockets!"

Before the General could respond, the huge black starship filled the bomber's wind screen, and moved lower and lower, almost to the point where the B52 crew's forward visibility was completely blocked.

"B52, we are a Techna Force 20 starship. We know your mission is to destroy Sardine Mountain with a nuclear device. In the process you will destroy Roswell and thousands of residents. Be advised that we will not allow completion of this mission. Abort now or we will force you to crash."

The B52 pilot stared at Schelhorne and said, "General, I say we abort. We abort now. It's wrong to bomb our own people!"

"And I say we go on, dammit! Sardine Mountain is enemy territory!"

The pilot looked at Schelhorne in disbelief, then keyed his microphone. "TF20 starship, we will not abort."

Within seconds the starship settled onto the forward section of the B52, forcing the huge bomber to tilt into descent attitude. The two aircraft stayed locked together that way until it was too late for the bomber to pull out of the dive. The starship disengaged just moments before the B52 crashed in a huge ball of fire in the middle of the desert, miles from any civilization, with no survivors. But the nuclear bomb inside it did not explode; apparently it had never been armed.

"TF20 starship to TF20 base. We have succeeded. The B52 just went in. All that is visible is a huge burn spot on the desert floor, no survivors, no nuclear explosion. Returning to base."

* * *

That evening, CTS television news programs all over the United States carried the story of a greedy Air Force General's crazed, but failed, attempt. The news program named Schelhorne and talked about the 25 million dollars he was to receive upon completion of the mission. It went on to say, "we have learned from an impeccable source that Morton Lassiter, a powerful member of the SABER Group of corporate CEO's, initiated this deadly operation, with the full and complete approval of SABER. It appears SABER has a sizeable measure of control over our military. A group of corporations controlling a Federal Government military force? How can that be, you ask? We wonder, too. Had it not been for the prompt action of Techna Force 20, a group from Techna Planet that has shown time and time again that it is on Planet Earth to protect the American people, the City of Roswell and all forty-six thousand residents would have been incinerated....and with a U.S. nuclear bomb, no less. How utterly scary and incredible is that?"

* * *

The look on Pierce Morgenthaller's face did not change at all as he watched the CTS news program in his study that evening. He sat back in his plush red leather chair, took another sip of whiskey and another puff on his fat cigar. To him, the event was just another stone along the road of business, to be handled calmly, purposely. When the news program ended, he picked up the phone by his chair, called the head of his company's legal department, and ordered him to take care of this pesky problem.

362

"We have to rid ourselves of Techna Force 20 once and for all," he said. "And Lassiter's idea on how to do it was a disaster. It just gave us a bigger problem. Now we have to mend some fences fast. Get our Publicity guys involved, and anyone else you need. But do it quickly. I don't care how. Just do it."

* * *

Thor watched the news program on a monitor in his office. Truls was with him. At the end of the news report he said, "Truls, when CTS runs the story on SABER's involvement in 9/11, Morgenthaller will really come after us. We need to be ready. That will be the moment to take over big oil, the pharmaceuticals and banking. I think the best way to kick those projects off will be to announce our takeovers on *Sunday Review* the same night CTS presents the shocking 9/11 news. Do you agree?"

"Yes, Commander, I do. A CTS announcement gives us a perfect launching point."

"Very well. I will talk to Sam Fischer to see when they intend to do the 9/11 story, and I would like you to work with Erika, Arne and Guri so we are ready."

* * *

At eight a.m. the next morning, Margie appeared in the door way to Sam Fischer's office and announced, "Commander Berksten is on the line for you, Sam."

"Hey, Commander, how are you this fine July morning?"

"I am good, Sam. Listen, I have an idea I would like to present to you. It's rather urgent that we talk."

"Okay, I am free this afternoon. How does one p.m. sound?"

"I will be there Sam."

* * *

At five minutes to one Thor walked briskly from the 60th floor elevator in the CTS building toward the reception desk, and

Sarah. He smiled broadly as he approached her, and said, "My darling, any day I get to see you twice is the perfect day."

"Oh, Thor, how sweet, and what a nice surprise. You are not on the appointment calendar, though."

"Probably because this came up too fast, but I talked to Sam this morning and he is expecting me."

"I am sure it is alright. Let me announce you. Will you be home for dinner?"

"Most definitely, angel."

At that moment the door to Sam's suite of offices was opened by Margie, and Thor walked through it. Sam was standing near her desk with Mark Haddon. The three men shook hands warmly, and then entered Sam's office. When they were seated around the coffee table, Sam said, "Alright, Commander, what do you have for us this morning?"

"Sam, another bombshell, perhaps. This is about Big Oil, Big Pharmaceuticals, and Big Banking. Techna Force 20 has been planning the same kind of takeover in those industries as the one that is currently under way on Health Care. We would like to tie our takeover announcement in with any program you plan to do on SABER's involvement with 9/11, because all of the corporate leaders we will be dealing with are members of that elite club. My purpose for being here today is to find out what your plans are and when you might do a program on the 9/11 travesty. "

"Jesus!" Mark exclaimed. What a fantastic *Sunday Review* that would make, eh, Sam?"

Sam nodded agreement, and then said, "Commander, that would put TF20 in charge of the four largest chunks of industry in the United States. Do you think that would be wise?"

"Yes, Sam, I do. These four business fields form the core of what is literally corporate control of the U.S. Government today. They own your Government, in effect. They influence law making, trade agreements, tariffs, plus they dictate who pays taxes and who does not. They even determine who runs for elected office. Why? All in the interest of larger and larger profits, leading to larger and larger salaries and perks for their executives. And your people, your citizens, who depend on these companies for essential goods and services, pay far too much for them. Someone has to stop the corporate takeover of American Government. Who else but us—Techna Force 20—is strong enough, and responsible enough to do that?"

"Hmmm. Yes, Commander, I see your point, but do you realize what you're taking on if you do this? I mean, even I will admit that they are the biggest bunch of thugs and crooks in the entire world. Oh, they seem gentlemanly on the surface, but underneath they are the most vicious animals imaginable. They may slaughter you, man. Slaughter you!"

"Sam, they will try. I have no doubt of that. But we are equal to anything they try to throw at us. I truly believe that. The power of TF20 is enormous. You know, because you and Mark have seen it in action. But we need to let the American people know what we are doing and why. Your program is the best format for doing it."

"Sam," Mark said. "What bothers you about this? It is our job to inform the people, and doing that where TF20 is involved has made *Sunday Review* one of the leaders in news media. I think this proposal is a perfect tie-in for the 9/11 piece we were discussing this morning. It will inform the people, and it will damn well improve our ratings, for sure."

"Yeah, and we will lose advertising revenue big time, Mark. Many of these companies are major CTS clients. Don't forget that."

A thin smile played around Thor's lips. "Therein lies the problem, Sam. That is exactly how these corporate giants control things—like the Government—for example. Please do not worry about losing revenue. That will not be a problem. TF20 will advertise on behalf of these companies as much, if not more than they do now."

"You guarantee that, Commander?"

"Yes, as long as there is a need to advertise and your rates are competitive."

"Fair enough, Commander. How do we convince people— our own executives, and American citizens—that Techna won't do the same thing with Government as the corporations do now?"

"You tell them that Techna is only interested in fair and reasonable treatment of all Americans, and will never favor corporations over individuals. Corporations are not people, Sam. If anything, they should be subservient to people. That has always been our philosophy, and will always be."

"Okay, I'm sold. We will do it if you will be there on the program with us, Commander."

"Sam, I would not miss it. We can be ready August 14. How does that sound?"

"What do you think, Mark? Can we get everything ready in that time frame?"

"Count on it, Boss. Wow, is this ever gonna' be somethin' or what?"

*   *   *

Group 4 of Techna Force 20, under the direction of Assim Agassi, began patrolling the U.S.- Mexican border at sun down, July 30. In preparation for this assault, Assim divided the 1969 miles of border into three sectors and assigned one transporter to each sector. These transporters were equipped with powerful heat-seeking sensors capable of "seeing" warm blooded targets on the ground without the aid of light, and even distinguishing between human and animal targets. Bad guy images appeared as blips on a GPS-driven monitor in the transporter's cockpit, which could pinpoint their location within a foot or two. Because U.S. drug enforcement agents on the ground wore special patches on their uniforms that the sensors recognized, these sophisticated machines easily identified bad guys from good.

Once detected by sensors, the bad guys had no place to hide. They were completely visible, whether in open areas of the border or in dense brush, even on the darkest night. The transporter simply hovered above them with its super-powered, sensor-guided search light focused on them, while ground forces, called in by radio, closed in on their prey and made the captures. In minutes a new batch of illegal drugs was confiscated, and/or illegal aliens were in custody.

On some nights, illegal border crossings were extremely heavy, and the transporters would barely complete one take-down before they were tracking another batch of bad guys. The illegal traffic was so heavy on those nights that the action was virtually nonstop. But no person or bag of drugs slipped through the net. The end result was that many more illegal crossings were thwarted than before the transporters went into use, and the volume of drugs confiscated increased more than a hundred fold, a number only slightly higher than the number of aliens taken into custody. DEA was amazed at the success rate, and very pleased.

The transporters were just as effective in daylight. During those hours, when the transporter crews could often spot illegal movement on the ground with their own eyes, they still relied on the sensors to confirm targets. "Coyotes," as the people who moved illegal drugs and humans across the border were called, quickly discovered that they could no longer enter the United States illegally during daylight hours and simply hide out in the brush till nightfall, then move their cargo north. The sensors always found them.

In the beginning, the transporters operated in V-Mode, at altitudes of approximately 500 feet above ground level. But in a number of instances, Coyotes, who were always armed, watched for the transporters and fired at them on sight. Transporter crews countered such attacks with deadly laser fire that occasionally, and unintentionally, injured or killed illegal aliens who were just trying to make a new life, as well as their Coyotes. To solve that problem, transporters began operating only in I-Mode. That change made them even more effective, especially in daylight. Now they could see their enemy, and not be seen themselves, and their capture rate went even higher.

After just one full month of operation, not one illegal alien succeeded in entering the United States, and no drug shipment escaped confiscation. As icing on the cake, so to speak, millions of dollars collected by the drug cartels for prior drug sales, and additional millions of dollars in guns and ammunition, never succeeded in leaving the U.S. via the Mexican border. At least on that front, illegal alien and drug traffic was completely shut down.

Assim was elated and could hardly wait to give his report to Thor. "Commander," he said, those three transporters, manned 24/7, are completely effective against illegal drug and alien smuggling activity along the Mexican/U.S. border. Now, for the first time, the United States has a positive and practical solution to a terrible problem that has gone on for many years."

"That is, indeed, very good news, Assim. I will inform the President immediately. And we must make sure the American people understand the significance of this, as well."

"Commander, there is one more thing: The work we are doing along the border is very effective in stopping illegal entry of aliens and drugs, due in large part to the exceptional accuracy of the GPS sensor system we are using. But we can do more with this system. I do not recommend taking the three transporters off duty on the border, but if we had another transporter, or perhaps two, so equipped, we could track members of the drug cartels all the way from the border back to their lairs. Then we could put Techna agents on the ground at those places and terminate the ring leaders and anyone else involved then and there. It is quite possible that, using both the border measures and these tracking measures we can totally eliminate the drug problem once and for all. "

"An exceptional plan, Assim. I will see that you get whatever else you need to expand your work, even though it will probably deprive us of operating funds we have been getting through intercepted drug shipments. "

"Sir, the system I am proposing merely protects the United States. A huge percentage of drug shipments go to other countries, as well, and those shipments produce massive amounts of drug revenue that funnels back to the cartels. So it seems to me our revenue could be much , much larger using this system."

"A very good point, Assim. Very good, indeed."

* * *

Thor left Barnstable for Washington, immediately after his conversation with Assim, and was waiting in the Oval Office when the President arrived.

"Ah, Commander," New President Fields said. "So good to see you. What news do you bring me this morning?"

"Very good news, Mr. President.. We have developed a system to stop Mexican drug cartels from importing illegal aliens and drugs into the U.S. It has been in operation one month, and in that time not one entry attempt has succeeded. Now we are expanding the system so we can track drug traffickers from U.S. borders back to their bases in Mexico, and then neutralize the players and the facilities. I believe your drug problem is nearly over."

"Commander, that is not good news. It is fantastic news. I am very pleased."

"Thank you, Mr. President. I would ask that you make sure the American people hear about this—not that we did it, just that they need not fear the bad effects of illegal drugs any longer."

"I will take care of that immediately."

"There is more good news, Sir. As you know we have taken control of the American health care industry. I am happy to report that U.S. citizens are beginning to experience increased health care services at much lower costs, and every citizen is covered now, with no increase in taxes. No longer are people turned away because they cannot pay, or have pre-existing conditions."

"Also, if you happened to catch the news July 27, you already know we destroyed one of your B52 bombers. An Air Force General named Schelhorne, who commanded the bomber base at March Field, armed the B52 with a nuclear warhead and launched it in a destruct mission against our New Mexico base. We intercepted that flight and ordered it to return to base. The General, who was on board, refused. So, rather than risk destruction of, not just the TF20 base, but nearby Roswell and its 46 thousand residents, as well, we forced the plane to crash with no survivors. SABER was behind that incident."

"Yes, Commander, I know about that, and Defense Secretary Bertram Phillips is planning a formal press release. It will mention TF20, and the role your agents made in saving Roswell."

"I appreciate that, Mr. President. We are not looking for kudos, you understand. We just want the people to know that we are friends, not enemies."

The President nodded in agreement, and said, "Commander, I will see to that right away. Anything else?"

"Yes, Sir. We are preparing to take over your petroleum, pharmaceutical and banking industries soon. American citizens are really getting hit hard by the cost of products and services provided by these industries."

"Because of SABER?"

"SABER's involvement in the Roswell incident simply caused us to accelerate what was already planned. We did not know how much power over the American economy that organization wields—I doubt any one did—and we know we can do better by the people. In the interest of serving the Middle Class, it is time to transfer control."

"Commander, I support that effort, and applaud your courage. Those businesses will fight you hard, so be careful. And, I hope when the time comes you can give us—the Federal Government—ammunition to sell this very important change to our citizens, and to other businesses."

"Mr. President, I am certain we can justify our actions in this arena to your satisfaction."

"Good. My, you have been a busy bunch of bees, Commander. The magnitude of your accomplishments is astonishing. I know how you do it, yet am still amazed."

"Mr. President, it is not amazing, really. We select the most qualified agents possible then encourage them to use their brains, their sense of good and the powers all people of Techna Planet possess. They do the rest."

"Yes, I know that is true, but there are some very smart Americans; many with that same sense of good versus evil, yet they do not accomplish anything close to what Techna Force 20 accomplishes. "

"Mr. President, I think most Americans do what is best for themselves, rather than what is best for their fellow countrymen."

"Ummm, maybe that is so. Anyway, thank you, Commander. You make my job so much easier."

"The pleasure is ours, Sir."

*   *   *

On the weekend beginning July 31, Thor and Sarah were joined at their Barnstable, Cape Cod home by the entire Malloy family. Sarah had arranged the gathering as a business meeting to be held inside the home for the purpose of planning the rapidly approaching trip to Techna Planet for her marriage to Thor. But the weather at Cape Cod was so beautiful she decided to make the event a family picnic on the home's rear lawn, instead. Suddenly she became a party planner, or rather picnic planner, for 17 people, including Manta and Jens, and the first thing she did was give everybody—including Thor—job assignments. Her mother and sisters were to help her prepare the food; her father, brother and Thor were ordered to find and set up tables and chairs, then set the tables; Manta and Jens were assigned to watch and entertain the five Malloy family children , a task they took on eagerly on the sandy beach behind the house, where the children had a great time exploring for sea shells, and playing in the warm Atlantic surf.

The picnic lunch was traditional, with sliced baked ham, baked beans, potato salad, corn on the cob, lots of warm fresh bread, and apple pie with ice cream. As an alternative for the kids, there was a large platter of hot dogs in buns. Sarah was richly rewarded with numerous compliments.

After the meal, she asked Thor to brief everyone on the trip to Techna Planet. "I have given them suggestions about what to pack, and they know each family will have its own stateroom suite including private bath. I also told them about my personal experiences on Techna and what a beautiful place it is, but I left preparing them for the actual flight up to you, if that is alright."

"I will be happy to cover that, honey. Actually it will be very similar to an ocean cruise, except that you will be surrounded by outer space instead of water. Techna Planet is five million miles from Earth, so our journey will take about 100 hours, or five days, each way. Our starships travel at 50,000 miles per hour once we clear Earth's atmosphere, but you will experience the sensation of speed only when we lift off. That is because our lift off is vertical and very rapid; one second you are on the ground, and the next you are miles above it. In case you are interested, we travel in I-Mode for protection, which means we are invisible to everyone outside the ship."

"All meals are served in the dining hall, and special requests are accepted. If you need a between-meals snack or a coffee or soda, the kitchen and dining hall are always open."

"Our starships are rather short on entertainment. We do have televisions, but reception tends to be very spotty in outer space. However, DVD players are attached to each television, and you will find many, many movies in the ship's library." Unfortunately, you will find internet and cell phone access unpredictable, as well. However, you are welcome to use the starship's communications system in emergencies."

"Jens, here, will be our flight captain and will manage the flight. Since we travel 24/7, we have three flight crews, each working an eight hour shift. During our flight through space you will all have a tour of the ship, including the flight deck, or bridge, so you can see just how everything works. Once we reach Techna, Manta will be your tour guide. I can tell you she is very good at it, and will make sure you see as much of Techna as time permits. While there you will all be guests of my Father, the Prime Minister of our country, in his official residence. I think you will find the accommodations quite comfortable. As for the actual wedding ceremony, I know Manta has prepared you for how it is done on Techna, and she will be glad to help in any way she can. Are there any questions?"

"I have a couple," Sarah's brother, John, said. "First, what is the scenery like in space? Second, how do you handle any medical emergencies that may occur?"

"Excellent questions, John. On the subject of scenery, you will have a fantastic view of Planet Earth as we depart, but then only an occasional view of stars and other space objects we pass. In actuality, space travel is like traveling in an ordinary airliner. As for medical needs, we have a physician on board, as well as a fully equipped, fully staffed sick bay, or mini-hospital , and can handle just about any illness or injury."

"Sounds good. Thank you, Commander."

Sarah, stood and said, "Now remember, everyone, we leave for Techna Planet September 4, and return to Earth September 18. This will be a momentous occasion that Thor and I do so want you all to experience with us. Okay, if there are no other questions, let's all adjourn to the beach and enjoy the sun, shall we?"

Carol, Sarah's sister, said, "You all go. I'll clean up here."

"Oh, I will help you, Carol," Manta said.

"I've got a better idea." Ken Malloy said. "Let's all pitch in and help clean up, then we can enjoy the beach and sun together."

*   *   *

Guri Kohn, Group 6 Captain, contacted Thor on August 13, to let him know that doubles agents for the next three takeovers had completed their training and were ready for duty. "Great work, old friend." Thor responded. "I will alert Truls, Erika and Arne right away." After calling those three Group Captains, he phoned Sam

Fischer of CTS, to see if everything was on track for the *Sunday Review* show scheduled for August 15.

"We're dead on, Commander," Sam said. "We are ready to wrap the segment on SABER"s involvement in 9/11, except for your testimonial. Can you be here tomorrow for taping of that and your segment?"

"I will be there, Sam."

"Seven a.m.?"

"Seven is fine."

* * *

The taping of Thor's part of the SABER segment and his announcement of more corporate takeover plans went very smoothly, and Sam called the complete show a wrap just before noon. Margie brought lunch for Sam, Mark and Thor, and the three of them sat around Sam's office , eating and watching the show preview. At the end, Sam said. "Well, it is most definitely a bombshell, Thor. Do you have room for us in your hotel? I see nothing but sharks this time, and they are coming after all of us."

"Count on it,." Thor responded. "Same plan as last time. TF20 will spread its wings and protect you from harm. "

"Good," Mark said. "What you're doin' for this damn country is nothin' short of wonderful, but I see sharks, too, and they will be very hungry and very big."

* * *

The minute Truls, Erika and Arne received the news that the agents they needed for their part in the huge corporate takeover were ready for deployment they made their first move, jointly. It was to replace every member of SABER with a Techna agent. That effort began early Saturday morning. They already knew where to find their prey and, methodically but swiftly replaced all 25 with doubles. Some were in their majestic homes, still in their pajamas, reading the morning paper. Others had gone to their clubs for breakfast, three were already on their private country club golf courses, and two were still sleeping. Pierce

Morgenthaller, was having coffee while seated in the plush red leather chair in the study of his palatial home. The one thing they all had in common—other than being members of SABER—was that, in the blink of an eye they were vaporized and replaced by an exact look-a-like, talk-a-like, Techna agent. They felt no pain. They simply vanished. Their wives, if they had wives, never noticed the change.

That was step one. In step two, which followed step one immediately on that weekend, other key executives of these 25 corporations were tracked down and replaced. They were not vaporized; just rendered invisible and taken away to await the long trip to Prison Planet. So by late afternoon, on Sunday, August 15, 2010, an entirely new set of executive officers was in place in all 25 companies.

At seven p.m., *Sunday Review* was broadcast on all CTS television stations. 15 minutes later, the world learned the truth about 9/11: The attack was not the work of Osama Bin Laden, or any other Muslem group. It was the work of 25 American corporate executives intent on enriching their companies and themselves by any means, regardless of the pain and suffering their actions caused others. They simply put so many dollars in front of 19 Arabic men that those men were willing to sacrifice their own lives for gold—and for Allah.

At seven-thirty p.m., the world also learned from Techna Force 20's Commander, Thor Berksten, who was there on the *Sunday* Review program, that those same 25 American companies would be taken over and operated for the good of mankind, by his organization. "No more will American people be burdened by exorbitant fuel and gasoline costs," He said. "And no more will they be forced to do without medication they so desperately need, because they cannot afford it, or suffer financial ruin at the hands of greedy bankers. We put the American citizens and their needs first, once and for all. And we put a stop to control of the United States Government by these corporate vultures, once and for all. Techna Force 20 is your friend, Americans, not your enemy. We came to your land to protect our own land, Techna Planet. But we discovered that you, the American people, needed protection, too. Now you have that protection."

Thor watched the *Sunday Review* broadcast with Mark Haddon, Margie Peterson and Sam Fischer, in Sam's office. When it ended, Mark said, "Well ladies and gents, hold onto your hats, the bombs will hit us any minute. But the minutes past, and nothing happened, then an hour passed and nothing.

Thor, of course, played along and urged them to come with him to Barnstable, Cape Cod, and they eagerly agreed.

CHAPTER FIFTEEN

Union of Two Planets

Guided by Manta, all 19 members of the Malloy family boarded Thor's starship on departure day for their journey to Techna Planet. She led them to their staterooms and helped with unpacking, then took them to a section of the ship's main lounge where standard-appearing airline seats were installed, and said, "We must sit here with seatbelts fastened during lift off. I will let you know when it is safe to move about the ship." She helped the Malloy children with their belts then made sure all adults fastened theirs.

A minute or so later they heard Thor's unmistakable baritone voice over the intercom, saying, "Prepare for lift off," and just seconds after that the starship seemed to literally leap into the air. The children squealed and laughed while the adults gasped in wide-eyed wonder. Although they could not comprehend it at the time, they were on their way to a fantastic adventure. But soon it was, as Thor had said, much like being on a cruise ship. They quickly settled into daily routines, of meals, relaxing in the lounge, games with the children, and just plain conversation, for there was so much that was new to discuss.

The lounge had no windows, but there were three points around the starship's circumference where staterooms had been omitted to allow windows for viewing but, as they had been told beforehand, there was very little to see; just vast open spaces. What the adults marveled at most of all was the absolute silence within the starship due to the lack of motor noise, as well as the smoothness of the ride. It was far different than riding in an airliner.

On Sunday, their second day of space flight, Thor took everyone on a tour of the ship. They saw everything Sam Fischer and Mark Haddon had seen, including crew quarters, the combat information center (CIC) with its double set of doors and red lights, the ships bridge with its vast array of control panels, levers, switches and gauges which the bridge crew watched continually, and the great expanse of curving windows that gave the crew a panoramic view of the world through which they were traveling. This part of the ship appealed to the male members of the Malloy family who, in fact, could not get enough of it. "This is truly amazing, Thor," Ken said. "You explained it so very well before, but seeing it is most impressive. Can you fly this ship?"

"Yes, I can fly it, and I have many times. But any more my work takes me in so many other directions that I do not get that pleasure."

The remaining three days went just as smoothly. 150 other Techna agents were on board, going home on leave, and some of them mingled with the Malloy family members. The children were fascinated by these young men and women in their sharp gray uniforms, and the agents, including some with children of their own on Techna, welcomed the chance to play with little guys again. As one of them said to Carol Malloy, "we have not seen or talked to our families for six months. Playing with your children is wonderful—it is sort of a warm up to playing with ours."

*   *   *

On September 8, 2010, after a five day journey from Barnstable, Cape Cod, they arrived on Techna Planet, and for the first time saw the wonders of it in person. They rode one of the beautifully streamlined monorail trains from the starship base to the City of Techna, and eventually to the majestic home of the Prime Minister, who greeted them all warmly upon arrival, then ushered them into his state home. There followed a hectic day of preparation and, on September 10, Commander Thor Berksten, and Sarah Malloy became man and wife. They were married in the magnificent Grand Assembly Hall of the Prime Minister's residence, in a civil ceremony. Per Techna tradition, Rose Malloy, Sarah's mother, was her Matron of Honor, and Thor's father, Karl Berksten, Prime Minister of Techna Planet, was his Best Man. Sarah was radiantly beautiful in the full length white organdy gown she had received from Mrs. Charlot, the shopkeeper in the tiny village of the same name, on her first visit to Techna Planet. Thor was resplendent in his formal dress uniform, complete with gold braid shoulder epaulets and wine-colored breast sash. All members of Sarah and Thor's families, and hundreds of Techna citizens were present to witness this most historical ceremony.

Prior to the marriage ceremony, Thor was given official notification by his father that he would assume the mantle of Prime Minister of Techna Planet on September 10, 2011, exactly one year from the date of his marriage to Sarah. It was an honor Thor assumed he would receive some day, but did not expect quite so soon.

There was a reception in the same hall in which Thor and Sarah were married, immediately after the wedding ceremony. And they stood in the receiving line for many hours, greeting the hundreds of guests who attended. Darien Lachsa, who once refused Thor's marriage proposal, had tears in her eyes as she walked through the line.

The next morning, Thor and Sarah boarded a monorail train to spend three days in Charlot. They registered as Mr. and Mrs. Thor Berksten for the first time, at a quaint little bed and breakfast hostel on the village's single cobblestone road. For two days they were lost in exploring each other and no one saw them. At this very special time in their lives they needed no nourishment, or companionship other than each other. On the third day they reappeared to stroll arm in arm along the narrow street, pausing now and then to examine the wares offered by one shop or another, and especially to visit Mrs. Charlot, but it was plain to see that they were not interested in purchasing anything; they were still in their own private world, seeing only each other, oblivious to every one and every thing around them.

*   *   *

While Thor and Sarah were honeymooning in Charlot, Manta, accompanied by Jens, took all members of the Malloy family on tours of the city. They visited many of the shops, all of the museums and the public buildings, some of the factories, a number of restaurants—even the little lakeside park where Sarah and Thor had picnicked with the Berksten family. Manta and Jens kept them on the go from early morning until late afternoon each day; they marveled at the free monorail train system which served all of the Planet, the complete absence of automobiles and trucks, and the extensive reliance on bicycles by Techna citizens. And on no occasion did they ever see a police officer.

Each evening there was a reception and dinner at the Prime Minister's home. All who came met each member of the Malloy family. All who came enjoyed a fine dinner with wine and champagne. It made no difference what their station in life was. It made no difference whether they wore tuxedoes and ball gowns, or work clothes and house dresses. All were welcomed warmly by the Prime Minister, and all were treated with dignity. Though Ken and Rose Malloy, as well as all adult members of their family were immensely impressed by the sights they had visited, nothing impressed them more than how Techna's citizens were treated by all other Techna citizens and the Prime Minister at those receptions.

In spite of their hectic, event crammed visit, Ken and James still managed to meet with the Prime Minister to complete plans for the Berksten family trip to Planet Earth. As recommended by Thor, it was decided the Berkstens would depart Techna Planet on September 22, arriving Planet Earth on the 26th of September. Their return trip to Techna was scheduled for October 9. "We suggest you land your starship in I-Mode, on Thor and Sarah's property in Barnstable, Cape Cod," Ken said. "Jens will help prepare your flight plan from Techna, if you wish and, on the day of the wedding, he will guide you to one of the fields owned by a farmer friend of mine near Brookline. We will provide transportation to and from there. After the wedding ceremony and reception, Jens will guide you back to Barnstable. Mr. Prime

Minister, I apologize for these rather crude arrangements, but we are so crowded in Brookline there is simply no other convenient place to land a large aircraft."

"Please do not apologize, Ken," The Prime Minister said. "I am certain we will do just fine. It is the day and the people we will meet that is important; not how we get there or where we stay."

* * *

Acting on Thor's behalf, Ken also briefed the Prime Minister on the American political situation, saying, "Sir, I must admit that the incredibly courageous work your son has done to change our Congress has put us on a solid political footing for the first time in our history, and I happen to know he is planning even more changes."

"And how do you feel about that, Ken, as a U.S. citizen and as an attorney?"

"Frankly, I was very concerned at first, since TF20 is, in effect, an invader from a foreign country. But the more I think about it and, indeed, I have thought about it at great length, the more I realize that the political problems our country faced could not be solved any other way. Our two party system is in tatters, to put it bluntly. The members of each party seem far more intent on either keeping or regaining their office, and waste precious time and energy that could be better used to work out the problems of the country. As a result, while in office they rarely accomplish much. So, while doing so comes very close to being treasonous, I support TF20's fine efforts. Of course I would not want that known outside this room."

"Your secret is secure Ken. I, too, have been greatly concerned, for, according to natural law, the end does not justify the means, and we are, in effect, violating that law. But because I know Thor has the highest ethics and moral standards, I believe what he is doing is good for your people, and ours, by the way."

"Yes, I agree, as to our people. But how so, yours, Sir?"

"Did he not tell you why he went to your country?"

"If he did , I do not recall."

"It was because agents on his original expedition to Earth overheard members of your Government discussing plans to

380

destroy any other planet inhabited by intelligent human life. To him that would mean the extermination of Techna Planet and its people"

"My, God. No. I don't believe I knew that. But now I understand. That is even more reason to support his work."

"Then, my friend, we are of like minds. And what is your position on the takeover of American corporations, Ken?"

"Sir, the same answer applies. Our government has, quite literally, been taken over by large corporations. That situation must be reversed, and I truly believe no one but Thor can do it. So far he has taken over just the health care industry, and not really that long ago, either. Yet, there are already signs of significant health care improvements."

"We absolutely do not want our government running corporations, because it is very inept at running anything. Conversely, we do not want our corporations running our Government, because corporations always, and I mean always, have a selfish, profit-driven motive. TF20 is not profit driven; it is people's needs driven. That makes it the perfect business manager."

"Ken, it is amazing how much we think alike, you and I. You and your family impress me very much. I have already been impressed by Sarah who, in my opinion, is the perfect wife for my son. Now I see that her family is the perfect set of in-laws, and I welcome you all into our family."

* * *

Tuesday, September 14, the date set for the Earth members of the wedding party to return to Planet Earth, came much too soon for everyone. On the night before, the Prime Minister hosted their last dinner at his official residence, and plans were finalized for a reunion in Barnstable on September 26.

Days spent on the flight home to Planet Earth simply flew by for the Malloy women, since they realized how short was the time before the next wedding in Brookline, and how many details still remained unresolved. So, as women will, when an urgent task must be completed quickly, all of them—Sarah, mother Rose, sisters Celia and Ellen, and sister-in-law-Carol, working together smoothly, attacked this challenge with utmost vigor, and woe to the male who interfered. But the results of their efforts were astonishing, for by September 18, with their starship on final approach to Barnstable, all wedding plans were set, and work assignments were distributed.

*   *   *

While Thor was on Techna Planet for his wedding to Sarah, Siran Missirian held a series of meetings with members of Congress who were actually Techna doubles, in her starship while it was at rest in I-Mode in a Congressional parking lot. The purpose of these meetings was to develop a Congressional Bill that, when adopted, would alter in major ways, the way Congress conducted business.

The significant elements of the Bill, as hammered out, would:

1. Make it illegal for members of Congress to continue membership in political parties once elected.

2. Bar political influence over Congressional members.

3. Prohibit lobbying of Congressional members.

4. Provide that all future political campaigns for Congress and the Presidency be financed strictly through government funding.

5. Make it a serious legal offense for members of Congress, or candidates for Congress, to accept money or anything else of value from non-government sources.

6. Eliminate filibusters entirely, and require that all voting be done on a simple majority basis.

The proposed Bill was unanimously adopted in its entirety by the Congressional members who attended, and the consensus of that group was that they could convince enough non-Techna members of Congress to vote for passage. Three Techna doubles Congressmen were selected to sponsor and manage the Bill. They worked hard and fast to sell it to as many non-Techna members of Congress as possible, and on September 6, 2010, it was brought to the floor of the House. After just four days of debate it was approved by a margin of 330 to 105 votes.

On September 18, when the wedding party returned from Techna Planet, Siran was pleased to report its successful passage to Thor. "That is fantastic news, Siran," He said. "Now I think we will be able to make real progress on behalf of the American people. Though it may take a little while for this change to become truly effective, we should soon see the total absence of political infighting in this country."

"Yes, Sir. I agree. And in time, when we have even more Techna agents in Congress, we should experience ever more progress."

"Very true, Siran. And as you know, there is likely to be a huge influx of Republican winners in the November election. That seems to be the pattern for America's mid term elections."

Siran nodded in agreement, and said, "Yes. They will be elected as Republicans, but before being sworn in they will be replaced by Techna doubles who will never vote the Republican line. I am already preparing for that election, Commander."

Thor smiled, and replied, "Good work, Siran. Very good work. Indeed. I knew you were the perfect person for this assignment, and you have not disappointed me."

*   *   *

On Monday, September 20, Thor called a staff meeting so he could be updated on the various projects in process. He opened the meeting with brief remarks on Siran's work with Congress, then asked her to report on the details of the project. She concluded by saying, "Getting this Bill passed was so easy because we have 195 Techna agents functioning as doubles in Congress. a minority, on the surface, yes, but when they start urging the remaining 240 members with the determination our agents exhibit, amazing things occur. That is what happened in this case. As time goes by we will have a stronger and stronger presence in Congress for, as all of you know, we will never allow another Democrat or Republican to serve; only doubles acting as Independents, no matter how the election turns out."

"Very good, Siran. Do you have anything else?"

"Yes, Commander, I have three more points to cover. Two are on the American Military, and one on health care. On the Military, a Bill will soon be offered to reduce the number of American bases on foreign soil. There are currently almost 900 bases in 130 countries, and the cost of maintaining them is astronomical. Billions and billions of dollars each year. There is no longer a need for them, and the money they cost can be put to much better use. This will be the first step toward moving the U.S away from a wartime economy."

"Second, we are evaluating an informal proposition to transform the American Military into a starship-based force, instead of a force relying on thousands of humans with hand-held weapons, cumbersome tanks, relatively slow, ineffective aircraft, and huge surface ships. Techna would provide the starships and they would always be manned by Techna personnel. Instead of fighting Americans, they would fight for them. In my opinion, it would be a formidable force for good over evil. I am not yet ready to recommend such a change, because we still need to make certain our starships can never fall into the wrong hands."

"Siran, that is an interesting concept. On the positive side, it would end the U.S. war based economy. I will wait with enthusiasm for your recommendation, whatever it may be. Now, your third point?"

"Yes, Commander. On Health Care, our plan was to insert doubles into all the top executive positions in those companies. That was the key to success. It is not just because those executives are the ones who set policies workers must follow; they also set the tone and operating philosophy, which are so important to success of the venture. I am telling you all this because I know that is the approach you are taking with other industries, and it is definitely the best approach."

"Siran, I completely agree," Truls said. "Erika, Arne and I have already seen positive results with respect to our projects in the petroleum, pharmaceutical and banking fields. It is amazing that just 30 or 40 executives can so quickly alter the way thousands of employees in their organizations work. One would think making such drastic changes as we make would take years, but it works like a waterfall. The word flows from level to level, and does so with surprising speed."

Thor smiled. "We see it in our own organization," He said. The vast majority of workers want to please their superiors, beginning with their immediate supervisors and those higher up. So it seems we have hit on the most workable approach to very difficult tasks. Now, I would like to hear from you, Truls, and Erika and Arne, on the status of your targets. Truls, would you like to start?"

"Certainly, Sir. My project, or target, is the U.S. Oil Industry, which is composed of essentially six large corporations and dozens of smaller players. Literally hundreds, of products derive from petroleum refining, then make their way into many hundreds of other products manufactured by non-petroleum companies. So we are not talking just about gasoline and fuel oil production. For better or worse, oil is either an ingredient in other products or a source of fuel to make them, and transport them to market. Oil can almost be described as a basic element of life. Yet, it is a fact of life that the supply of oil is not unlimited; the world is consuming it faster than nature can replenish it. Oil companies are fully cognizant of this and, rather than find substitutes for it, they are taking every opportunity to maximize profits on the existing supply, while spending far too little time and expense on research to find replacements. Oil companies seem always to take the easy road. Instead of drilling new wells on American soil, where they own or control millions of acres of oil leases, they buy the crude they need from OPEC, an arrangement that makes Middle Eastern Nations rich beyond imagination."

"But oil company executives are opportunists by nature. When OPEC needed oil drilling technology not already possessed, it looked to American oil companies, all of whom are expert at finding and drilling for oil. The American companies came running, and in short order were producing oil on the sands of

Arabia. For that effort they were richly rewarded with shares in the wells they drilled and the refineries they constructed. So then, every barrel of oil they brought out of the ground paid not only OPEC a nice profit, it paid the American oil company a nice profit as well. That is still the arrangement today. From the very beginning, this OPEC oil combine has had the power to alter crude oil prices around the world by changing the supply/demand mix, and it does so routinely to maintain its desired profit level. OPEC's American partners do not object because they share in those profits. Of course, artificially high crude oil prices impact the price of every product derived from oil refining, as well as every product that uses oil derivatives as ingredients. Thus, American oil companies profit not only from crude sales, but from refined product sales as well, which is why their annual reports show such huge profit figures."

"One of our major takeover objectives is to eliminate the OPEC oil combine's influence on any crude production and refining that affects the U.S. To accomplish that objective, we had to activate other sources of crude oil, including the millions of acres of dry land oil leases the oil industry already owned. Another source considered was off-shore drilling, but after the disastrous oil spill in the Gulf of Mexico earlier this year we decided that source of oil is potentially too damaging to the environment and could virtually obliterate the fishing industry and other business that rely on the sea. So we have ruled that source out altogether. There was some concern in the beginning that oil shortages would occur, forcing a return to OPEC for supplies. However current supplies are sufficient to meet demand for at least a year, and it appears new U. S. wells coming on line will more than offset the loss of OPEC oil."

"What about other energy sources, Truls?"

"Commander. We have resurrected the extensive research programs started then dropped by the oil companies a number of years ago, to determine the viability of other energy sources, such as solar, wind, nuclear, and hydrogen, and those projects are showing great promise. All factors indicate that the U.S. may not need as much fossil fuel in the future as it consumes today, and of course, that is exactly our objective, because the fossil fuel supply is limited at best. And, as you all know, Techna Planet has no oil and manages very nicely using little more than nuclear power. If we can do it, Planet Earth can do it."

"Who do you see managing other forms of energy?"

"Sir, to keep the oil industry from becoming an even larger giant, energy sources other than crude oil and natural gas will be managed by companies that are, and will remain, completely independent of the oil industry."

"So, that is where things stand on the energy supply side of the equation, but we are also working to reduce operating costs in all the oil companies we are taking over. There was a time when this industry spent wisely for offices and office furnishings, always providing top quality equipment, without any display of ostentation or opulence. Private offices were rare and only allowed for top executives; all other employees worked in open spaces, or 'bull pens,' and every desk, whether in a private office or open area was the same gray metal with a matching linoleum top. All chairs were the same gray metal, a low backed swivel desk chair, and a matching side chair. That was the typical décor."

"But how things have changed, especially in the executive office suites. Now there seems to be no limit to what an executive can spend for his office; $500 thousand dollars for a single office is not uncommon. On top of that comes executive compensation, in the form of salaries and bonuses, expensive cars or car allowances, fat expense accounts and stock options. and almost obscene buy-outs, or golden parachutes, if the executive is forced out. Think multi-millions of dollars for these packages; ten million for the lowest level executive, to 30, or even 40 million for the CEO."

"That philosophy has ended. We are going back to the 1950's thinking on furnishings—back to substantial metal chairs and desks, and fewer private offices. And we are going back to common-sense compensation packages--the 30 or 40 top executives are now Techna agents, of course, and they are quite comfortable earning $400 thousand a year, instead of $30 million. Nor do they miss the bonuses, buy-outs, and stock options. In addition, our new executives do not get fancy cars or allowances, or private jet planes—their transportation vehicles, which we provide, are transporters."

"I think that makes a lot of sense, Truls. I can confirm that $400 thousand is adequate compensation, because that is what I earn, and each of you earn only a few thousand less. I have no problem meeting my personal expenses, even with a wife to support, and if any of you have a problem, you have not informed me of it. It is common knowledge that people—especially American people--eventually become dissatisfied with their salary, no matter how large it is. They come to believe the work they do is worth more money That is just human nature, and it does not mean there is an actual need to pay them more. So I like that thinking, and hope it is being applied to all takeovers."

Siran said, "Commander, my Group has addressed the compensation question as it applies to health care. We see the exorbitant salaries and bonuses as almost insane, and have done exactly what Truls is talking about doing: getting back to sensible compensation systems. I believe you will hear similar themes from Erika on pharmaceuticals, and from Arne on banking, when it comes to compensation. We all share a common belief that the current system is neither necessary nor effective."

"Siran, I am certain we are all on the same page with respect to the four corporation group takeovers currently underway. My comments were meant to establish a policy with respect to takeover in the future."

"Thank you, Commander," Siran responded. "I believe I speak for everyone here when I say we understand and agree with your wishes."

"Truls, I Am Sorry. I think I took us a bit off the subject. Would you please continue?"

"Certainly, Commander. I have only one other area to cover, and that is the practice of using various excuses to raise retail prices on gasoline and diesel fuel. In the past, those prices went up just at the start of every summer vacation and on every major holiday. Oil companies have also used, as an excuse to raise prices, claims that this or that refinery had to be taken offline for repairs or modifications. We have ended the practice of raising prices during vacation and holiday periods,. And we now know refineries go offline routinely, and such down time events are almost always planned well in advance, with backup always assured, making it totally unnecessary to raise prices. So we will not be doing that, either. Gasoline prices will remain a constant

$1.00 per gallon all year. Diesel, which is slightly more costly to produce, will consistently sell for $1.10 per gallon.

As every American who drives a vehicle with a combustion engine knows, these products have been selling regularly for up to $5.00 per gallon. That ends my report. I thank you all for your patience and attention, and turn the podium over to Erika Varda."

"Thank you, Truls. I am pleased to be able to report significant progress in reorganizing the pharmaceutical industry. I think the most significant changes my doubles agents have brought about fall under the headings of (1), cost reductions to the consumer; (2), greater compliance with FDA rules; and (3), production of safe prescription drugs that do what they are intended to do for consumers, and which consumers can trust."

"As Truls discovered, our operating costs also plummeted just by switching to Techna business philosophies—no ridiculously high salaries and bonuses; no extravagant offices, fancy cars or expensive air travel. In fact, as he discovered, we realized a huge drop in travel costs simply by requiring the use of Techna transporters in lieu of airlines and private jets, plus, our traveling personnel are safer, more comfortable, and reach their destinations in much less time, than ever before."

"In addition, we discovered some terribly sloppy research and production practices that were causing contamination of various drugs, thus jeopardizing the health of consumers. Not only that, these practices were in outright violation of FDA requirements, all in the interest of reducing costs and sending the result to officer perks. Those practices have been stopped cold forever. So, now we deliver to the consumer, prescription drugs that cost less, do more, and can be completely trusted.

Favorable reports are already flowing back to us from patients, pharmacists and physicians, and our year end projections call for net earnings after taxes of at least ten percent, a number we consider very acceptable."

"So do I, Erika. Congratulations. Great work."

"Commander," Siran said. "I would like to add something to Erika's report, if I may."

"By all means, Siran."

"As you know, pharmaceutical companies work hand in hand with health care companies to provide prescription medicine to patients through Medicare at very low cost. So, while reviewing procedures and records on this joint effort, Erika and I discovered that the pharmaceutical companies were invoicing health insurance providers amounts that far exceeded the over-the-counter price of those same medications. The health care providers either did not notice this practice, or simply looked the other way, and billed Medicare the higher amount. Patients paid according to the much lower payment schedule for whatever drug was prescribed, but the practice led Medicare to pay untold extra millions of dollars for years for health care costs. We have stopped that practice now, of course, and doing so is reducing health care costs substantially. Erika and her team deserve much of the credit for this discovery, Commander."

"Thank you, Siran, for pointing that out. And Erika, again I say great work. Now, Arne, what is happening with our takeover of banking? "

"Commander, the United States has experienced a major evolution in banking within the past ten years, not so much with the smaller banks—those serving small towns and cities—but certainly with the six or seven large, multi-office banks. This evolution is due to an exodus of business—primarily manufacturing—to other countries, in search of ever greater profits—greed, in other words, and to some extraordinarily bad real estate mortgage loans that, in actuality far exceeded the property's value in the very beginning—also a matter of greed."

"This movement of manufacturing out of the country, over and above the terrible loss of jobs, has had a profound impact on banking. In the old days, banks and manufacturers worked together as a team, with the banks financing production of their customer's products, and receiving payment, in the form of interest, when the product sold. That is no longer the case. Now, corporations self-finance their operations, leaving banks out in the cold, searching frantically for other sources of revenue. That has led banks to go far beyond their traditional revenue sources, even into the stock and bond markets, to derivatives, and to other, far more risky and volatile investments. All of us have heard stories about banks going under due to making bad mortgages and very bad market investments."

"Having lost most of their business customers, banks are struggling. If they limit financing activities to the only things left—a dearth of home sales, and therefore far fewer home mortgages, a lower volume of automobile loans because of a lower volume of automobile purchases, and a very real slowdown in home appliance purchases—they cannot survive. But in taking that dangerous investor road they violate their SEC charters and risk closure. Most bankers know this, so they look for other sources of revenue. That leads to all types of fees on savings and checking accounts, including high fees on NSF checks, that is, checks written without sufficient funds to back them, automatic teller use fees, checking account retention fees, and on and on. There seems to be no limit to their creativity in the fee area. But that only leads to angry customers who retaliate by pulling their money out and trying another banking institution."

"I have stayed awake many nights with this problem, and have finally concluded that the solution is to bring business home—back to the United States—and reestablish the traditional banker/corporate head relationship that existed before the exodus, then exert great pressure on bankers to give up their risky current habits."

"Yes, Arne, I see the problem, and I agree with your proposed solution. But how do we force corporations to bring production back to the States?"

"By enacting stiff tariffs, Commander, and that means Government intervention."

"How do you see that helping, Arne?"

"Sir, as you know, corporations move their production offshore to take advantage of far lower labor rates in certain foreign countries. Then they bring their foreign made products back to the States. The U. S. currently has no tariffs to restrict such activity. Millions of American jobs have been lost to this practice. Furthermore, the U.S. has lost a huge portion of its technical and manufacturing capability because of out-sourcing, and, as I have stated, banks have suffered virtually irreparable financial losses. Tariffs are the answer. It comes down to using the old carrot and stick approach. Government offers the carrot in the form of reduced taxes to corporations who do their manufacturing in the U.S., and the stick in the form of very high duties on every piece of every product brought back into the country for sale, if they do not. We say to the corporation in effect, bring your production home or we will not allow you to sell it at a profit in your former home. You will become a foreign corporation."

"What if they do not respond, Arne?"

"Truls, then they go out of business here, and other companies, willing to comply, take their place."

"It is a beautiful solution, Arne. It certainly solves the banking problem and, as you point out, it has the collateral advantage of bringing tens of thousands of good paying jobs and skill back to the U.S."

"That is true, Commander. It is a win, win situation."

"Yes, indeed it is. Siran, how should we handle this?

"Sir, it is a job for Congress, and I will see to it immediately. I think Arne has performed an excellent analysis of the problem, and has not only given us the solution, he has even given us the language of the law we must create."

"Excellent. Now, Truls, what has happened to the 25 SABER members who engineered the 9/11 attack on the World Trade Center?"

"Commander, we put them on a starship bound for Prison Planet but, unfortunately, they did not survive the journey."

"I see. Well then, justice was done, I think."

"Yes, Sir. Justice was done. In the American legal system, few high executives ever pay a sufficient price for their crimes. These men did."

Thor nodded in agreement, and turned to look at Assim Agassi. "Last but by no means least, Assim, how is it going with the Mexican drug cartel problem?"

"Commander, I believe we are closing in on a solution. The border crossing problems have been solved by using our transporter patrols, though I feel we must make that a permanent procedure, for as soon as we stop, the cartels will be at the border again."

"Consider it done, Assim."

"Thank you, Sir. However, our most pressing problem at the moment is the virtually complete breakdown of law enforcement in the Mexican Interior, primarily in very large metropolitan areas. The Mexican Government no sooner appoints new Mayors, Provincial Governors, Police Chiefs and Police Officers, than the cartels begins to slaughter them. I have agent teams in all Mexican cities and towns, and their instructions are to shoot to kill any cartel members they encounter. We have executed more than 250 drug gang members, and I believe we are slowly gaining on the problem by using their technique; they scare officials so much by killing many of them that those remaining simply walk away from their posts. Now we do the same thing; we kill every drug thug we encounter without mercy. The cartels know us well now, and are having a much more difficult time recruiting drug runners. There are still many targets down there, so it will take time. I think, though, that until we find alternative ways for Mexican people to make a decent living, we will not succeed completely."

Thor nodded in agreement, and said, "I think you are correct, Assim. The U.S. tried NAFTA, and I am not sure why that failed. It seemed to be a good idea, because it created jobs for Mexicans in Mexico, without taking jobs away from the U. S. TF20 must give that problem more attention in the near future. Siran, I am afraid I must add this burden to your already overloaded shoulders, for this seems to me to be another job for Congress."

"Not a problem, Commander. I will bring it up with the Chairman of the Foreign Relations Committee when I meet with him next week."

"Very well. These have all been excellent reports today, which does not surprise me at all, for you are the cream of the crop when it comes to getting things done right and on time. It is obvious that we made the right decision when we decided on these takeovers, and it is just as obvious that, thanks to all of you, we are succeeding in efforts to provide a new beginning for the United States. I hope this new United States will see the true value of having Techna Planet as a friend, and forget about trying to destroy us."

Now, if there is no other business, I have an announcement. First, I am sorry none of you could go with us to Techna for my wedding to Sarah. I really wanted you all there, but totally understand why you could not be there. However, now we will be married according to American customs, in Brookline, Massachusetts, on October 2, and all of you, including, of course, Manta and Jens, are invited. In fact, I have asked that you be in the wedding party. Please set aside all work for that day, because I truly want you there."

"We will be there, Commander," Truls responded. "Congratulations on your appointment as Next Prime Minister, and on your Techna marriage to Sarah. We all love her."

"As do I, Truls. As do I."

------///------

CHAPTER SIXTEEN

A Fine Beginning

On September 26, the starship of the most powerful man on Techna Planet, Prime Minister Karl Berksten, landed on the rear lawn of his son's home at Barnstable, Cape Cod, in the state of Massachusetts. With him on the voyage were his four daughters, with their husbands and children, and all six members of his Cabinet and their wives. They came to witness, and be a part of, the wedding of the Prime Minister's only son, Thor Berksten, to Sarah Malloy.

During the first five days they were at Cape Cod they were tourists. They took full advantage of the four long black chauffeur-driven limousines Thor had provided, and eagerly explored all the sights and sounds of the many quaint villages and historical sites the Cape offered, including Hyannis Port and the Kennedy compound, Sandwich and the Daniel Webster Hotel, Plymouth Rock, Provincetown, and the Island of Martha's Vineyard. They seemed unable to get enough of the magic of the Cape, and were especially fascinated by all the cars, trucks, busses and trains, together with the noise those vehicles made, for this was more foreign to their eyes and ears than anything else they discovered.

On Friday, the first of October, Thor took his father to Washington to meet New President Fields. As was his custom, they arrived in the Oval Office in I-Mode, and were waiting when the President and Jack Brill entered. Brill was waving his arms and talking in urgent tones on some point he was trying to make, but the President seemed not to be listening, and Brill soon left the Office. At that point, Thor and Karl made themselves visible, and, the President came around his desk to welcome them. "Commander," He said. "So good to see you. And Mr. Prime Minister, it is an honor to see you again. Perhaps you will not recall, but we met some years ago, when you inspected my graduating class at Techna Military University."

"Yes, Mr. President, I remember, but then you were Captain Damien Moss, I believe."

The three men laughed, and Karl said, "I knew you would rise to great heights, but you have exceeded all my expectations."

"Sir, my job here is easy, thanks to Thor. Whatever I need to happen, he accomplishes for me; assuming, of course, it is something ethical and legal, and with him, there is never any question of that."

"Or with you, Sir, I assume."

"Indeed. It is the way we were brought up on Techna Planet. I find it most unfortunate that most Americans were not brought up the same way. Now, is there anything I can do to make your visit more pleasant?"

"No, Mr. President. We are being treated very special, I assure you. I just wanted the opportunity to meet you, and I hope everything continues to go well for you and the United States.

"Thank you, Mr. Prime Minister."

The three men shook hands, and Thor and his father left the White House and flew directly to Brookline.

*   *   *

For the second time in her young life, Sarah Malloy prepared to marry the love of her life, Thor Berksten. The first time was on Techna Planet where, as required by the traditions of that society, any citizen of Techna who chose to marry a non-Technian, in a non-Technian ceremony, would be required to consummate the union in a formal Techna ceremony. She had complied with that requirement happily, but with little emotion, for it gave her

396

no feeling of having been married. For one thing, it was a civil ceremony, not the "church" wedding she had always imagined.

Now, on October 2, 2010, with her sisters, Celia, Matron of Honor, escorted by Captain Truls Heyerdahl, and Ellen, Bridesmaid, escorted by Captain Assim Agassi, leading the way, Sarah was making the long walk down the aisle of Gates Of Heaven Catholic Church, on the arm of her father. She looked very different this time, not because of how she was dressed, for she was wearing the same Charlot wedding gown, the same shoes and the same lace veil she wore on Techna Planet. The difference was in the great joy that shown in her lovely blue eyes, the almost triumphant smile playing around her lips, and the near angelic glow that made her even more beautiful. She walked slowly, in measured steps, and her eyes were focused exclusively on her husband-to-be, waiting just to the right of the long main aisle, that stretched before her toward the alter rail. Everything about her said to the world, this time it is for real. This time the whispered words I uttered so many months ago (*I intend to spend a great deal of time with you*) will soon be true, and I will realize my dream of becoming Mrs. Thor Berksten.

Outwardly, she was the epitome of the confident, happy woman about to be fulfilled, but she was thankful for her father's strong arm and for the long dress that concealed trembling knees, so reminiscent of the trip she once made on Thor's arm down the staircase of his father's residence. And all the while she was trying to store in her memory every sight, sound and aroma that existed in the church at that moment, for she never wanted to forget any part of this magic day.

At last she and her father reached the alter and Thor. Her father raised her veil and kissed her goodbye tenderly, then moved to the pew assigned to him and her mother, Rose. Thor took her arm and smiled, then together they walked through the alter rail gates and up the steps to stand before the waiting Priest. They listened to his words as he recited the traditional Catholic wedding ceremony, responded "I Do," when he asked them whether they would take each other for better or worse, in sickness and in health, till death, exchanged wedding bands when he asked them to do so, and then, after what seemed an eternity, they heard his magic words, "I now pronounce you man and wife," followed by, "Ladies and Gentlemen, may I present Mr. and Mrs. Thor Berksten."

* * *

More than 400 people attended the reception and dinner at the Brookline Country Club to celebrate Thor and Sarah's marriage. In addition to the new couple's immediate families, Many dignitaries attended. The Prime Minister of Techna Planet's Cabinet members and their wives were there. Manta Sames, Jens Petersen, and all of Thor's Group Captains were there. Ken Malloy's law partners, as well as judges, and lawyers from many other firms came. The Speaker of the House, The Senate Majority Leader, The House Minority Leader and House Minority Whip were there, and last but not least, The President of The United States was there with his adoring wife.

In addition, Sam Fischer, Mark Haddon and Margie Peterson of CTS were there, along with at least a dozen other reporters from local and national news media, for what they commonly referred to as *The Wedding of The Century, for it was also the wedding of two great Planets.*

Finally, there were the numerous close friends, distant relatives, and many, many other well-wishers, who came just to see the very first marriage of an American woman and a man from outer space.

The reception lasted well into the night, and Mr. and Mrs. Thor Berksten did not break away for their honeymoon trip to Solvang, California until nearly two A.M. the next morning.

* * *

Meanwhile, The Techna Prime Minister and his family members, plus the Cabinet members and their wives, and Manta Sames, were guests of Sarah's parents, Ken and Rose Malloy, and their family.

Ken and Rose, with much help from their children, James, Celia and Ellen, seemed determined to show their visitors everything there was to see in Boston, one of the oldest cities in the United States, perhaps the most historical, certainly the most picturesque, so there was much to see. They kept the four limousines rolling almost from daybreak until dusk every day, from the day after the wedding until their guests left for Techna Planet, on October 9.

* * *

Thor and Sarah spent the days of their first week as a married couple touring the beautiful, quaint village of Solvang, which was so Scandinavian, and so much like his country that at times Thor felt as if he was home again.

For Sarah, Solvang was a fairyland filled with beautiful chinaware, paintings, silver and gold jewelry, lace linens and ornate, high-quality home furnishings, to say nothing of the numerous shops selling delectable homemade pastries, candies, cakes, and breads. The aromas that drifted out of the shops and along the streets was enough to make one constantly hungry. As they moved from shop to shop, Thor became ever more aware that he had married a woman who loved to shop—especially for bargains, and it amused him greatly to watch her in action as she negotiated with this or that shopkeeper.

What few meals they took time to enjoy were in the Viking Restaurant, just off the main street, where the smorgasbord was fabulous, and during those times they lingered and talked for hours.

They spent the nights in their tiny Norwegian bed and breakfast hostel, though none of the other guests ever saw them at meal time, for solid food was not a requirement, they needed only time to explore each other.

Sometimes, while Thor was deep in slumber, Sarah propped her head up on one hand, watching him, listening to his soft, almost silent, measured breathing, marveling at his ability to relax and put aside all the problems he faced. He had such great ability that way. She had seen him when he was all business and would let nothing else interfere, but when they were together he put his business problems in a drawer deep in his head somewhere and concentrated entirely on her. It was as if she was the only thing on his mind, and indeed, she knew she was. That pleased her immensely. She was perfectly willing to share him with his duties, so long as he put her first and only first during their special times together. She usually fell asleep after those moments of observation, contented and overwhelmed with happiness.

And then, before she knew it, their honeymoon was over and they were back in their beautiful Barnstable home, ready to finally begin a life together. It was so different now. Before, when they were simply girl friend and boy friend, and later, after Thor had asked her to marry him and they were an engaged couple, Sarah liked to pretend that she really was his wife, and he really was her husband. But now there was no need to pretend any longer. She *was* Mrs. Thor Berksten. She *was* the mistress of this house. And in a moment alone she put both hands to her breast, tilted her head upward, and said silently, "Thank you, my Lord."

Marriage brought other changes to Sarah's life. She no longer worked for CTS; being a homemaker was all she wanted, and she looked forward to that new adventure eagerly. Also, she would no longer be living in her New York apartment, at least not permanently, so the decision was made to keep the apartment, but to move most of her clothing and personal items to Barnstable.

But the greatest adjustment she had to make by far was to being an agent of Techna Planet. That was something to which she had paid little attention, yet she was, in fact, an agent, by reason of being married to Thor. She would not be called upon to perform the work of other agents, but she would need to constantly be on the alert to danger for, as Thor was quick to point out, there were people in her country who resented anyone from Techna Planet, and would not hesitate to do her harm, given the chance. So he made her realize that she had the same powers of personal protection as other agents, the same personal laser weapon, and he taught her how to use that weapon, though she did not willingly become a student of the art of killing, and prayed she would never have to do that.

*   *   *

Thor was aware that he would have new responsibilities after marriage, long before the wedding ceremony. He knew Sarah would make more demands on him as his wife than she ever did before marriage; she would expect him to make time for her in his life, to confide in her as much as his work permitted, to be loving and respectful of her private needs, to help her around their home, to be there for special occasions, and to never forget their wedding anniversary, or to be a partner in the hundreds of other things so important to women. He understood the importance of all of these things, and promised himself never to minimize a single one.

*   *   *

When they returned to Barnstable, Thor saw that his staff members had been very busy. A new building was being constructed at the rear of the Barnstable residence, to house his and hers transporters, and provide living quarters for Jens, and for Sarah's pilot, when necessary.

Also, his starship was no longer there, having been moved back to Sardine Mountain along with all the others, and new satellite offices been prepared for him and for Manta, along with a new conference room in the Barnstable home for those times when he would be working there. Living quarters for Manta were being incorporated into the new hanger building under construction behind the home.

Later, as he was going through status reports that had accumulated during his absence, he received a call from Siran Missirian. "Good afternoon, Commander," She said. "And welcome back. It was such a beautiful wedding. Do you have a moment?"

"Certainly, Siran."

"Sir, I have good news regarding the problem of American Corporations out-sourcing manufacturing. I brought the problem to the attention of the Speaker Of The House, Katherine McDonald, and learned from her that the House has been struggling with it for months without success. When I gave her Arne's suggestion regarding the levying of tariffs on companies who refuse to bring manufacturing back to the States, she really jumped at the concept. She said that, incredibly, it was a solution the responsible House Sub-Committee had never considered, and she promised to talk to the Chairman of that Committee right away. That was on Monday, the fourth, just five days ago. This morning, she called to let me know that a bill has been drafted to enact stiff tariffs on off-shore manufacturing, and that it will be brought to the floor of the House next Tuesday, the 12th of October. She is confident the Bill will pass by a large margin."

"That is great news, Siran. Have you informed Arne?"

"Yes, I have, Commander, and he asked me to call you. As soon as we hear the results of the vote, I will let you know."

"Thank you, Siran. Great work."

*   *   *

On the evening of that same Friday, Thor and Sarah had their first meal in their new home as husband and wife. It was a seafood dinner consisting of Boston clam chowder, shrimp cocktail, and broiled filet' of sole. It was served with a very crisp chardonnay wine. Sarah designed the menu and prepared everything herself. They ate by candle light while listening to soft, Cape Cod music and afterwards strolled arm in arm to the boat dock at the end of their expansive rear lawn, where they sat for the longest time, saying little, listening to the waves gently slapping against the dock. It was very dark when they returned to the Barnstable house.

*   *   *

Ending corporate out-sourcing and bringing jobs back to the United States was proving to be much more difficult than Siran expected. As drafted, the Bill was a bitter and totally unacceptable pill for American businessmen. Its main provision would require American companies engaged in manufacturing products in foreign countries, with intent to sell them to other companies in the United States, or to American citizens in the United States, or for use in America's national defense program, to conduct such manufacturing operations on American soil, using American labor. Any American business choosing to ignore this law and out-source manufacturing to other countries, would be required to pay a tariff amounting to the equivalent of marking up the retail price of any item offered for sale in the U.S., at the port of entry, by 50 %. That markup would place the retail price far above the price of similar products made in the United States, and in effect make them unmarketable.

A second provision would set minimum and maximum limits for employee compensation at every pay grade, limit bonuses, if any, to 20 percent of base salary per year, specify that all compensation, including non-cash compensation, be subject to Internal Revenue Service employee tax rules, and set a maximum limit of $450 thousand in total annual compensation from all sources per employee, per year. This provision was especially galling to top executives, for it would ban multi-million dollar salaries and bonuses, and put business compensation packages more in line with Government packages.

Even the provision in the Bill cutting Federal income taxes by 50% for five years for businesses that agreed to return manufacturing operations to the United States failed to win favor for the proposed legislation.

Upon reading the Bill, American business leaders realized they could not compete in the U.S. market using foreign labor. In fact, they would need to sell their products at a substantial loss, and that would be fatal. They would either have to comply with the law, if passed, or forego the lucrative American market altogether. Neither option was acceptable so they decided to fight the Bill with every weapon at their disposal, including legal litigation.

The knowledge that passage of the Bill would likely trigger legal action did not faze Congress. On November 8, the Bill now known as "Jobs For Americans" won in the House by a wide margin. The Senate then passed it by a vote of 80 yea's to 20 nay's one week later, and sent to the President. He signed it immediately, making it the most historical Law of the Land ever.

But American business was not quite ready to roll over and accept the new law without a fight, and fight they did. Even before it passed, and in complete violation of lobbying restrictions, they worked the halls and cloakrooms of Congress, to get sympathetic members to vote against the Bill. When that effort failed they resorted to outright bribery—offers of huge sums of money, lavish vacations, future powerful and lucrative positions on their corporate boards, and every other enticement they could conceive of to defeat the proposed law that, in their minds, would reduce massive profits to a pittance, rob them of stockholder allegiance and destroy their huge companies. But none of their ploys worked.

In desperation they turned to the Supreme Court for relief. But Thor had anticipated the possibility of just such corporation action months before, with the result that five of the nine Supreme Court Justices were now Techna doubles. Thus, when 50 U.S. corporations joined in a petition for relief to the High Court on November 22, the Court refused to hear their appeal, stating that the law was a just, necessary and appropriate effort to restore to the United States its right to retain essential skills and protect its sovereignty.

Following that failed attempt, all but a handful of businesses accepted the terms of the new law without exception, and agreed to return operations to the U.S. as quickly as logistically possible. While complete return would take months to accomplish--if not years in some cases—one could almost hear the happy chants of workers long deprived of a steady income, and read the hope in their faces for *A New Beginning.*

* * *

In spite of its great victory with the Jobs For Americans legislation, and due largely to Siran Missirian's near constant urging, Congress discovered that its work for the time remaining before the Christmas holidays was far from complete. Siran wanted decisions on two other very important Bills, one ending political party representation in Congress, and one ordering drastic reductions in U.S. military bases in foreign countries. She got her way.

The Bill prohibiting members of Congress from holding membership in a political party was signed into law by the President, and would become effective January one, 2011. It specified that they could be supported by and campaigned for, by a political party, but could have no allegiance to that or any other party once elected. Every member of Congress became, in effect, an Independent.

The Bill reducing the number of American bases on foreign soil passed in a special session of Congress December 6, 2010, with the stipulation that designated bases must be closed by the end of 2011. 500 of the 830 U.S. bases operating in foreign countries were specifically scheduled for closure, a move that was expected to reduce U.S. military spending by nearly one trillion dollars each year when fully implemented. The House Armed Services Committee was specifically charged with oversight, to insure that scheduled closures were carried out as intended, and Siran Missirian would be there to make sure that Committee carried out its responsibility.

She had, of course, kept Thor current on all Congressional activity and during one status meeting with all his Group Captains he praised her highly for her good work and said, "Siran, Congress has performed exceptionally well this year. I think they have earned their Christmas recess."

"I agree, Commander, but when they return there will still be many more problems to resolve."

"Ah, Siran, I sense that you feel a bit of dissatisfaction with our progress, so let us take a moment and look back at what we have accomplished so far:"

"We ended the wars in Iraq and Afghanistan, saving perhaps hundreds more soldier's lives, and billions of dollars."

"We brought nearly 200,000 service men and women home safely, and put them to work guarding the U.S./Mexican border until better-paying jobs become available for them."

"We control the Presidency, Congress and the Supreme Court, and will never give up that control."

"We have ended lobbying entirely, and have forced private enterprise out of Government."

"We have begun, and will diligently pursue, the return of policies guaranteeing much higher standards of ethics and morality in every business and Government entity."

"We have stopped political party control of Congress at the doors of Congress. Political parties can campaign for candidates, but if and when elected, those candidates may not claim political party affiliation, and will not be bound by allegiance to political parties."

"We executed thousands of capital crime prisoners who should have been executed soon after conviction, instead of storing them in prisons for from a few years to life."

"Now, so far I have addressed just our Government accomplishments. There are many more. Thanks to you Siran, and you, Truls, we now control the American health care industry, and can guarantee low cost health care to every American, and still reduce overall health care costs significantly."

"Thanks to the fine work of Assim and his Group, we have made great progress toward elimination of illicit drugs sales in this country. The remaining drug lords have been chased back to Mexico and are being executed by our agents on sight."

"Arne and his Group put an end to televangelism that was sucking the life blood out of poor Americans eager for miracles they would never see."

"In the area of successes to come, we heard from Siran that outsourcing of jobs by U.S. corporations ends with full implementation of the 'Jobs For Americans' program. That will help greatly in putting the nearly nine million out of work Americans back to work. The Bill that will make this happen also provides significant limits on executive compensation and, for the first time, sets mandatory compensation standards for every level of every industry, thus guaranteeing fair and adequate earnings, plus raises and promotions where appropriate, much as is already done in Government. "

"Siran also told us about successful passage of the Base Limitation Bill, which will close 500 bases saving nearly a trillion dollars a year when completed. More needs to be done there, but this is a fine start."

"Trul's Group will soon take control of the petroleum industry, ending dependence on foreign oil, and setting the stage for replacement of petroleum-based fuels with other, more plentiful, less costly alternative fuels, such as hydrogen, nuclear, solar, and wind."

"Erika's Group will control the pharmaceutical industry very soon, at which time drugs will be safer and far less costly."

"Another wonderful bit of news is that Arne's Group will control all U.S. banking by the end of the first quarter of 2011."

"Finally, let me remind all of you that without the fantastic support of Guri and his instructors in Group 6, many of our accomplishments would not have happened. Great work, Guri. To all of you, I say you should be extremely proud of what you have accomplished. Yes, there will always be many more problems to resolve, not just for Congress, but for the rest of the U.S. Government, and for all members of Techna Force 20. We came here to save our planet. We discovered that, in order to do that, we needed to overhaul virtually the entire U.S. Government, a task that is now almost complete. Therefore, I think it is safe to say we have saved Techna Planet. Our force, TF20, though small, has the most powerful arsenal in the universe, and the most proficient group of warriors. It is equal to anything any Earth country can throw at it. With diligence, we can be sure to keep it that way. So, while all of you have performed far above the call to duty, and we have come such a long way in less than one year, there is still much to be done here on Planet Earth. I do not see our progress to date as the end. As that great British Statesman, Winston Churchill, said during perhaps the lowest point in Great Britain's war with Germany, *'This is not the beginning of the end, it is the end of the beginning.'* Techna Force 20 must fight on. It must fight on."

"Commander," Truls said, "With all due respect, you left out one major accomplishment."

"Oh? What is that, Truls?"

"Your marriage to Sarah."

Everyone laughed. Thor, who was slightly red-faced now, responded "Ah, yes. Well, that was not part of my original plan, I assure you. But, as another famous man once said, 'Things work out.' I was not consciously searching for a wife when we came here, but I suppose my sub-conscious saw the need in my life for a mate and pushed me into making room for Sarah, who is absolutely the best thing that has ever happened to me, personally."

"And to Techna Planet, Commander," Manta added.

There was a chorus of cheers for Sarah and for Thor, and the meeting ended.

------///------

The End

CAST OF CHARACTERS

Thor Berksten	Commander, TF20
Manta Sames	Executive Assistant to Thor
Truls Heyerdahl	Captain, Group 1, Government
Siran Missirian	Captain, Group 2, Corporations
Arne Klein	Captain, Group 3, Religion
Assim Agassi	Captain, Group 4, Legal Sys.
Erika Varda	Captain, Group 5, Middle Class
Guri Kohn	Captain, Group 6, Reserves
Jens Petersen	Thor's Personal Pilot
Sam Fischer	CTS Sunday Review Producer
Mark Haddon	CTS Sunday Review-Sr. Correspondent
Margie Peterson	Sam Fischer's Executive Assistant
Sarah Malloy	CTS Receptionist
Howard Fields	President, United States of America
Damien Moss	Captain, TF20, Special Assignments
Jack Brill	President's Chief of Staff

President's Cabinet

Bertram Phillips	Secretary of Defense (I)
Margaret Bridges	Secretary of State (R)
John Dawson	Secretary of the Treasury (R)
Richard Perkins	Attorney General (R)
Linda Foxworth	Secretary of Interior (R)
Robert Morgan	Secretary of Agriculture (R)
Sylvia Patterson	Secretary of Commerce (R)
Alphonse Parks	Secretary of H.U.D. (R)
Sol Pinella	Secretary of Energy (R)
Morris Levine	Secretary of H. E. W. (R)
Pierce Clemons	Secretary of Homeland Security (R)

Congressional Leaders

Katherine McDonald	Speaker of the House (D)
Edward Reynolds	Senate Majority Leader (D)
John Raider	Senate Minority Leader (R)
Murray Rosenthal	House Minority Whip (R)

Cast of Characters, cont'd

Other Players

Darien Lachsa	Thor's first love
Karl Berksten	Thor's father (Prime Minister-Techna
Kenneth Malloy	Sarah's father
Rose Malloy	Sarah's mother
James Malloy	Sarah's brother
Carol Malloy	James' wife
Celia Brightmann	Sarah's sister
Kurt Brightmann	Celia's husband
Ellen Miller	Sarah's sister
Peter Miller	Ellen's husband
Kirsten Tesler	Thor's first sister
Ivan Tesler	Kristen's husband
Birgit Unger	Thor's second sister
Krause Unger	Birgit's husband
Erika Bonnet'	Thor's third sister
Jean Bonnet'	Erika's husband
Dana Ibsen	Thor's youngest sister
Soren Ibsen	Dana's husband
Pierce Morgenthaller	CEO-North American Energy Ind.
Harley Failes	CEO-Globe-Pacific Oil
Morton Lassiter	CEO-Kansas Petroleum
Bart Willis	CEO-Armbruster-Snyder Oil
Kermet Beech	CEO-Maggellian Oil and Gas
Leonard Boswick	CEO-Scanlon-Rogers Oil
Dean Wallis	CEO-Hummer Oil Co.
Walter Schelhorne	Air Force General

High Desert Club

Caroline Crawford-Smith	Board President
John Henderson	Board Member
Samuel Bromstein	Board Member
Erik Krause	Board Member
Peter Kasperian	Board Member
Mark Harshfeld	FBI Agent